Readers Love Rose Bend

'*The Road to Rose Bend* is what romance reads are all about'

'I would definitely recommend *Christmas in Rose Bend* for anyone who likes books that are immersive, romantic and have a Christmassy atmosphere'

'A heart-warming story about love, loss and new beginnings. If you want to fall in love with a new romance novel get yourself a copy of this amazing book'

'Naima Simone is a brilliant author and writer'

'I can't adequately convey how much I loved this book'

'A lovely Christmas read'

'An adorable, quick and easy read that I really enjoyed. A cute plot, endearing characters and a great setting, I loved it'

D1352643

Published since 2009, *USA Today* bestselling author **Naima Simone** loves writing sizzling romances with heart, a touch of humour and snark. Her books have been featured in *The Washington Post* and *Entertainment Weekly*, and described as balancing 'crackling, electric love scenes with exquisitely rendered characters caught in emotional turmoil.'

She is wife to Superman, or his non-Kryptonian, less bullet proof equivalent, and mother to the most awesome kids ever. They all live in perfect, sometimes domestically-challenged bliss in the southern United States.

Also by Naima Simone

The Road to Rose Bend
Christmas in Rose Bend
Slow Dance at Rose Bend (Novella)
A Kiss to Remember (Novella)
The Love List (Novella)

*

The Billionaire's Bargain
Black Tie Billionaire
Blame It on the Billionaire
Vows in Name Only
Trust Fund Fiancé
Ruthless Pride
Back in the Texan's Bed
Secrets of a One Night Stand
The Perfect Fake Date

For additional books by Naima Simone, visit her website, naimasimone.com.

Naima Simone

With LOVE from ROSE BEND

MILLS & BOON

This novel is entirely a work of fiction. The names, characters and incidents portrayed in it are the work of the author's imagination. Any resemblance to actual persons, living or dead, events or localities is entirely coincidental.

Mills & Boon
An imprint of HarperCollins*Publishers* Ltd
1 London Bridge Street
London SE1 9GF

www.harpercollins.co.uk

HarperCollins*Publishers*
1st Floor, Watermarque Building, Ringsend Road
Dublin 4, Ireland

This paperback edition 2022

1

First published in Great Britain by
Mills & Boon, an imprint of HarperCollins*Publishers* Ltd 2022

Copyright © 2022 by Naima Simone

The Love List Copyright © 2022 by Naima Simone

Naima Simone asserts the moral right to be
identified as the author of this work.
A catalogue record for this book is
available from the British Library.

ISBN: 978-1-84845-854-3

MIX
Paper from
responsible sources
FSC
www.fsc.org
FSC C007454

This book is produced from independently certified FSC™ paper
to ensure responsible forest management.

For more information visit: www.harpercollins.co.uk/green

Printed and Bound in the UK using 100% Renewable Electricity at
CPI Group (UK) Ltd, Croydon, CR0 4YY

All rights reserved. No part of this publication may be reproduced,
stored in a retrieval system, or transmitted, in any form or by any means,
electronic, mechanical, photocopying, recording or otherwise,
without the prior permission of the publishers.

This book is sold subject to the condition that it shall not, by way of trade
or otherwise, be lent, re-sold, hired out or otherwise circulated without
the publisher's prior consent in any form of binding or cover other than
that in which it is published and without a similar condition including this
condition being imposed on the subsequent purchaser.

To Gary. 143.

To Connie Marie Butts. I'll miss you forever,
and I'll love you longer than that.

With Love from Rose Bend

CHAPTER ONE

THE WORD NO is a gift not only to yourself, but also to others.

Leontyne "Leo" Dennison grimaced. Yeah, of all the rules that governed her life, she had the damnedest time following that one.

Hence the reason she sat parked outside the house of Rose Bend's newest resident and town recluse, stalling.

"What the hell?" she muttered. After pushing open her car door with more force than necessary, she stepped out.

She didn't *stall*. Didn't *hesitate*. Leo Dennison made decisions then executed them with confidence.

Apparently, she spoke about herself in the third person, too.

Shit.

It had to be Moe's breaking her ankle that had Leo so indecisive and weak. Yes, weak. Because nothing else could describe this uncharacteristic uncertainty. But damn, it wasn't every day she saw seemingly indomitable Lucille "Moe" Dennison, matriarch of the Dennison clan and her mother, as...mortal.

Okay, fine, to some a broken ankle might seem small in the grand scheme of calamities that could befall a person. But to see the woman who epitomized formidability suddenly looking so fragile...her face taut with pain, eyes glassy with the effort to hold back the tears she knew would upset her kids...

Leo's chest seized, and she lifted a palm to rub the suddenly tight, burning spot.

True. The injury might only require a cast, crutches, elevation and several weeks of healing. But the memory—the memory would leave its mark on Leo long after her mother ditched her crutches.

Which also explained why Leo stood on the curb outside this regal slate blue Victorian that sat on the edge of town like an elegant but judgmental spinster. Perched on a small rise, a ways from the rest of the neighborhood, it was a grand old lady—three imposing stories and a steep, gabled roof, rounded turrets, pointed towers, dark bay windows, white shutters, a wraparound porch and decorative trim.

From the gossip Leo had heard about the house's reclusive tenant, some kind of football or basketball or baseball player—hell, one ball looked like another to her—the house and the temporary owner had a lot in common.

They both screamed, "Get off my lawn!"

Only the love of a daughter for her injured mother could have Leo here, braving this obvious No Man's Land. Well... love and pride.

God knew she had her fair share.

And according to the Bible her ex-boyfriend loved to thump and quote, that same God didn't look too kindly on it, either. Still, pride wouldn't permit her to return home without bagging this celebrity as the newest judge for the wildly popular chili contest in Rose Bend's annual spring Honeybee Festival. Especially since she'd taken Moe's place on the festival committee—approaching the reluctant ball player was her first assignment.

She *had* to acquire his agreement.

Failure was not an option or in her vocabulary.

Failure is impossible.

Another of the rules she lived by.

All right, fine. So Susan B. Anthony said it first, but still, Leo claimed it, so that made it hers.

Rolling her shoulders back, she hiked up her chin, repeated the mantra in her head and marched up the front walk bordered by a tidy lawn.

Having spent most of her life at Kinsale Inn, first observing and then working alongside her parents, she noticed the little things about the stately home whose dark blue steps she climbed. Though the porch and its white columns and railings were immaculate, no rocking chairs with cushions slightly worn from sitting occupied the vast space. No wooden swing swayed in the early-afternoon breeze. No small tables claimed the corners. No lush green plants were tucked under the windows.

If she had to conjure up a word to describe the place it would be…lonely. The place was lonely.

She fought the urge to rub her chest again. Her mind argued that coming from her large, boisterous, nosy and loving family there was no way she could understand the empty ache of loneliness.

Yet, her heart—the heart of the girl who'd faded into the shadow of her more brilliant, vibrant siblings—told her brain it had no idea what it was talking about.

"C'mon, girl, the town hermit's porch is not the place for a counseling session," she muttered to herself, shoving aside the guilt at her uncomfortable thoughts.

She came from a home with adoring parents and sometimes pains-in-the-ass, but for the most part wonderful, brothers and sisters. Complaining insulted all of them.

Inhaling a deep breath, she tugged open the storm door and knocked on the front door with the beautiful stained-glass windows. It slowly opened and she locked her knees.

Not since the early hours of a morning a little over a year ago had she experienced such a strong urge to bolt. But bolting had been her reaction to an utter loss of control on *that night*. She shook her head. Hard. The fewer thoughts on all of *that*, the better...

Holy. Shit.

She closed her eyes in an unnaturally long blink.

Lifted her lashes.

Nope.

The man was still there.

Standing at the front door of this lonely house was the man who'd transformed her into a wild, hedonistic being on *that night*, the one she'd just been thinking about.

It'd been a little over a year, and even though the door concealed half his chiseled features and dense, dark scruff covered the lower half of that beautiful face, she hadn't forgotten the one person who'd made her burn every one of her rules on a pyre of sex.

Control.

That was what her rules were about. Control over her actions, her words, her expectations, her future, her heart... If she had control over all of those, mistakes were minimal.

Yet, she'd lost complete control that night and the man looming in the doorway right now, like a brooding giant, was a glaring, neon *mistake*. A mistake that had sent her running out of that hotel room in the dark without leaving her name or a way to contact her.

"What?"

His brusque—okay, no, *rude AF*—question snapped her out of her memories. Swallowing a curse, she scrounged for a smile and forced it to her lips.

"Well, this is awkwa—" The man she knew as Patrick shifted in the doorway and shock slammed into her. A gasp escaped. Hurt for him swelled, submerging her surprise, and she moved forward, lifting her arm toward him. "I didn't know—"

"What do you want?" He cut her off, those hazel eyes that had been so warm and flirtatious during their night together in Boston now glittered like chips of cold amber.

She lowered her arm, embarrassment keeping company with the unease, but neither could outrace the pain. The pain for him.

For the sensual, laughing, charming stranger who'd gifted her with hours of abandonment and freedom. Such abandonment and freedom she'd run scared from it.

Because he'd obviously suffered. A person who'd survived whatever tragedy had left the scars marring the left side of his face must have suffered. And horribly.

If not for the slip of the door, she wouldn't have guessed. The right half of his face remained exactly as she remembered—a perfect study of symmetry, angles and beauty. Dark, arching brows that somehow conveyed both wickedness and elegance. Slumberous, thickly lashed hazel eyes. Cheekbones that an artist would despair of perfecting. An arrogant blade of a nose softened by a too-lush, carnal mouth that could stretch wide in a charismatic smile or harden in sensual promise. A year ago, both had her willing to give him anything, do anything, become anything...

Yet, now that symmetry... Another gasp crawled up her throat, but she locked it down. That symmetry no longer existed because a long, raised, dark pink scar bisected his cheekbone, stretching to, and cutting through, the corner of his mouth and slightly drawing it down. Smaller marks scattered along his cheek and jaw as if maybe glass had shattered and sliced into his skin.

No, he was no longer the perfect man she'd met, but the scars didn't detract from his masculine beauty. In a way, they highlighted it.

And God, did her fingers itch to trace the evidence of his pain. To assure herself that the vibrant, vital man she'd met in that hotel bar was still full of life. To imagine otherwise... Even though she'd once run from him, she now wanted to shift closer. Her chest seized, twisting so hard she swallowed a whimper. She curled her fingers into her thigh, preventing herself from reaching out to him.

"Have you had a good enough look yet? Or should I turn more to the left so you have a better angle?"

Shit. She briefly closed her eyes. The only way she could mess this up any worse was if she'd walked up here with a manual on *How to Offend and Other Social Faux Pas.*

"I'm sorry. Can I please start over?" She shook her head, offering him a rueful smile. Which he returned with a flat stare. Okay, that was fair. She tried again with a small, tight chuckle. "You have to admit this is a little shock—"

"A shock for who? Me? You showed up on my doorstep unannounced and uninvited." His gold-and-green gaze dipped down over her as if she were something the neighborhood mutt had dropped on his porch. Something hot, stinking and waiting to be pooper-scooped.

Irritation curled in her chest, mingling with and darkening the sympathy. Inhaling a deep breath, she held on to her smile.

"What I mean is neither of us expected to...to..." She trailed off as he arched a dark eyebrow.

Horror and the truth collided inside her in a cataclysmic bang. It mushroomed, filling her head with a deafening roar and shoving against her chest, as if trying to escape this humiliating situation.

Run. Run far away from the mortifying fact that *he had no idea who she was.*

He'd gifted her with the most intense, earth-shattering sexual experience of her existence and she hadn't even rated a space in his memory bank.

That. Fucker.

Anger surged, hot and bright, and she welcomed it. Better than hurt and that godawful humiliation. Anything was better than that.

"Neither of us expected to be here today," she quickly amended through gritted teeth. According to Vanessa Perkins, chairwoman of this year's festival, Patrick was a football player. Not an English teacher as he'd told Leo. And apparently, emphasis on the *player*. But wait… Vanessa had called him by another name. Owen…something. Definitely not Patrick. So not only had she been a forgettable footnote in his sexual history; he'd given her a false bio and name, too. Wow. *So* not her greatest moment. But damn if she would remind him of it. Her pride might be sprinkling the porch like ticker-tape confetti, but hell, she still had it. "But if you'll just give me a couple of minutes of your time, I'll let you get back to your afternoon."

"Look, Ms.…"

"Dennison. Leo Dennison."

Yep, that burned. Once more she inhaled a deep breath, held it. Then quietly, deliberately released it. And it did nothing to ease that scorching ache inside her.

This was what she got for breaking her rules. He was a living, breathing reminder of why she had rules in the first place. If she hadn't loosened the reins—if she hadn't forgotten that being emotionally out of control held irreversible consequences—then she wouldn't be in this predicament. If she had remembered the penalty for inhibition, she wouldn't be standing here now, convincing herself she wasn't wounded. This was her fault for not following the rules. For letting her guard down.

Lesson learned.

Again.

But it would be the last time.

"Look, Ms. Dennison, I don't know if this is some belated Welcome Wagon, but fine. I consider myself welcomed." His hand rose and gripped the edge of the door, fingers tightening in preparation to shut it in her face. "If you'll excuse me…"

"Not the Welcome Wagon. Sorry to disappoint, but that's not an actual thing." She shifted closer, ready to sacrifice her foot and slide it in the doorway, if necessary, to prevent him from closing it. She'd come here on a mission. She might be a disappointment at being a notch on his bedpost, but getting him to judge this contest? *This* she wouldn't fail at. She *couldn't*.

"Listen, Mr. um, uh…"

Shit. She couldn't call him Patrick. And Owen was a little too forward. But for the life of her she couldn't remember what Vanessa said his last name was.

Annoyance flickered across his face. "Seriously? You don't even know my name?"

She swallowed a bark of incredulous laughter at the irony.

You can't snap on the football player because you need him.

"I apologize," she shoved out between gritted teeth. *Moe's counting on you. And so is the rest of the committee. And think of the revenue this festival will bring in for the inn. So shut up and get through this.* "It's been a long day."

"It's only one o'clock."

Good Lord, this man could try the patience of a saint.

And considering what he could do with his tongue, he was far from being canonized. "It's five o'clock somewhere, right?" she said. And she could use a happy hour drink right about now. "Anyway, I'm here representing Rose Bend's Honeybee Festival committee. It's our annual spring festival, and it's a pretty popular event for the town as well as the region."

"Honey. Bee. Festival," he repeated, and she couldn't quite hide her wince.

"Yes, I know, the name is a little…cutesy." She shrugged, holding up her hands. "But let me tell you. There's a helluva lot of honey at this festival. People come from all around to sell homemade wild honey, honey soaps, honey candles and lotions. We have a honey cake contest, and every year Melba Dinkins wins. And she's smug about it. Although, I'm pretty sure it's not just the honey that gets her that win but the bit of rum she adds in, too. Want to know an interesting fact, though?"

"No."

"The honey doesn't actually come from directly from honeybees or beehives," she continued, ignoring his refusal. "It's from the lavender that grows wild on a farm a couple of towns over. Crazy, right? But Honeybee Festival sounds better to the ear and makes more sense than Honey Lavender Festival. Speaking of the festival," she segued without taking a breath or permitting him a chance to interrupt. "We really would love if you'd agree to be a judge for our chili contest. It's one of our most popular contests, aside from the Lavender Pageant and aforementioned honey cake contest, and you would be doing us a huge favor. With a celebrity as one of our judges, the crowd you'd draw would be fantastic. More people would mean more money for the town and the…"

His flat "no" couldn't get her to shut up, but the blanching of color from his face accomplished it.

She'd read of people paling, just going white, but in all her twenty-nine years, she'd never witnessed it. Alarm crackled through her like bad static, and she moved farther into the doorway, afraid he might faint. What she, at five feet seven inches and one hundred and forty-five pounds, could do to catch him, a huge athlete who stood well above six feet and had to exceed two hundred pounds of pure muscle if her memory served her well—and unfortunately, it did—she didn't know.

Yet, she stretched a hand toward him, and if possible, more color bleached from his skin as he stumbled backward. Away from her.

Hurt blasted through her in a hot torrent, and she snatched her arm back, clutching it to her chest. But moments later she burrowed deep, searching and finding that reservoir of "you can't hurt me because I don't care" that she never went anywhere without. Some people never left home without a pack of tissues, gum or clean underwear; she was never without her armor.

Just for situations like these.

Leaping before you think only leaves you with a dirty, sore ass.

Another of her rules. One that when she broke, she always suffered the consequences.

Forcing a smile, she deliberately dropped her arm to her side and stepped back. And took another. And another.

"I'm sorry, I didn't mean to offend," she said, proud of her even tone. Especially when she still throbbed inside from his obvious aversion to, well, *her*. That shouldn't sting as much as it did. Just as his not remembering her shouldn't. But fuck it all, it *did. Just get this over with and leave.* That was what she needed to do. Now. "Anyway, the festival and chili contest are in a few weeks. And we wouldn't require anything of you but to pose for a couple of promotional photos and show up the day of. Like I said, we would really appreciate—"

"No."

She snapped her lips closed, really, *really* tired of his interrupting her.

"If you need time to think about it, that's fine. I can come back later."

He shook his head, his lush mouth hardening. His hand gripped the edge of the door again, and he turned, giving her a view of his profile—the unscarred side.

"I don't need to think about it. No. Goodbye."

He shut the door.

Leo stared at the white-painted wood, frozen.

And numbly recapped the past few minutes.

The hermit football player turned out to be the unforgettable one-night stand she'd foolishly indulged in a year ago.

Said one-night stand hadn't found her so unforgettable because he didn't remember her at all.

He'd refused to be a judge in the contest, and she'd failed at the one job she had on this committee.

And now he'd slammed the door in her face.

Well, damn.

CHAPTER TWO

HE REMEMBERED HER.

Hell, yes, he remembered her.

Heaving a leaden sigh, Owen Strafford scrubbed a palm down his face, the scars and pockmarked skin abrading his palm.

"Fuck."

He flung his arm down and his hand away as if it'd offended him. And it had. For a blissful second, he'd forgotten. But just one accidental pass over hard tissue and pitted skin and reality plowed into him like a linebacker. He tried not to touch his face. Hell, in the shower, he just tipped his head back and let the water run over it. That was a particular kind of torture, too. Anything glancing over that marred flesh... The nerve endings had long since deadened, but in his mind—in his mind, a thousand needles jammed under the thick surface waiting for the slightest stroke to come alive...

Come alive and remind him of the excruciating pain of that night. Of the paralyzing fear. Of the yawning, aching loneliness.

"Fuck," he said again. Lower. Softer.

Shaking his head, he thrust his fingers through his hair, dragging the chin-length strands out of his eyes. Not that he should've bothered. As he headed back across the wide foyer, he purposely didn't glance to his right at the wide, gold-framed mirror hanging over the mahogany entryway table. He quietly snorted. Used to be he couldn't pass a reflective surface without taking at least a glimpse of himself in it. Now? He avoided mirrors like a goddamn vampire.

Just one more change on top of a dog pile of them in the past year.

His footsteps thudded on the hardwood floor, the high ceilings and white walls of the old Victorian home carrying the echo of his heavy tread through the house. Four months he'd been living in this dream house in a picture-perfect town after leaving his New York penthouse.

Leaving. What bullshit. Sneaking out. That was what it was called, after all, when a person crept out in the middle of the night like a thief to avoid being seen. Desperation caused a man to do things he usually wouldn't. Like abandon the bustling city for a small town, and his high-rise, state-of-the-art penthouse for a turn-of-the-century house with fireplaces that weren't strictly for decoration. Not for the first time Owen asked himself why he'd agreed to hide away in Sherrod Forrester's hometown. Sherrod was his best friend and teammate, and he'd let Sherrod completely arrange his living accommodations.

Oh, right.

Because Owen didn't give a fuck.

If Owen ever allowed his mother to visit—which was a big fat "never"—she would lose her mind over the high ceilings, ornate woodwork, the fireplaces big enough for her husband and son to stand in, the stained glass and bay windows, deep archways, the library and the honest-to-God crystal chandelier in an honest-to-God parlor. Truthfully, he didn't mind the library. Packages filled with books *might* show up on the regular on the front porch.

Why shame and fear still skulked through him at the

thought, he couldn't explain. He was thirty, not a boy afraid of being caught reading by his sneering dad, and he didn't have to hide his books. Yet, he never read those books in the living room where the sun streamed through the huge bay windows, providing light—and exposure.

Some habits died hard. And other habits? Well, they lingered like the ghosts he was nearly certain haunted the attic of this house.

The peal of his cell phone disrupted his thoughts. Gratitude didn't ripple through him. Honestly, he'd rather muse over who might've died in one of the upstairs bedrooms than who called him. After all, he'd come to this small Berkshires town that he'd never heard of—and prayed no one of his acquaintance had ever heard of—to disappear.

Disappear from the rabid press.

From his parents' relentless concern…and demands.

From his agent's hounding calls.

From life.

Except for the press, he hadn't managed to avoid dick.

Stalking down the hall, he cut a sharp left into the formal study that he'd turned into what could only be called a man cave. Mounted eighty-five-inch flat-screen LED smart TV with surround sound and gaming systems. Built-in bookshelves and wet bar. Black leather sectional couches. Matching recliners. Walnut coffee and end tables. Fireplace. He spent most of his time back here or in the parlor room off the master suite that he'd turned into a home gym.

Still, none of the calm that usually entered his body invaded him as he stepped into the room. Not when the cell stopped ringing…then immediately rang again seconds later.

His stomach curdled like sour milk, and the fucking shame of that only served to sicken him more.

Yeah, Owen Strafford, former all-pro, two-time Super Bowl championship—winning quarterback, who'd faced down countless defensive linemen intent on crushing him to the turf, and he was afraid of a goddamn phone.

An image of Leo Dennison—until ten minutes ago, he'd only known her simply as Leo—flashed across his mind's eye. Of her at his front door, reaching out to him with that delicate, fine-boned hand that had once caressed his unscarred flesh, concern darkening those beautiful blue-gray eyes. Of the shock and hurt that had flashed across her gorgeous features before disappearing behind a smooth doll's mask that revealed nothing but a polite smile.

He'd been afraid then, too. Been afraid of her touch. Of the pity she'd been unable to hide. Of *her*.

So he'd rejected her. Pretended not to know her. Shut her out—literally.

And now, staring at that phone as if it'd sprouted scales and fangs, he hovered on repeating the same actions.

But something wild, feral and wholly unexpected—something that had been absent for a long while—surged inside him, propelling him across the room to snatch up the phone.

The temporary bravery gave way to a flood of relief at the number on the phone's screen. Thank God. Because if it'd been anyone else but that person, he didn't know how far his courage would've stretched. Maybe not far enough to answer.

Good thing he didn't have to find out.

He swiped his thumb across the screen and lifted the cell to his ear.

"Hey, man."

"Oh, good. Now that I know you've answered the phone…" Sherrod announced seconds before the ring for a video call chimed in Owen's ear. In the next second he was staring back at his own face.

Fuck.

"Don't even think about not answering. If you believe for one second that I won't put Celeste on this phone and make you hang up on her, then you seriously underestimate me," Sherrod threatened. Cheerfully.

Owen's grip tightened. For a second he considered hanging up anyway, but his best friend knew him too well. Sherrod, he had no problem offending. That was why they were closer than brothers. They could go at each other one minute and pound beers with each other the next. But Sherrod's wife, Celeste? Yeah, he'd never do anything to disrespect her. Not even in a joking manner. And not just because she was his best friend's wife. Celeste Forrester was one of the kindest, most generous and beautiful souls in this world.

No, he'd never hang up on her. And Sherrod knew it.

Asshole.

"Well played, motherfucker." Owen stabbed the answer button on the video call and Sherrod's face filled the screen.

His friend's wide, white grin flashed, completely unrepentant. His dark brown dreads swung forward as he dipped his head. "Thank you, thank you. I thought so. Getting you on the phone is like wrestling a bag full of wet cats, so I'm not afraid to play dirty. Besides, you already know if you hurt my wife, I will fly up there and beat that ass six ways to Sunday. Ooh. Speaking of six ways to Sunday. Have you tried the ice-cream place yet? They have the best salted caramel you've ever tasted in your life, bruh!" His dark eyes rolled as if sampling the cold treat at that moment. It was frankly disturbing. "Not to mention their malts. Thick with bits of real fruit that get stuck in the straw. You could give yourself a headache trying to suck 'em through. To die for. To. Die. For."

Owen stared at Sherrod as the other man's eyes glazed over in pleasure. Anyone looking at the wide receiver who'd hit every Sexiest Athlete List in the past seven years running—and the team had mercilessly teased him about it for the past seven years running—would assume someone with his looks, talent and fame would be arrogant and a player. But there was a reason he and Celeste were the perfect match. She might be sweet and giving, but Sherrod matched her. The man was a living, breathing teddy bear.

Except on the football field.

On the field, he was a total beast.

"Oh, wait." Sherrod narrowed his eyes. "Let me guess. You're still doing your Quasimodo-bell-tower shtick so you haven't been to the ice-cream shop. Or anywhere else, for that matter."

And sometimes he was mean as fuck off the field, too.

"Your skill is wasted on football. Comedy, that's your calling."

Sherrod snorted, and the walls behind him changed from cream to a light blue as he walked through his New Jersey home. "Truth. I'm all about truth. Hell, I suggested my hometown so you wouldn't have to sneak around like a masked psycho about to break out in song…or murder."

"You're mixing up your literature, and that's not sexy." Owen rounded the end of his couch and dropped down. The motion dragged up the sleeve of his black Henley enough to glimpse the thin jagged scars left by flying glass and twisted metal. With more strength than required, he yanked the material back into place, hiding the evidence of his accident, of the end of his life as he'd known it. "At least you have the mask part right, though. I should probably invest in one so I don't terrify the locals."

"Not funny, bruh."

"Not meant to be."

Sherrod glared at him, mouth thinned into a hard line. "When you say shit like that it pisses me off. There's nothing wrong with you a foot in your ass, an attitude adjustment and a ball back in your hands wouldn't fix."

Owen groaned, pinching his forehead and rubbing it. "Not this again. Have you been talking to Byron?"

Fucking Byron.

"Yeah, Byron called and asked me to talk to you," Sherrod admitted, and once again Owen silently cursed Byron Shaw, his agent. "But it's not something I hadn't already planned on doing myself. Or hadn't already been thinking about for a long time. Man, I love you like a brother. Hell, given the right circumstances, I might love you more, although I will deny that shit until my dying day. That said, I can be honest with you when others will lie to make you feel better." He paused and his solid, clean-shaven jaw hardened. "You belong back in the game. It's time to come out of that bullshit retirement."

"Bullshit retirement." His fingers ached with how tightly he clutched the phone, and his throat burned with the roar that demanded to be released. "Just because you and Byron don't want to believe I'm no longer fit to play doesn't make it true."

"This is me, Owen," Sherrod snapped, his thick, dark eyebrows a plunging V over his nose. "I was there when you woke from that coma. I was there when the doctor gave you the laundry list of your injuries. I was there when he gave you the percentage chance of a recovery. And I was right fucking there, pushing and shoving your ass through rehab. So the only person who knows more about how fit you are to play, other than your doctor, is me. I know even more than you, apparently, because you're in denial."

All true. Every word. Even when his parents hadn't been there—they lived nearly twelve hours away in Indiana, and even if his mother could take off all that time from her job, which she couldn't, his father had no desire to sit useless by a sick bed. His words, not Owen's. So yeah, Sherrod hadn't left his side through the hell of the accident and the purgatory of recovery.

But Owen wasn't the one in denial; Sherrod was. Byron was.

"Physically, you're recovered. The ACL tear is fully healed. You finished rehab and the doc cleared you. There's no reason you can't be back out there on the field with your team—"

"Isn't there?"

He looked away, and out of habit, he gave his friend his unblemished side. His good side. But he didn't need to see the left side of his face to feel the tug on his scar. To feel the pull at the corner of his mouth that prevented his lips from fully flattening. Or smiling. Or just goddamn moving.

Yeah, Sherrod was right—his knee had healed. But what about the fear? The paralyzing fear that was as debilitating as an amputated limb.

"Owen."

"I'm not doing this," Owen chewed out. Hell, he didn't know which was worse—the subject or the soft, sympathetic note that had crept into his friend's voice. Both churned the nausea in his gut. "Drop it. There's nothing more to talk about. Why else are you calling?"

For a long moment Sherrod didn't answer, just stared at him. And even through the phone with hundreds of miles separating them, the impact of that gaze sliced into him.

But then Sherrod glanced over his shoulder, freeing Owen, and he sighed in relief.

"Celeste and I were thinking about heading that way soon."

"Checking up on me?" Owen scoffed.

"No. You gotta check that ego, bruh. Not everything is about you." He tsked, shaking his head. "Training camp starts in a couple of months and we need a vacation before then. She loves Rose Bend, and for some reason she loves you, too. Don't ask me why. And the spring festival is in a few weeks, too. We love that thing." He snorted. "Besides, you should be grateful we're coming. We'll be the only people you've probably seen in the four months you've been there."

"That's not true," he objected, irritation flashing through him. At the dig at Owen's hermit tendencies or the mention of that damn spring festival, he couldn't say.

"Yeah?" Sherrod arched an eyebrow. "Name one."

Owen's mind blanked. And he blinked.

"Un-huh," Sherrod drawled, nodding. "Just what I thou—"

"Leo Dennison."

It was Sherrod's turn to blink.

Dammit. Mentally, Owen clapped a hand to his forehead. What the hell? Why had he said *her* name? True, he had most of his groceries and other necessities delivered. But the things he couldn't have dropped off on his doorstep, he ventured out of the house to purchase. So he had bumped into a few people. The late-night clerk at the supermarket in the next town over. The cook and waitress in the late-night diner here in town. Maddox Holt, the owner of the local dive bar who had become something of a friend. Sort of.

And yet, the name he threw out there was Leo's.

What the hell had he been thinking?

That was easy. He hadn't been.

"Leo Dennison as in sister to Cole and Wolf Dennison? As in the Dennisons who run the Kinsale Inn? *That* Leo Dennison?" Sherrod cocked his head to the side, surprise thick in his voice.

Owen shrugged, regretting his slip more than ever. And yet, somehow, he found himself saying, "I don't know about that since I didn't ask about her family tree. But it was the same woman from Boston."

"What wom— No, *the woman* from *Boston*?" Sherrod honest-to-God gasped. Christ. The only thing missing was a hand pressed to his chest, fingers splayed wide.

"I don't know about this *the woman* shit, but yeah, it's her," Owen muttered.

Sherrod's eyes narrowed. "You never mentioned her name was Leo."

"I forgot," Owen muttered.

He hadn't forgotten shit about that night. Not one moment and definitely not her name.

There'd been several things he hadn't mentioned about the woman he'd approached in the Boston hotel bar that night last year, still high on their Super Bowl win from the previous week. Hell, he'd only said anything to Sherrod in the first place because he'd been shaken by the hot-as-fuck encounter with the beautiful stranger who hadn't known who Owen was and who'd ghosted him the following morning.

Beautiful.

He smothered a snort. He might've graduated from Indiana University with a bachelor's in liberal studies and just three credits shy of a minor in literature, but words still had failed him when he'd initially laid eyes on Leo. Since he'd turned thirteen and Rosie Baxter had cornered him between her bushes to kiss him, Owen had understood his appeal to the opposite sex. And he'd enjoyed the benefits his face, build, talent and popularity had garnered him. All that to say, he knew beautiful women.

Yet...

Yet, there'd been *something* about the woman perched on the wine-red leather bar stool. Maybe the small but intense frown that wrinkled her brow. Maybe it'd been the light yet adorable smattering of cinnamon freckles that contrasted with the bold, red lipstick painting her full mouth. Or maybe it'd been the slight widening of her eyes when she'd realized his gaze was on her even as that wrinkling of her brow returned. As if asking him, *What the hell do you want?*

She'd been a study of intriguing contradictions. As cliché as it sounded, even across a crowded bar, she'd fascinated him. And once she'd opened her mouth and asked, "Can I help you?" he'd been hooked. From the lure of those blue-gray eyes to that good-girl-next-door-who'll-take-you-to-her-bedroom-when-her-dad's-not-home vibe. And the aphrodisiac of her not knowing him as Owen Strafford, quarterback of the Jersey Knights, but as Patrick, a New Jersey high school English teacher visiting Boston for the weekend.

He'd lied.

Guilt had gnawed at him, but not enough to give up the intoxicating freedom to just *be* with this woman. He hadn't been that liberated in...well, so long he couldn't remember. It'd all culminated in the hottest, best sex he'd had in his life. And he'd had a lot of sex.

But every woman, every dirty fuck, had been reduced to a distant memory as he'd driven himself inside Leo's tight body. Buried his face in the lilac-, rain- and sweat-scented crook of her neck. Surrendered to the sweetness of her embrace.

She'd rocked his world and had left it cold when he'd woken to empty, tangled sheets the next morning. But he'd been determined to find her.

Then the accident happened.

And he lost his career, his life...himself.

"So what happened?" Sherrod demanded, yanking Owen from his morose thoughts. "That first meeting had to have been...memorable."

Memorable. Funny he should choose *that* word.

"Yeah, you could say that. She came here to ask me to be the guest judge for some contest for the spring festival. I think it's safe to say she was...surprised."

"Surprised," Sherrod slowly repeated. Squinting into the phone, he leaned forward, his face filling the screen. "All right. I know that shifty tone. You're hiding something. What happened, bruh?"

Owen sighed. Sometimes having someone who knew you better than you knew yourself was a blessing. This was not one of those times.

"I might have pretended not to remember her."

Sherrod blinked. Blinked again. "Say what, now?"

"I said I might have—"

"I heard you!" Sherrod's chin jerked back toward his neck and if a glare could set a person on fire, Owen would be rendered to barbecue by now. "Why would you make such an asshole move? What? She didn't remember you?"

"No, she knew me." An image of the shock and hurt that flashed across her face wavered in front of him, and again guilt slithered through him.

"Then what the hell, Owen? Why would you deliberately humiliate her like that? I mean, yeah, you've become a moody, grumpy bastard since the car accident but to be intentionally mean? That's not like you. So there must be some—"

"Because I'm not the same man she was with!"

The truth exploded from him in a hot torrent that scalded his throat and tongue, and he shot to his feet. Thrusting his fingers through his hair, he dropped his arm, not caring that Sherrod would now have an excellent view of the floor. He paced to the other side of the room, the chaotic tumble of anger, frustration and grief swirling inside him until it burned a hole in his gut.

Goddammit.

They didn't understand. None of them did. Not his parents. Not his agent. Not his coach. Not even Sherrod.

The man he used to be—the man they still insisted he was—didn't exist anymore. That easygoing, laughing, no cares in the world except for the next game, the next party, the next good time…that handsome, unscarred man had died in that car crash.

There was no resurrecting him.

No matter how much the people in his life might wish or hope otherwise.

"Owen."

Briefly squeezing his eyes closed, Owen tried to block out the sound of his best friend's voice. Despair mingled with anger, and for a second, in his mind, he saw the phone smashing against the wall, ending the call. Permanently.

He didn't want to hear the platitudes, the assurances that he was the same, that nothing had changed.

Everything had changed. Every-fucking-thing.

In the end, he didn't hurl the phone. Didn't howl his pain and outrage.

No. In the end he inhaled, shoved down the emotion that did him absolutely no good and lifted the cell again.

"What?"

"I'm sorry."

Owen's head jerked back. "What?" he repeated.

"I'm sorry." Sherrod shook his head. "I know you better than that. And I should've thought that one through before I opened my mouth and made an ass of myself. But—" he paused, and if his friend had been in the same room with Owen, the impact of that dark gaze couldn't have been any heavier "—what are you going to do to fix it? I'm just thinking back on how you reacted to her, to that night. You were never one to carry tales about the women you were with, but you talked to me about her. She made an impact, bruh. So I'm just imagining it must've been the same for her, even if she did dip the next morning. So if that's true, for you to not even remember her…"

"I get you," Owen murmured.

He'd been a dick.

No, worse. He'd been a coward. Afraid of her pity, of her…revulsion. Shit, he couldn't decide which turned his stomach more. But what he'd said, or rather yelled, had been true. Leo didn't know the man who'd stood in the doorway and kicked her off his porch.

She remembered a ghost.

And in spite of what Sherrod said, it was best for both of them if Owen allowed things to stand as he'd left them— her on one side of his door and him on the other. At this very moment she might be calling him an asshole with community dick but there wouldn't be any further contact between them. It was for the best.

For both of them.

After all, he'd come to Rose Bend to disappear.

And with Leo Dennison, he felt entirely too visible.

CHAPTER THREE

LEO STARED AT the young, pretty, *crying* woman sitting across from her, and worked hard to conceal the panic welling inside her.

Not saying Leo was a stone-cold bitch. But displays of emotion tended to make her...itchy. They were so messy. Moe possessed that warmth, and it'd skipped a generation.

Leo had no idea how to handle emotions.

Considering the loud, often chaotic clan she'd grown up in, she should have had plenty of practice. Sinead and Flo going head-to-head over bathroom availability. Sonny settling into a fantastic brood over his football team's latest loss.

Cole losing his wife and son in childbirth and watching him drown in grief for two years.

In all those situations, Moe had waded in, doled out calm wisdom and comfort where needed. And Leo, uncomfortable and lost, proceeded with what she did best—action. She came up with a bathroom schedule. Arranged to have her brother's favorite snacks waiting for him when he arrived home from practice. And with Cole? She'd organized meal deliveries and cleaning services for his cottage and law office. Contacted his colleagues, who agreed to assume some of Cole's caseload until he could return to his practice.

She might shy away from the tangle of emotion, but she

did. She controlled the environment, arranged people. And she was the best at it.

But as Gina Riley sat in the chair next to her, tears filling her pretty brown eyes, Leo drew a blank. The woman was a bride-to-be. Weren't brides-to-be supposed to be happy? *Oh, God.* Was Gina having second thoughts? Leo offered wedding venues, not premarital counseling. *Please, Lord, don't let her ask me for advice on how to break up with her fiancé. I'm not built for that.*

"Gina, sweetie." Leo turned to the small table under the inn's office window and nabbed a couple of tissues, then held them out to the other woman. "Are you okay?"

Leo inwardly cringed at the question. Uh, obviously not.

"No." Gina shook her head, her blond ponytail swishing over her shoulder. Pure misery coated her voice as she accepted the tissue and dabbed at her eyes. "I'm sorry, Leo. I didn't mean to come here and unload all this on you," she apologized in her soft drawl that still carried the flavor of Georgia. She'd moved to Rose Bend about five years earlier.

"It's fine, Gina. Really. Besides, not only are you our client, but you put up with the twins their sixth grade year. Shoot, we might owe you." Leo grinned when a reluctant smile curved the teacher's mouth. "Is there anything you want to talk about? I don't mean to brag, but I'm a great listener."

She was. Again, growing up in her family, she didn't have a choice. Besides, in order to figure out how to solve a problem, one had to first hear it.

Another of her rules.

Gina dipped her chin, staring at her lap for several seconds before lifting her head and meeting Leo's gaze. More water filled her eyes, her bottom lip trembling.

"It's nothing you can do, and honestly, it's a little selfish of me to dump this on you."

"How about you let me decide that?" Leo tilted her head. "If you need someone to talk to, I'm here. I don't think we're going to get much done until you get whatever it is off your chest."

"My grandmother doesn't approve of Derrick," Gina finally whispered.

Leo cocked her head, frowning. Okay, now *that* she hadn't expected.

From the meetings she'd had with Gina about the upcoming wedding at Kinsale Inn, Leo had discovered that the other woman's fiancé had made the trip down to Georgia to meet Gina's side of the family. And even though Leo was currently on a man hiatus, she had to admit Derrick Holmes was one of the good ones. Manager of the bank in town, one of her brother's football coaches and just an all-around nice guy, Derrick deserved someone as sweet as Gina. Leo had been happy for them when she'd found out they'd started dating.

"Are you serious? But why? As one who has dated more than her fair share of frogs I can attest that Derrick's one of the princes. What could she possibly disapprove of?"

This time Leo's attempt at humor didn't elicit a smile from Gina. What appeared to be shame shadowed her eyes before her lashes lowered and her fingers twisted the tissue on her lap.

"My grandmother…" Her voice petered out, then she softly continued. "She's old-fashioned and steeped in, well, Southern tradition."

Leo's shoulders tightened, her brain wrapping around what Gina tried *not* to say. She stared at the petite blonde, and though she hated to consider it, she couldn't ignore the obvious.

"Is it because Derrick's Black?" Leo gently asked, although inside, anger scalded her like a living flame.

"Worse," Gina whispered, her shoulders hunched as if bearing the weight of her grandmother's bigotry. "He's Methodist."

Leo blinked, the flames of rage guttering to sparks before extinguishing. And only by the grace of Derrick's Methodist God did she manage to control her face.

"Uh." Leo cleared her throat. "He's...Methodist." When Gina nodded her bowed head, Leo shook her own, not even bothering to hide her confusion. "I'm sorry, Gina, but I don't follow. What's wrong with that?"

Gina sighed and finally met Leo's gaze. "He's not Southern Baptist."

Leo snickered. It escaped her, and she clapped both hands over her mouth, horrified as another slipped out, muffled but there.

Oh, shit.

Her reaction was most definitely inappropriate.

Gina stared at her, brown eyes wide. Then the corner of her mouth twitched. And a snort echoed in the small office. Then another. In the next moment her soft laughter filled the air, and Leo joined her.

"Oh, that feels good." Gina dabbed at her eyes again, but thankfully, for a different reason this time. "Thank you for that."

Leo smiled and covered Gina's hand, gently squeezing. "Listen, Gina, I don't want to trivialize your family issue. That's not my intention at all. I, more than anyone, understand how important family is, and how much we want to please them because we love them." Or crave their approval.

"Still, finding that person who adores, protects and cares for you seems to be rarer and rarer these days. And, Gina, the way Derrick looks at you? It's like you either walked on water or created the game of football. Which, to him, might be the same thing."

Gina laughed, a pink flush staining her cheeks even as delight sparkled in her brown eyes.

"Yeah, it's kind of annoying, actually." Leo grinned. "When love like that comes your way, you grab ahold of it, cherish it and count each day as a gift," she said, thinking of her brother Cole and the wife he'd unexpectedly lost. And the wife and baby daughter he now had. "Your family, if they want what's best for you, will eventually come around. If they don't," Leo said, shrugging, "well, that's their heart issue, not yours. And if that does end up being the case, well, then, thank God they live a thousand miles away."

Gina chuckled. "You're right. Of course you're right. I love Derrick, and that's all that matters." A dimple flashed in her cheek. "And as the bride, I'll use my prerogative and assign my mother to deal with Nana."

"Good thinking." Leo laughed and squeezed Gina's hand again. "Now, let's talk about table arrangements and tent rental just in case of bad weather."

An hour and no more breakdowns later, Leo closed the inn's entrance door behind Gina. Okay, crisis averted. And, they'd managed to settle on the details for tables, tents and rooms for guests coming in from out of town.

"You did really well back there."

Leo whirled around, frowning at her mother.

"One." She ticked up a finger. "Is it some parent super-power that allows you to sneak up on your children even while on crutches?" She waved her other hand toward the bright pink cast encasing Moe's right foot and the aluminum crutches under her arms. "And two." She popped up a second finger. "You should be sitting down and elevating that ankle, not hobbling around on it. And definitely not lurking around office doors, eavesdropping."

"You have a really funny way of saying thank you." Moe squinted her green eyes. And though her fingers curled around the handles on the braces, Leo could easily imagine them fisted on her slim hips.

Snorting, Leo said, "Thank you... Now, could you please go sit down and stop making me have to reach for my blood pressure pills?"

"You don't have high blood pressure," Moe grumbled, but wheeled around and dutifully moved down the hall, past the spacious living area with the wide, nearly floor-to-ceiling windows, overstuffed couches and a fireplace, and on to the kitchen at the back of the inn.

"Not yet," Leo muttered, following behind her.

"I heard that."

"Of course you did, with your freakishly bionic ears." Leo paused next to the small cedar reception desk that her brother Wolf had built. She flipped open the sign-up book and skimmed a finger down today's sheet.

Two of their expected guests had arrived. That left the Harrisons, a couple from New Hampshire, and Ronald Merritt, an author who reserved a room every April for about a month for his annual "writing retreat." They had more reservations for the coming weekend, and as the spring festival loomed, the rooms would become more and more booked. Still...

Still, as Moe would often say about Leo, she was never satisfied.

And she wasn't. She wanted *more*.

More for the inn. More for her family.

More for…herself.

This inn and everyone under its roof—it was her world. All she had. Making sure it was the best, healthy and well… That fell under her responsibilities. And she couldn't fail. She *wouldn't* fail. If achieving it meant she worked harder, spent longer hours, exorcised relationships… Those sacrifices were worth the cost.

Moe tapped a crutch on the floor to catch Leo's attention. "C'mon and let me fix you a cup of tea. Tell me about how the rest of your meeting went."

"No." Leo flipped the book closed. "You'll sit down, and *I'll* fix the cup of *coffee* while I tell you how the meeting went."

"Fine." Moe huffed out a breath, telegraphing quite eloquently how she felt about Leo's bossiness.

Not that Leo cared. Well, that was a lie. She did care. But with her mother, who'd been running the inn since moving to Rose Bend over thirty years ago, one had to be firm. But not *too* firm, because broken ankle or not, Leo still retained a healthy respect for the woman. Billie Thomasina "Moe" Dennison had never lifted her hand to the seven children she'd raised, yet the woman had instilled the fear of God into each of them. She'd patented side-eye before it'd become a thing.

The fear of ever causing their loving and fiercely protective mother any hurt or disappointment, that, more than anything, kept her and her siblings in line—for the most part.

A little while later, with Moe settled at her cherished kitchen table where she'd fed her beloved family and served many a guest, Leo relayed the details of her meeting with Gina.

"The wedding and reception are going to be beautiful," Moe said, sipping her steaming cup of coffee. "I'll be the first to admit I was a little worried if wedding planning would be too much for you and the inn. But you've really taken the initiative, and I believe Kinsale Inn is going to be the newest destination venue for weddings. I'm always proud of you, Leo. That's a given. And this just reinforces why."

Leo ducked her head over her cup of coffee on the pretense of spooning in another serving of sugar. But pleasure bloomed inside her, pouring into her cheeks. Neither Moe nor Leo's father, Ian, had withheld affection or approval. Yet, she seemed to crave it. She was ugly-honest with herself about that. It wasn't pretty; that relentless need drove her in a silent competition with her brothers that they didn't even know existed. She wasn't brilliant like Cole or artistically gifted like Wolf, but she'd tried to make herself indispensable by working hard at the family inn and taking it to the next level.

That included reimagining Kinsale Inn as not just the local picturesque bed-and-breakfast with excellent service, but also as a coveted wedding destination venue in the Berkshires.

And what better event to broadcast this new venture at than the spring Honeybee Festival when people from all over the state would travel to Rose Bend? The inn would host their annual booth where they sold several of Wolf's carpentry pieces along with Moe's baked goods. Leo already had gorgeous brochures planned with the wonderful pictures Flo had captured of the inn and the new gazebo Wolf had built for them. Oh, yes, the festival would be the perfect time to promote...

The coffee she sipped soured in her belly and she set her mug down on the table, staring into the light brown depths.

As if Moe was a mind reader—and at one time or another Leo had questioned the veracity of that—she eyed Leo over the rim of her cup.

"Vanessa Perkins called me. She hasn't heard from you about the guest judge for the chili contest. I told her you probably were sidetracked with inn business and would contact her today." Moe tilted her head, her dark brown-and-gray hair falling over her shoulder. "You never did mention how that went. Did everything go okay with the football player?"

"Sure." When her mother arched an eyebrow, Leo grimaced. "Maybe *sure* is a bit too strong of an answer."

"Leo."

"Moe." She stretched an arm across the table and grasped her mom's free hand. "I don't want you to worry. I promised I'd handle it. And I will. He just needs a little... persuading."

Moe snorted. "Define *a little*."

The thud of Owen Strafford's door slamming in her face echoed in her head. She fought not to betray that humiliation on her face. Instead, she forced a smile that her mother seemed to find suspect.

Smart woman.

"Moe, when I took your place on the committee, it was to alleviate you from worries about the festival so you could focus on healing—"

"I broke my ankle, not my brain!"

"So therefore," Leo carried on as if her mother hadn't interrupted with narrowed eyes and a scowl fierce enough to iron the wrinkles from her linen pants, "let me concern myself with convincing a reluctant athlete to perform his civic duty to the town he's adopted as his home, and you concentrate on—"

"Concern yourself with the festival. Concern yourself

with getting this guy's agreement. With the inn. And who is supposed to concern themselves with you?"

Leo's lips parted, but then they snapped closed, her pat answer drying up under the warm worry in her mother's green gaze. Denial scraped at her—the words and the emotion. She didn't need looking after. Didn't require sleepless nights or anxious hand twisting. She was the one Dennison her mother could count on not to give her those moments.

Leo busted her ass to make it that way.

To be...perfect.

Failure is impossible.

Her golden rule.

And the silver rule? *"Perfect is unobtainable" is a copout.*

Because if she wasn't the organizer, the manager... If she wasn't as close to perfect as she could possibly be... Then what good was she to Moe, to her family?

Hell, *who* was she?

"I'm fine, Moe." Leo shook her head, smiling, though something tiny and jagged had lodged itself between her ribs.

"Un-huh." Moe studied her, and Leo fought not to fidget. "So tell me. What happens if you can't convince this athlete to judge the contest? Are you going to accept his answer and move on? Or are you going to beat yourself to a bloody pulp? Because as strong as your will is, Leo, this man saying no is a possibility. And so is you not achieving one of your all-important goals."

Not happening.

Because this was about more than Owen Strafford—or Patrick or whatever name he decided to go by—and his decision to guest judge a chili contest. The festival counted on every dime it raised not only as revenue for the various businesses in Rose Bend—including the inn—but also because those funds benefited Purple Heart Homes, an organization that built homes for disabled vets and their families. And with Wolf being ex-military, the cause was dear to her heart.

So nope, this was bigger than her reluctance to be in the same vicinity of the one-night stand she'd ghosted. Or his desire to disappear.

Besides, the people here were football crazy. So Owen/ Patrick would be the perfect publicity draw.

She got it. He'd probably come to Rose Bend to get away from...people. Yes, she might've googled him since returning home yesterday. Owen Strafford. Heisman Trophy winner. Graduated from Indiana University Bloomington. First round draft pick to the Jersey Knights, number-two pick overall. All-pro. Two-time Super Bowl champion. League MVP. All this in an eight-year career.

And if not for a rain-slicked night and a new dad falling asleep at the wheel, it wouldn't have ended at eight.

He'd lost his career. A torn ACL, the articles had detailed. Owen had retired after the accident that had left him injured and scarred, and she could only imagine the hole ripped in his life. Could understand why he'd sought the relative obscurity of Rose Bend considering how...unkind the press, social media, even football fans could be. Some of those comments when he'd announced his retirement... She ground her teeth together. God, you'd think people owned the title and registration to his ass and soul.

And yet, here she sat across from Moe determined to get him to do her bidding. She should feel guilty. And okay, yeah, there was a slight twinge.

But if she had to beg the man who'd rendered her to a faceless booty call for a favor, then he could damn well do this for charity. Besides, he'd made her lose complete control once, and a small part of her had never forgiven herself for it. She had a point to prove—to herself and to him—although he didn't remember her. She could be around him and not break her rules, not lose herself...again.

But the only way to prove it was to get him to judge the contest. So Owen was going to say yes to this festival, dammit!

Of course, she said none of this to Moe.

It might come over as a skosh insensitive.

"And what about you, Leo?" her mother continued. "If you give so much time to everything and everyone else, where do you come in? You said you're fine, but it's my job as your mother to worry about you. You haven't mentioned Gregory once in the last two weeks. And I've let it go. But since you seem bound and determined to devote all of your time to other projects, it makes me think you're deflecting from something else. Would that something else be Gregory?"

"Gregory who?"

Moe's face softened as did her voice. "Oh, Leo, sweetie..."

"No, it's fine—I'm serious," she insisted, when her mother tipped her head and pinned a look on her that fairly screamed *bullshit*. "We just...weren't a good fit," she finished lamely.

But how could she say, *We were actually a perfect match. God couldn't have created a more flawless set of bookends. Gregory cares about his accounting firm as much as I do about the inn. Which, unfortunately, means we were more like pen pals rather than a couple.*

No, she couldn't say that. Mainly because she didn't want to hear yet another lecture on balance. On prioritizing the "important things in life." That was what Moe and the rest of her family didn't get. The inn was the most important thing in her life.

The inn didn't criticize.

It didn't change.

It didn't leave her.

She could depend on the inn to always be there, to remain stable and immutable.

People couldn't promise the same.

"You were seeing each other for three months. How can you be just *fine*? I swear I'm beginning to hate that word. That's what Cole would always tell me. 'I'm fine. I'm fine.' As if I don't have eyes in my head and I can't see that you're anything but *fine*."

Leo's breath stalled in her chest, and she stared at her mother, not even blinking as Moe's last vehement note quivered in the silence.

"Shit." Moe blinked. Then huffed out a heavy sigh. "I'm sorry, sweetie. I didn't mean…" She clasped her hands around her cup and lifted it to her mouth, taking a sip.

"Moe," Leo whispered, worry tarring over her irritation.

Shallow puffs of air whistled through her lungs, and she studied her mother, for the first time noting the delicate lines fanning above her mouth and creasing her forehead. Shadows dimmed her eyes. Pain and fatigue. It'd only been a week since she'd had that freak fall down the back steps and broken her ankle.

"No." Moe held up a hand, palm out. "I'm sorry. It's this stupid ankle. I—"

"You're so used to being independent and doing everything on your own, and now being grounded and having to depend on others has you feeling helpless, frustrated and just a wee bit angry?"

Moe squinted at her. "Since when did you get so smart?"

Leo shrugged. "I blame it on my mother. She's something of a know-it-all, too, but don't tell her I said so."

"Shut it." Moe snorted. "Smart-ass."

"I get that from her, too." Leo grinned, reaching across and squeezing her mother's hand again. "I think it goes without saying, but…" She paused, meeting Moe's green gaze. "I get my strength from you, Moe. That's why I'm fine. And it's why you might be on those crutches for the next six weeks, but it doesn't diminish how much you're needed around here."

"I know, I know." Moe waved her free hand. "I'm just feeling a little…mortal." She chuckled and flipped their hands, squeezing Leo's. "Thanks, sweetie. I appreciate the pep talk. Now, if you don't mind, I'm going to take my coffee up to my room and prepare the menu for Lorraine. I love that woman—God knows I do," Moe muttered, slowly pushing back from the table and rising to her feet…or rather foot. "And I appreciate her helping me out in the kitchen while my ankle heals. But if she tries to rearrange my refrigerator and cabinets one more time, I'm going to clothesline her with my crutch."

"Ooh, hold up on that and I'll get Sonny to film Kitchen Smackdown Five and we can sell it as part of the summer package along with tickets to the motorcycle rally."

She rounded the table, picking up the crutches and handing them to Moe, while her mother arched an eyebrow.

"Make sure he gets my good side. And that the curtains are pulled back to add natural light so my skin looks nice and dewy while I make sure she remembers to keep her hands off my spice rack."

Leo barked out a loud crack of laughter, picking up her mother's coffee.

"Damn, Moe. You're savage."

"And don't you forget it."

"Yes, ma'am."

Still grinning, Leo followed behind Moe, a keen eye on her mom as she slowly hobbled toward the family wing of the inn. Her humor faded as Moe's outburst flickered in her mind. And a dogged determination welled inside her, solidifying.

She refused to give Moe one more thing to feel helpless and worried about. Her mother had entrusted her with the inn and her position on the spring festival. Leo wouldn't let her down with either one.

So Owen Strafford should brace himself.

Because she was coming for him.

CHAPTER FOUR

THROUGHOUT HIS CAREER, Owen had been known for keeping his head in stressful situations. For maintaining his cool under pressure.

Case in point.

Last year. Third and seven, final drive of the playoff game against Baltimore. One hesitation, one wrong move, could've meant he'd end up under a dogpile. Instead, he'd evaded the blitz from an all-pro defensive end to hit the receiver for the first down to seal the game.

That was then.

But only a day ago he'd stood in the doorway of his rental home, faced a five-foot-six-inch slip of a woman and panicked.

And now, as he listened to that same woman knock on his door again, he hovered on the verge of royally fucking up once more.

Because, with everything in him, he did not want to open that door.

Did not want to look into the beautiful, guileless, *perfect* face of the woman who'd known him as the man he used to be.

Didn't want to remember the white-hot passion they'd shared and know with every inch of his scarred being that she would cringe if he tried to touch her like that now.

Yeah, he needed for her to go away.

And if that meant hiding out until she got the picture, well, he had nothing but time on his hands.

"I'm not going away, so you might as well answer." Another sharp rap against wood that he swore carried a note of impatience. "And I can see the shadow of your feet under the door so I know you're there and can hear me."

No, she couldn't... *Fuck.*

Owen scowled down his body. Goddammit. His feet did cast a long-ass shadow. Or maybe she was just playing him so he'd answer the door. Serve her right if he called her bluff—

"I'm not bluffing."

Well, *damn.* Was she a mind reader now?

Irritation blasted through him. This was *his* house. If he didn't want company, that was his damn prerogative. And his damn prerogative was no company. Especially pushy, won't-take-no-for-an-answer, sexy-as-fuck, I-know-what-you-sound-like-when-you-come company.

Another knock echoed in his foyer. And goddamn, if it didn't strike him as a threat.

The woman seriously underestimated his spirit of rebellion.

He pivoted and headed back in the direction of his study just as Leo Dennison hit the chorus of a Chaka Khan song. Loudly. And horribly off-key.

Jesus Christ.

The neighbor's dog down the street howled in a plaintive plea for her to shut the hell up.

"That is not how that note is intended to go."

Leo cut off mid-*whoa* and smiled at him. "Oh, good. I'm so glad you decided to answer the door."

He arched an eyebrow, crossing his arms over his chest.

"I usually don't give in to terroristic threats, but I'm making an exception in your case."

The corner of her full, sensual lips curled just as her gaze dipped to his arms. His bare arms. *Shit.* He'd forgotten about the sleeveless tank and long basketball shorts he'd thrown on after his post-workout shower. The light pink scars crisscrossing his forearms and distorting his sleeve of tattoos hadn't affected his muscle movement or range of motion. Unlike those on his face, the glass hadn't scored deep enough to damage his nerve endings. And yet at this moment, the touch of her eyes on his skin burned, and hot pinpricks danced along his flesh.

He detested the sensation.

Resented her for glimpsing what only doctors had seen in all these months.

Hated feeling so exposed...so vulnerable.

He unfolded his arms and stepped back, out of the suddenly glaring sunlight and into the safer shadows of his foyer.

"You've shown up at my house, *again*, unannounced and uninvited. And now you're doing something that's masquerading as singing at the top of your lungs and torturing my neighbor's dog. What do you want, Leo Dennison?"

The wattage of her smile brightened, but it didn't touch her eyes. Those blue-gray depths remained smoky, obscuring any emotion that he might read. Such a difference from a year ago, when he could read every feeling—excitement, humor, insecurity, lust—in that lovely gaze.

Something tight twinged in his chest. Something that almost felt like...loss.

"We didn't finish our conversation yesterday—"

"We did."

"—so I thought I'd give you some time and return to continue it today."

Only the drone of a bee buzzing around one of the bushes by his front steps and the distant bark of a dog— probably in gratitude—disrupted the silence between them.

Finally, he sighed and resisted the urge to dig the heels of his palms into his eyes. "You're not going to leave, are you?"

"Not until you hear me out."

Owen sighed. Yeah, it was rude as hell, but then again, so was showing up on a person's porch and bogarting an "invitation" into their house by means *all* foul. But given how he'd treated Leo the day before—pretending not to know her after he'd spent hours inside her—he could at least listen to whatever she was hell-bent on pitching.

Then he'd kick her out.

"Five minutes," he growled.

"Perfect," she said. Triumph glittered in her eyes, curved her lush mouth.

And fuck if that didn't make him want to stalk forward until her back hit the railing of the porch behind her, bend over her and take that mouth. Hear and taste that delicious moan etched into his memory as it hit his tongue. Curl his fingers around those sexy hips. Tip them forward so he could grind his cock into the welcoming softness of her belly...

Shit.

He stepped back. And back again, granting her a wide berth to enter the house. As if that could somehow distance him from the lust working its way through his system. Impossible.

But physical space was a good thing. There would be no accidental brushing of arms or inhaling of that elusive lilac-and-fresh-rain scent. This wasn't about a deep dive into a night that had marked his soul.

No, this was about temporarily giving in to the skirmish of hearing her out so he could win the battle of getting rid of this beautiful, breathing reminder of the man he used to be.

The man she'd once stared at with shy desire and not rank pity.

The man he could never be again unless God was suddenly into handing out "do overs." And since he'd prayed for that very thing hundreds of times in that dark, hazy time before true wakefulness hit, and yet still woke to the horror of the present, Owen doubted that would happen. There was no returning to a time when he was whole, had the career of his dreams and knew who the fuck he was.

Bright anger, dipped in helplessness, surged hard inside him.

Get out.

The command beat at his throat, barreled onto his tongue. And only the tight clench of his teeth trapped the bitter words. He needed her gone. For his pride. For his self-preservation.

For his fucking sanity.

Body pulled taut as a rope seconds away from snapping, he stiffly turned toward the door and closed it, allowing his eyes to follow suit. Just for a second. He needed this moment to…breathe. But that might be asking too much.

Because even as Leo moved into the living room off the foyer, her heady, sensual scent lingered, teasing his nostrils, filling his lungs. Carrying him back to when he'd sought out the places on her sweetly curved body where that fragrance was richer, more condensed. Addictive.

That thought shattered his paralysis and propelled him forward. He stalked into the large, airy living room as if chased—yeah, that wasn't far off—and immediately cursed her choice of rooms.

Three large, rectangular windows graced one of the three walls, the top arches halting just short of brushing the ceiling. Since he didn't spend time in this room, he hadn't really noticed the sheer panels that covered them, doing nothing to block the natural sunlight from streaming into the room like a goddamn spotlight.

His skin prickled, and phantom pain throbbed through his scar. As if he were a vampire and the sun hitting his face burned. Only flames didn't set him afire. Humiliation did. Shame did.

Only the scraps of his pride prohibited him from charging across the floor like a madman, snatching the cords from the burgundy drapes and letting them enshroud the room in deep shadows.

But when her gaze once again dropped to his arms then lifted to his face, and he spotted her compassion, he almost abandoned those scraps of pride.

"Go ahead and get a good look. Maybe you should get your phone out and snap a picture. But be advised, you've wasted thirty seconds of your five minutes."

She cocked her head, narrowed her eyes on him. "Since I need your help, I'm going to let that slide. Still, that's the second time you've accused me of gawking at you like you're some sideshow at a circus. Sorry to disappoint you, Mr. Strafford, but while I'm sure you're accustomed to people falling all over themselves to stare, take pictures and basically make asses of themselves over you, not my circus, not my monkey. Now," she said while gracefully sinking onto the couch behind her as if she wore a couture ball gown instead of a white shirt with a side bow at the collar, khaki linen pants and nude heels, "can we get back to why I'm here?"

He stared at her, shock and annoyance dancing in his gut, sparking in his chest. What was her game? Was this payback for pretending not to know her?

Right after his accident, he'd had some women act as if his disfigurement didn't bother them. But actresses they weren't, and they couldn't pull it off for long. Not when their gazes would land somewhere over his shoulder. Not when they would brace themselves before brushing their mouths over his because of the scar that bisected the corner of his mouth.

The first time he'd tried to have sex after the accident...

Disgust, pain and grief coiled low in his belly, and he glanced away from Leo, an ache blooming along his jaw at the tight clench of his teeth.

"You're right." He moved to the mantel above the fireplace and stared at the empty wood where the previous owners had no doubt filled the space with framed pictures of family and friends. Even before the accident, he wouldn't have been able to do that. Turning around, he leaned his back against the shelf, crossing his arms. "Why don't we get down to what you want so you can get on with your day and I can get back to my—what did you call it?—circus."

Emotion he couldn't decipher flashed in her eyes, and once more he ruthlessly squashed the curiosity to unearth the thoughts in her head.

"Before I begin, let me apologize for ambushing you today. It wasn't fair, and I'm sorry for that."

She paused and inhaled. Her head dipped to her lap and for a moment, she studied her clasped hands. The man he'd once been would've either cracked a joke to put her at ease or even crossed the room, knelt before her to cover her hands and gently urge her to talk to him.

But he wasn't that man anymore, so he remained standing against the mantel, arms crossed. Ignoring the tingle in his palms.

Finally, she lifted her head and hit him with those blue-gray eyes that had haunted him for ten long months.

"Yesterday— I didn't explain very well about the spring festival. Yes, it's an annual event. And yes, people host all manner of booths. There are contests, games, music and even a pageant. It draws not just the members of our community, but those from neighboring towns and cities, as well as tourists. It's a source of revenue for many of the businesses in Rose Bend, including Kinsale Inn, the bed-and-breakfast my family owns and runs. Yet, it means more than that."

A small wrinkle creased her brow, and she flattened her hands over her thighs, spreading her fingers wide. For some reason he couldn't tear his gaze away from the short, no-nonsense nails with their pale pink shade. Jerking his attention from them, he swept up over the pretty but conservative shirt to the slightly darker shade of lipstick and light makeup.

It all contrasted sharply with the woman whose lips had once boasted a bold fuck-me red, whose eyes had appeared brilliant and mysterious with smoky eyeshadow. Even her nails and toes had been painted in the same vibrant shade of her lips. And he would know because there hadn't been one centimeter of her body that he'd left unexplored.

Which version reflected the true woman?

The passionate, vivacious woman who'd not only branded herself on his memory but also caterwauled a classic song on his front porch?

Or the polite, reserved and nervous businesswoman perched on his couch?

Maybe a fascinating combination of both?

Yeah, he needed her gone.

Five minutes be damned.

Because fascination threatened the isolated construct he'd erected here in Rose Bend. The numb existence he'd carefully built for himself in the past few months, just to survive.

Fascination was his nemesis.

He pushed from the mantel, straightening. "Ms. Dennison—"

"Leo," she corrected and thrust up a palm, shaking her head. "And you promised me five minutes. I still have three left. Please hear me out."

His muscles locked, screaming with the need to usher her from his one safe place.

There was nothing safe about Leo Dennison.

"I have a confession—I googled you before coming here today."

Body already pulled taut, now Owen tried to mimic a mannequin. His breath froze in his chest.

It wasn't the invasion of privacy that had panic creeping through him. He was an athlete. An expectation of privacy had ceased to exist around middle school when scouts from colleges had started to show up at his games, and reporters from ESPN had taken notice of him at football camps.

No, it was what he knew she'd seen when she'd entered his name in the search engine. What articles and images would've popped up. That was what had acid loitering in his veins.

"I read that your uncle and a couple of your cousins served in the armed forces. I also know you've financially supported organizations in honor of our troops. The festival not only supports the town, but a substantial part of the funds is also donated to Purple Heart Homes, which builds houses for local disabled vets and their families. This organization holds a special place in my heart. My brother served, too. In Iraq. And he lost his best friend over there. So making this festival a success is important...and personal."

"I've heard of Purple Heart Homes. It's a worthy cause. They do admirable work."

She nodded, her face lighting with a warm smile. Rising from the couch, she took a couple of steps toward him, then stopped, but her enthusiasm animated her face, her hands.

"It's true. With more disabled veterans returning home, this gift is just a small token for their service and their sacrifice. If the vet already owns a home, then PHH retrofits it and completely assumes the cost. If they are building a brand-new home, then the veteran is only responsible for fifty percent of a small mortgage while Purple Heart Homes gifts the other half of the debt. Either way, our servicemen and their families are honored with homes that are totally accessible, with larger doorways, sliding shower doors, medical railings and seats for bathrooms, mechanical chairs that transport them from one room to another, if that's needed. And that's just to name some of the necessities they make possible. With the festival, we raise funds to help offset those costs."

He didn't speak—couldn't speak—just stood there, damn near *enthralled* by the passion that vibrated in her voice. It burrowed past skin and bone and brushed over something shriveled in his chest. That something he'd intentionally buried and ignored since finishing rehab and announcing his retirement.

Even more evidence of why he needed her out.

Two minutes and thirty seconds.

"I'm imposing. Believe me, I understand this, and again, I apologize, because you came to Rose Bend for your own reasons. And I truly respect those reasons, Owen. All I'm asking for is a little of your time. A couple of hours and one afternoon. A couple of hours for promotional pictures and one afternoon to judge a chili contest. A chili contest may seem trite and silly to you, but it's one of our most popular events, and having a celebrated professional athlete will be an incredible draw. Tons of people will attend on that day alone just to see you, which means they will browse the other booths and hopefully spend money. And that in turn will benefit Purple Heart Homes. Not only would I appreciate you volunteering your time, but the town would—"

"No."

The word burst from him, harsh and abrupt. Leo blinked at him, her head snapping back.

He would've tempered his response, softened it…if he could've. *If.* But with panic clawing at him, he couldn't manage it. Hell, with blackness encroaching into his peripheral vision, and his breath soughing in and out of his lungs, deafening in his ears, he could barely stand. Only the press of his back into the mantel grounded him, propped him up, because his feet had gone out right around *tons of people will attend…*

A panic attack.

It'd been a while, but he still recognized the signs.

Lurching forward on feet with no feeling, he half-walked, half-stumbled across the room toward the windows. Toward the semblance of space, of air. Sweat popped on his skin and rolled down his spine. He pressed his palms to the glass. Bending his elbows, he pressed his forehead to the glass as well, focusing on the coolness and inhaling a deep breath. Holding it. Releasing it. He repeated the exercise until the claustrophobic tightness in his chest eased and his heartbeat didn't pound in his ears. Until he could trust his legs to bear his weight. Until his skin expanded back to its normal size instead of seeming two sizes too small for his frame.

"Owen?"

A small palm settled on his back, and he flinched away from the too-gentle touch as if scalded. Pain flashed in her eyes, and regret knotted his gut. Responsibility for that hurt lay heavy on him, as did the apology he couldn't shove past his constricted throat.

Humiliation licked at his skin, leaving scorch marks behind that blistered under her too-perceptive gaze.

"Owen, are you okay?" she asked, not putting her hand on him again.

No, she'd placed space between them, and damn if that careful distance didn't send bile surging for the back of his throat. She no longer treated him like a lover she regretted. Now, she handled him like a wounded animal that might lash out, bite.

And the sad part? She wasn't wrong.

"I can't. I'm sorry," he rasped. And he was. God, he was. "I wish..." He swallowed, hard. "But I can't."

He lifted his lashes, but only blindly stared out the window. He couldn't look at her. Afraid of what he'd glimpse. That ever-present pity. Disappointment. Fear. Disgust. He couldn't chance discovering which would darken her features.

Coward.

Yeah, well, he was used to this development in the past year.

"Owen, I don't know what I said to upset you, but I can see I did. Why don't I give you time to think on it—"

"I'm not changing my mind." He shoved off the window and paced across the room, still avoiding her gaze. "Do you mind letting yourself out? I need to make a phone call," he lied.

He didn't wait for her reply. His scar pulled tight as his mouth flattened and he rushed from the living room, charging down the hallway toward the study, his hideaway.

Before he crossed the threshold, though, he caught the soft, firm closing of the front door. And he paused just outside the study, his hands gripping the frame, head bowed.

They seemed to be making a habit of running from each other.

She'd started it in Boston.

He'd continued it the first day she'd shown up on his porch and kept it going today.

Worry eddied inside him like the spring storms that had been swirling through the April afternoons.

What if Leo Dennison became a hard habit to break?

CHAPTER FIVE

"Um, tell me why I'm making beds and cleaning rooms again?" Sydney Dennison frowned at Leo as she tucked the corner of a forest green fitted sheet at one end of the mattress. "Especially when I don't even like to do this in my own house?"

"Because." Leo expertly finished folding her side under and grabbed the matching top sheet, snapping it open.

"Because what?" her best friend pressed, brown eyes narrowed.

"Because it's part of the best friend contract. Page three. Paragraph four, clause B, section C. You really need to read that thing. I'm tired of having to explain your duties and responsibilities to you."

Sydney cocked her head, her dark curls brushing her shoulders. "Shouldn't you be downstairs making schedules? Or managing promotions? Or corralling vendors for weddings? Why're you up here cleaning the inn's rooms anyway?"

"What?" Leo propped a fist on her hip and arched an eyebrow. "Are you too good to make a bed now?"

"Heffa, please," Sydney scoffed, tugging on the sheet again and shooting Leo a side-eye. "Have you met my mother?" As Sydney and Leo had been best friends since they were little girls, the question was rhetorical. "She's the reason why I hate the domestic arts now. You know good and well I'm not a snob when it comes to cleaning. But I also know that you have in your employ two people whose jobs are to do this very thing. Which tells me—" Sydney jabbed a thumb at her chest "—that you—" this time the finger jab was aimed in Leo's direction "—are avoiding someone or something. Or you're trying to stay busy to avoid thinking about someone or something. Or both. So give, Leontyne Barbara Dennison. What's going on?"

"God, I hate having a best friend sometimes," Leo muttered, snatching the sheet up the mattress before folding the top half back in concise, irritated movements.

"Right?" Sydney grinned, following her lead. "But don't try to change the subject—" A knock on the door echoed in what was named the Limerick Room after the western county in Ireland. "Hold that thought," she said, popping up a finger.

As her friend crossed the room to answer the door, Leo gathered up the comforter off the floral upholstered armchair. It had a matching ottoman and sat next to an oak bedside table and reading lamp. This room happened to be one of her favorites, and when she went on one of her cleaning/ruminating jags—damn Sydney for being a know-it-all!—she usually hit this room first. With its framed photography of scenes from the famed Irish county, the feminine vanity, dresser, scrolled desk and sleigh bed, the room wouldn't have been out of place in a film set in the Irish countryside. The sweet elegance and simplicity of the space calmed her. She'd never stopped moving long enough to take a vacation—a sad indictment for a twenty-nine-year-old—but if she ever did, it would be to the lovely county that had inspired this room.

"Hey, Sinead," Sydney greeted Leo's younger sister. "Is this little one giving you trouble?"

Leo paused, the comforter weighing down her arms, as

she stared at her friend's beautiful face, lit up with love. The ache warned her to glance away until she got herself under control. But those same stirrings—tugs of pain and yearning—didn't allow her to look away from her friend and the baby she now cuddled against her chest.

"No, not this angel," Sinead said, her usually serious expression softened by a smile as she swept a hand over baby Patience's thick, tight curls. "But when she started patting my chest, I figured she was hungry. I can change a diaper, keep her entertained and love on her, but getting milk out of these?" Sinead waved her free hand over her breasts. "Not going to happen. So I had no choice but to bring her to you. But," Sinead said, squinting at Sydney, "I get my niece back after you're finished."

Sydney laughed, brushing a kiss over Patience's chubby cheek even as the five-month-old baby turned her head in search of that elusive nipple.

"Deal."

"All right. Don't make me have to come looking for you. It won't be pretty," Sinead teased, handing Sydney a yellow diaper bag.

Or maybe she wasn't teasing. With Leo's younger sister, it was sometimes hard to tell.

All the Dennison kids had their roles. For instance, Wolf was the teddy bear they could all confide in. Leo, the overachieving perfectionist. Which was just wrong. What was so terrible about striving to be the best? And wanting everything in its place? Nothing. Nothing at all. Life was more stable that way. It was…safer.

And Sinead? Well, Sinead was their resident Thinker. Quiet, reserved, in her head. Dependable and steady as they came. Still, seeing her sister lose some of that aloofness with the baby continued to stun Leo.

"Am I excused from my domestic duties to feed my off-spring?" Sydney asked, already crossing to the window seat as Sinead closed the door.

Leo shrugged a shoulder, dropping the comforter on the bed. "I suppose. But only because I'm afraid what havoc my niece will wreak if you don't pop that nipple in her mouth."

Snickering, Sydney skillfully maneuvered her shirt, and when her friend went for the cup of her bra, Leo turned back to making up the bed, granting her privacy. In moments, the soft, hungry sounds of her niece feeding punctuated the room, and though that dull throb in her chest persisted, Leo smiled.

"When is Daniel coming up to see her?" Leo glanced over her shoulder.

"Next weekend. He and his wife are staying for a week since it's spring break for him."

Leo paused in the middle of folding the cover back and sat on the mattress, facing Sydney. "You and Cole okay with that?" she murmured, studying Sydney's face for a hint of discomfort.

But Sydney shook her head, lifting the blanket she'd tossed over her daughter to check on Patience before meeting Leo's gaze. "No, we're good." Sydney wrinkled her nose before rolling her eyes. "And I mean it, so you can get that look off your face."

Snorting, Leo didn't bother asking what *look*. It was the one that called bullshit. But she didn't sense any hurt or resentment from Sydney. Which kind of made sense. Sydney and her ex-husband, Daniel, had gone through a rough patch when she'd been pregnant with Patience and first returned to Rose Bend—threatening to take custody of her baby would do that. But with the support and love of Cole, she'd mended that relationship and enjoyed co-parenting with Daniel. Her ex-husband had even moved from Charlotte, North Carolina, to Boston to be closer to Patience. Still…

"A week, though?" Leo arched an eyebrow. "That's a lot of time away from her."

"When he came for Christmas, it was for about a week, and we managed. It actually went well. It meant pumping more breast milk, which don't let anyone lie to you, is not all that fun." The corner of her mouth curled up, but her eyes held a hint of sadness. "Besides, this will be practice for when she's older and our custody agreement changes. Then she'll be with him for several days at a time and for holidays. Before I know it, that time will be here," she whispered.

"And Cole will be here to get you through that first visit. And the second one. And the fifth one. We'll be here, too." Leo leaned forward, holding her friend's gaze.

"Thanks, Leo." Sydney dipped her head, caressing her daughter's hair. Several quiet moments passed, and then Leo found herself pinned under her friend's frown again. "But don't think this sweet, sensitive moment has distracted me from my original question. What the beep is wrong with you?"

"The. Beep?"

"I'm trying to clean up my language around the baby."

"Oh." Leo nodded. "Good luck with that."

"Again. Deflecting. You might as well confess, chick. You're not very good at this."

Leo huffed out an aggrieved sigh. "Fine."

Good Lord, why had her pulse started revving like a race car? Maybe because a pair of shadow-filled hazel eyes flashed in front of her. And tightly muscled, inked arms with thin, white scars declaring the pain inflicted on that body.

"Leo?"

Blinking, Leo refocused on her friend.

"Sorry." Pinching the bridge of her nose, Leo grimaced. "See, what happened… God, I have no idea how to even say this," she muttered.

"Hey, this is me. Safe space 'n' all that. No judgment. And whatever you tell me stays here."

"I know, I know. That, too, is in the friendship contract. Seriously, Syd, do you just use the thing as a coaster?"

"Out of curiosity," Sydney said, seamlessly switching Patience from one breast to the next without flashing Leo. "What are the consequences of breaking this contract?"

Leo gave a full-body shudder. "It's best we don't talk about that…unpleasantness."

They stared at each other. Grinned widely.

"You're so full of shit," Sydney said.

Tsking, Leo wagged a finger back and forth. "I thought you were curbing your language in front of the baby."

"And you're still avoiding the subject. Stop stalling and spill, Leo."

"Okay, it's just you're the first person I've told about this." She shoved her fingers through her hair but drew up short as they bumped into her ponytail. With an impatient grunt, she yanked the band from her hair. "A little over a year ago, I traveled to Boston for a convention, and that Saturday night I went to the hotel bar for a drink. I met a man. A really hot man that I couldn't believe was looking at me across a crowded bar, as cliché as that sounds. With a face like his, he could've easily been a self-entitled, arrogant ass. But he wasn't. Sweet. Funny. Self-deprecating. We talked for hours, and though I'd never, ever done anything remotely like it before, when he asked me up to his hotel room, I said yes."

Sydney didn't utter a word, but her eyes widened so far Leo could glimpse a reflection of damn near the whole room in them.

"Just go ahead and say it." Leo twirled a hand at her. "Go on and get it out."

"You sure?"

"Might as well. I can practically see the hamster on that wheel in your head."

"Okay." Sydney nodded. Glanced down at her baby, who'd slipped into a milk coma. *"Oh, my God,"* she whisper-yelled. "You picked up a stranger in a bar and had a one-night stand! You're such a badass, Leontyne Dennison! Was it hot? Was he a grower or a shower? Could you walk straight the next morning? Details, woman!"

Leo blinked. Then snickered. Then laughed, a cleansing outpour.

Tipping her head back, she huffed a breathless chuckle to the ceiling. "You're crazy, Syd. I don't know why I was nervous to tell you about this."

"I don't know why, either." Sydney scoffed. "I'm the least judgmental person I know. But especially with you. You're my best friend. Hell, closer than that, you're like a sister to me. And now I'm just staring at you in awe because you got hot stranger dick."

"Hot stranger dick? Really?" She snorted. "And to answer your questions, hot as hell, none of your business and again, none of your business."

Sydney pouted, moving Patience in a carefully choreographed dance as she shifted the baby to her lap and slipped back into her bra and shirt. "You're such a Debbie Downer. I'd give you the details of my sex life."

"Oh, God." Leo gagged. "Since those details would include my brother, I *appreciate* you keeping them to your-self."

"Whatever," Sydney grumbled. "Well, can you tell me about the morning after? Did you get his number? Have you called him? Have you seen him again?"

The next morning? Well, I snuck out of that hotel suite like a thief with my shoes in my hands, my panties in my purse and my heart in my throat. And no, I didn't get his number or give him mine—I just wanted to get the hell out of there. Because anyone who could make me throw my in-hibitions and rules to the wind would entice me to be just as reckless with my heart. And I can't afford that.

The too-honest answer floated through her head, but she locked it down. How could she admit that to Sydney when she could barely admit it to herself?

"Hmm." Leo grimaced. "Funny you should ask that."

"Uh-oh. I sense this is where the story takes a turn."

"Yeah, well, remember I told you I assumed Moe's place on the spring festival committee? And that I had to go ask our resident recluse, who happens to be some kind of pro athlete, to be a judge for the chili contest?" When Sydney nodded, she continued. "Well, through some bizarre twist of fate, the pro athlete and my hot stranger happen to be the same person."

Sydney's loud gasp bounced off the walls.

"The hell you say. So hot stranger is hot celebrity ath-lete stranger? Good Lord, Leo, you sure know how to pick 'em." Delight gleamed in her eyes as she gently laid the baby over her shoulder, rubbing her back. The sweet ma-ternal movement did not match up with the lascivious, ma-niacal grin she aimed at Leo. She glanced away from both. "Spill, woman. What did you do when you realized who he was? What did he say? This is *so* delicious!"

"Well, funny you should ask *that*," Leo muttered, her shoulders curling forward before she was conscious of the embarrassed gesture. Then she deliberately straightened her posture. This wasn't on *her* but all on Owen Strafford. "He didn't remember me."

Sydney's chin tucked in toward her neck, her eyes gathering enough storm clouds to blot out the sun in the sky.

"Say what, now?" she asked in a voice that contained a fair share of offense. And a note of menace.

Leo smiled. She wouldn't have thought the tiny sparks of humor in her chest possible, but there they were. All because her best friend sat there, murder in her eyes and retribution in her voice for the man who'd dared to hurt Leo.

This was what she'd missed when Sydney had left Rose Bend over eight years ago. Yes, Leo's family unconditionally loved and supported her. But a part of Leo believed they had to; that was what family did, after all. But Sydney had no such obligation.

She'd been Leo's friend, her sister-of-the-heart, simply because she liked *her*. Not because of her brothers and despite Leo's compulsive pursuit of perfection and need for control. Sydney had accepted her. With her best friend, Leo had belonged. And when she'd left, and hadn't kept in contact, Leo had felt adrift, like debris on wind-tossed waves. She'd battled the sense of abandonment that had hounded her for years afterward. But when Sydney returned to Rose Bend last summer, it'd been like a homecoming and the hurt had sloughed off like dead, dry skin.

Even if faint echoes of the pain resonated deep in her chest sometimes.

Leo shook her head, both in response to Sydney's question as much to clear her head of her sober thoughts.

"He didn't remember me," she repeated. "Not my name,

my face, not that night. I was just another random one-night stand, apparently."

"Asshole," Sydney snapped. Her moratorium on cursing must not count if the baby was sleeping. "Did you remind him? Hopefully with a couple of middle fingers to get your point across."

"Not quite. I pretty much followed his lead. Besides, I couldn't say, 'Hey, remember me? I'm the woman you gifted four orgasms. Thanks for that. Such a shame it's not even a blip on your groupie radar.' But considering I snuck out of the hotel room while he was sleeping—that might be why I didn't claim any space in his memory."

Well, damn. She hadn't meant to let that slip.

"Four orgasms?" Sydney gaped at her. Then silently mouthed the two words again, eyes wide with disbelief. *"Damn."*

"You see my problem now?"

"Yes." Sydney nodded. "No wonder your relationships haven't worked out since then. How does anyone compare with one, two, three—" she popped up corresponding fingers "—*four* orgasms? Poor saps never stood a chance."

"No, you goof." Leo frowned, throwing her hands up in the air.

To be fair to the poor saps, her relationships hadn't been working out *before* that night, either.

Although… No. She mentally shook her head. No way. She had *not* been unconsciously comparing the last two men she'd been involved with to Patrick—or rather, Owen. It'd been mere hours she'd spent with him. Not enough to truly know him. Certainly not enough to form a standard by which to judge other men. That was just…farcical.

But none of those men had threatened her carefully constructed world.

"My problem is that I'm in the position of begging a man I'm biblically acquainted with to volunteer his time to the festival. And pretend that I don't know what he looks like naked."

"Yeah, I see your problem. But…" Sydney tilted her head to the side. "Can I ask you a question?" Not waiting for Leo's acquiescence, she forged ahead. "Why did you leave the next morning?"

Because I was afraid of seeing regret on his face.

Because my utter loss of control terrified me.

Because I wanted to stay too badly. And if experience has taught me anything, it's that whatever I desire too much will be snatched away. Such as you staying in Rose Bend. Cole's son and wife not dying… My baby.

But again, she said none of that. Instead, she shrugged a shoulder. "Because it was a one-night stand. Nothing more. As he proved when he didn't remember my name or face."

"Okay, Leo, I love you. You know I do. And I also know you better than most. So I'm calling bullshit on that answer. I think you ran scared. What happened? Did he make you feel too much? Did you want more than a one-night stand with him?"

Anger flashed inside her, hot and bright. Eight years Sydney had been gone. Eight years she'd abandoned her with barely any phone calls. How could she claim to know her better than most?

No one did.

No one knew about her darkest secret. Her deepest pain.

No one…

Then, as quick as the anger appeared, it burned away, scattering like ashes. In spite of lingering hurt, Leo would always love Sydney. Simply because she'd brought Cole back to Moe, to the family. They'd all feared he would never heal, never return to the smiling, *alive* man he used to be before losing Tonia and their baby in childbirth. And having her best friend back brought Leo joy.

"Right now you're being one of those women who are so blissfully in love they want all their friends to fall in love, too." Leo smirked. "And I adore you for it. But no. I wasn't running scared. I just recognized it for what it was. One night. Admittedly, one good night, but still…"

"Okay. If you say so. That's also in the best friend contract, too, y'know. Agreeing even when we disagree."

Sydney grinned, then something outside the window caught her eye and she gasped. Patience started, her little body wriggling on Sydney's shoulder. Patting her daughter's back, Sydney didn't remove her gaze from the view that overlooked the front yard of the inn.

"Tell me something. Does your athlete have long-ish black hair, a body that would give The Rock insecurity issues and a walk that promises four orgasms? A promise we both know he can deliver on?"

Leo jackknifed from the mattress, her pounding heart lodging in her throat. "What the hell? Owen is here?" She didn't wait for Sydney's response but charged over the few steps to the windows. "Oh, my God. He's here," she whispered, gaping down at his tall, wide-shouldered, slim-hipped, utterly perfect frame. "What is he doing here?"

"I'm no expert on these things," Sydney drawled. "But it looks like he's talking to your brother."

"Sonny? *Oh, damn.*" She groaned, pivoting on her heel and bolting for the door. "I need to get down there." God knows she loved her baby brother, but he could either charm the pants off a person or scare the shit out of them. It just depended on the day.

"Not without me you're not," Sydney muttered.

But Leo had already hit the hallway.

There was no time to waste.

"WHAT THE HELL am I doing here?"

Owen pinched the bridge of his nose, the question bouncing back to him in the interior of his Range Rover. Yeah, he could sit here for hours and the answer would not be forthcoming. Sighing, he dropped his arm and stared out the windshield at Kinsale Inn.

The building could've graced the pages of a fairy tale. Clean steps swept up to a wraparound porch and a wide, red front door with sparkling glass panes. Dark green shutters bordered the many windows that adorned all three stories, including the smaller dormer windows of the third, smaller level with its slanted roof that topped the inn like a red cap. With the coming of spring, gorgeous pink and yellow flowers and lush green bushes added to its beauty.

Funny how he could easily imagine Leo here. Under her don't-take-no-shit care, those flowers didn't dare not bloom.

Shaking his head, he pushed the car door open. Just as he stepped out, his phone vibrated. Pulling his cell from his hoodie pocket with one hand, he shut the driver door with the other. He glanced down at the screen, part of him already knowing whose name would appear there. Very few people had his private phone number. His parents didn't bother to text; they called with their complaints. Sherrod definitely texted, but Owen had just talked to him earlier this morning. That left one other person.

Byron Shaw.

His thumb hovered over the notification, but he pressed the message before he could rethink it. Before the knot twisting his stomach could convince him differently. Because he could easily guess what Byron wanted. His agent hadn't been quiet about his opinion on the direction of Owen's career. And the pressure weighed on Owen like an anvil on his chest. There were days he couldn't breathe.

Owen, the Colts and the 49ers just reached out to ask about you. Wanting to know if you plan on coming out of retirement for the upcoming season. That's now six teams interested including the Knights. We need to make a decision soon with the draft coming up at the end of the month and training camp in June. Call me.

After scrubbing a hand down his face then dragging it over the nape of his neck, he dropped his arm by his side, his cell banging against his thigh. Again, that weight pressed down on him. The pressure of knowing other people relied on him. Byron. His parents. His personal assistant. Physically, there was nothing preventing him from returning to the game he loved and had been playing since he was six. But emotionally?

Emotionally, the thought of stepping back onto that football field in front of thousands of screaming people…no, sitting behind that table at a press junket with all those glaring, merciless cameras and greedy reporters with intrusive questions had chills breaking out over his skin.

He couldn't do it.

Not even for the game that made a part of his soul fly.

Closing his eyes, he sucked in a deep breath.

Jesus, when would that need, that *hope*, die? When would he have some relief from the heartache? Dammit, what he wouldn't give to feel…empty.

Stuffing the phone back into the front pocket of his hoodie, he took a step forward, only to draw up short again. *Damn.* He blinked. The Fates. God. Karma. He must've done something to piss off one or all of them, because he couldn't seem to avoid the kicks in the ass they kept throwing his way.

Two teenage boys stood on the front lawn, throwing a football back and forth. Within seconds it was clear to Owen that the taller kid with the light brown skin and close-cut brown hair had talent with his arm.

Quarterback. He'd bet his autographed Josh Groban CD that if the teen played on a team, his position had to be quarterback.

An inner voice howled at him to just walk past them. March up those front steps, go into the inn and take care of the business he'd come here to do.

Yet, his feet remained rooted on the pavement. Unable to move. Even if watching them enjoy a simple thing like throwing a ball sliced into him like a thousand tiny cuts.

"Dang it." The kid Owen had been studying linked his hands behind his head, his eyebrows pinched into a fierce scowl. "If I don't get this throw right, Coach will never pick me over Tyson for quarterback."

"Nah, man." His friend, a slightly shorter teen with long twists that hung to his shoulders, tossed the ball back to him. The quarterback plucked it out of the air. "Tyson only has seniority over you. That's the only reason Coach Wilson would choose him. But no way Tyson's better than you. And Coach wants to win with the best."

"I'm not the best if I can't even throw the ball to the right receiver."

"Your arm isn't the problem. Your footwork is."

The boys jerked around to stare at him, and shit, Owen didn't know who was more surprised. Them or him. He hadn't meant to speak. Hadn't meant for the words that drifted through his head to pop out of his mouth. Especially now, with the boys' stupefied gazes cemented on his face. The scars there seemed to tingle. He braced himself for their curiosity, the innocent questions that would punch a hole in his chest.

"Holy…" the quarterback whispered. "You're *Owen Strafford."*

"Daaaaamn." The other teen shook his head. "No one's going to believe this. *The* Owen Strafford."

For a second Owen froze, his breath stalling in his lungs. Both of the boys' eyes sparkled with pure excitement and neither seemed to give a damn about Owen's scars. Hell, they didn't even appear to see them.

"Yeah." He strode forward, coming to a stop in front of them. "I'm Owen. Nice to meet you…?"

After several more seconds of gaping at him, the taller kid thrust out a slightly shaking hand. "Sonny. Sonny Dennison."

Owen's brows jacked high. "Leo's brother?"

Sonny grinned, and his dark eyes squinted with it. "Yeah. And don't hold that against me, okay?" He jerked his head toward his friend. "This is my friend Mack Young."

"Hey." Mack hiked his chin up and held out his hand.

"Nice to meet you, Mack." Owen shook his hand.

"Wait until the guys hear we've met Owen-freaking-Strafford," Mack muttered under his breath.

Mentally, Owen winced. Okay, for someone who'd craved anonymity, outing himself to two teenage boys might not have been the smartest decision.

"What're *you* doing *here*?" Sonny asked, the same awe coloring his voice.

Owen tried not to fidget under that familiar note of wonder. Even though he'd been a regular on sports highlight reels, celebrity magazines and gossip sites since he'd hit college, he'd never become completely comfortable with that "superstar" status. In a lot of ways, he could never see himself as anything other than the scrawny kid from Pine Village, Indiana, who lived for waking up, suiting up and running onto that field. Football and books, those had been the places where he'd felt safest, where he was happiest. Where he belonged.

"Actually, I came by to see your sister. But I couldn't help overhearing your conversation." Tucking his hands into his hoodie pocket, he nodded at the football Sonny held. "You guys are trying out for the team?"

Sonny scrunched up his face and dropped his gaze to the ball. "Yeah, tryouts for the high school team are soon. We don't have a JV team, so we're competing for spots against upperclassmen. Mack is going for wide receiver and I'm trying out for quarterback. But I'm an incoming freshman so the odds..." He shrugged a shoulder, but Owen caught the longing in his eyes.

"Well, from one quarterback to another, you're good, Sonny. Real good. I don't know what this Tyson kid looks like, but you have a natural talent any coach will see."

"Seriously? You're not just saying that?"

Disbelief weighed down Sonny's question but underneath, Owen heard the telltale whisper of hope. Hope that Owen wasn't lying to boost his confidence. Thankfully, Owen didn't need to. The kid was that good.

"Not in the habit of lying."

Sonny's eyes narrowed. "You could be if you're trying to get next to my sister. Which, let me give you a heads-up, isn't going to work with Leo. She has a radar for bull that's eerie."

A snort escaped Owen before he could swallow it. He'd

only spent a handful of hours with Leo Dennison, but Sonny's description struck him as pretty damn accurate.

"I could be," Owen conceded, "but I'm not. Can I see your ball?" More awe slackened the kid's features as he slowly handed the ball over as if offering the Holy Grail. Jerking his chin to Mack, Owen said, "Run a hook route."

At first, Mack stood there, staring at him, unblinking. But after a moment he jolted into action and ran straight down the yard. Damn, the kid was fast.

Cupping the ball, fingers perfectly aligned on the laces, Owen positioned his feet, twisted his waist and launched the ball in a flawless spiral toward where he wanted Mack to be. In seconds the teen leaped, nabbing the ball out of the air and gracefully landing, the football cradled in his arm.

The catch was a thing of beauty, and Owen felt the grin sliding across his face without his express permission. A quiet joy rose up in him, like a hymn, and he inhaled, briefly closing his eyes. Saving it.

But then, in the next moment, the smile ebbed until it faded altogether, sadness eclipsing the delight. That was the first time he'd thrown a football in fourteen months. The first time that particular elation sang inside him like a soprano nailing an exquisite aria. He'd missed it. Like an amputated limb, he'd missed it.

He also feared its return.

Feared opening himself up to the longing that could rip him open and leave him even more broken than he already was.

Mack loped back up the yard, a grin splitting his handsome face. Whereas earlier, he'd tried to act cool, now he'd shed that teenage ennui, and his excitement shined through.

"That was fire!" He tossed the football back to Owen, fairly bouncing on his toes. "Let's do it again."

"I'm going to let Sonny throw the next one. Here." Owen passed the ball to the teen. "Now, like I said before, your arm isn't the problem. Get in position as if you're about to throw." Once Sonny did, Owen pointed at the ground. "Look at your feet. They're not up under you. And if they're not, you're not balanced. Which means a loss of control and power over the ball. If you're not balanced, the ball won't go toward your target. Look at me."

Owen mimed pulling his arm back then sharply forward before scrambling to the right and abruptly stopping, throwing an imaginary ball down the field.

"See? Whether you're in the pocket or you need to scramble, positioning yourself is everything. Get rooted and sure about the position of your feet. Come here." Once Sonny stood next to him, Owen had the teen go through the motion of throwing several times. "That's good, Sonny. Remember not to throw off your back leg because that, too, takes power off your arm. And always follow through, finish that throw. Got it?"

Sonny nodded. "Yeah, I think so."

"Don't think. Know. Half the battle of being a quarterback is confidence, believing you can make every throw on the field. Ready to hit Mack with some?"

This time Sonny's answer sounded firmer, stronger, and he pulled his shoulders back. "Yeah, I'm ready." Turning to his friend, Sonny yelled, "Mack, run a slant route."

Mack shot off down the yard, and Sonny shot the football like a perfectly aimed missile into his friend's hands.

"Beautiful." Owen smiled. "Absolutely beautiful. Try it again. This time get out of the pocket."

For the next ten minutes the teens ran through several routes, Owen offering a couple of tips here and there. For the most part they were a well-oiled machine. By the time both of them jogged back to him, Owen grinned and held out a fist. They grinned, bumping their knuckles against his.

"You guys are ready for those tryouts. I wouldn't worry about them. Just remember one thing. It's what my high school coach told me, and it was one of the best pieces of advice I was ever given. You're always going to hear 'make sure your fingers are on the laces.' Or 'always keep your eyes on your receiver.' Or 'have your internal clock turned on.' And don't get me wrong, all of that is true, but it means nothing if you don't get this one thing."

Both boys stared at him as if he was about to drop knowledge on them straight from Mt. Sinai.

"Shut up. Listen. And learn. This Tyson kid might have seniority over you, Sonny, and Mack, same goes for the other returning players who are trying out for your position. But sometimes, when you've been on a team, or playing for a while, you start to believe you know it all. That you have all the answers. Like I said, I don't know the other players, but you will always have an edge on anyone else if you keep learning. Because the truth is you'll never know more than your coaches. Stay teachable. Be like a sponge. And you'll win that spot."

"Thank you, Owen." Sonny stuck out his hand, his face solemn. "We appreciate you taking the time with us today. You didn't have to. And we'll remember everything you've taught us."

"Good." Owen clasped the teen's hand in his, firmly squeezing it before letting go. Turning to Mack, he clapped a palm to his shoulder. "See you around. And good luck with tryouts."

"Thanks, Owen." Mack nodded. Then, after a brief hesitation, he asked, "If Ms. Leo has your number, can we let you know how it goes through her?"

Nothing changed about the boy's it-is-what-it-is expression. Same with his voice. Yet, underneath that teenage indifference, Owen detected the note of hope. Of...need.

He was familiar with that note. Intimate with it.

Even now, an ache pulsed dead center in his chest. That ache had nothing to do with background or how many parents were in the home. Hell, Owen had been raised in a middle-class, two-parent home with a *too* involved father. And yet, he'd still damn near throbbed with that need for affirmation, for someone related to him through hard work and merit to be proud of him.

For acceptance.

That kinship with this teen had sweat rolling down his spine under his hoodie. Had him fighting the urge to back-pedal away from the hero-worship in the eyes staring up at him. He didn't deserve it; he knew his feet had been fashioned out of clay, not gold.

Owen Strafford was no one's hero.

"Hey, Leo! Look who's here to see you." Sonny pointed the football at Owen as if it were a blinking red arrow. "Owen. Strafford. *The* Owen Strafford."

Owen whipped his head toward the front steps of the inn, desperate to look anywhere but at the two young faces that reminded him of when he'd been their age. When he'd possessed a love of the game and an idealistic view of the future. When the taste for freedom had been an unquenchable thirst.

His heart thudded in his throat at the sight of Leo Dennison standing on the porch surrounded by hanging plants and flowers like some kind of militant fairy.

"Yeah, we've met." She crossed her arms over her chest and tilted her head to the side.

"Ooh. Yikes." Sonny winced. He shook his head and pseudo-whispered, "I don't know what you did to earn that look, but I'm praying for you. Go with God, Owen."

Then the little traitor shifted backward and disappeared around the side of the inn with Mack.

"What are you doing here, Owen?"

Okay, *brr*. Not that he didn't deserve this icy treatment, considering the way he'd tossed her out of his house—twice now. But damn. His balls were in danger of frostbite.

Pasting on a smile that tugged on his scar, he moved toward her and the lovely woman with a baby cuddled to her chest who'd joined her.

"I came to see you, actually."

"Then what was that?" She tipped her chin up, indicating where her brother and Mack had been before they'd hightailed it out of sight.

Once upon a time, he'd been known as a charmer, a player with a golden tongue. Since the accident, his confidence, and yes, his ego, had taken a hit. Yet, no one—not the most ruthless reporter, not the cruelest woman, not his own father—could leave him as tongue-tied and fucking unsettled as this five-foot-six woman.

And dammit, he didn't like it.

Hated it.

Could resent her for it.

"It's definitely not whatever you're cooking up in that suspicious head of yours," he growled.

"Really?" she drawled, uncrossing her arms and propping her hands on her hips. "And what exactly am I *cooking up* in my suspicious head, pray tell?"

Her friend—hell, he hadn't even been introduced to

her—stared at them, lips parted in a small "O," head swinging back and forth between them, as if observing a fierce tennis match.

"Sarcasm duly noted." He shifted forward until he stood on the bottom step. "Only God knows, and I'm sure He's shaking His head right now. But let me take a shot. You saw me talking to your brother and his friend and you think I had some kind of angle, right? That I couldn't possibly offer to help him just because I know the game and gave some advice out of the goodness of my heart?"

"Oh." Her eyes widened and she splayed her fingers wide over her chest. "You have one of those? And here I thought it had absconded for parts unknown. With your memory."

Well, damn. That hurt. But he couldn't acknowledge it without admitting he remembered who she was and where they'd met. And he'd already stuck his foot so far in it with that, confessing would only make him look like more of an asshole. Besides, he couldn't do it.

Fuck it. Fine. He didn't *want* to do it.

He'd rather she believe him to be a manwhore than someone to pity.

So self-centered manwhore it was.

"I guess I'm supposed to know what that means," he lied through gritted teeth.

Her eyes narrowed on him, but he still caught the flash of hurt in the blue-gray depths. What kind of man did it make him that he'd sacrifice her pride to save his own? He disgusted himself.

Screw this.

His father might've raised an athlete, but his coaches, Sherrod… They'd raised a man. One who had some honor at least.

He inhaled a breath. "I'm—"

"I repeat, what're you doing here?" she asked, if possible, her voice colder, flintier.

He sighed, dragging his fingers through his hair. "Not to do this. I'm sorry for whatever this—" he waved a hand back and forth between them "—devolved into. That wasn't my intention when I came by. I really did want to talk to you."

Leo dropped her arms by her sides and glanced away, her dark brown hair swept back into a high ponytail, revealing the graceful column of her neck and the stubborn yet delicate line of her jaw. And the tiny muscle ticking there.

When she turned to meet his gaze again, the corner of her mouth curved in a small twist.

"No, I apologize. I might be a little sensitive after yesterday."

"A little?" her friend muttered.

"Okay, more than a little." She shot the other woman a healthy dose of side-eye. "And I'm sorry for jumping down your throat. I'm not usually that..."

"Abrasive. Aggressive. Snarky. Out for blood." Once more her friend helpfully jumped in.

"Owen, let me introduce you to my best friend and sister-in-law, Sydney Dennison, since she insists on joining our conversation." Leo leveled a scowl on the smiling woman who rubbed her baby's back in wide circles. "Although, I'm seriously considering rescinding the best friend title at the moment."

Climbing the last two steps to the porch, Owen smiled and extended his hand to Sydney. "Nice to meet you."

She shook his hand with the one not holding her infant, eyes squinted. "Hmm. The jury's still out on that one. I got both my eyes on you, Strafford." To emphasize the warning, Sydney pointed two fingers toward her eyes, then jabbed them toward his. "Two." She bumped her hip against Leo's. "I'm going to put Patience down for a nap. I'll be inside if you need me." With one last narrow-eyed glance at him, she disappeared inside the inn.

Owen stared after her, bemused. "Do I want to know what that's about?"

"Eh. Probably not." Leo waved a hand toward the two rocking chairs with the green-and-yellow plaid cushions. Beautiful hand-painted vases his mother would've fought someone at a flea market to own flanked both chairs. Yellow and orange flowers spilled from them.

"Do you mind sitting out here? Ordinarily, I would take you in the office, but my mom is using it. And since it's been taking a minor miracle to get that woman to stay off her feet, I'd rather not disturb her if she's actually complying. Even if it is to disrupt my perfectly organized vendor system. It's for the greater good. I keep telling myself that. It's all for the greater good."

Laughter bubbled up like water from a hot spring. He turned away, biting the inside of his lip as he sank down into one of the rocking chairs.

"How long have you been keeping that bottled up?"

"Oh, my God, *days*." She groaned, closing her eyes.

And shit. He needed her not to do that again. He gripped the arms of the rocker and pressed his feet hard into the boards of the porch, grounding himself in the here, the now. So that luxurious, satisfied sound wouldn't transport him to the past. To a time when he'd been clasped in those long, golden limbs, cradled within the vee of those rounded hips, welcomed in the tight, wet sheath of her sex. A similar groan had bathed his ears when he'd first sunk inside her. Similar, but not the same. Then, hers had been deeper, needier...

Fuck.

He tore his eyes away from her face. Pinning his gaze on the bushes that bordered the front of the inn, he inhaled, held the breath, then exhaled it. Briefly closing his eyes, he replaced the memory of the lust that had tightened her beautiful features that night with horror, rejection...sympathy.

Yeah. He slowly lifted his lashes. That killed his lust. Almost like it'd never existed.

"Owen?"

Her delicate, smaller hand covered his and he flinched, barely subduing the urge to snatch his away. And from the smooth mask that dropped over her expression, she didn't miss it.

God. He kept messing this up. Once more he shoved his fingers through his hair, and he fiddled with the strings of his hoodie, on the verge of tugging it up, hiding behind it.

"Don't," she murmured.

He paused, his hands falling to the arms of the rocker. Out of habit, he twisted to look at her, giving her his good side—his perfect side.

"And don't do that, either."

Anger beat at him, threatening to engulf him. Irrational anger. Hurt anger. That she dared to bring up the elephant on the porch that he'd prefer she left alone. The anger swirled inside him, a twister that gathered strength with each rotation, ready to spew out destruction... But then she touched him.

A light dance of fingertips across the back of his hand. A courageous, sweet touch that completely stole the force from his emotional storm.

"Will you look at me?" she asked, and only then did he realize he was studying those slim, fragile-looking fingers on his larger, scarred hand.

He jerked his head up at her request, peering into eyes that reminded him of the purest moment of dawn. When the world was at its most fragile, hovering between greeting a new day or slipping back into the dark of night.

That was what terrified him when he stared into her eyes.

Would he remain in the dark, relatively safe cocoon he'd erected for himself? Or would she convince him to emerge as a new creature, adapted to a world where he wasn't seen as…golden?

He glanced away.

Leo Dennison was someone to fear.

"I wanted to talk to you about the spring festival," he said.

"I'm not going to talk to the side of your face."

Because you can't stand looking at the view. I get it. Me, neither. The sarcastic comment burned on his tongue, but deliberately, he extinguished it. Lashing out wouldn't get him anywhere.

Slowly, he turned to face her, their gazes meeting. She arched an eyebrow, her lips curving in a faint smile.

"I like looking into the eyes of the person I'm talking to. You can tell if they're being honest, shifty, holding back something. Windows of the soul and all that." She leaned forward, propping her crossed arms on the rocking chair's arm. And he pretended not to notice how her breasts plumped against her silken shirt. Or how a hint of black lace peeked through.

Shit. He wasn't that good of a pretender.

"Now continue." She twirled a hand in the air. "You were telling me you changed your mind about judging the chili contest."

That forced his attention back into focus with a cold

snap. "No." He cleared his throat. Again, his answer had emerged hard, abrupt. "No," he said again, softer this time. "I still...can't do it. But after you left, I thought over everything you said about the festival and Purple Heart Homes. I would hate for the organization to possibly lose donations because I couldn't do my part." He lowered his hands to his thighs, dug his fingers into the muscle. "I asked my friend Sherrod Forrester if he would take my place, and he agreed. Sherrod would be as much of a draw, if not a greater one, than me. He's an all-pro, Super Bowl–winning wide receiver and is currently the Knights' all-time leader in receptions. Not to mention he's been voted Sexiest Man Alive several times." He snorted. "And he's a Rose Bend native. I'm thinking you can really play up that angle."

"I remember Sherrod. He was in my brothers Cole and Wolf's class. Everyone is super proud of him. Thank you for arranging this with him."

"You're welcome. Like I said, it's the least I could do."

Message delivered, this was his cue to get up and leave. To escape that penetrating stare. But his need to study the smattering of freckles across the bridge of her nose and cheekbones kept him rooted in the chair like one of those cheery yellow flowers. His desire to inhale that delicate lilac-and-fresh-rain scent just one more minute glued him by her side. The thick ropes of lust tightening his gut and wrapping around his cock forced him to remain still.

"Don't take this the wrong way, and I don't want to seem ungrateful." She leaned back and crossed her legs; the sight of the light green wide-legged pants whispering over her skin had a shudder working its way down his spine. "But why did you go to the trouble?"

Yeah, he'd been afraid she would ask this question. And

avoiding it had been high on his to-do list. How could he give her an answer he didn't know himself?

Because it was the right thing to do.

Because you needed someone, and I had the connections.

Both were true but somehow too pat, too trite.

Because it was important to you.

Because for some uncomfortable, unfathomable reason, I couldn't stand the idea of letting you down.

Still true. But too fucking personal. Too...intimate. And he didn't do intimate. Didn't want it. Especially not with her.

So he shrugged a shoulder and did what he did best. Smiled. Trivialized.

"Maybe I'm trying to stock up on points that will get me out of whatever doghouse you've stuck me in."

"Does that work?"

Owen blinked, taken aback as much by her calm, curious tone as by her words. "Excuse me?"

"No, I really want to know. Does the—" she circled a finger in front of his face "'—aww, shucks, I'm a harmless player' smile and bullshit excuse usually work for you?"

Well, goddamn. He didn't know whether to be offended or turned on.

His gaze dropped to the lush curves of her lips, and his cock stirred, hardening against his zipper.

Apparently, his dick was Team Turned On.

Only Sherrod talked to him like that—straight up, no chaser. Damn sure not women. In his experience, they'd been too busy trying to get in his bed, his wallet or his spotlight.

Once more Leo Dennison had set herself apart. What the hell was he supposed to do with that? With her?

Hands off. Keep your distance. She's not for you.

The reminders flitted through his mind, and yet, it required more strength than he'd ever exerted in a weight room to drag his scrutiny from her mouth.

"Yes, it does."

Where had that come from? He hadn't given his tongue permission to drop the ugly truth.

Leo smiled, propping an elbow on the chair's arm, her palm cupping her chin. "Do tell."

Heaving a loud huff, he dragged a hand down his face, his scars providing a bitter reminder that his "aww, shucks" smile wouldn't get him far now.

"Honestly?"

"I practically insist on it."

"Does *that* usually work?" He turned her own question back on her, flicking his fingers toward her. "The bulldozer thing."

She scrunched her face as if pretending to think it over. "In business, most of the time. In relationships? Not so much."

Now, if *that* wasn't a loaded answer.

She shot up a hand, palm out. "But we're not talking about me," she said. "So stop deflecting."

Owen chuckled, and the unfamiliar sound scratched his throat. "That's rich."

"What does that mean?"

"It means, the *reason* is deflection. And it works because people see what they want. Every time."

Except for her and Sherrod.

And his father. God, it'd driven his father insane.

But smiling and throwing out random comments had been one of the most effective weapons in Owen's arsenal when it came to disarming Troy Strafford when he strapped up for one of his epic rages about his son's career. Or his son's ungratefulness. Or his son's carelessness.

"I don't understand." She frowned. "What is it they want to see? Or a better question, what is it you're so concerned about them seeing that you'd go through the trouble of putting on a show?"

He laughed again, but it didn't conceal his cynicism. Shoving out of the chair, he stalked to the railing and surrendered to the urge to tug up his hood. Not caring what she read into the gesture. Relief flooded into him, and as he wrapped his fingers around the wood, he exhaled.

"One of the first things you learn in the football business—because it is a business—is to guard yourself. There are people whose sole purpose is to take advantage of you for your money, your fame, your connections, your body, your success. It's all about what you can do for them, what you can give them, what they can access through you. Only a fool leaves himself vulnerable when every word or action has the possibility of being recorded or relayed to a reporter or a gossip site or even another team player just to cause dissention. One of the first things you learn is to perfect your public face and accept that you'll wear it ninety percent of the time because you can only afford to wear your private one when you're completely alone or with the very few people you can trust."

"That sounds incredibly...lonely." Her heady, sensual scent announced her arrival next to him. "Having to constantly protect yourself like that. To have to continually be vigilant and suspicious of people's agendas? It must be exhausting. Why do you do it?"

He shook his head, never removing his gaze from the tranquil view of the perfectly kept lawn and tree-lined driveway. "That's easy. The game. I love it. There's nothing like it."

Talking too much. You can shut up now. But for some reason his lips kept flapping. Like a valve letting the steam seep out. "I've never felt more…free, more myself than when I'm on that field. Some people were born to teach. Others to sing or work on cars. Me? I was born to be on that field, with a ball in my hand. It's where I'm my best self, where I'm whole."

A chasm cracked wide inside him and despair rushed in. "Yeah, I don't believe that."

He jerked his head toward her, disbelief, surprise and, yes, anger battling it out for dominance in his chest.

She calmly stared back at him, unaware of the war going on inside him. Either that or she didn't care. It was so damn hard to tell with Leo.

"Excuse me?" he asked, though he'd heard her crystal clear.

"I don't believe that we're born to be certain things. I do think that we're all blessed with gifts and talents. But to say we were born to do just this thing? Well, what happens if that mechanic loses his hand and can't work on engines anymore? Is he now purposeless? What if the singer is no longer able to sing? Are they worthless? What if the athlete is injured and can't play? Is their existence meaningless now? No, no and no. It's not their careers that gave them identity or determined who they were, but their gifts, their character, their talents."

She shifted, leaning her hip on the railing, facing him fully and folding her arms under her breasts. This time he didn't have to fight to keep his attention on her face. The thoughtful expression arrested him.

"The mechanic might lose his hand, but he still possesses

his technical knowledge, his experience, his education, that can break down the many parts of a car and put them back together again. The average person can't do that. His hand was a tool, but his brain, his vision, those are his true gifts. A singer might lose her voice, but she still has her ears that can tune into pitch, tone, nuance. She can hear things that you and I would never catch. Music is her gift, and no one can take that away. And the athlete might no longer be able to play, but he's so much more than a pair of legs or an arm. He's a leader, a strategist, a visionary. He's intelligent. A risk taker, a quick thinker. That's who he *is*, and that has nothing to do with a ball or how many yards he can run. And with those qualities, he can do anything he desires."

Owen stared at her, his mouth dry. He tried to swallow. He tried to clear his throat. But it proved impossible. So he said nothing. Did nothing. Heard nothing but her words ringing in his head.

The resentful, shriveled soul in him bellowed, *What do you know in your perfect town, your perfect house and your perfect family?* Nothing about her—from her flawless golden skin to her white blouse and spotless pants—shouted suffering, loss or even inconvenience. She couldn't possibly understand his world. Couldn't understand *him*.

But then… The man who should've left this porch, this woman, minutes ago but couldn't, wanted nothing more than to jerk down his hood, force her to peer at his face and ask her to repeat her words. Force her to tell him these scars didn't matter. Ask her if she still saw the same man she did a year ago.

Then wrap himself around her and beg her to hold him. Beg her to not let him fall further apart than he already had.

So of course, he did what he did best. Smiled. Trivialized. And weaponized.

"And what about you, Leo?" He propped a shoulder on the post behind him, arching a brow. "What were you not born to do?" He waved a hand toward the inn. "Run this inn? Dole out unsolicited advice? What have you discovered about your own self?"

Her soft, sharp inhale didn't get by him. He hadn't learned much from his mother since she'd left a lot of his raising to the harsh "tenderness" of his father, but one thing she had instilled—never hit a girl or woman. And though he'd never physically laid a hand on a woman, he'd just broken that rule. Because his verbal hit had landed a direct strike, and Owen hated himself for it.

"I've learned I'm better at giving advice than taking it," she murmured. "You must have a dick of gold, Owen. Because I can't imagine a woman putting up with that shit for any length of time. I don't care how pretty you are."

Shaking her head, she pushed off the railing and walked away. Seconds later the front door to the inn opened and closed with a quiet but firm click behind her.

Because no slamming of a door from Leo Dennison.

Class all the way.

And him?

Alone as always.

Because that was what happened when you were an asshole.

CHAPTER SIX

"WELL, WE ARE definitely on track for a fantastic festival this year," Vanessa Perkins, chairwoman of the committee announced with a bright smile and a "go team" fist pump.

Leo bent her head, but not before she caught the smirk of Maddox Holt, owner of Road's End, the local dive bar. Vanessa's enthusiasm was contagious and cute, if not a wee bit corny. But the very proud grandmother and long-time clerk at the Blooms 'n Things flower mart had chaired the spring festival for years. It'd always been a great success, so no one saw a reason to rock the leadership boat. Plus, no one else had stepped up to volunteer, either. So there was that.

"Granted," Vanessa continued, "I was a little worried about low turnout since we had a dip in attendance last year, but thanks to Maddox corralling more people to donate more food and beverages—" she winked at him, and Leo swallowed a snort because one of those beverages was beer from his bar, "—and Leo wrangling up our very own football celebrity judge for the chili contest, I think attendance is no longer a concern. As a matter of fact, I believe we're going to have record numbers!"

"Really, Leo?" Declan Howard, recent transport to Rose Bend, asked, a gleam in his eyes. The man was ridiculously good-looking. Like, the kind of good-looking that had a person tossing their head back, glaring at the heavens and yelling, "C'mon, God? Really? Is all that beauty really necessary?" Remi Donovan, his wife and librarian at Rose Bend Public Library, was a very lucky woman. "I heard that Owen Strafford moved here a few months ago, even though I've never seen him around. Is it him?"

Just the sound of his name had a shiver skipping its way down her spine in delight even as her belly tightened in aggravated knots. It'd been a week, but her last encounter with Owen still had the power to send the burn of humiliation to her face.

What were you not born to do? Run this inn? Dole out unsolicited advice? What have you discovered about your own self?

His words wouldn't haunt her so much if she could answer those questions. Wouldn't taunt her if those very concerns didn't keep her up too many nights to count. Wouldn't mock her if she didn't feel like such an imposter, because to her family, friends and the people of this town she had it all together.

Because no one knew more than she did how *imperfect* she was.

The thing she strove so hard to do? Drag the wool over everyone else's eyes so they didn't perceive the cracked, guilt-ridden creature beneath. It was why she fought so hard to protect that facade of perfection, of self-discipline. So no one would guess the ugly truth.

He'd exposed her secret shame with his pointed words.

Owen had warned her he used his smile and words to deflect. And he'd come out swinging, defending himself like an injured, terrified animal, protecting his wound.

"Leo?" Vanessa asked, tilting her head and peering at her, concern and curiosity in her brown eyes.

Giving her head a hard shake, Leo offered the other woman and Declan a small, apologetic smile. "I'm sorry, my mind wandered for a moment there. To answer your question, Declan, no, it isn't Owen Strafford."

"I'm not surprised." Jenna Landon snorted. "He was in a bad car accident, wasn't he? I heard he isn't as pretty as he used to be. I wouldn't want to be seen in public, either."

Anger pressed against Leo's rib cage like a feral cat, hissing to jump on the beautiful but mean redhead across the table. The woman must have some redeemable qualities somewhere. Like deep, deep down inside. It might take a hobbit's journey through Middle Earth to find them, but hey, Leo was the eternal optimist. In the meantime, she'd continue her deep breathing and depend on her mantra of *Orange is not a good look on me. Orange is not a good look on me*, to tide her over.

"Well, I just don't know how to follow that totally sensitive, heartwarming comment." She shot Jenna a sharp smile that had Maddox snickering and Cicely Moreno covering up a laugh with a cough. "Anyway, Owen arranged for Sherrod Forrester to be the celebrity judge of the chili contest. It was very nice and gracious of him since he didn't have to do it," she added, sliding Jenna a narrowed glance that dared her to say one more word about the man.

Leo might be calling him about fifteen different kinds of asshole in her head, but damn if she'd allow the ex-mayor's spoiled daughter to get in any digs. The woman didn't know him, had never met him.

Hold up. Was Leo actually being *protective* of the jerk? Lord help.

"Sherrod Forrester?" Maddox scrubbed a hand over his auburn beard. "Wow. That man is a beast on the field. League VIP last year." He hiked his chin. "You did good, Dennison."

"Forget all that. The man is gorgeous." Cicely fanned

herself, and her mouth widened into a lascivious grin. "*Dios mio.* I can't even lie. I only watch football because of him. Oh, yes, he is the Sexiest Man Alive."

"I know absolutely nothing about football except it has touchdowns instead of home runs...I think." Olivia Allen laughed. "And even *I* know Sherrod Forrester." She curled her fingers into claws and emitted a mock growl.

The room erupted in laughter.

All except for the redheaded joy snatcher, of course.

"Owen, is it?" Jenna scoffed, as soon as the chuckles quieted. Flipping her hair over her shoulder, she peered down her nose at Leo, eyes glittering with spite. "Already familiar and cozy? Why am I not surprised? You always did have a thing for rejects."

The gibe jabbed Leo in the stomach. Sydney. The other woman referred to Sydney. Jenna knew just where to strike to hurt Leo. Family.

Well, screw that and screw her.

Leo had never been one of those "turn the other cheek" folks.

"Olivia and I seem to have that in common, then," she said, adding a saccharine-sweet smile, mentioning Jenna's best friend.

How they were friends, Leo had no idea. Olivia might be her brother Wolf's ex-girlfriend, and her rash actions last Christmas almost cost him his now fiancée, but she was still a nice woman. Too kind to be the BFF of Jenna "The Hellbeast" Landon.

Jenna's mouth thinned until it almost disappeared, and her fingers curled around the table's edge. Huh. Wondered if the redhead was imagining Leo's neck between her hands.

"Well, let's, uh, let's get back to business." Vanessa

coughed nervously, glancing back and forth between Leo and Jenna before switching a pleading look to Maddox. As if begging him to intervene just in case one or the other of them leaped across the table. Good call. There was a reason she'd been the chairwoman for years running. "We've had a bit of a snafu with the Lavender Queen Beauty Pageant."

Of all the events held during the festival, Leo hated the annual pageant the most. Arguments about women being objectified, sexism and promoting unrealistic beauty standards aside, she just found the whole thing silly as hell.

And when Jenna straightened in her chair, shoulders rolling back, her perky breasts greeting the entire room, Leo hated the idea just that bit more.

"What kind of snafu, Vanessa?" Jenna asked, frowning. "I spoke with Scarlett Ross a few days ago and she didn't mention a problem."

Leo fought not to roll her eyes. As if the pageant coordinator was obligated to disclose all information to Jenna.

From the spots of pink staining Vanessa's cheeks and the slight flex of her jaw, it appeared she possessed the same opinion.

"Scarlett let me know this morning that one of the contestants had to drop out of the pageant."

"Why?" Jenna demanded.

"I. Didn't. Ask," Vanessa said through pursed lips. "Anyway, we need a replacement. And soon, because rehearsals start next week."

"This isn't a catastrophe." Leo shrugged a shoulder. "Just go forward with the women you have. I don't see the issue."

"The bylaws specify there must be twelve contestants," Vanessa explained.

"Get out." Leo's lips parted in surprise. "There are actual bylaws to this thing? What's next?"

"A constitution. With amendments," Cicely added, a dimple flashing in her cheek.

"Very funny." Jenna stared at them, her gaze as flat as her voice, before dismissing them with a flick of her hair. "Olivia, you should join the pageant. You would be perfect."

"Uh, Jenna, you're my best friend and I love you like a sister, but—" the other woman's mouth curled into a dry half smile as she patted Jenna's hand "—if I want to keep that friendship, there's no way I'm entering. Not with that competitive streak of yours. Sorry, hon."

Jenna's eyebrows slammed down over her nose, and her lips parted in preparation to argue, but when Olivia shot up a hand, she leaned back in her chair, letting it go. Probably because she admitted to herself Olivia was right.

Vanessa glanced at Cicely, hope a gleam in her eyes, but Cicely was already shaking her head. "I can't. My little cousin is in it. Can you imagine the war it would start in my family if I entered, too? It would make the Hatfields and McCoys look like a petty playground fight."

"What about you, Leo?" Declan cocked his head and propped his elbows on the table.

She took back what she'd said about him being good-looking. He was dull and ordinary. Take that.

Traitor.

"I'll enter when Remi does." Leo jutted her chin out, crossing her arms over her chest.

They both knew the logical, fiercely independent and feminist town librarian would never do something as antithetical to her beliefs as join the local beauty pageant.

"Well, get your talent ready, Leontyne, because my wife is already signed up." He smirked.

It was official. The world was turned upside down.

And she was quoting *Hamilton*.

Shit.

"You're lying." She gaped at him, her arms dropping to her lap.

"Nope. She submitted her application and was chosen in the first round." From one blink of an eye to the next, his smile dropped, and he jerked his head toward Jenna. "Say one word about my wife, just one, and I'll forget my mother raised a gentleman."

His low warning vibrated in the room, and not one person breathed. Probably all of them hoped—just a wee bit— that Jenna would test the Boston-born wealth manager so they could witness his sharp tongue slice a strip out of her hide.

But it seemed even sharks had self-preservation instincts. She glared at him, sniffed and turned away.

Leo silently sighed, disappointed, and then her current dilemma roared back to the forefront. Her dilemma and a shitload of terror.

Her mouth had just written a check her ass couldn't cash. This was her nightmare. As much as she craved control, this was the exact *opposite* of it. Rehearsals didn't mean a damn thing once people were out on that stage. In front of an audience. Live. Lines could be forgotten. Lighting could go wrong. Cues could be missed. People could trip.

Awful, bone-chilling stage fright.

Oh, she should know.

Being the center of attention... She hated it. The background, turning the cogs in the machine and ensuring they ran smoothly. That was her thing. People like her brother Cole and even Jenna, for God's sake, they could bask in the spotlight where all eyes were on them. Just the thought—a shudder tripped down her spine. God, no.

With running the inn—overseeing the bookings, managing the inventory, making sure the inn remained clean, supervising promotion and the new wedding venture—Leo could control the outcome, the results. Of course, everything didn't always go perfectly. But because she always had plans in place, she could contain the damage. Even prevent it.

Not so with an unpredictable setting like a pageant. Especially when she was a mere participant instead of the coordinator.

No, she couldn't do it.

"You would be saving us a lot of trouble if you agreed, Leo," Vanessa said.

"I thought people had to apply, though." And here she was, grasping at straws, very applicable straws. "It wouldn't be fair if I didn't go through the same process."

"Good point." Vanessa nodded. "Submit your application and we'll fast-track it. That'll make everything on the up and up."

"But— But—" Leo sputtered.

"If she doesn't want to be in the pageant, she shouldn't. Besides, maybe there's a good reason. Are you scared...or do you know you'll just embarrass yourself?" A taunting smirk tipped the corner of Jenna's mouth, and damn if Leo didn't long to smack it.

She narrowed her eyes at the smug redhead. "I can't tell if you're using reverse psychology or if you really believe the crap you're spouting."

Jenna shrugged a slim shoulder, that "cat ate the bird" smile on her face.

With the bet she'd stupidly thrown down and lost, Vanessa's plea and Jenna's challenge, Leo couldn't back down.

An image of Moe before Leo had left for the meeting snapped into her head. Her mother, lines bracketing her mouth even as she worked to give Leo a smile and try to put *her* at ease. Her mother, being strong even when tired and in pain. Just as Leo had pulled through with acquiring a celebrity judge, she couldn't let Moe down now.

Fuck.

She was doing the Lavender Queen Beauty Pageant.

CHAPTER SEVEN

"IS THAT LEO DENNISON?"

Maddox looked up from wiping down the bar and glanced over at Owen. On the other side of the dance floor, four women crowded around a table, beer bottles and cocktail glasses littering the surface. Even though they were too far away to catch the sound of their voices, their faces were alit with laughter.

"Yep." Maddox chuckled, and Owen wondered what the wicked edge was about. "We were at a committee meeting for the spring festival together earlier today. It was... interesting."

Another chuckle, and Owen's curiosity was officially pricked.

"What happened?"

"Well—" A hand hailing Maddox from farther down the bar caught his attention, and he rapped his knuckles on the bar top. "Be right back."

Impatience strummed through Owen and he picked up his Sam Adams, downing a healthy gulp. With Maddox gone, that feeling of exposure returned full force. Ducking his head, he allowed the long strands of his hair to conceal the scarred side of his face from view.

Road's End was one of the very few places he ventured out to in Rose Bend, and he only visited the dive bar— one of the nicest and cleanest he'd been in—on the slowest nights. Like tonight, a Tuesday. Only it seemed everyone else in town must've had the same idea, because more people packed into the bar than usual, and it had Owen jumpy. On edge. For a man who used to be surrounded by people 24/7, he didn't like it anymore.

That's a lie.

As if she were a magnetic force and he a powerless piece of metal, he peered back in Leo's direction through the long strands of his hair.

Regret and disgust with himself mingled with an unfortunate, inevitable delight at seeing her. It'd been a week, and he couldn't count the number of times he'd thought about driving over to the inn and apologizing for his thoughtless words.

No, he couldn't use that crutch. They hadn't been thoughtless. They'd been premeditated and designed to strike with well-aimed precision.

He took another sip of his beer, but the cold liquid did nothing to wash away the shame on his tongue.

The only thing that had kept him from going to Leo was that he had no idea what he would've said. The truth couldn't do. *I was so afraid of you getting too close to my own insecurities that I lashed out.* Yeah, that sounded healthy and well-adjusted.

Yeah. Better to end...whatever had been happening between them now rather than continue and have her find out he was too broken—inside and out—for her to fix.

If only his eyes and dick would get the message.

Sighing, he lifted his beer again, draining the last of the alcohol. Time to call it a night. The bell over the front door jingled, announcing more customers, and his arms itched under his black Henley. Out of habit, he reached for his hood, but cursed when he nabbed air. He'd forgone the added armor because the bar should've been mostly empty.

Shit.

He needed to get the fuck out of here.

As if she were a mentalist, Leo's head jerked toward him just as he slid off the stool. Even at that distance, her eyes pinned him. At least that was how it felt. Like that blue-gray gaze immobilized him, locking him into place. Her smile slipped, and goddammit, he didn't blame her. Not considering how their last encounter ended.

This was her night out with friends. He didn't want to ruin it. He'd just leave—

A wide, not maniacal—but okay, *maniacal*—grin spread across her face, and she waved an arm at him. Waved enthusiastically. *So* enthusiastically, she almost hit the woman sitting next to her in the head.

What the hell?

After jumping up, Leo strolled across the dance floor sparsely littered with couples and wound between tables until she reached his side. Tilting her head back, she beamed up at him.

"Hi!"

Oh, fuck.

She was drunk.

Maybe not stumbling down, flat-on-her-ass drunk, but from the sparkle in her eyes, the flags of pink painted across her cheekbones and the *really* happy demeanor, she most definitely was tipsy.

Laughter strangled in his throat. That and horror. 'Cause, good God. Leo drunk was as unpredictable as a skunk with mad cow disease.

"Uh, hey. You good, Leo?"

"Psshh." She swatted at his chest. "Of course I am. I'm grrrreat!"

"Cool." He cupped her elbow and her waist and guided her to the bar stool he'd just vacated. "Why don't you sit down?"

Especially since that *great* had sent her weaving on her feet. Catching Maddox's eye, Owen flicked a hand, signaling him over when he had a chance. In moments the owner was there, a smile hovering over his mouth, but a hint of concern in his blue eyes.

"Hey, Leo. How're you doing? Having a little too much fun?"

"Nah." She waved off his concern with a hard shake of her head that nearly sent her tumbling off the stool. Only Owen's grip on her elbow prevented the spill. "Whoops." She gifted both of them with another brilliant grin that really shouldn't have been so damn adorable. "Maddox, bring me another of those cranberry vodkas. And one for my friend here." She patted Owen on the arm. Then paused. Frowned. And squeezed his biceps. "I swear to God, these things must be made of rocks. Like stacks and stacks of 'em."

Okay, he was reevaluating just how smashed she was.

Water, he mouthed to Maddox, positioning his body so his back faced the bar.

Not bothering to hide his snicker, Maddox walked off.

"What're you doing here?" she asked, leaning her head to the side until it nearly touched her shoulder. "I thought you didn't come out of your house. Y'know, like the hermit's code or something."

"Yeah, the code allows for free time after dark."

She nodded, expression solemn. "Good for you." She patted his hand. "Fresh air is good for the lungs."

For fuck's sake.

He turned away, wiping a hand down his face and choking on laughter. So they were really having this conversation.

Her heavy, dramatic sigh tagged his attention, and he schooled his features before looking at her again. A way-too-cute moue scrunched up her face, and his fingers itched to trace the full, sensual lines of that pouty mouth. To smooth out the wrinkling skin above the bridge of her nose. To count each freckle with the tip of his finger...or the tip of his tongue.

For the first time since his accident, he found himself thankful for something. Grateful that while he might've lost sensation in his face, he hadn't in his hands. Because to not have the possibility of feeling her silken flesh... That would be torture.

But hell, who was he kidding? Given the odds of her allowing him to ever touch her again, he might as well have lost that sense.

Curling his fingers into his palm, he asked, "What's wrong?"

"You mean Maddox hasn't spilled the beans?"

"Uh, is this about that festival committee meeting?"

She huffed a loud breath. "Hell, yes, it's about the festival committee. And the goddamn Lavender Queen Beauty Pageant," she fairly wailed, head dropping forward along with her shoulders.

"Lavender. Queen. Beauty Pageant." Owen repeated it slowly. Because surely this wasn't a thing. But then, he was in a small town that held an honest-to-God spring festival. So yeah, this tracked. "I'm guessing from your cry of dismay that this is a bad thing."

"Yes, it's a bad thing. Keep up, Football Casanova." She scooched forward on the bar stool, grumbling, "Where's Maddox with my drink? I need my libations."

It seemed she'd had plenty of *libations* tonight.

Speaking of...

He glanced over his shoulder toward the table where she'd been sitting, and three women stared back at him. One, a Black woman with a shaved head on one side and long, dark hair on the other, waved at him. He tentatively returned it. Another, an Asian woman, possibly Filipina, smiled widely at him. Sydney, though, gave him another two-fingered "got my eye on you" warning.

Turning back to Leo, he said, "You need to get back to your friends?"

"Nah, they know this story." Picking up his beer, she lifted it to her mouth, but scowled when she realized he'd emptied it. And he silently ordered his dick not to get hard at the sight of her mouth on the same spot that his had just covered. "And it's a sad, sad story." She slapped her hands to her face, and Owen winced in sympathy. That had to *hurt*. "Mn nn th pgnth."

"I'm sorry. What?" He peeled one of her hands free of her face. "Say that again?"

"I'm in the pageant!" She plopped crossed arms on the bar and dropped her head onto them.

Owen stared at her. Confusion swirled inside him. He glanced from her bowed head to seek out Maddox for some kind of clarification, but his friend was busy serving drinks to customers. All right, so he'd have to wing this one. But dammit, he didn't see the problem.

Leo was gorgeous. Sexy. Confident. One of the most poised women he'd ever met. Did she have some moral stance against pageants that had her upset about participating? But would that impel her to get this lit? There had to be more going on here.

"Since I have a really bad habit of shoving my size

twelve in my mouth around you, I'm going to just listen this time. You want to tell me why being in this pageant is so horrible?"

At that moment Maddox appeared with a tall glass of water with a pink umbrella and thin, red straw in it.

"Here you go, Leo."

She lifted her head and frowned. "This is *not* a cranberry and vodka, dude."

"In the immortal words of Shaggy, wasn't me."

Then the traitor jabbed a finger in Owen's direction and walked off with a smile.

Her lips parted—most likely to deliver a stinging diatribe on how she was grown enough to order a drink for herself—but he cut her off by nudging the glass closer. "Drink, Leo. It's been a long night, and I want to get a coherent story out of you. Without you falling off the bar stool."

She glared at him. Then picked up the drink and sipped until only half the water remained.

"That's fair," she grumbled.

"Okay, why don't you start at the beginning?"

She groaned, and he twitched behind his zipper. Tipsy, sober, his dick didn't care. It was an equal opportunity lecher.

"The beginning? Okay. The beginning is in the second grade when Ms. Dinkins announced we would be putting on a performance of *The Tale of Peter Rabbit* for the school and our parents. I was cast as Elm Tree Number One. Moe helped sew this fantastic costume complete with a realistic-looking trunk and leaves with a little hole in the middle for my face. It was awesome. I had no lines, but I was ready to be the best damn Elm Tree out there. And I was. Until the lights came on. I got woozy with all those people out there looking at me. I tried to pretend they weren't there. But as soon as Peter Rabbit hopped by me, I threw up all over his fluffy white tail."

"Wow."

Don't laugh. Don't you fucking laugh.

"Yes, wow." She shook her head, misery stamped on her features. Forgoing the straw, she drank the rest of the water. "But it didn't end there."

"It didn't?" Owen blinked. This got worse? Double wow.

"No." She heaved out a breath, blinking rapidly. Oh, shit. Was she going to...cry? "I thought Vomit Gate might've been a fluke. So I decided to give acting another try. It just so happened my high school drama department was putting on a production of *Romeo and Juliet*. Surprisingly, I was cast as Tybalt, Juliet's hothead cousin. All the rehearsals went well, and I was thinking, I could do this! I could actually do this! Then came opening night."

She hung her head, her chin resting on her collarbone, and Owen shifted closer to hear the rest. Because, by God, he was *invested*. This was better than, well, theater.

"While putting on my costume in the girls' bathroom, I knew it was going to be bad. My hands wouldn't stop shaking. My stomach kept cramping and my legs couldn't seem to hold me up. Jelly. I'd heard the term before, and thought it silly, but at that moment I got it. My legs were jelly. I tried deep breathing, but soon I just started hyperventilating. But I couldn't back out. And, oh, Jesus. It was a fucking nightmare. Like a repeat of *Peter Rabbit*. As soon as the lights hit me, with all those eyes on me, I froze. I mean, like a statue. And then the laughter started. Low at first. But every time I fumbled a line or tripped over a prop or nearly killed myself choking on that damn feather on my hat, it got louder and louder. But then... Then when I was supposed to stab Jack Houser, who was playing Mercutio, under his arm, I accidentally jabbed him in the balls. He almost died on the stage. Just keeled right over." She added a demonstration with her arm and a whistle. "And the audience almost died laughing. I just ran off the stage."

"Oh, fuck," Owen wheezed.

A crack of laughter escaped him before he could contain it even as he squeezed his thighs together, sympathizing with poor ol' Jack. Jesus Christ, he would've paid good money to see that high school play.

But then she lifted her head, and her obvious misery doused some of his humor. And when her bottom lip trembled as if she held back tears, the rest of his hilarity completely disappeared. And he surrendered to the need he'd caged ever since he'd first opened the door to her on his porch.

He touched her.

Cupping her jaw, he gently brushed his thumb over her soft skin. And as her lashes fluttered down and she turned into his palm, something inside him, in a place buried so deep he'd barely acknowledged its existence, sighed. That something relaxed. As if it'd waited for this moment. Had been waiting for this moment for fourteen months.

Romantic bullshit, he chided. He didn't entertain it, didn't believe in it.

But right now, sweeping her silken skin again, remembering how he'd trailed his fingers and his lips over this flawless landscape once upon a time, he thoroughly enjoyed it. And like the greedy, entitled bastard he was, he wanted more.

So he dropped his hand.

One. This wasn't about him and his desires.

Two. Wanting more of anything, but especially her, only meant trouble.

Briefly closing her eyes, she huffed out a laugh that held more than a fair amount of chagrin. "I'm a sad drunk."

"An adorable sad drunk, though."

She shot him a look that he couldn't begin to read before she lifted a hand, signaling for Maddox. When he approached, she pointed at her glass. "A refill, please. With another cute umbrella."

"You bet."

Within seconds he placed another water in front of her and she downed a good amount before turning back to Owen.

"I'm sorry I laughed."

Leo waved a hand, almost smacking herself in the nose. Apparently, the sobering-up thing was going a little slow.

"Forget it. You're much more sensitive than my brothers, who for weeks would cup themselves anytime I walked by them." The corner of her mouth curled up as she leaned over her glass and aimed for her straw. On the third time she found victory. "Anyway, do you see my dilemma? I can't get up on another stage. I haven't since *Romeo and Juliet*, and the thought of doing so now scares the shit out of me. And considering my disastrous past, that is a definite possibility."

He grimaced. Because damn. She wasn't wrong.

"Leo, you are one of the strongest, most self-possessed, articulate and poised women I know—"

"I'm not. I'm really not. And we've just met so you can't possibly know that."

A note of vehemence and hint of desperation colored her voice and he managed not to frown. Barely. But his curiosity wanted to squeeze and squeeze until the truth emerged. Ironic and more than a bit hypocritical.

He hungered for her truth but hoarded his.

"Sometimes you don't need to be in the presence of someone for months or years to be familiar with their character," he argued. "Tell me your biggest fears about this pageant."

"Haven't you been listening?" She threw up her hands. "Projectile vomiting. Imminent fainting. Paralysis. Stabbing of testicles. Does there really need to be more?"

"Well, first of all, it's an all-women beauty pageant so we can cross potential castration off the list." At her glare, he shrugged. "But everything you've named are the possible outcomes of your fears but they're not *your fears*. What are they?"

She huffed again, propping her elbows on the bar top and pressing the heels of her palms into her forehead.

"I don't know…"

"Yeah, you do, and *in vino veritas*, right?"

"I didn't have wine, I had cocktails."

He snorted. "Stop avoiding the question."

"Fine." Popping the straw out of the water, she drank until not a drop remained. Settling the empty glass back down, she frowned down into it. Deliberately not looking at him. "I have a horrible case of stage fright. As you can tell. But it's deeper than that. All the preparation in the world and I can't determine the results…can't control them. That terrifies me. And what if…" Her voice dropped to barely a whisper. "What if I fail? What if I make a fool of myself? It's not in private. It'll be in front of everyone. *Again*."

Owen stared at her profile. At the elegant slope of her nose. The regal slant of her cheekbones, softened by the smattering of cinnamon freckles. At the lush curve of her lips and the deceptively delicate line of her jaw. How could someone so beautiful, seemingly so self-confident, doubt herself and her ability to get up on any stage and captivate an audience? Past experiences aside, she was now a full-grown woman. He possessed zero doubts that she could enter and win this pageant. By a fucking landslide. By sheer willpower alone.

Daring to touch her again—because hell, why not press his luck?—he pressed two fingers to her chin and turned her head toward him. When her gaze met his, he dropped his arm back to his side.

"Have you ever heard the phrase 'any given Sunday'?" She shook her head, and he said, "In football any given Sunday means, on any Sunday—any game day—any team can beat another team. A team with the worst record in the league could possibly beat the team with the best. Despite the preparation during the week... Despite having the best coach in the league... Despite having the best facilities... An upset can happen. It's what makes the game so exciting. Because it's not about the bigger dog. It's about whether there's more dog in you than in them. On any given Sunday, anything is possible."

He edged closer to her, bending his head over hers. God-damn. Yes, he was playing a cat-and-mouse game with his own self. Tempting himself when he had no business doing so, but when her eyes widened a fraction and her faint gasp teased his ruined mouth, he couldn't move back. Even though every self-protective instinct in him screamed that he do just that.

"You asked me before why I continued to play football. Here's another reason. Because going out on that field, I knew there was no one else I could control but me. As the quarterback, I could influence and lead, but not control. I could throw the perfect throw and my receiver could still drop it. I could throw for three touchdowns and the defense could still fuck up and we could still lose the game. Or we could win it all. That's the thrill of it. The not knowing. The laying it all out there on the field every Sunday. Leo—" he picked up her hand, held it and studied the size difference between them. Found it hot as hell "—this hand is too small to hold the weight of everything in this world. The responsibilities. The outcomes. The results. And I don't know why you'd want to. I had a…strict upbringing with my father. Football was the one place where I could be free. It taught me that things won't go perfectly in this life, and we adapt, roll with the changes. Do we strive to be perfect? Hell yeah, we all want to win or else we wouldn't be out there. But when we fuck up, we shake it off and look to the next opportunity to get it right."

"So…" She inhaled a trembling breath, her gaze trained on his hand enfolding hers. "You're telling me to forget about the past and do the pageant?"

"No." He returned her hand to the bar and slowly straightened. But that didn't remove her scent from his nose. Didn't erase the clawing desire to bury his face in the curve of her neck and inhale directly from her pulse. "I'm saying cut yourself some slack. And let go of that need for control. Any given Sunday, Leo. This pageant doesn't have to mean disaster. It could mean the biggest comeback in the history of Rose Bend drama and theater. Because when it comes to any dog in the fight, I'd put my money on you any day."

She blinked, clearing her throat and glancing away from him.

"Thank you."

"You're welcome."

"I didn't tell you what for."

He scratched his unmarred cheek. "Uh, okay."

A faint smile ghosted across her mouth. "Thank you for

taking the time and helping my brother and Mack. I never did say that last week. I was actually ungrateful and I'm sorry for that. He hasn't stopped talking about you yet. He made the team. Both of them did."

Warmth seeped into his chest and spread as if he'd just downed a tumbler of top-shelf whiskey.

"Again, you're welcome. Your brother and his friend are good kids. And Sonny has a great arm."

Leo's smile bloomed into a grin, and that warmth in his chest flashed into a full-out fire.

"And thank you again. For tonight. For listening. And for your kindness. I'll think over what you said. When I'm sober."

It was on his lips to give her another "you're welcome" when she hopped down off the stool and shifted into his space. Closer. Closer still, until her firm breasts grazed his chest. His breath disappeared from his lungs, and he stiffened. *All* of him stiffened. And he stifled a groan that climbed its way up his throat with sharp claws.

She brushed his hair away from his cheek—his damaged cheek—and planted a soft kiss directly on the scar.

Shock rippled through him in icy waves, breaking over and over. He fisted his hand, preventing himself from tracing his fingertips over the deadened patch of skin that he could swear tingled with Leo's kiss.

That had been deliberate. She hadn't been that drunk. No, Leo had intentionally placed her lips on his scar.

But why?

Bending his head so his hair once more concealed his face, he forced himself not to glance over his shoulder at the alluring, sexy, confusing woman who refused to be evicted from his head. Without waving goodbye to Maddox, he headed down the hallway, toward the bathrooms and the back exit of the bar.

Pushing through the door into the night, he inhaled the clean air into his lungs as well as the heavy scent of rain that hadn't started pouring yet. It reminded him of Leo. Of her skin. Of sweet, wet sex.

He shuddered, lust shivering through him, leaving him hard, aching.

Shaking his head, he shoved his feet forward, away from the bar.

Away from temptation.

Away from Leo.

CHAPTER EIGHT

"LEO, MY LOVE!"

Leo groaned, cradling her poor abused head between her hands. When the pounding settled to a dull pulse instead of the battering of a thousand hammers, she glared at her brother. But not too hard because a frown hurt her head, too.

"Wolfgang, do you think you could keep it down to a low roar, please? I'm trying to die a peaceful death in here, and I'd like to do it without your foghorn of a voice in my ears."

Wolf stepped farther into the office, a wide grin splitting his beard.

"So the rumor is true. My little sister went out and got smashed. When Nessa told me, I didn't believe it. I had to come over and check it out for myself."

"Your wife is a narc, and she broke about three girl codes by passing on that information," Leo mumbled, fumbling for her cup of coffee.

"Well, if it makes you feel any better, I was stopped by no less than four people who either told me they had no idea you could suck back so many drinks or to compliment your lovely singing voice."

He dropped into the chair in front of the desk, his grin never slipping. If possible, it widened.

"Surprisingly, that doesn't make me feel any better."

"Huh." He scratched his jaw. "Makes me feel good."

"Ass."

He laughed. "Oh, this is perfect."

"Oh, my God." She clutched her head again. "Use your inside voice. What the hell are you doing here anyway? Shouldn't you be outside in your he-shed or picking up my sister-in-law from school?"

The *he-shed* was the workshop in back of the inn where Wolf created the most beautiful furniture and woodwork as part of Dennison Carpentry. In the past few years, Wolf had transformed his love of working with wood and gifting those pieces to those he loved into a small business whose products were heavily in demand. And not just in their region, but across the country, too. She was proud of her big brother and that he'd finally found a woman and child whom he loved.

And if there was a tiny twinge of envy over Wolf's and Cole's finding the ones who so perfectly completed them, well, that just showed she could be a petty bitch sometimes.

"I just sent Trevor into town with our last order, so I'm finished for the day. And Ivy has play practice after school." No one could miss the note of pride in his deep voice as he spoke about his wife Nessa's twelve-year-old sister. "She has the lead role, and why wouldn't she with that voice?"

This time the pitching of her stomach had nothing to do with her hangover and everything to do with the reminder of her *illustrious* past with plays. A groan slipped free, and Wolf's grin ebbed until a soft, sympathetic smile remained.

"Nessa also told me about you being conscripted into the pageant." He leaned forward in his chair and stretched his long arm across the desk, covering her fist with his large palm. "If you really don't want to do it, Leo, just tell them. Cole and I were shitheads after the whole stabbing of the Montague jewels incident, but we understand how hard it is for you to be up on a stage. No one would think badly of you if you decided not to be in this thing. But for what it's worth," he said, squeezing her hand, "I think you would totally rock it. When you put that brilliant, scary mind to something and place that will of steel behind it? Nothing can stop you, Leontyne Dennison."

She flipped their hands over and captured his in hers. "Thanks, Wolfgang," she whispered. "I needed to hear that."

Nodding, he leaned back in his chair and that grin widened into what she could only describe as "shit-eating."

"My wife also shared that you might have received some advice from a certain quarterback." He waggled his eyebrows.

"I really need to have a talk with Nessa about the sanctity of the sister circle," she muttered. "And don't try to make something out of nothing, Wolfy." She snorted. "Besides, you probably have more of a crush on him than I ever could."

He shrugged. "I'm comfortable enough in my manhood to admit you're right. Have you ever seen that man throw? I've never seen anything as beautiful in this world."

"I'll make sure to mention that to Nessa."

"I'll deny it and then take her home and blur her mind with fantastic sex."

"Oh, eew." She gagged. "I just threw up in my mouth a little."

Wolf laughed, the sound echoing in the office, and despite needing to erase the image of her brother and her friend getting biblical, she smiled, too. Happiness sat well on him.

"Anyway, you sure nothing's going on between you and Owen Strafford? I read the news just like everyone else, and he's been through a helluva lot this past year. Things that could make a man angry and bitter with the world. At the risk of having my advice shoved in uncomfortable places—" he held up his hands, palms out "—just be careful. Disappointments and pain can…harden a man's heart. And I don't want to see you hurt."

The hot denial sputtered out on her tongue.

Because one glance into Wolf's eyes and she knew they both thought of Cole. In their brother's grief over the deaths of his wife and son, he'd fought love for so long that he'd almost lost it.

Leo cleared her throat, and Wolf bowed his head.

"You don't have to worry about me, Wolf. There's nothing between me and Owen Strafford."

Not a lie. He didn't even remember that night, so to him it didn't happen. As for last night…

Funny how some things from the bar were hazy, but her conversation with Owen remained as clear as a window freshly cleaned on a spring morning. All of his words. His patience. His tenderness.

His touch.

Before she could stop herself, she grazed her fingertips across the hollow of her cheek where his thumb had brushed. As soon as she realized what she was doing, she dropped her hand and clasped it with her other one. As if trapping it, punishing it for its wayward actions.

And of course, Wolf didn't miss a thing. His green eyes narrowed on her, and she braced herself for the inquisition…

"Hey, Leo, you have a couple of visitors asking to see you." Danielle, one of their employees who helped the front of the house and also assisted in cleaning the guests' rooms, rapped on the door frame and leaned into the office. Catching site of Wolf, she smiled. "Hi, Wolf."

"Hey, Danny." He waved at her with a friendly grin.

"Thanks, Danny. I'll be right out." Rising from her chair, Leo rounded the desk and paused next to Wolf as he stood, too. Rising on her tiptoes, she balled her brother's shirt into her fist, dragged him down and smacked a kiss on his cheek. "You're a good man, Wolfgang. Thank you for worrying about me."

"I knew you loved me, Leontyne. And you're welcome."

Chuckling, she exited the office and smoothed her palms down the front of her high-waisted light blue pants. Pausing just outside the doorway, she made sure her ruffled, blue-and-white-striped shirt was neatly tucked in. Satisfied, she headed down the hallway, her blue heels clicking on the hardwood floor. As she approached the end of the corridor, she curled her lips into her professional smile…and froze.

Owen stood in front of the sign-in desk tucked next to the curving staircase.

And he wasn't alone.

A gorgeous woman accompanied him. Dark hair cut close to her head, bold, fierce bone structure and full lips. She reminded Leo of actress Danai Gurira. A sexy but classy olive green jumpsuit clung to her tall, tightly toned body, and her beautiful ebony skin fairly gleamed under the ceiling's lights.

The woman was stunning.

Leo tried valiantly not to resent her on sight. Not for being beautiful. But for being beautiful *and* standing with Owen.

Sigh.

At some point Leo needed to send a search party for her maturity.

Deliberately brightening her smile to compensate for her internal pettiness, Leo moved forward in full hostess/manager mode.

"Well, this is a surprise," she said to Owen.

Him in a dress shirt and slim-fitting black pants should be freaking outlawed. His dark hair still hung over the left side of his face. His discomfort radiated off him, from the stiff set of his shoulders to the outline of his fists in his pants pockets. Unlike in the bar last night, the lights weren't dim, and they had an audience.

Given he rarely ventured out of his house, Owen must feel…exposed.

"How about we go back in my office?" she offered.

Owen gave a sharp nod and his heavy footsteps echoed behind her when she turned to retrace her path back down the hallway.

When she reached the doorway of the office, Wolf no longer occupied it, and though she loved her brother, she breathed a sigh of relief. Meeting Wolf when Owen might already be overwhelmed, could've proven too much.

As soon as they stepped in, she closed the door, granting them privacy. Then she turned to the woman with him and stretched out her hand.

"I haven't introduced myself yet. Leo Dennison. Welcome to Kinsale Inn."

"It's a pleasure to meet you, Leo," the beauty said, wrapping Leo's hand in a surprisingly firm grip. "Owen has told me so much about you. I'm Celeste Forrester."

Forrester. Why did that sound familiar?

"Well, now I don't know whether to assure you that he exaggerates or ask you to put all of that aside and form your own opinion." Celeste chuckled, and even that was pretty. Smiling wryly, Leo rounded her desk and waved toward the two visitor chairs. "Please, sit. What can I do for you?"

She arched an eyebrow at Owen.

He shifted in his seat, and if Leo didn't know better,

she'd believe nervousness flashed across his face. But she *did* know better. Someone possessing his level of arrogance didn't do nervous.

But then Celeste poked him in the arm, and he scowled at her. Oh, yeah. Something was definitely up.

"Leo, before I begin, I ask that you hear me out first."

Oh, God. Nothing good ever started with that.

Frowning, she nodded.

Leaning forward, he propped his elbows on his thighs— thighs that appeared extra powerful in those pants—and dangled his clasped hands between his spread legs. His hazel eyes met hers, intense and focused.

"Last night when we talked about the pageant, I heard you regarding your fears. The pageant is out of your wheel- house, and you have every right to be nervous and uncom- fortable."

Hold up. Record scratch. He'd spoken to this woman, a stranger, about something she'd confided in him? Anger and betrayal welled inside her, and she struggled to keep her face from outing her.

But either she wasn't that good at concealing her emo- tions or maybe he'd started to know her too well... Nah. Her face must've snitched. Because he held up a hand in the age-old sign of "stop."

"Hold on. I didn't go spreading your business behind your back. There's a reason I shared with Celeste. You might not have recognized her name, but she's Celeste Forrester. Not just wife of my best friend, Sherrod, but a past Miss Teen USA, Miss Illinois and Miss America. She knows beauty pageants."

Well, damn. I guess she does.

"That's, uh, amazing," Leo said, switching her atten- tion to Celeste.

And it was. Not that she should be surprised. Looking at the woman was like staring at the sun. Hard to do for too long without glancing away, afraid of being blinded by her gorgeousness.

"But you're wondering what that has to do with you." Celeste softly smiled, her dark brown, upturned eyes bright with humor. "I promise you I wasn't prying, but Owen knows that I've also coached girls before. He shared with me because he wanted to know if I would be willing to help you prepare for the pageant."

"What?" she whispered. No, gasped. Shock seized her and she jerked her gaze from Celeste to Owen. "What?" she repeated.

An impassive mask slipped over his face, and he reclined against the back of the chair. As if adding distance between them.

"You're worried about failing. About not being ready."

What if I make a fool of myself?

Her words from the night before echoed in her mind. How diplomatic of him to phrase her words differently. Had he told Celeste…everything? She studied him, but his eyes—amber chips flecked with green—gave nothing away.

Embers of humiliation kindled within her. *Concentrate on the here and now. Burn with embarrassment later.*

"Celeste can help you, train you. She's one of the best. What I want for you, but more importantly, what I know you want for yourself, is to be as prepared as possible, to be as in control of your chances as you possibly can. That's what she can give you. Every advantage. Right now I have zero doubts you're calling me an insensitive asshole, but you can do that and still accept her help."

"Why?" Leo murmured, momentarily forgetting Celeste's presence. "Why would you go to all this trouble for me?"

His mouth firmed, and he briefly glanced away. The thick, black strands of his hair fell away, revealing the scar crossing his cheekbone, slicing through the corner of his mouth as well as those dotting his cheek and jaw. Last night she'd deliberately kissed that dark pink one arcing down his cheek. To show him it didn't repulse her. Didn't make her turn away from him in disgust.

Quite the opposite.

If only she did revile him.

Then maybe she could erase the feel of hard flesh and silken skin against her lips. Maybe she could get rid of his scent, which reminded her of leather seats in a sinfully expensive car. Maybe she could evict the wicked curl of smoky heat low in her belly and the tight, almost painful, ache in her nipples at just the memory of her breasts stroking his wide, hard chest.

He looked back at her, and an emotion flashed in his eyes, there and gone so quick she questioned herself. Because she had to be projecting. No way in hell did she glimpse heat flare in those whiskey-colored depths.

No. Definitely projecting.

"Leo?"

Leo dragged her regard from Owen and focused it on Celeste.

"Is it okay if I call you Leo?" Celeste asked. When Leo gave a jerky nod, Celeste smiled, linked her hands on her knee and continued. "We've just met, and I don't want to assume anything about you as a person, so I'll just talk about me. It's hard for me to accept help. One, that's just how I grew up. You didn't go around asking for handouts or assistance because then you invited people into your business. And two, admitting you need help is like conceding a weakness. And when the world expects you to project strength, when any kind of vulnerability is viewed as a fault, we avoid asking for help at all costs. But again, I'm just talking about me."

Leo snorted, and Celeste's smile widened.

"My husband and I are here in Rose Bend for the next several weeks on vacation until after the spring festival. Let me coach you, give you tips. However you want to put it. Actually, you'll be doing me a favor. I like the quiet and time to relax...for the first few days. After that, I go stir-crazy without something to do. So give me something to do. I beg you."

"You're good." Leo squinted at her.

"I would say it's my talent, but I killed 'Bohemian Rhapsody' on my violin."

"Queen is life." She'd been on the verge of crushing on the woman before, but now the adoration was deep and profound.

Such was the power of Freddie Mercury.

"I feel super close to you right now." Celeste rose from her chair in a graceful move that slammed Leo with a sudden desire to work on her core muscles. The other woman extended her hand. "So, Leo, do we have a deal? Do I help you win this thing?"

"I'll settle for not fainting, puking or neutering anyone, but..."

For most of her adult life, Leo had combated her anxiety with control. The more control she could exert over a situation, the better she felt. Not exactly healthy, but considering what had happened the two times in her life she'd thrown caution to the wind, it was how she coped. And it was the only option she had now. She slid her palm over Celeste's, squeezing.

"Yes, we have a deal. And thank you. I appreciate you giving up your vacation to train me."

"Honestly, it's no problem at all."

"And thank you, too, Owen," Leo said to the man standing to his feet. "Again. It seems like I'm saying that to you a lot lately."

"You're welcome, Leo."

For a long moment his eyes met hers, and the intensity reached past skin and bone to the heart that she desperately guarded with polite reserve, smiles and snarky humor.

Maybe she and Owen weren't that different after all.

"Do you want to start the day after tomorrow, Leo? We're staying with Owen. If you want to call me and let me know a good time for you, I'll make sure I'm there."

"That sounds perfect."

Leo plucked a business card from the holder on her desk and handed it to Celeste.

"If you'll text me I'll have your number in my phone. I'll check my calendar to make sure I don't have any appointments, and I'll message you this evening."

"Wonderful. It was awesome meeting you."

Waving her fingers, Celeste exited the office, and with a dip of his chin, Owen followed after her.

Leo stood staring after them—after him—for several moments.

What in the world just happened?

CHAPTER NINE

LEO CLIMBED THE front steps to Owen's porch, smothering a groan.

This would mark her third time visiting his house, and seriously, she should collect frequent-flyer miles at this point. And Rose Bend being what it was, the gossip wouldn't be too long in coming.

Leo's at it again. Wink, wink. Nudge, nudge.

A shame she can't seem to hold a man.

That biological clock is probably ticking louder and louder 'cause she's latched on to another one.

Hell, there'd even been a betting pool going at the local Elks lodge on the longevity of her last relationship. That'd been an asshat move... But those wagering on three months had made a killing.

Funny how she was labeled a maneater when no one castigated the assholes who'd been gaslighters, cheapskates or cheaters. Romantic feelings tended to dry up when you walked in on your boyfriend pounding away at his sister-in-law on the chaise longue you helped pick out for his office.

Sighing, she pulled open the storm door and knocked.

Within moments the front door opened, and Owen filled the space.

One time. Just *one time* she would like to see him and not have her breath stumble in her lungs like a drunken bachelorette.

Instead of the dress clothes from yesterday, he was back in a long-sleeved gray hoodie and black track pants. And for a moment all she could see was the memory of endless taut golden skin pulled tight over hard muscles.

It didn't take much to drum up the taste of earthy musk, sandalwood and *him*. God, she'd overindulged on that taste, that scent, getting punch-drunk.

She fisted her fingers then straightened them in a futile attempt to shake off the sensation of hair-dusted abs and thighs under her fingertips.

His gaze dropped to her restless hands, and she stilled them, pressing her palms against her legs. But when he lifted his scrutiny to her face, she met it, pretending she didn't glimpse the question there. The flicker of…something. That same something she'd seen and dismissed in her office a couple of days ago.

"Leo." He shifted backward, granting her space to enter. "Come on in."

"Thanks."

She eased by him, inhaling his scent, wishing she could cut back on such unnecessary vices. Like breathing.

Silence fell between them, and the foyer echoed with the awkwardness. Owen shoved a hand through his hair, dragging the black strands away from his face. But then, as if he'd forgotten she stood there, he tugged the long waves back into place, hiding the left side of his face.

"You don't have to do that. Especially with me." She'd meant for her voice to emerge strong, even a little reprimanding. But somehow, it came out whisper soft.

Heat raced for her face at what that tone could betray. Or what he could perceive from it.

"I'm sparing you." His sensual lips twisted into a hard, nearly cruel, smile. "I find when people don't have to look at reminders of pain and imperfection, they're more comfortable."

"That might be true for some. But I think the person you're really trying to *spare* is yourself."

Owen stiffened, his eyes narrowing on her. This time she had no problem deciphering the emotion in those hazel depths. Anger.

Before he could answer, though, Celeste descended the stairs, with a tall, gorgeous Black man with long, shiny dreads behind her. Jesus. Did all the beautiful people travel in packs?

"Hi, Leo," Celeste greeted. "I'm so glad you could make it."

"Leontyne Dennison!" Sherrod Forrester boomed, grinning and swooping in to wrap Leo in a hug that lifted her off the floor. "It's good to see you! How're those brothers of yours?"

"It's nice to see you, too." She smiled back at him. How could she not? His enthusiasm was contagious. As was his friendliness. Hell, she hadn't even been aware Sherrod knew she existed outside being Cole and Wolf's younger sister. Yet, he greeted her like a long-lost friend. She hadn't expected someone so famous and pretty to be so...well... nice. "And Cole and Wolf are doing great. Both recently married, actually."

"That's amazing. I'm glad to hear that. Especially for Cole. He's a good brother and deserves a second chance at happiness." Sherrod nodded, and those words had her liking the football player even more.

A confused frown pulled Owen's eyebrows down over his nose, and he studied Leo closely.

She ducked her head, not ready to face the question in that gaze. Later maybe, but not now.

"I hear you're about to grab the pageant world by storm,"

Sherrod continued and hooked an arm around Celeste's waist, dragging her into the side of his body.

"Whoever you heard that from is really optimistic. And has probably had a lot of wine."

Owen snorted as Sherrod and Celeste laughed. Glancing down at his wife, Sherrod swept his mouth over hers, and they shared a look that had envy entwining around her ribs.

"With my baby in your corner, you have this on lock." He planted a kiss on the tip of Celeste's nose and slid his arm from around her waist, jerking his chin at Owen. "Give me about five minutes? I'll meet you by the truck."

Owen nodded. "Yeah, sounds good."

"And, Leo, if you'll give me the same five minutes there are a few things I want to get ready for us in Owen's man cave. I thought we'd start by assessing your qualities and talents so we can reinforce your strengths. And refine whatever areas need improvement. Okay?"

The thought of being criticized and found lacking had Leo's stomach cramping. "Okay," she said.

Inhaling a breath, she watched Celeste disappear down the hall, anything to avoid looking at Owen. But that tactic could only work for so long. And dammit, she was twenty-nine not nine.

"They seem like a great couple—"

"Leontyne? That's your name?"

Their words crashed together like wrestlers caught in an armlock. She blinked. And that quickly, irritation replaced awkwardness. Nothing could extinguish the ever-present hum of desire that seemed to define her every interaction with him, but irritation? Irritation was good. It kept her from picturing how she'd licked the strong column of his neck to that delicious vee where his torso and thighs met.

Because, dammit, he'd had his dick in her three times.

Had been in her company at least four times now here in Rose Bend. And he *still* didn't know her name.

"Yes." She crossed her arms over her chest. Arched an eyebrow. "You know, I realize CTE is a real thing with football players, but having to remind you of my name is tiresome."

"In my defense, you've only introduced yourself as Leo." He paused. "Your parents named you after Leontyne Price, the opera singer?"

With a dramatically exaggerated sigh, she dropped her arms. "Yes." She narrowed her eyes. "Is there a problem with my name?"

"No." Again, he paused. "Other than... Hell, I'm trying to be delicate about this..."

His face scrunched up in a manner she absolutely refused to find adorable. She knew exactly what he was trying to edge around, and with an unholy glee refused to bail him out.

"Delicate about what?"

"Leontyne Price is..."

"Fierce and fabulous? I know," Leo supplied, nodding.

Owen scrubbed a palm across the back of his neck. "Of course she is. Her performance as Aida at the Met was incomparable. *She's* incomparable. She's also..."

In spite of the surprise rippling through her at his description of the soprano classical singer, Leo squinted up at him. "A trailblazer? Also true."

Owen dropped his arm, stared at her. Hard. "You're fucking with me."

"Only 'cause you're so fuckable."

Silence plummeted between them, and though it was impossible, she could've sworn the temperature plunged to below freezing. One glance at the forbidding but expressionless mask on his face, and "Leo, girl, you messed up" boomed in her head.

She rewound her last words and only needed to hit Play before she mentally slapped a hand to her mouth.

Shit.

She'd been teasing him about trying to be so politically correct, but he hadn't taken it that way. It was only a guess, but the jeweled chips of his eyes assured her that she wasn't far off the mark. Owen believed Leo had referred to his scars, being sarcastic about his fuckability. As if they diminished his magnetism, his beauty, in any way. If anything, they made him sexier. More attractive. This was a man who'd suffered, who'd endured pain and had survived. He was a fighter. And what woman didn't find that hot as hell? Because if he'd go to war like that for himself, what more would he do for the woman in his care?

In the next instant, images bombarded her. Images of just how he *cared* for a woman.

Images of just how *fuckable* Owen was.

Clearing her throat, she ducked her head, pushing a strand of hair that had escaped her ponytail behind her ear.

"What you were trying so hard to say was, yes, I'm named after a Black opera singer when I'm so obviously not Black. There. See how easy that was?"

She tilted her head and forced herself to meet that glacial gaze with a smile. Forced herself to hide the shiver that worked its way through her. Eyes that cold shouldn't send *that* much heat coursing through her. Jesus, heatstroke from lust wasn't a thing, right?

"You've only met Sonny, not my other brothers and sisters," she continued...or babbled. She'd done the same that night in Boston. Babbled under the warm light from those hazel eyes and his single-minded focus. "But we're all named after musicians. Coltrane. Wolfgang. Florence as in Ballard. And on and on. There are seven of us."

Still, he remained silent, but the sheet of ice coating his gaze started to thaw, and she caught the spark of curiosity in the gold-and-green depths.

"Seven?"

"And my baby sister is the only musically inclined soul in the bunch. A singer. How about you? Any brothers or sisters?"

Other than looking up the car accident, she'd deliberately not researched anything else about him. At the time she'd convinced herself she was respecting his privacy. But truth be told, she was proving she was definitely *not* interested in knowing anything beyond the info required to persuade him to judge the chili contest.

In the words of Dr. Phil, *How's that going for you?*

"It's just me." The corner of his mouth curled, and Leo couldn't call it humorous. "Unfortunately."

Don't ask. It has nothing to do with chili, judging or a festival, so don't you dare ask.

"You've always wanted siblings?"

Dammit, woman.

She didn't think it possible, but the bitterness in that not-quite-a-smile deepened.

"The more moving targets, the odds of getting hit goes down."

Her horror must've shown on her face, because he shook his head. "Not physically."

"So you wanted more siblings as cover?"

He shrugged. "More like strength in numbers." Slipping his hands in his front pockets, he asked, "But you never answered my original question. Why did your parents name you after Leontyne Price?"

Nice deflection. This time no smile included. They were certainly a pair. Experts at avoiding uncomfortable conversations and situations.

"My mother is a huge fan. And that's putting it lightly. She was able to see one of the last performances of *Aida* at the Met in '85. Moe still talks about it. Says she never heard anything as beautiful, as powerful, as important. When Dad and Moe found out they were pregnant with me, he didn't even have to ask what my name would be." She laughed softly. Then tilted her head. "My turn. How do you know so much about Leontyne Price?"

He snorted. "What? Because I'm a football player I'm only supposed to listen to rock or rap?"

"Defensive much?"

"I happen to love...music. All music."

She gasped. Why this delighted her, she decided not to delve into. "You listen to opera! Admit it."

"I'm pretty sure that's what I just did."

"No, you hedged. You. Love. Opera. How in the world did that happen?" And how did that make him ten times sexier?

He sighed, a hand emerging from his pocket to once more thrust through his hair. But he abruptly stopped short and dropped his arm. Not meeting her gaze, he sharply pivoted and strode toward the front door.

"My quarterback coach in high school was a huge fan, and he made us practice to it. Insisted football was more about grace and strength than brute force. Especially my position. So we listened to opera, moved to it while we ran through our plays."

"And..." Leo pressed, dogging his heels.

"And what?"

"And you love it. Your coach might've made you practice to it, but he didn't make you research the soloists. Just go on and admit it."

Owen drew up short and spun around. With an undignified squeak, Leo just managed not to collide into him. As it was, her palms slapped against his chest, and *dear Lord*, her fingers needed to learn some self-control because they curled into the dense muscle.

Instead of inserting space between them—or at least between him and her shameless hands—Owen leaned into her palms, pressing against them. As if giving her permission to go ahead and feel...

His heart thudded like a bass drum under her palms, and that rhythm echoed low in her belly—between her thighs.

Oh, damn.

"I love opera," he murmured. "My coach might have introduced me to it, but I fell for it after that. It uplifts, it mesmerizes. It helps me to escape." He paused after that last telling but enigmatic admission. What did Owen need to escape? "Now, give me something, Leontyne. Something no one else knows since you demanded the same from me and wouldn't let go until I surrendered it. What do you secretly love?"

Like a light switch, her mind shut down, instantly rebelling.

Information was power. And what idiot willingly handed over their power? To feel potentially exposed, betrayed? Weak? She'd felt all three before. Promised herself never to be in those positions again.

It's a game. He's teasing. Asking for something simple. Not your deepest secrets.

Nothing's ever simple. Nothing's ever too small. Trust no one.

Her mind warred. Her heart battered her rib cage.

And breathing? It became a luxury, not a necessity.

"Leo?" Owen's sharp voice penetrated the white noise that filled her head. He cupped the back of her neck. The shock of his touch, those calloused hands on her skin, vibrated through her body like an electric jolt to her system. "Sweetheart, breathe. What's wrong?"

The order and the question breached the fog and she blinked. Once, twice, focusing on his worried frown. On the scar that ran through his mouth, pulling one corner down. Her fingertips itched with the need to trace that mouth, that scar.

She'd blame it on the surreal moment, but she gave in to that need.

As if from a distance she watched her hand lift toward his face, hover above his lips, then lower, lower.

The instant the pads of her fingertips touched his soft flesh, any disassociation evaporated with a resounding, almost painful, snap. A sigh climbed her throat, broke free.

Just as she remembered.

Waves of erotic heat shimmered inside her now, like water sizzling on fire-warmed rocks.

She shifted her fingers, skimming them over his scar. What would it be like to kiss him now? To feel that contradiction of textures against her lips? To feel it drag over her skin? Over her sex?

She shivered.

Leo lifted her gaze to Owen's, awareness trickling into her head for the first time in minutes. Good God, what must he think? About her entirely too-forward actions? About *her*? She'd violated his personal space, not to mention the question of consent.

Did he—*oh, fuck*.

Flames. Flames burned in his eyes, transforming them to an amber-lit forge.

No.

No, it didn't seem he minded her actions at all.

A throat cleared behind them. "Leo, I'm ready when you are."

She sprang away from him as if scalded. And hell, in some ways, she was. Her fingers still bore the phantom singe marks of contact with his mouth.

Turning, she spotted both Celeste and Sherrod standing behind them. Christ. How long? How much had they witnessed?

Never mind. Ignorance was not only bliss but sanity saving, too.

Or pride saving anyway.

"Yes, I'm ready." Drumming up a smile for the Forresters, she waved a hand. "Lead the way."

Without glancing over her shoulder at Owen, she followed Celeste, avoiding Sherrod's curious scrutiny.

Another of her rules.

Pretend it didn't happen, then it didn't happen.

Because she was mature like that.

CHAPTER TEN

"ARE YOU REALLY going to wear that damn thing in there?" Sherrod rounded the hood of the Range Rover, eyes narrowed on Owen's hoodie.

More specifically, the hood pulled up over Owen's head.

"Shut up. And yes."

Sherrod rolled his eyes. "Y'know, it's fundamentally unfair. If I went out looking like this—" he swept a hand up and down Owen's hooded and sweatpants-clad figure "—I'd be either Karen-ed or shot for jogging down the street. You, on the other hand, it's probably an endorsement for some new brand of casual wear. Also the unfair part? Well, besides the systemic racism. I'm better-looking with a far tighter body. I tell you, man, it's hard being a Black man in America."

He wasn't wrong.

But at the moment Owen couldn't focus on his friend's social commentary—or on the shade he'd just thrown. His heart lodged in the base of his throat, while his stomach made a break for his esophagus. Hell, every organ inside him was rebelling.

Swallowing to dredge up any kind of moisture for his suddenly dry mouth, he squinted at the fence that stretched out behind the aluminum bleachers and the squat concrete building that had CONCESSIONS painted across it in huge, red block letters.

What had he been thinking to agree to this? Well, he hadn't *exactly* agreed to come over here, had he? When Coach Matt Wilson had reached out to Sherrod and asked if he and Owen would come to a practice, Owen had balked. But Sherrod being Sherrod wouldn't take no for an answer. And he'd threatened to truss Owen up, stuff him in the back of his own SUV and drive him over here.

But now, standing here in the high school parking lot, a whistle blaring in the distance, the air in his lungs roared in his head.

He was scared.

No use denying it.

Most of these football players had probably looked up to him, admired him. Hell, had played video games with his image on them. They most likely saw him as an invincible, perfect, charmed quarterback who was a beast on the field, a winner.

Not this defeated has-been who hid from the world.

He had no place here. What could he say to them? It was one thing to give Sonny and Mack tips, but this? *Do what I say and not what I do?*

Persevere.

Press on through the pain.

Don't quit.

It would all be laughable if it wasn't so damn pathetic.

"You belong here, Owen. As much as I do. You being out of the game for a year doesn't change that. And believe me, these kids don't think that, either." Sherrod cupped his shoulder, squeezing tight. "Now, let's go shape some young minds."

Owen snorted. "You sound like a PSA."

But he started walking toward the field.

"Don't be jealous of my oratory skills."

"Please. I'd rather not hear about your and Celeste's love life."

Sherrod barked out a loud crack of laughter. "Fuck you."

Moments later they strode through the gate and to the edge of the field. The nerves in his gut didn't abate. But lessons he'd learned during his career surged to the forefront. Showmanship. He could bullshit with the best bullshitters.

The coach spotted them and blew his whistle, calling a halt to the practices going on with the different positions. The quarterbacks, offensive linemen, wide receivers, running backs, defensive linemen, defensive backs and linebackers, all with their coaches, jogged over to Coach Wilson and gathered around.

"Take a knee, guys. I have a treat for you today." He grinned at Owen and Sherrod, and they walked toward the team. "It's my honor and pleasure to have all-pro, two-time Super Bowl–championship quarterback and wide receiver Owen Strafford and Sherrod Forrester from the Jersey Knights. They're doing me a huge favor, spending practice with you, offering some advice."

"The pleasure is ours, Coach." Sherrod grinned and jerked a thumb toward him. "I played for him, guys. So he knows a little something."

That got the laughter Sherrod had been aiming for.

"I'm glad to help. Nice to meet you all," Owen said. Spotting Sonny kneeling at the front, he jerked his chin up. "What's up, Sonny?"

"Hey, Owen," Sonny murmured, eyes wide, but obviously trying to play it cool. Especially with most of his teammates' gazes fixed on him. Probably wondering how the freshman knew the professional quarterback.

Owen bit back a smirk.

"I really appreciate you donating your time, knowledge

and experience with us today. It's invaluable. And I'm sure these guys appreciate it, too. Don't you, fellas?"

A loud chorus of *yeah*s responded, and Owen bit the inside of his mouth to prevent a smile at Coach Wilson's glare as a few *hell yeah*s trickled through.

"All right." He clapped his hands. "Let's go to individuals. Coaches, go with your players. Sherrod, if you'll join Coach Merritt and the receivers, and, Owen, if you'll go with Coach Holleran and the quarterbacks, that would be awesome."

Wilson blew his whistle, and they all broke off in their groups.

"Hi, Mr. Strafford. I'm Marion Holleran, the quarterback coach for Rose Bend High." The pretty, petite Black woman with a curvaceous, athletic build stuck her hand out to him. "My dad and I had the opportunity to see you play against the Eagles the year before last. You competed twenty out of twenty-five passes for three hundred and fifty yards with three touchdowns. An excellent game."

"Owen, please." He shook her hand. "And thanks. How long have you been coaching with the team?"

She nodded toward the boys who'd started running plays. "The last three years. It's not as rare as it used to be for women to coach high school football teams. Still... Not as common as it should be. But Coach Wilson gave me a chance. I love the game. It's my passion. I went to college, earned a degree in kinesiology and my teacher's certificate, all with the goal of returning here and coaching for this team."

"Head coach?"

She grinned at him. "When Coach Wilson retires? That's the goal."

Noting the steely determination in her light brown eyes, he wouldn't bet against her.

"Save me a seat at your first home game."

She laughed. "You got it."

"I'm not here to step on your toes. Let me know where you need me."

But Coach Holleran was already shaking her head. "Oh, no. One thing about being a leader is knowing when it's your turn to follow. And I'm here to learn as much as possible from you today so I can give even more to my boys. As a matter of fact, if you have a few minutes after practice, I'd consider it a favor if you'd let me pick your brain on a couple of things."

"No problem at all."

"Awesome." She waved a hand toward the small quarterback team. "They're all yours."

And she meant it.

For the next hour he took over position as coach and ran the four teens through several plays, offering advice, giving suggestions and corrections and an equal amount of praise. Soon, his hood came down, and he forgot about his face. Like Sonny on the day he'd helped the teen at the inn, none of the players seemed to pay any attention to Owen's scars. They focused on his words, what he had to teach them. Since they didn't make a big deal out of the marks, neither did Owen.

It was…freeing.

And as on that day with Sonny, Owen found his love of the game flickering in his chest again, that flame dancing in exhilaration. That joy allowed him to focus more on the boys instead of his own insecurities. They were all good players. But there were two standouts—the Tyson he'd heard so much about and Sonny.

He studied the older kid as he simulated the snap, faked the ball to where the running back would be, rolled out to the left, planted his feet and threw the ball to the player running routes for him.

Yeah. Really good.

But he had a cockiness about him. He liked to showboat. And even as Coach Holleran blew her whistle and called him over, correcting him on squaring his shoulders more when propelling the ball down the field, he fidgeted, not meeting her eyes. As if she annoyed him and he wasn't listening to her. Wasn't respecting her advice, her authority.

Everything in Owen itched to snatch the kid up and get on his ass about deference, humility and good ol'-fashioned things like not being a dick.

But it wasn't his place. And long after he left, Coach Holleran would have to deal with little shits who didn't believe she deserved their respect simply because she had a vagina. Just from having Sherrod as a friend, he also acknowledged that wouldn't be the only battle she'd have to fight.

Yet, if anyone had the warrior spirit to go to war and not let anyone break her, he suspected it would be Marion Holleran.

Soon, Coach Wilson called all positions together and the team practiced as one, running through plays they'd gone over individually. Both Owen and Sherrod interjected periodically to call out mistakes and corrections, but for the most part left the coaching up to Wilson. Owen immediately saw why Sherrod loved the man and jumped when he'd called. Firm but fair, he seemed to rule with a calm, no-nonsense head. He didn't yell, but didn't need to. The players and coaches highly regarded him.

After Coach Wilson called an end to practice, Owen sought out Sonny. Seeing the youth standing near the edge of the field with Mack and a couple of other guys, he strode over to them.

Clapping Sonny on the shoulder, Owen said, "You looked good out there, Sonny. You, too, Mack. Sherrod mentioned you had strong hands and caught the ball with your hands not your body. And you had a nice crisp route. That's high praise coming from him."

Both teens grinned wide, their chests puffed out.

"Thanks, Owen." Sonny held out his fist to Owen and he bumped it. "Did you get my message telling you we made the team?"

Owen nodded. "I did. Your sister told me. I knew you would."

This earned him even wider grins.

"You two have rides home? Sherrod and I can give you lifts if you need them."

Several gasps and murmurs from their friends swirled, and Sonny and Mack stared at each other before their heads whipped back toward Owen.

"He— I mean, sure," Mack said, catching himself when Owen arched an eyebrow. But in the next instant, his face clouded. "Sonny and I were actually going to stay after and run through some more plays with our coaches and get some laps in. But we can do that tomorrow..."

Owen shook his head, admiration for these two and their work ethic rising. "No, we'll wait for you to finish. And if you need to call anyone to let them know we're giving you a ride, make sure you do that."

"Cool!" Sonny elbowed Mack and they ran off.

Twenty minutes later Owen stood on the sideline with Sherrod, studying the two teens and a couple of others as they practiced as hard as they had when the full team had been there. He'd finished talking to Coach Holleran, and she continued to impress him with her insightfulness. Her heart might be here at this high school with these kids, but she had the talent to compete for a position in the NFL if she desired it. There might only be eight female coaches in the league, but they were opening doors for more. And Marion Holleran could be one of them.

"Who's the kid? The one you said hi to when we first got here? The same one I saw you talking to after practice."

"Leo's little brother. Sonny. Apparently, she and her brothers and sisters are all named after musical greats. I'm afraid to ask, but I think his namesake might Sonny Bono."

Sherrod stared at him. Blinked. "Nah. That can't be right."

They continued to study the players, arms crossed, then Sherrod asked, "So speaking of Leo… What's going on there?"

"Nothing."

Sherrod scoffed, sliding him side-eye. "So my lying eyes just saw you two cuddled up at the front door with her fingers all over your mouth? Now, I'm nearsighted as fuck but that doesn't make me hallucinate."

Owen didn't dare glance at his friend because he didn't trust his face not to betray him. Memories of that hot-as-fuck moment played through his head. He could still feel her stroking over his mouth, exploring it as if greeting an old friend and yet discovering something fantastically new. Something that fascinated her. Unable to help himself, he slicked the tip of his tongue over his bottom lip, encountering the toughened skin of his scar.

That hungry part of him desperate for human contact—no, for *her* contact—needed to believe in that flare of desire he'd glimpsed in her blue-gray eyes.

But the sensible half of him dealt with reality, with reason. And that half argued he'd seen what he'd wanted to see. What he'd been projecting.

Because one, he'd injured her pride by pretending not to

remember her. And second, she hadn't given any indication of interest in rekindling what had flashed out of control in Boston a year ago. Hell, then his status as a football star hadn't even impressed her. Now? He had even less to offer. Scarred, broken and, as far as she was concerned, an asshole with multiple personalities—sometimes broody, sometimes a jerk, sometimes actually nice.

If he was half as smart as his coach claimed him to be, he'd stay away from her. Stop finding excuses to show up on the inn's doorstep. Stop playing savior with chili contests and pageant coach saves. He'd stay in his damn house with his gym, video games, opera and books. Revert back to avoiding people and life.

Because in the end, she would discover what his father had known all along, what his agent was beginning to suspect and what Owen lived in fear of everyone else realizing.

He was irrelevant without football.

He had absolutely nothing to offer her or anyone. And what would a strong, capable, powerful woman like Leo need with a man like that?

His arms tightened across his chest. To keep his emotions trapped inside? Or to prevent them from pouring out?

He honestly didn't know.

"There's nothing to tell," he belatedly said in response to Sherrod. "I can't even say we're friends."

"You're not friends but you arranged for my wife to be her pageant coach?" The arch of his eyebrow called bullshit on that. "We've been friends for how long? Eight years," he continued, not granting Owen time to answer. "And I can confidently claim to know you better than anyone else. I've never seen you like this around any other woman."

Don't ask. Do not entertain or encourage this shit.

"What are you talking about? Like what?"

"Indecisive. Uncertain. Skittish." Sherrod dropped his

arms, turning to fully face Owen. "You've never had to chase a woman. Probably not in your life, but definitely not since I've known you. And now, this one isn't falling at your feet. Not to mention she ghosted you once already. There's some unfinished business there. You can't wrap your head around Leo Dennison, so you're running scared."

More than a little smugness tainted his tone, and if Sherrod wasn't his best friend, Owen would tell him where he could stick his theory.

Eh. Screw it.

"What psychologist you blow to come up with that theory?"

"Fuck you." Sherrod jabbed a finger toward him. "There's that toxic masculinity raising its ugly head. I'll have you know there's absolutely nothing wrong with a man being emotionally mature and able to communicate his feelings openly and honestly, without being afraid to be compassionate and empathetic. This is me being compassionate and empathetic, motherfucker."

Owen snorted. Then snickered. "I can see."

"Shut up."

Sherrod turned back to the players as they started to wrap up. He'd claimed to know Owen well, but Owen could claim the same. So he waited for Sherrod's second wind.

He didn't have long.

"You do realize I'm like the cliché in this lil' second-chance romance you have going on, right? The Black best friend? To hell with that. I'm leading-man material." Sherrod thumped his chest.

Owen cocked his head, squinting at the wide receiver. "Where do you come up with this stuff? Second-chance romance? How do you know so much about it?"

Sherrod sighed. "Celeste. She sure does love her Hall-mark movies." He shrugged. "I can't even lie. They're kinda addictive once you start watching."

"We're really going to have to find you hobbies, man."

"Damn that," he scoffed. "I love hanging with my wife. She's amazing company. Just wait until you find a woman who stimulates your mind as well as your dick. Oh, wait." He widened his eyes to a comical degree. "You already did—"

"Shut it."

His friend laughed, the sound evil and not the least bit repentant.

"All right, all right. I'm done. Promise. For now." He held up a hand as if taking a vow that they both knew he'd break in a New York minute. "On to more unpleasant topics that you're probably going to shut down because you're touchy as Celeste when I start talking about her putting too much damn mayo in her potato salad."

Ouch. Owen had witnessed the attitude Celeste got about her grandmother's recipe for potato salad. He wasn't that bad… Right?

"Have you been giving any serious thought about coming out of retirement? I'll take any casual thought, too. Just…any thought."

Ice trickled through Owen's veins. As if drawn against his will, he studied the kids on the field again. Lingered on their laughing faces as they shrugged out of their pads and engaged in horseplay. So young. So idealistic. So…free.

He'd been like them once.

God, how the years since then sat on his shoulders like boulders. Weighed him down until he felt like a hundred years old instead of thirty.

Except…that heaviness had disappeared when he'd been on the field during practice, helping them, guiding them. Because for the first time in so long—fourteen months, to be exact—he'd been part of a team again.

His soul had been complete instead of scattered in flyaway pieces that had no hope of ever being whole.

"Yeah," he breathed, his gaze not moving from the teens.

"Yeah?" Surprise echoed in Sherrod's voice as if he hadn't expected that answer. But pure delight vibrated beneath it. A hard hand squeezed Owen's shoulder, dragging his attention to his friend. "Are you serious?"

"Yeah, I've been thinking about it." Not a lie. Until this moment, he hadn't acknowledged to himself that he had been. But now that he'd put it out there, he couldn't deny it. "I don't know if I am—I can't give you or Byron an answer either way. There's a lot to consider. But it's been on my mind."

"As long as it's not a no." Sherrod grinned. "Goddamn. I feel like I've won the lottery. I don't even care if you decide to play for a team other than the Knights. I just want you back. Beside me or on opposite sides of the field. Doesn't matter."

Sherrod's voice thickened and Owen blinked against the sudden sting in his eyes. Clearing his throat, he nodded.

"Well, like I said, I've just been thinking on it. I'll call Byron later and let him know I haven't given up on the idea. I just…don't know if I have the courage to pull the trigger."

"You do," Sherrod quietly said as Sonny and Mack ran over to them. "And it's okay if you don't believe it right now. I'll do the believing for both of us until you catch on."

Smacking Owen on the back, Sherrod called out to the two teens and the four of them turned and headed toward the parking lot.

I'll do the believing for both of us until you catch on.
Until you catch on.

Sherrod sounded so certain Owen wouldn't fail him.

Too bad Owen didn't share that same faith.

Hadn't in a long time.

CHAPTER ELEVEN

"How am I exhausted when all I've done for two hours straight is walk, pose and turn?" Leo whined, sprawled out on Owen's bowl-shaped chair on his back porch. Oh, yes, *whined*.

The cool, late-afternoon breeze brushed over her damp, warm skin, and she closed her eyes and turned her face up into the airy caress. She sighed, welcoming it. No doubt, in minutes, she would venture back inside the house for her jacket as the spring breeze would become too chilly. But now?

Nope, they would have to scrape her complaining body from this amazingly comfortable chair with a human-size spatula.

"Don't forget transition," Celeste said from the chair next to her. "Walk, pose, turn and transition."

"Believe me. I'll be saying it in my sleep."

Celeste chuckled. "Then I consider day one a success."

They sat in a companionable silence, and Leo flipped through mental images of her afternoon with the former beauty queen. As Celeste had informed Leo earlier, she'd taken Leo through several exercises ascertaining just how hopeless she was—not Celeste's words, but therein lay the gist of it.

Answer: hopeless squared.

All this time Leo had believed she walked just fine. Her

feet always managed to carry her from Point A to Point B without any major incidents. Who knew how wrong she'd been? At least for pageants.

Elegance is key. A slow, elegant walk. Methodical movement and turns. Always keep a soft smile on your face. And remember, remember, do not look down at your feet. It's instinctive to do so, especially with that long gown, and that's going to require a lot of practice. Once we buy your evening gown, we'll make sure to rehearse in it to reinforce this.

For an instant a powerless sense of drowning swamped her. She was overwhelmed. The panic ran down her throat like mouthfuls of dark water. No matter how hard she swam for the surface, her heavy limbs hindered her.

Her head jerked toward the door, and she stared at it like a mouse desperately seeking an escape out of a maze. The inn. She wanted to be back at the inn. There, everything was familiar. Safe. She was competent.

She couldn't fail there.

"Hey." A slim, strong hand covered hers. "Breathe."

Leo opened her eyes, met Celeste's dark brown pair.

"It's okay, Leo," Celeste said, voice soft. "Breathe."

Oh, shit.

What had just happened? For the second time in a day, she'd spaced out. Earlier with Owen, and now again with Celeste. Sharp fingers inched up her chest, farther up her throat. Clutching. Squeezing...

She'd only experienced this one other time. Right after...

Her body stiffened, and any air left in her lungs evaporated. Sparks spun in front of her eyes, disorienting her.

Oh, God.

She couldn't... She was...

A face appeared in front of hers. Suddenly, her hand pressed over the thud of a calmly beating heart.

"Focus on me, Leo. Focus. You're not alone. Listen to my heartbeat. Feel it. And breathe with me."

She grasped on to that relaxed pulse, to the composed voice like a...well, like a drowning woman afraid to go under a third and final time. And after struggling through the noise in her head, the chaos in her body, she soon found herself following the soothing pattern.

Minutes that seemed like an hour passed before Celeste lowered their arms, and she enfolded Leo's hands in hers. The tightness in Leo's chest had loosened, but humiliation stung her cheeks.

"Leo, I'm going to give you about fifteen more seconds of avoiding me and then the badass innkeeper who mouths off to arrogant football players is going to lift her head and look me in the eye."

Well, hell. When she put it like that...

Inhaling a deep breath, Leo met Celeste's judgment-free gaze.

"That's better." Celeste rose from her kneeling position and reclaimed her chair, pulling it closer. She also reclaimed her grip on Leo's hand. "You don't have to tell me what was behind the episode—"

"I wouldn't call—"

Celeste threw up a hand, palm out.

"Don't bother trying to deny it. Or maybe you don't even realize what just happened. But I recognize anxiety when I see it. I've experienced it myself. Suffered it."

Another denial died on Leo's tongue, taken out by astonishment.

"*You* have *anxiety*?"

Celeste smiled, the curve a cynical twist. "I was a Black woman—a dark-skinned Black woman, at that—competing in a predominantly white system. Oh, yes, I had anxiety. It didn't make me weak, though. Didn't mean I was damaged or somehow less worthy to be there than the other contestants. I just needed to pinpoint the triggers and then find alternate methods of coping."

Leo stared at the flawless, poised woman before her. It stretched the bounds of her imagination to envision Celeste shaking or frozen in place, helpless.

"It's nothing to be ashamed of," Celeste continued softly. "As a society, we've been taught that emotional or mental illnesses are stigmas. Scarlet letters. With women, especially, we've fought to overcome labels like the weaker sex or being emotional or hysterical. So to show any weakness is tantamount to admitting we're not strong enough. That we can't hack it. That yes, society was right all along. We weren't built to compete on the same level as men. When this—" she waved a hand back and forth between Leo and herself "—isn't about power or character flaws or bad upbringing or weaknesses. Anxiety is one of the very few equal opportunity things in this world, and it happens to so many of us. Being a superwoman isn't about being infallible. It's about having the courage to embrace your imperfections and move forward with your head held high, not allowing anyone to shame you for them."

Leo squeezed her eyes shut. Tiny prickles stung her eyelids, and she squeezed tighter. Celeste's words both pummeled and petted her, bruising and soothing her. She curled in on herself, avoiding them and stretching toward them like a plant seeking the nourishing sun.

But in the end, Celeste couldn't understand how her words wounded her. Leo courted no illusions about her flaws, of just how fallible she was. No, she fought to maintain the charade so no one else guessed the truth.

It was a long game of sleight of hand. Keep everyone's

gaze on the persona of cool, controlled, have-it-together Leontyne over there so no one perceived secretive, imperfect Leo over here.

It was exhausting.

But necessary.

She couldn't afford to be less than perfect. To loosen the reins.

To let go.

"Leo." Celeste tilted her head. "Have you—"

"Hey, everything okay here?"

Leo startled, jerking against Celeste's hold at the sound of that voice. She twisted around to meet Owen's narrowed hazel gaze before it dipped to her and Celeste's clasped hands. When his scrutiny rose to her face again, questions shadowed it, as did concern.

"We're grilling out, babe." Sherrod strode over to his wife and planted a quick kiss on her lips. Straightening, he slipped an arm around Celeste's shoulders and aimed a Sexiest Man Alive smile her way. "I would ask if you're staying, Leo. But we stopped by the inn to drop off your brother after his football practice, and your mother gave us a message to deliver to you. 'Stay where you're at and don't even think about coming home until well after dinner.'" He cocked his head to the side. "I'm sure she meant that with more love than it sounds."

Leo snorted. "Probably. But I'm not going to push it." She rose from the chair. "I won't impose, though. I can head over to my bro—"

"That was an invitation, so you're not imposing," Owen said. After a moment he dipped his head in a nod. "Stay."

Are you asking me or telling me?

Smothering a sigh, she murmured, "Okay. Thanks."

Then because she couldn't help herself, "Is there anything I can do to help with dinner?"

"Woman, grilling is for men," Sherrod announced, his deep voice resonating with his offense. "All you need to do is sit back, relax with a fruity drink and be amazed at our prowess."

"Huh." Celeste frowned, tapping a perfectly manicured finger to her full bottom lip. "I could've sworn the last time you grilled, the fire department had to be called out. That huge funnel of smoke really worried our neighbors. So I had to man the grill during our last get-together with my parents."

"No loyalty, Celeste. None."

"Of course I'm loyal, babe." She patted his ass, tipping her head back and smiling up at him. "Now, Leo—" Celeste turned a wicked grin on her "—how do you take your steak?"

"Medium rare." Leo squinted at Sherrod. "If you're in charge of the fruity drinks, I love my margaritas with extra sugar around the rim."

Sherrod sniffed, jerking his chin up. "Noted."

Behind Leo, Owen softly snickered, but apparently not soft enough, because his friend shot him what she could only describe as the stink eye.

"Pay him no mind, babe. You go take a shower and when you come back down, I'll let you season the meat," Celeste offered, standing and brushing her lips across his jaw.

Sherrod wiggled his eyebrows. "Oooh. I would love to season your meat."

"Oh, Jesus." Owen gagged. "Don't ruin a perfectly good steak for me. I beg you."

"What?" Sherrod widened his eyes, aiming for innocence—and failing. "I could've said let me beat the m—"

Celeste slapped her hand over her husband's mouth. "Okay, you're going too far now. Bye, Sherrod."

Cackling, he kissed his wife's palm and strode across the porch. "Promise you won't start without me." He pointed a finger at Celeste and when she held up a hand, fingers parted between the middle and ring finger and thumb extended, he sighed. "That is the Vulcan greeting not the Scouts' honor. And you know it."

When he disappeared into the house, Owen arched an eyebrow at Celeste.

"You just enjoy tormenting him, don't you?"

Celeste shrugged a shoulder. "It's included in our wedding license. Not my fault he didn't read the small print."

Chuckling, Owen shook his head. "I'm headed up to take a shower, too." He switched his attention to Leo, and she struggled not to surrender to the image of him naked, with water pouring over him like some golden, earthbound Adonis. "Are you going to be here when I get out or am I going to have to tie you down to a chair before I leave?"

Hell. Now she had *that* picture in her head. Liquid heat slid through her veins, swelling her breasts and pooling between her thighs.

Apparently, her nipples and vagina were aaaaall on Team Tie Me Down.

"No need for that. I'll be here." How she managed to sound so calm astounded her.

"I think we might've found your talent for the pageant," Celeste said after Owen disappeared. "Acting. Because you almost had me convinced that you didn't want him to pull out the ropes and go all *Fifty Shades* on you."

Horrified, Leo jerked her gaze toward the other woman, her hand climbing toward her throat. "Don't tell me—"

"That he noticed?" She scoffed. "He's a man. Of course

he didn't. Like I said, you're a good actress." She narrowed her eyes. "Maybe we should consider a dramatic monologue for the talent section." Celeste waved a hand. "We have a week or so to think on it. But no, he didn't notice, and I don't see you denying you find him hot, either."

Shit.

Her stomach churned with embarrassment. Celeste couldn't know about that night a year ago, but still… Acknowledging she found anything attractive about the man seemed tantamount to admitting that secret—especially since she was the only one who remembered it. It would be like confessing to the time she discarded all her strict, self-imposed rules and allowed emotion to rule instead of her head.

And look how that had turned out.

Disappointment flashed in Celeste's dark eyes, but she smiled, nodding. "Let's go prep the food so when they come back down, we can get started."

Celeste didn't wait for her reply but moved past her into the house. After a moment Leo followed.

Feeling like she'd let the other woman down.

And in some odd way, herself.

"ARE YOU SURE we shouldn't be up there helping?" Leo asked, frowning at Owen's wide back as he led her across his backyard.

Since before today she'd never made it past his living room, this oasis behind his home struck her as a surprise. A huge, lush yard that stretched to a high, white fence that afforded him whatever privacy the stands of elms didn't. A rickety, rust-spotted playset from another era claimed one side of the lawn and large, towering trees with a tire swing occupied the other.

He was a self-declared hermit, and she couldn't exactly

picture him sitting on his back porch sipping a cup of coffee and enjoying the peaceful view. Or walking his yard in his bare feet, enjoying the morning dew between his toes or the fresh, cool air on his skin.

She might not be able to picture it, but staring at the stiff set of his shoulders and the wide back that seemed to carry the weight of the world, she wanted to envision it. Wanted that for him.

Shaking her head to get rid of the fanciful thought, she hurried to catch up to him as he glanced over his shoulder at her.

No, not her.

At the side patio with the grill, small table and chairs where they'd left Sherrod and Celeste.

"Very sure. Trust me. We're safe over here."

"It's going to get that ugly between them?"

"Ugly?" Owen snorted. "Hell, that's foreplay. C'mon." He took her hand in his, sending fiery shivers of shock and desire rippling through her. "When's the last time you took a ride on a swing?"

"More recently than you, I bet."

The corner of his mouth kicked up. "You'd no doubt win that wager." Tugging on her hand, he led her to the mammoth tree with a tire suspended by chains from its thick branches. Holding the swing steady with one hand, he patted the rubber with the other. "Jump on."

She stared at it, more than a little dubious, then shifted her gaze to him. "Pass."

"Why, Leontyne Dennison, are you scared?" he mocked.

"Using my full name does not goad me into doing what you want like I'm twelve years old."

He cocked his head. "Will that spider crawling behind you do it?"

"Shit!"

She bolted forward, her shriek ringing across the back-yard. With an agility she'd later attribute to adrenaline, she leaped up onto the tire, balancing both feet on the rims and clutching the chains.

"Where? Where, dammit?" She scanned the space she'd occupied just seconds ago.

"Wow. That was…wow. I haven't seen receivers move that fast. Did your feet actually touch the ground?"

She jerked her gaze from the potential spider-ridden area to peer over her shoulder.

"Hello! Forget that. Kill the damn spider!"

"Fine, fine." He moved around her, and no, she didn't miss his low chuckle. Bastard. "But to be fair, you were in its natural habitat. Why must the spider be murdered?"

"Because it's an abomination against nature, and right now it's probably plotting my demise. Take it out before the hit on my life can be carried out."

Owen threw her a look as his bark of laughter echoed between them. "Well, that's not over-the-top dramatic at all."

Reaching up, he cupped his hands over…something. Leo squeezed her eyes shut, unable to watch. Good Lord, she hated the things. Had ever since Wolf brought home that freaky *Charlotte's Web* book from the library and then made her watch the cartoon. A spider that spun names? *Unnatural.* That had triggered her irrational phobia of the little terrors.

Moe assured her God didn't make mistakes, and Leo believed that. Yet, she had questions about His creative decisions behind the eight-legged freaks…

"Are you done yet?" she ground out.

"Yes, you big baby."

His voice reached her from a distance, and she cracked an eye open to peep at him squatting down across the yard.

"Don't tell me you just let it go," she yelled. And gasped. Because what the hell was he thinking?

Rising to his full height, Owen turned and strode back over to her, a smile flickering around the unmarred corner of his mouth. Not answering, he gently but firmly cupped her elbow and guided her down to the tire, her ass fitting in the hollow center. Only once he had her gliding through the air, her legs extended, the early-evening breeze coasting over her, did he reply.

"I did release it into the wild," he said as if the spider was an endangered species instead of the spawn of Satan. "And it's not going to travel all the way back over here to torment you. But I promise you, if it does, it forfeits its second chance at life."

She didn't have to lean back and glimpse his face to know a smirk rode that sinful mouth. Whatever. Manners demanded she thank him. But that'd have to wait until she could say for certain the little abomination wouldn't pop up again.

Several moments of silence passed between them. Though she'd originally balked about climbing onto the swing, the tension from the day—work at the inn, her first pageant practice with Celeste, the conversation afterward—slowly ebbed from her body. Tipping her head back, she allowed her lids to lower. Savored the whisper-soft caress of the breeze on her face, throat, over her jacket- and jeans-clad body.

It seemed impossible, but for an instant, she'd become a child again. Carefree. Unburdened.

"I haven't met all of your family, but Sonny and your

mom are really nice people. And Sherrod speaks highly of your brothers Cole and Wolf."

She opened her eyes, peering straight ahead at the lush green lawn.

"You met my mother?"

Why *that* stuck in her head she couldn't explain. Not even to herself. But it did. And left an uncomfortable ache in her chest.

"Why does that bother you?"

"It doesn't." The denial came, immediate and fake as a hockey player's teeth.

Instead of sending her sailing through the evening air once more, he gripped the chain and edge of the tire, halting her flight. In one instant, he was behind her out of sight, and in the next, he stood in front of her, hands still claiming the chains. Pulling her close to him.

She tried not to stare—just as she had after he'd returned downstairs earlier. But with him inches away from her, there remained nowhere else to look. At least that was how she consoled herself. Dark hair still damp from his shower and curled around his face. His hazel eyes seemed to gleam in the setting sun, casting shadows in the hollows under his impossibly sharp cheekbones. She forced herself to glance away before her gaze dropped to his wicked lure of a mouth.

Nothing good came of those firm, lush lips.

Nothing good for her control. Her common sense. Her sanity.

"Leo."

Sighing, she shifted her rapt attention from over his shoulder to his golden eyes. "Owen."

"Since you touched my mouth earlier, I've been fighting not to call, text—*fuck*—skywrite and ask if you're okay... If it disgusted you. How did it feel? Did you rub your fingers against your leg to get rid of the feeling as soon as my back was turned? The masochist in me wants to know while the coward in me would rather pretend it didn't happen."

Her heart thudded against her chest. The pounding resounded in her head, and she clutched the chains tighter so she didn't press her palms over her ears.

"You're not a coward," she whispered. "That's self-preservation, and it's smart, not weakness."

"It's denial, Leo," Owen countered, shifting closer so his thighs brushed the tire and her calf. He didn't loom over her, didn't intimidate her with his big body, but her breath still lodged in the base of her throat. Simply because he blocked out everything else and, in this moment, her world narrowed down to *him*. "And I am the master of it. But we can only be ostriches so long before we either get horrible cricks in our necks or we admit to ourselves that denial and self-preservation are excuses to hide from not just the world but ourselves."

She gaped at him. "Since when did you become so self-aware?"

He grunted, giving the swing a small push. "Oh, I'm insightful as fuck. But am I going to do anything with this wisdom? That is another question."

"Why are you telling me this?" she murmured. "About me touching…you earlier. Which I apologize for because I did it without your permission. And now this? Why?"

"First, there's no need to apologize for touching me."

He didn't push her again, clutching the chains and holding on. His intense gaze tugged her even closer.

"Not even your scars?" she pushed, voice no higher than a whisper. Gentle.

"Not…you," he said. "You seem to get a free pass with me."

A ripple of heat shivered through her. She'd had that

free pass once. Had used it for hours on one hot, uninhibited, delicious night.

But now? Now she couldn't ever take it again.

"As for why I'm admitting all this to you? Because I'm hoping if I give you honesty, you'll return the favor. At least for today or even for the next thirty minutes while we wait for our steaks to be done."

"Why?" she breathed, finding herself captured by the sudden…need in his hazel eyes.

"Honesty is rare in my world. Even more so finding a safe space—a safe person—to be open with. Give me thirty minutes, Leo. Please."

She didn't need to think. "Okay."

"Okay," he said, and she caught the soft hint of wonder.

Slowly, he released her, stepping back and moving behind her again. Seconds later she swung through the air, legs pumping.

"I guess I should mention that your mom invited Sherrod, Celeste and me to Sunday dinner."

Once more that curious constriction gripped her chest, but this time she paused and analyzed it.

"What're you thinking?" Owen murmured.

She'd promised him truth, but theory and practice were two different animals. Wetting her lips, she willed her throat to loosen, her tongue to move. The words to come.

"I…" She paused. Tried again. "I'm thinking that my mother has never invited a man connected to me to Sunday dinner."

A beat of silence passed.

"Have you?"

"Have I what?"

"Have you invited a man to dinner before?"

She closed her eyes, exhaled. "No."

What did that say about her? Because she'd been in several relationships—some more serious and lengthy than others. And yet, she'd asked none of them to the Sunday dinners at the inn that were reserved for family. Cole, Wolf, even Sinead and nineteen-year-old Florence had brought significant others to the table through the years. But Leo? No.

Did that make Leo emotionally unavailable, which was what her ex, the middle school teacher, had said? Or did she have a fear of intimacy as her other ex, the certified public accountant, had accused?

Why hadn't she noticed before?

Better question.

Why hadn't it bothered her before?

"Then I'm honored."

She blinked. His deep voice vibrated near her ear. Lust whipped through her like a hot wind. And not even the gentle evening wind could cool her.

Good Christ.

Owen Strafford had every potential of being her next big mistake.

Again.

"Sherrod said something about dropping Sonny off after football practice. Were you two there with him?" she asked, tasting the desperation to switch the subject on her tongue.

"Yeah," he said after a brief pause that telegraphed she wasn't fooling him. "Sherrod's cool with the coach, and he asked us to stop by."

Whoa.

Helping Sonny and Mack was one thing, but heading over to the high school and…helping a team full of boys and adults when he'd lived most of the past year as a recluse? That had to have been terrifying.

"Are you okay?"

His inhale broke the quiet that settled between them.

"Yes." Another push of the swing. Another short silence. "I didn't think I would be. And the only reason I went was because Sherrod refused to take no for an answer. But my fears..." He didn't name them, but he didn't have to. Gawking. Pointing. Whispering. Snickering. Or for a man like him, even worse, sympathy. "In the end, none of them mattered. I had fun."

"And that surprised you."

"Yeah, it did." A soft, self-deprecating chuckle. "I remember high school. I went in there braced for those kids to give me shit. But when I got caught up in the game, in coaching, and the hood came down, they never said a word about the scars. And I know they saw them. I mean, how can you miss them? They glanced at them, but that's all they did. Like me, all they cared about was football, and what they could learn."

"No." Leo tilted her head back, briefly meeting his gaze as the tire tipped toward the sky. "They cared about learning from their football hero. Scars or no scars."

He scoffed. "I'm no one's hero, Leo."

"Keep telling yourself that if it makes you feel better."

As the tire swept back toward him, he twisted it around and in the next instant, she faced him. His body shifted forward, and her knees and calves cradled his hips and legs. Palms flat on either side of her hips, he leaned forward, steadying her and infiltrating her personal space.

He loomed too close.

She should tell him to back up. Give her space. Space to think. To breathe without inhaling his intoxicating scent.

Any minute now she would order him to move...

"I've said it before. That tongue of yours is like a sledgehammer." He studied her, his gaze so piercing Leo wouldn't have turned down body armor right now. "And yet I find it one of the sexiest things about you. What in the hell does that say about me?"

A bomb of lust detonated low in her stomach and radiated to her throat, breasts, sex, thighs, hell, even toes. It throbbed in a heavy beat that eliminated reason and threatened her precious control.

She tightened her grip on the chains, focusing hard on the links pressing into her palms. The cool steel anchored her. Provided her something concrete to cling to so she didn't do something monumentally stupid like throw herself at him.

"It says that either you're the masochist you believed you might be or this reclusive lifestyle you've been living has you really hard up."

"Again with the mouth."

She snapped her lips closed with an audible pop.

He laughed softly—darkly—and it stroked over her skin, tickled a caress down her spine to the sensitive base.

"Oh, it's a little too late for that."

As if God hit the half-speed button on some celestial clock, time slowed. Suddenly, every hitch in her breath knocked against her throat like a tiny hammer. Every breeze drifting over the nape of her neck caressed her like a lover's gentle fingers. The distant chirp of a cricket resounded in her head like a foghorn. And when Owen leaned forward, raising his arms above her, grabbing the chains then gently pressing his forehead to hers, his luxurious woodsy-and-sex scent rushed her in a tender attack of the senses.

One she had no hope of evading.

Didn't want to evade.

Move, fool. Distance. That's what you need to not repeat old mistakes.

But she didn't *move.* Not one inch.

"Tell me," he whispered, the dense fan of his lashes lowered, hiding his eyes from her. "When you touched my mouth earlier. How did it feel? Were you…? Did you…?"

His lips flattened, grooves forming brackets on either side of them. He shook his head side to side, and the shadow of pain, of embarrassment, that flickered across his face shredded her. The guards she'd carefully erected took a direct hit, and rather than hurry to patch them up, she delivered more blows by leaning back and daring to cup his face.

He flinched, but he didn't jerk away from her.

Taking that as a positive sign, she exhaled and lifted one hand from his jaw. Slowly, deliberately, she traced his lean, powerful features. The thick, dark brows. The patrician slope of his nose. The bold cheekbones.

The long, slightly raised scar that bisected that cheekbone.

She followed its dark, pink path, lightly, as if she could harm him all over again with a too-firm touch. Logic argued the silliness of this. Yet, she didn't chance it.

Owen deserved gentle handling.

Their breath broke on the quiet early-evening air like precious china against a floor. Loud. Jarring.

And as she trailed her fingertips over him, leaving no part untouched, undiscovered, the volume turned up. The shattering grew louder. His chest heaved, tension in his body winding tighter. Yet, he still didn't shift away from her.

He trusted her not to hurt him.

Not to reject him.

A whimper scrambled up her chest, and when she

brushed the tip of the scar… Well, locking down that needy sound became wishful thinking.

An answering growl rumbled in his chest, and even though it rolled through her, she didn't lift her gaze to meet his. Sinking her teeth into her bottom lip, she stroked the smaller marks dotting his cheek and jaw. But like a magnet, his mouth drew her attention, her touch.

"I thought your lips were soft," she murmured. *Just like I remembered.* "And perfect. It didn't—and doesn't—seem fair that a man should have a mouth this perfect."

He scoffed, his puff of breath warm, moist on her skin. "We both know I'm not—"

She pressed a finger to his lips. "This—" she swept her thumb over the scar crossing through the corner of his mouth "—doesn't detract from it. No, this adds to that beauty."

Disbelief and pain spasmed across his face, and his arms dropped, his hands circling her wrists. To pull her away. To walk away. From her.

Damn that.

She scooted to the edge of the tire then jumped off, the rubber bumping into the backs of her thighs. Still, she didn't loosen her hold on his face. Instead, she took a step closer. And another until only body heat separated them, and a deep breath from either of them would graze her breasts against his chest. A slight stumble forward would press her thighs to his.

God, she was tempted to fake that stumble.

"Leo," he said, his grip on her wrists gently tightening in warning. A warning that he intended to remove her hands from him and didn't want to hurt her.

Well, too bad. She wasn't letting go. Not until he listened to her.

Sometimes being stubborn as hell came in handy.

"No. You don't get to ask me a question then shut me out because you don't like my answer. You're the one who wanted honesty."

"Honesty, not pity," he said, voice low, but she caught a tattered edge of bitterness.

Pity?

Pity?

Fisting the front of his T-shirt with one hand, she tangled her fingers in the thick strands of his hair at the back of his head with the other. She hauled him down as she rocked up on her toes and crushed her mouth to his.

Shock ricocheted through her. Shock peppered with a healthy dose of *What the fuck are you doing?*

For a moment, she froze, paralyzed by her own rash actions that were so out of character.

Are they, though?

She didn't have time to respond to her subconscious, though. Because the heat, the overwhelming, crackling heat, chose that moment to flood in, pick her up in its current and sweep her away.

A whimper she hadn't even been aware of holding in broke free, and she softened, melted, surrendered. Her lips parted of their own volition, and she licked at the seam of his mouth. With a growl that rumbled against the tips of her breasts, the vibration drawing them to taut, aching beads, his tongue met hers halfway, tangling, sucking...taking complete control.

He angled his head, and though she still retained her grip on his hair, she didn't fool herself into thinking she retained the reins on this kiss.

Kiss.

Hah.

That was laughable.

He might not remember their night together, but he took her mouth in the furious fucking of well-acquainted lovers, not like two people sharing a first, tentative exploration. Had he been worried about his scar hindering him? God, no. He handled her like the pro he was, with skill, with confidence. And just as she imagined, the ridge of his scar provided a fascinating contrast of lush and hard, a sensory delight. It was different than before.

It was better.

His large hands...positioned her—there were no other words for it—for optimum taking. One cradled the back of her neck, holding her steady for each stroke, lick and thrust. While the other gripped her hip, aligning her curves along his hard, tall frame. Every muscle, every plane, pressed against her.

The wide, thick length of his cock branded her belly.

A dark chasm yawned deep inside her, and a flutter of delicate butterfly wings filled it. And underneath? Underneath was a bottomless pool of desire that she could willingly drown in and still never be satisfied.

Helpless, she rocked against the evidence of his lust for her. Bit his bottom lip, his top lip, soothed any hurt she might have caused with a glide of her tongue over that soft but firm flesh. She shifted to the scar. Licked it. Grazed her teeth over it. Fully expecting Owen to jerk away from her, she tightened her grip on his hair, but he didn't.

No, he leaned into her. Demanding more. Insisting she do it again.

Lust burst inside her, a fiery, combustible ball that razed her inhibitions to ash. Lifting her other hand to his hair, she snatched back the reins of this fierce mating. Dove deep between his lips, twisted her tongue around his, claiming his mouth. All of it.

Who was this wild creature who nipped and sucked at a man's mouth? Who clutched him so close, she could be part of his body?

Who moaned and whimpered with a delicious, unful-filled ache?

"Steaks are done!"

Sherrod's announcement, yelled to them from across the yard, penetrated the blanket of passion that enshrouded her. Blinking, she slowly untangled her fingers from his hair and rolled back down to the soles of her feet. Their quick, ragged breaths punctuated the air as they stared at one another.

Did the same shadowed swirl of desire and astonishment darkening his eyes eclipse hers?

Hopefully, she did a better job of concealing the fear that coalesced in her chest.

Fear that he still wielded the same power over her that he had in Boston. To transform her into this stranger who cared only about her pleasure and giving him his and willing to forget everything else.

Stop, no. That wasn't fair. She couldn't blame him for her weakness. The root of that fear lay in her willingness to betray herself and throw all her rules out the window. When experience had cruelly taught her the rules were in place for a reason. She *needed* them for a reason.

She took a step back.

Owen wasn't a rule breaker.

She was.

And that was why she couldn't trust herself.

Or anyone else.

"I don't pity you," she murmured. "You're a strong, healthy former athlete who—I'm just guessing here—could probably live two lifetimes off the money he earned on endorsements alone. So no, I'm not crying you a river." She shook her head, softening her words with a small smile. "I stand by what I said about the scars adding to your beauty. You and so many others have this ideal about perfection. You equate it with flawlessness. And you're wrong. That kind of perfection is not only boring, it's a lie. Fake. No one is perfect. I have to wonder, what is a person who needs to be impeccable on the outside trying to keep other people from seeing on the inside?"

She'd wondered the same about Owen that night in the hotel, too. His wide, beautiful smile. His playful charm. His masculine beauty that teetered on Greek god status. His subtle yet noticeable deflection from any personal subjects or details. Now, that could've been him concealing his identity as a famous quarterback. But he'd still been hiding...lying.

And maybe that had been the least of his secrets.

"These—" she dared to touch him again, a glancing caress over the tight, puckered skin of his cheekbone, the scattered marks over his jaw "—tell a story. They speak of your strength, your fight, your resilience. They relay the tale of a man who could've shut himself off from the world—and maybe even tried to—but couldn't. Didn't. He battled to recover and, even though he might still be in that battle, he's not quitting. That, Owen, makes you beautiful. Makes those scars beautiful, and you should wear them with pride, not shame. And I think, just like you learned from the players at the high school today, that if you gave people the chance, most of us would look on them the same way."

He didn't speak, but his Adam's apple worked in his throat. And how far gone was she that even in this moment where he clearly struggled with emotion, she yearned to lean into him and press a kiss to the front of that strong column?

Best not answer that.

"We should head back to the house before Sherrod and Celeste come looking for us." She nodded in the direction of the back patio.

Turning, she granted him several seconds of privacy and strolled in the direction of the house. She didn't have too long to wait before he appeared by her side, his longer strides shortening to match hers.

Sliding a glance at him, she gently nudged his arm with her shoulder.

"Hey."

He looked down at her, arching a dark eyebrow.

"The Addams family called. They want their playset back."

The unscarred corner of his mouth twitched. "How long were you holding that in?"

She released a dramatic sigh. "Oh, God, you have no idea. Forever."

His low chuckle drifted on the night air, and she dipped her head, hiding her smile.

Ignoring the blare of warning in her head that this man's laughter had lightened the weight off her chest.

Never invest more in another person than they're willing to invest in you.

Another of her main rules, and for a damn good reason. As nice a man as Owen might be, in several ways he was as broken as she. And she suspected he harbored as many secrets. Neither one of them had the emotional reserves to spend on another person.

They barely had enough for themselves.

Best she remember that.

And follow her own rules.

CHAPTER TWELVE

"So I TOLD Tara she needed to find another song for the talent show. She chose the same one as me and Ivy on purpose." A beautiful teen with mahogany skin and light brown curls, whom Leo had introduced to Owen as her sister Cher, scowled at the dinner table as she announced her gripe with the allegedly sneaky Tara.

Sonny and Cher.

Wow.

On the other side of Cher, Ivy nodded, her cloud of dark curls bouncing on her shoulders. "It's true. And knowing Ms. Young, if we can't agree on a solution, she's going to pull a King Solomon and make us sing it together. And Tara sounds worse than Nessa in the shower."

"Hey!" Nessa, who Owen recognized from Road's End as one of the women at Leo's table, glared at the girl. "Where's the loyalty to your sister?"

"What?" Ivy blinked, eyes wide. "When Wolf is in there with you, he helps you sound a skosh better."

A beat of silence descended over the dinner table, then it erupted in loud cackles and hoots of laughter. Flags of color streaked Nessa's cheekbones and she continued to glare at her sister, who grinned at her. Wolf leaned back, winding an arm around his wife's shoulders, his wide smile flashing in his thick beard.

"What can I say?" He shrugged. "My baritone is to die for."

More laughter, and Owen shook his head, his own smile reluctantly pulling at his lips.

The Dennison family was...unreal.

Honest to God, if he wasn't witnessing them with his own eyes, he wouldn't believe they existed outside a TV series.

Considering several members of this family were brown-skinned and others, including Moe and Ian Dennison, Leo's parents, weren't, they couldn't all be blood related. But that didn't seem to matter a damn. He shared his parents' DNA, and yet when he sat down to share a meal with them, there was none of this affection, acceptance and genuine enjoyment.

Jealousy flickered in his gut, but it wasn't the prevalent emotion.

No. It was sorrow, for not only what he and his parents didn't have...but for what they'd never had. This easiness. Camaraderie. Joy.

Trust.

Hell, while he believed his parents loved him, he couldn't claim with certainty they even liked him. Especially if Owen didn't have a football in his hand.

You make sure he's okay. He's nothing without his arm.

The words uttered in his father's distinctive churned-up-gravel voice rebounded off his skull. Though spoken years ago, they still ripped through him like claws tearing old tissue paper. His own father considered his sum worth no more than his ability to hurl a ball down a field. If the man whose number one purpose was to unconditionally love Owen didn't, how could others...

Unbidden, Owen glanced across the table at Leo.

The athlete might no longer be able to play, but he's so much more than a pair of legs or an arm. He's a leader, a strategist, a visionary... And with those qualities, he can do anything he desires.

Her words rose to combat his father's in his head. Funny how he'd so easily rejected her encouragement, her praise, but clutched his father's criticism like a hoarder.

Maybe because one made more sense to him, and the other... Well, the other filled him with too much fear. Fear and...hope.

Both were dangerous.

If that didn't sum up his feelings for Leo Dennison in a nutshell. His gaze dipped to her mouth, shaped around a smile at something Sonny said. Not all his feelings. There remained this inconvenient lust that wouldn't abate no matter how many times he lectured himself on the futility of it or fucked his fist when reason failed.

And now that he'd kissed her again after a year of abstaining from her... Shit. He was like an alcoholic falling off the wagon. It'd been a few days since her tongue had been in his mouth and his in hers, and he damn near shook with his need for that next shot of her. Leo tasted like *her*—strong, sharp yet sweet and heady. Addictive.

Owen shifted, tearing his gaze away from her. Getting hard at her family's Sunday dinner table wasn't only embarrassing but also rude as hell.

"Uh, Cole and Sydney. I love my niece, but you got to get your daughter. She's absolutely ripe." Flo wrinkled her nose, jabbing a thumb in the direction of the baby's high chair. "I can't eat peach cobbler and smell that at the same time. And I'm not passing up Moe's cobbler for no one. Not even the cute munchkin."

Already digging into her own bowl of cobbler, Sydney swallowed her mouthful and waved a spoon at Cole. "Your turn."

Cole hiked both eyebrows at his wife. "I could've sworn the last two times were *my turn*."

"So sad how the mind goes. Must be the stress from all that mayor-ing," she tsked.

He snorted, rising from his seat but bending to press a kiss to the top of her curls. "You better be glad I love you."

Tipping her head back, she beamed up at him. "You do, don't you?"

As Cole lowered his head to brush another kiss across his wife's lips, the rest of the table groaned and shouted everything from "Get a room" to "There are children present!" to "My eyes!"

Owen dropped his scrutiny to his own dessert, convincing himself the hard wrench behind his sternum was due to the amount of food he'd indulged in this evening, not envy. Definitely not longing.

Don't you fucking look up. Don't you do it.

And somehow, he didn't. But still, an image of Leo—in his backyard, hand brushing his scars, desire brightening her eyes—flickered in his mind.

"Owen, I hear we have you to thank for arranging pageant lessons for Leo," Moe said, drawing him out of his thoughts. Thoughts he had no business thinking about her daughter at her table. "I appreciate you looking out for her."

"You're welcome." He nodded toward Celeste, uncomfortable with the praise. "Though it's Celeste who really deserves your thanks. She's amazing. She agreed to coach, even though she's here on vacation."

"Oh, I agree." Moe leaned forward, crossed arms propped on the table. "Celeste, you have no idea how thankful I am, especially since the committee just sprung the pageant on Leo on such short notice. And I have to admit I've been desperate to find out how Leo's doing. So please, spill. Leo won't tell me a thing. All she says is *fine*." Moe rolled her eyes before sliding a smile in her daughter's direction. "We want the dirt."

Celeste grinned, catching Leo's narrowed stare and hard shake of her head.

Shrugging at Leo as if to say, "That's your mom," the other woman turned to Moe. "She's doing great. Leo's picking up everything really quick, especially considering the limited time we have. I don't think I have to tell you how hard Leo can be on herself." Celeste paused, throwing Leo a telling look, but after a moment switched her attention back to Moe. "But she's doing really well with her walk, presence and interview questions. We're still going back and forth on her talent, though. As in, we can't settle on one."

"As in, I don't have one," Leo grumbled.

"Are you kidding me?" Wolf frowned. "You have plenty of talents."

"Name one."

"Magic," Sydney blurted, waving her spoon again. "Literally. Remember in the sixth grade, you used to do magic tricks at kids' birthday parties? I was your assistant."

"The *kids* were my brothers and sisters and you," Leo drawled.

"Still," Sydney muttered.

"Something to put in our back pocket," Celeste said.

"You can dance," Flo added.

Owen's chin jerked up and he gaped at Leo. Honest to God *gaped*. "You *dance*?"

"It was one praise dance in church when I was sixteen," Leo bit out.

"But you were great," her sister insisted.

"She can put a hundred-piece puzzle together in ten minutes flat!"

"She can do a mean cartwheel."

"My girl is wonderful at Irish stepdancing."

"She can rap!" When everyone halted in the volley of Leo's talents to stare at Sonny, he crossed his arms over his chest and grinned, sheepish. "Well, she can. I mean, she's no Cardi B, but..." He shrugged.

Sherrod leaned over and murmured, "Best. Dinner. Ever."

Swallowing a laugh, Owen couldn't agree more. Studying Leo, who'd covered her face with both hands, he had a much harder time concealing a smile at her expense. On the surface, it might seem like her family was poking fun at her, but they weren't. They genuinely wanted Celeste to be aware of Leo's talents—and the pride in their daughter, sister and friend couldn't be mistaken.

They loved her.

"She can act," Cole announced, striding back into the kitchen, his daughter cradled in his arms.

Owen frowned, remembering the horror story Leo had relayed to him that evening in the bar. The same thoughts must've jarred her as well, because she lowered her hands and scowled at her brother.

"That's not funny."

"Not trying to be," he said, handing the baby to his wife then sliding his hands into his pants pockets and leveling a calm gaze on his sister.

"Do I really need to remind you of what happened the last time I was on a stage? The fumbling of lines? The near neutering? You should. You and Wolf teased me for weeks afterward."

"Yeah, we were little shits back then." Wolf grimaced.

"Language," Ivy sang, side-eyeing him.

"Sorry," he whispered. "But we definitely were."

"Yeah, we were. Sorry about that, Leo." Cole shook his head. "Opening night might've been a disaster, but before that? You were great. Remember, I attended the audition to support you and went to some of those rehearsals. Forget great. You were wonderful. I always said the only reason you didn't get the Juliet role was because of seniority. Nerves got the better of you that night, but it doesn't negate how good you were—are. I think you should try again."

"That's, uh, something we can consider," Celeste said into the thick silence.

Even though Leo's expression shouted a definite *hell no*. Owen warred against the urge to shove back his chair, round the table, scoop her up and plop her down on his lap. Shield her from whatever emotion caused that bleak dullness in her eyes.

No personal attachments.

He didn't do them.

Because of this right here. Too complicated. Too messy.

As someone who'd been raised in an emotionally barren household, he didn't get…this. The undercurrents, the nuances. Lust, he got. It was simple. Like that kiss. He understood the language exchanged by tongues, hands, bodies. Yet, even then…

Leo had been trying to prove a point. She didn't pity him. She didn't find his scars revolting. Message received. But he didn't want to be her project, her good deed. In the hotel in Boston, healing him hadn't been her concern.

He wanted that back.

"I ran into Randall Wilson down at Sunnyside Grille earlier this week," Ian Dennison said in an obvious switch in subject. Owen looked down the length of the table at the family patriarch and met his blue-gray eyes, identical to his daughter's. "He mentioned how you guys have been coming out to football practice and helping with the team. He's really appreciative."

"I'm not going to ask in polite company what you were doing down at Sunnyside Grille. But rest assured I will be asking later," Moe grumbled.

Sherrod grinned. "We've been having fun doing it. Shoot, it's keeping me in shape, too. Especially if I'm going to be eating a ton of chili in a few weeks." He patted his stomach.

"That's right." Ian leaned back in his chair, a slow smile sliding over his face. "You're the celebrity guest judge for the chili contest. I'm entering my famous five-alarm chili. It's absolutely delicious. And hot. Everything chili should be."

"Dad, you shouldn't be trying to influence the judge. It's against the rules," Cole admonished.

"Who's trying to influence him? I'm just having a conversation with a guest in my home... And telling him the truth."

"Let me save you from being disqualified, old man," Wolf interjected, and received a scowl in return. "Sherrod, are you and Celeste going to hang around until the spring festival?"

"Yes, it's been a while since I've been back. Even though Mom and Dad have moved to Florida, Rose Bend is still home. And with my best friend here—" Sherrod clapped a hand on Owen's shoulder "—it's even more reason to hang out and enjoy some downtime before OTAs start in June."

"You plan on staying on in Rose Bend, Owen?" Cole asked. "You've been here for several months already, right?"

"A little over four," Owen confirmed.

Of course, he'd spent the majority of those months holed up in his house, but...semantics.

"Have you been bitten by the Rose Bend bug?" Nessa asked him, a wry smile curving her mouth. "That's what this town does if you stay here long enough. It infects you. Like the flu. And suddenly, you don't want to leave."

"Ah, my woman. Such a romantic." Wolf sighed, smacking a loud kiss on his wife's cheek.

Laughing softly, Owen shook his head. "I can't say I have been." He refused to glance in Leo's direction while he uttered that. Especially when his mind provided evidence of her literally *biting him*. Without his permission, his thumb brushed over his bottom lip, the ruined corner of his mouth. And though he still kept his focus trained on Nessa, Leo's gaze seared him. He dropped his hand to his thighs under the table. "But to be fair, I haven't spent much of those four months in town."

Dammit. Why had he said that? What, did he want them in his business, asking why he'd been a hermit? Hell, he must be drinking the whole sitcom-family vibe like the Kool-Aid.

"Well, if I have my way, Owen won't be around much longer. Hopefully, he'll be leaving with me and Celeste after the festival." Again, Sherrod clapped Owen on the shoulder, grinning wide.

"You're leaving?"

Owen jerked his head toward Leo, hearing the turbulence beneath those two calmly spoken words. Confusion. Surprise. Hurt.

The last one had his fingers curling in on themselves, and he cocked his head, eyes narrowing on her. Did her family glimpse the telltale signs behind that perfect, serene mask? Or were the signs so small, they missed those details? The dimming of her eyes. The slight tautening of her full lips. The tensing of her shoulders.

I have to wonder, what is a person who needs to be impeccable on the outside trying to keep other people from seeing on the inside?

It'd taken him some time to notice, but Leo boasted a flawless facade. So according to her own words, what was she trying to hide?

And why did he hunger to find out? Want it more than any championship ring or game trophy?

"I might be," he said to her, voice low and just for her, even though they sat at a dinner table full of people. "Nothing's decided yet."

"Holy—" Sonny yelled from the other end of the table. "You're returning to football!"

Owen didn't remove his gaze from Leo as he answered her brother. "Maybe. I'm considering it."

Excited chatter erupted around him, and he responded to the questions and comments, but his attention never wavered from the silent woman across from him. The woman whose expression never shifted. But those eyes...

Those eyes told a completely different story.

"I'M NOT A psychic but judging by the emoji hearts that just replaced Celeste's eyes, I'm guessing you're going to have a vow renewal scheduled at the inn soon."

Owen switched his gaze from his best friends, who stood in the white gazebo behind the inn, to the woman standing on the bottom step of the back porch. At the sound of his voice, her spine stiffened, and he caught the reaction to him. Since that first day she'd arrived on his doorstep, bursting back into his life, there was very little he didn't notice about Leo Dennison.

And fuck if her tense shoulders didn't punch him in the chest.

"I'll make sure to upsell, then. We're trying to promote the inn as a destination venue for weddings and receptions. A pro athlete having his ceremony here would be an advertisement you can't place a price on."

"I can't decide if you're trying to sound cold for my benefit or not."

She finally glanced over her shoulder, her eyebrow arched. "That's mighty arrogant of you to think that I'd do anything just for your benefit. What would be the purpose?"

"The same reason you accused me of using a bullshit smile to deflect. To push people away. So they would leave me alone and see only what they wanted to see."

"You said that, not me."

"The truth's the truth. Or is our truce over? No more honesty between us?"

She didn't answer but turned around to continue studying Sherrod and Celeste as they descended the steps of the gazebo and followed a paved path alongside it.

"Why didn't you tell me you were returning to football?"

"I'm not. I'm considering it. I haven't decided on anything yet." He hesitated then climbed down the few steps separating them until he stood in front of her, giving her no choice but to look at him. "What's bothering you most, Leo? That I might be returning to the game? Or that I didn't share the news with you?"

She sank her teeth into her lush bottom lip, briefly closing her eyes, and he thanked whatever deity happened to be listening. Because with those thick lashes lowered, she missed the instinctive lifting of his hand toward her mouth to free that lip. To press his own thumb against that abused curve and soothe it. By the time she opened her eyes, his arm hung by his side, his hand a fist, and back under his control.

"I don't know. Both, maybe." She shook her head. "I thought you were injured and couldn't play anymore. Isn't that why you retired?"

"I tore my ACL in the accident and had surgery to repair the ligament. After months of rehab and weight training to build up the strength in my leg, the doctors and team trainers cleared me to play again. But I just couldn't... I lost my joy in the game. In everything. So I voluntarily retired."

"Why return now?"

"My agent and Sherrod have been on me to come out of retirement for a while." He shrugged a shoulder, looking away, but then he met her gaze again, unable to confess this truth without staring into her eyes. Allowing her to see *his* truth. "Because I came here and remembered why I loved the game. I recaptured that joy of being on the field purely for the fun, the camaraderie, the freedom, the escape. And I missed it. I missed how it was before the business, the politics, the press—" *the pressure of being perfect* "—became involved."

"You know all those things will be waiting for you if you go back."

He nodded, his mouth twisting into a humorless smile. "Of course. I stopped being an idealist a long time ago, Leo. But I've been through hell this last year. And after going through that, after tasting these perfect moments?" He sighed. "Some players have lucky socks, necklaces and other charms. Maybe mine can be these memories to keep me steady and not jaded." He huffed out a short, harsh laugh. "Or maybe I should stop being so fucking fanciful."

"You call it *fanciful*. I call it hope." She studied him in that too-damn-perceptive manner that pierced deep. "And I answered my own question about why you didn't mention returning, didn't I?" she murmured. "Because telling anyone besides Sherrod makes it real. It means the dream isn't vague or unclear anymore. It's concrete, and you have to face it." She nodded, an emotion flashing across her face so fast, he could almost convince himself he'd imagined it. Almost. "I get that."

"I'm scared." The confession burst out of him before he had time to consider it. Fuck that. Before he had time to trap it.

She frowned. *Frowned.*

He'd never figure this woman out.

"Hell yeah, you are. I'd think you were an idiot or an egotistical asshole if you weren't. We might've had a rough start of things, but I've never thought you were an idiot or a narcissist."

"But an asshole?"

"Take the win, Owen. Take the win." Then she smiled, her hand covering his hand, gently squeezing it. "Make the best decision for *you*. Not for Sherrod. Not for your agent. Not for…anyone else. But don't make it out of fear. That's a prison you'll build with your own hands. And escaping it isn't easy. Make that decision from a position of strength, Owen, not weakness."

Who imprisoned you?

What secrets are you keeping, Leo?

Let me help you break free.

The questions and plea crowded into his head, but he didn't voice any of them. Not only because he knew she wouldn't answer. But because asking meant being responsible if she did reply.

Entanglements.

Strings.

Connections.

Now more than ever, with the possibility of his days in Rose Bend numbered, he couldn't afford them. Had to avoid them.

Didn't want them.

Liar.

Staring at Leo, into her luminescent eyes, his hands damn near shaking to follow the slender lines and wicked curves of her body, he ached to become…entangled.

Owen glanced over his shoulder in the direction his best friend and his wife had disappeared, rummaging up a smile. "I better go save Sherrod. It's my duty as his best friend— and probably his best man…again."

Leo nodded, returning his smile, but it didn't reach her eyes. Yet, Owen couldn't call her on it.

Because he was pretty sure his didn't, either.

CHAPTER THIRTEEN

A BEAD OF sweat raced down Leo's spine. The forerunner of the others that gathered under her blouse. Oh, how she wished she could attribute the perspiration to a sudden late-April heat wave. But nope; even Mother Nature conspired against her by treating them to a pleasant and sunny fifty-nine degrees.

The bitch.

Dragging in a deep, and hopefully quiet, breath, Leo scanned The Glen—the wide-open field at the end of Main Street where all the festivals were held in Rose Bend. The Honeybee Festival wouldn't be any different. Already, the pounding of hammers and chatter of conversations and laughter filled the air as volunteers worked on building booths and stands. The main stage, where she stood, had been one of the first constructions erected. The live bands, presentations and pageant would be held on it.

Hence Leo standing on the platform now, running through a rehearsal. And the runaway train of sweat traipsing down her back.

Jesus, this was her nightmare.

The only things preventing her from making a break for it were the stress creasing the pageant coordinator Scarlett Ross's face, Celeste perched on one of the chairs in front of the stage and Jenna Landon staring a hole in the back of

Leo's head. If not for those three factors, though, her word and pageant bylaws be damned. She would be *out*.

Scarlett frowned in the direction of Main Street and the entrance to The Glen. Obviously anxious to see if the twelfth contestant would eventually show. She'd apparently thought disaster had been averted by Leo's joining the pageant, but now, on the first day of rehearsal, they were again down a person. And much too late to conscript someone else into entering.

Was it terrible that Leo hoped, prayed, that the person continued to be a no-show? Her mind shouted *yes*, but her stomach twisted with a vicious knot, and she translated it to mean, *nah, not at all*.

"Okay, let's go through the first category again. This is evening wear. Then we'll move on to talent," Scarlett announced.

Shit. Leo had barely made it through evening wear the first time without stumbling. And she did mean *barely*. No matter how many times she ran Celeste's lessons in her head, Leo couldn't get out of her own damn way.

Don't trip.

You're going to make a fool of yourself.

Everyone's going to laugh at you.

You have to do this perfectly.

You have to.

With all that shit charging through her head, how could she hear Celeste's voice? Simple. She couldn't. All she heard was her own failure and humiliation.

Fuck, she needed out of here.

Maybe Celeste noticed the whites of her eyes, because she rose from her chair and strode over to the side of the stage. While the other women lined up to start the walk-through, Leo moved to the edge of the platform.

"Hey," Celeste said, concern bright in her dark eyes. "Are you okay?"

"Sure," Leo lied. "Don't I look okay?"

"No, that's why I'm asking. For a moment there I thought I might have to throw my body in the path of the escape you were about to make."

In spite of the coils of fear still twisting inside her, she snorted. That wasn't a far-off assessment.

"I'm good. Only… The sooner this is over with, the better."

"You got this, Leo. You did great the first time. Just like we practiced. Behind you, a couple of jaws dropped in shock." She grinned. "I don't think some people were expecting you to bring it. 'Cause, babe, you were fierce."

"I don't know about that," Leo muttered, although Celeste's praise loosened the knots in her belly a fraction.

"Well, I do. Now, go do it again, and whatever your brain is saying to you in that head of yours, tell it to shut the fuck up." Celeste arched an eyebrow and strode off, every inch the beauty queen.

Biting back a grin, Leo headed over to the other contestants and slid to the back of the line.

"I have to admit you've surprised me, Leo. Getting a Miss America to coach you for this pageant? Smart. And to think I didn't consider you competition." Jenna sidled next to Leo, giving her a slow up and down, from the top of Leo's ponytail to the tip of the silver stilettos she'd donned just for rehearsal. "I don't think I'll underestimate you again."

Leo heaved a loud, drawn-out sigh, crossing her arms over her chest. Moe would've been very proud of her that she didn't roll her eyes.

Then again, maybe not. Moe always did appreciate a good eye-roll.

"Does this make me your nemesis?"

Jenna laughed, and the sound contained genuine delight. Hell, Leo didn't know whether to be amused, too, or offended.

"Please, let's not get ridiculous. You're just learning to crawl where I've been running."

"Then what's the point of this conversation, Jenna?" Good God, the woman would make a saint cross over to the dark side.

"What?" She held up her hands, palms out, striving for an innocence she couldn't obtain. Especially when a cold glitter sparkled in her blue eyes. "Can't two friends have a nice talk? You're so suspicious, Leo."

Don't take the bait. Don't take the...

Screw it.

"Can I ask you a question?" Leo turned, her back toward the rest of the women, tuning out Scarlett, the music pouring out of the sound system—everything but the beautiful, mean woman before her.

Jenna arched an auburn brow, flicking a hand in permission.

Gritting her teeth at the haughty gesture, Leo leaned forward. "You're a bitch. And you know it." Surprise flared in Jenna's blue eyes, but she didn't interrupt. Didn't snap back or get in her face. So Leo continued. "You cultivate that image on purpose. Why? What does it get you, except for most people avoiding or fearing you? Or is that what you want?"

Silence writhed between them. Jenna stared at Leo, that frigid blue scrutiny moving over her face, leaving icicles behind. Leo would be a liar if she claimed the same ice didn't trickle through her blood. Jenna stood taller than her by inches and while Leo had her by several pounds, the other woman made up for the difference in pure nastiness.

But damn if she'd allow Jenna to see it.

Yet, when a slow, hard smile carved across Jenna's face, Leo might've rethought her position. Damn. Where was Ms. Eva when you needed her? Sydney had told her how the town matriarch had delivered an epic verbal smackdown to the redhead months ago. Leo might need the elder woman to glove up...

This smile was terrifying.

"You have it all figured out, don't you, Leo? You think I don't notice how hard you try to be liked, to be so perfect? Have you asked why that is? I bet our reasons are the same. No one messes with the bitch just like they don't mess with the good girl. They leave both of us alone, because they're afraid of us for different reasons. So that doesn't actually make us very different, does it?" Her smile twisted into something ugly and...sad. "Maybe remember that when you play armchair psychologist."

Jenna didn't wait for Leo's reply, but swept past her, lining up behind the next woman to walk onto the stage. Leo couldn't move even if it was her turn. Not with that smile branded in her head, along with Jenna's haunting words.

I bet our reasons are the same. No one messes with the bitch just like they don't mess with the good girl.

They leave both of us alone, because they're afraid of us for different reasons. So that doesn't actually make us very different, does it?

The words clung to her like cockleburs, stubbornly refusing to turn loose. Pivoting, she gazed at the proud set of Jenna's shoulders, the arrogant tilt of her head and the immaculate fit of her emerald knit dress.

They leave both of us alone. They leave both of us alone.
They leave both of us alone.

Leo's throat constricted, closing around a snarl of emotion she couldn't begin to untangle. But it clawed at her, smothered her, choked her…

No. People weren't afraid of her. She didn't have anything in common with Jenna… She didn't want people to…

She blinked hard, battling back the sudden sting of tears. The sting of truth. The sting of…loneliness.

"Oh, thank goodness! Cut the music, please!" Scarlett yelled, snapping Leo out of her downward spiral.

Inhaling a breath that scraped her tender throat, she lifted her head, focusing on the coordinator as Scarlett tossed her clipboard to the stage and advanced on the two young women walking across The Glen.

"Aileen, where have you been? I was starting to panic, thinking you'd quit." Scarlett enfolded the younger woman in a quick embrace, then did the same with the other, taller woman, whom Leo recognized as Carla Grayson, one of Sonny and Cher's middle school teachers. "I'm too relieved to scold now, but it's coming." She laughed. "We still have about thirty minutes left in rehearsal. We've gone through evening wear. Are you ready to run through it?"

Aileen nodded, but didn't move toward the stage. Instead, she beamed at Scarlett, pink dusting her light brown cheeks. "I have some news first, if that's okay?"

"Of course," Scarlett said, though she glanced down at her watch.

Aileen turned to Carla and slid her arm around her waist. "We're pregnant!"

Scarlett's head snapped up, her mouth forming an "O." "What?"

"Yep." Aileen nodded as Carla wrapped her partner in

an embrace, her blond hair blending with Aileen's straight, dark brown strands. "We're having a baby!"

"Great. They're just dropping like flies out of this pageant," Jenna muttered.

The woman gave absolutely zero fucks about anyone but herself.

"Oh, my God!" Scarlett threw her arms around both women, dragging them close. "Are you serious? I'm so thrilled for you!" She smacked kisses on both of their cheeks, laughing. "Did you just find out?"

"We did," Carla said, still grinning. "That's where we were. At Dr. Collins's clinic. Aileen's thirteen weeks."

"That's the best excuse to be late ever!" Scarlett whirled around, arms thrown wide. "Did you hear? My best friends are pregnant! And I'm going to be a godmother!" She spun back around. "Oh, I'm going to be a godmother," she demanded.

"That's a given." Carla smiled.

"It's a given!" Scarlett announced to all of them on the stage.

All the contestants streamed off the stage to gather around the happy couple and Scarlett. Everyone except Leo.

She couldn't force her feet to move. The excited chatter, squeals and laughter eddied in her head, rebounding off her skull and sinking like a lead weight in her stomach. Taking her with it. Tugging her under the dark waves of bitterness, of anger...of grief.

Selfish. You're being so fucking selfish, making this about you. Move. Paste a damn smile on your face, move and congratulate them.

That was what she should do—would do. Because this wasn't about her. She could get through this. Hell, if Cole could survive losing his wife and newborn baby in childbirth, she didn't have *the right* to seize up and panic when she'd never even held...

She gave her head an almost violent shake.

Not going down that road.

That'd been so long ago...a lifetime ago for her. She was no longer that scared girl.

No longer that weak girl.

Curling her fingers into her palm, she pressed her nails deep into the flesh, welcoming that small bite of pain. Savoring it. The tiny sting loosened her paralysis. Ordering herself to get her shit together, she stalked forward, looking down as if to ensure her feet obeyed her demand. And once she reached the ground, she tried to melt into the back of the small group, hoping no one noticed her brief lapse.

But then her gaze clashed with a bright blue one.

She wanted to look away, but Jenna's intense scrutiny narrowed on her like a stoplight—or an accusation.

"Hey, I was looking for you," Celeste said, appearing at her side and distracting her from Jenna. Thank God. Dipping her chin in the direction of the women crowded around Aileen and Carla, Celeste smiled. "Great news, huh?"

Leo mirrored her smile, so used to masking her feelings, it was second nature. "Yes, I'm really thrilled for them."

And she was.

Despite the murky, grimy guilt and pain that saturated her, she was happy for them. Prayed they would one day hold what she could never have.

Unconsciously, her hand rose to her belly, cupping it. Feeling the emptiness that would never be filled.

Why she glanced in Jenna's direction again, she couldn't say, but she did. And the other woman still stared at her, her gaze lowering to the hand that cuddled Leo's stomach. As if scalded, Leo dropped her arm with a soft gasp.

Dammit. She had to be more careful. For eight years she'd safeguarded her secret...her heart. She'd already learned the harsh, cruel lesson of what happened when someone walked away. Another lesson she'd been taught. As a matter of fact, she'd invoked her first rule during that time in her life.

Protect yourself at all costs.

"I know I asked you before, but are you sure you're okay?" Celeste tilted her head, and in a move straight from Moe's handbook, she pressed the back of her hand to Leo's forehead. "I'm already loving you like a play cousin, but you're not looking great. You might be coming down with something. Or it could be the nerves from the first rehearsal. Maybe you should head back to the inn and rest."

Affection for this woman rose within her. True, they hadn't known each other long, but with the amount of time they'd spent together, Leo had come to really like and enjoy her. Celeste had become a good friend.

Reaching out, Leo captured Celeste's hand and squeezed it.

"I promise, I'm fine. A little tired maybe, and okay, overwhelmed with all of this. But I'm good."

"If you say so." But her frown telegraphed her doubts.

"Excuse me. While I'm delighted for the happy parents," Jenna drawled, her bored tone belying the congratulatory words, "I have to ask the question that's on everyone else's minds. Aileen, are you still going to be in the pageant? We need twelve contestants, and it's much too late to find another person if you drop out. Sooo..." She shrugged, flipping up her hands.

Celeste leaned over, whispering in Leo's ear, "She can't possibly be that—"

"Oh, yeah, she is."

Scarlett spun around, brown eyes narrowed and her lips stretched into a very tight smile. Sharks probably offered a school of fish that smile. Right before they devoured them whole.

"Actually, I don't know if that question was on *everyone else's minds* at this moment, considering it's not as important as Aileen and Carla's *baby*. But Aileen doesn't have to make that decision right now. And if she chooses not to continue, then it's just that—her choice. Her health and that of her baby comes first."

"Calm down, Mama Bear." Grinning, Aileen laid a hand on Scarlett's back as Leo silently applauded the petite coordinator who'd suddenly seemed ten feet tall in defense of her friends. "No, Jenna, I'm not dropping out of the pageant."

"Are you sure? You don't have to—"

Aileen wrapped an arm around Scarlett's shoulder. "I'm sure. Carla and I discussed it on the way over here. I'm not showing yet, and I probably won't be for a few more weeks, so I can still fit into my evening dress. Besides being a little tired, I'm okay. And I don't want to leave you in a bind. Also, I've been looking forward to this. Being pregnant isn't a disease. I'll double-check with Dr. Collins, but I'm sure it'll be fine."

"Well, great. Now that that's settled..." Jenna clapped her hands. "Are we going to continue rehearsal or is this it for the day?" She made a show of twisting her wrist over and peering down at her slim, rose-gold watch. "I have an appointment."

"Don't let us keep you," Scarlett purred.

"I won't." Tossing the coordinator an ice-cold smile, she strode off, retrieved her purse from the side of the stage and exited The Glen.

"That woman makes Cruella de Vil look like a candidate for Humanitarian of the Year," someone muttered.

Laughter danced through the group, followed by more excited chatter. But Leo didn't join in; instead, she stared after Jenna's retreating figure.

The Cruella comment hadn't been far off. With the exception of their freshman year, Jenna had been a bully ever since they'd been in high school. Sophomore year, she'd returned mean as hell, and she'd been outdoing herself ever since. Most people outgrew that behavior as an adult, but not Jenna. She'd just honed her spiteful skills.

So why, watching Jenna walk away, no one by her side, did Leo have the inane urge to run after the other woman and join her so she would no longer be by herself?

They leave both of us alone.

Right.

She had to remember Jenna was alone by choice.

Just as Leo was.

CHAPTER FOURTEEN

LEO RECLINED ON one of several white benches with black wrought iron arms and legs scattered around the town square. Set right smack-dab in the middle of downtown, the square represented an oasis in a picturesque town that could grace the front of any postcard, small-town romance book or one of those cute Christmas movies. Norma Howard and her book club had started a campaign to petition one of those production companies to come visit Rose Bend for just that purpose. And if Norma ended up as an extra in one of those movies? Well, that probably didn't have anything to do with her zeal...

Snorting, Leo closed her eyes, tipping her head back. Her hair brushed the leaves of the bushes behind her, but she didn't straighten. A weariness weighed down her bones, and she needed a couple of minutes to herself before returning to the inn. Scarlett had ended the rehearsal thirty minutes ago and after telling Celeste she needed to run a couple of errands, she'd come here. And hadn't moved yet.

She'd tried and tried but she hadn't been able to scrub free from her mind the events from the practice. Not her small panic attack. Not Jenna's haunting, *convicting* words. Not Aileen and Carla's announcement. Not the door to the past Leo hadn't been able to slam shut as quickly as she usually did.

Something was happening to her. Something she couldn't define, couldn't understand. Couldn't fix.

And it scared the hell out of her.

"I don't care how small or safe this town is supposed to be. You shouldn't fall asleep out in the open like this."

That voice. Good *God*.

Her heart leaped, as if hurling itself toward that voice like a virgin sacrifice. As much as she wanted to judge the organ for its complete lack of dignity, she couldn't blame it. Not when her body damn near trembled with the need to follow suit.

Just from the sound of. That. Voice.

Slowly, she tipped her head down, lifting her lashes to meet his steady hazel gaze.

"What are you doing here? In town during daylight hours? Aren't you violating the sacred hermit's code?"

Her favorite corner of his mouth—the one with the scar—twitched. And that was when she noticed that his dark hair was tucked behind his ear instead of hanging in his face.

What the hell is going on?

Owen cocked his head to the side. "I came here to ask you that."

Dammit. I said that aloud.

Owen snorted. "Said that aloud, too." Concern darkened his gaze, the golden brown nearly eclipsing the green. He lifted a hand and after a hesitation, trailed his fingers over her hand then stretched his arm along the back of the bench. "What's going on, Leo? And don't tell me *nothing* or *I'm fine*."

Her lips parted, the objection heavy and prepared to be delivered on her tongue. But it didn't come.

But "I'm so fucking tired" did.

Surprise didn't flicker across his face. Pleasure did. Pleasure and a fierce determination that she could easily imagine him wearing on a football field. Still it declared, *I got this.*

This being *her.*

And the shiver low in her belly assured her she hungered to be *got.*

"What are you tired of?" he asked. And when she wavered, he leaned forward, an impatient sound rumbling in his chest. "Don't think, Leo. Don't analyze your feelings, your thoughts or the question. Just answer. What are you tired of?"

She wanted to grant him what he requested. Desperately. But she couldn't. That first rule was imbedded into her. *Protect yourself at all costs.* She couldn't escape it.

If she answered him without thought, without censoring herself, she would remind him of their night together even though he didn't remember her. Confess that he'd marked her and she couldn't forget him, couldn't forget how he'd made her lose control...lose herself. And how that terrified her. That even though she had a disastrous track record with relationships, she still couldn't force herself to avoid him, her next and biggest disaster waiting to happen, knowing he was not for her.

He was the antithesis of who she needed in her life—an athlete, retired or not, a playboy charmer, scars or not, who was richer than Midas and, most importantly, not planning on staying in Rose Bend. Her heartache was written all over him in neon Magic Marker. Scratch that. Glow in the dark, neon Magic Marker. His confession the other night about coming out of retirement... She was happy for him that he'd rediscovered his joy for the game and had an opportunity to return to the career he loved. But it was only a matter of time before Rose Bend was a memory for him.

Before *she* was a memory for him.

That was why she worked so hard for the inn.

Men would come and go, as her past had shown. And Cole, Wolf—they had their families. Her other brother and sisters, one day they'd have their wife, husbands and kids, too. But Leo would never have that. She'd have the inn, though. It wouldn't leave her. Fail her.

Crush her.

So no, she couldn't just *not think* with her reply to Owen, because she couldn't risk exposing herself. Not again.

But she could give him some truth. It would be like twisting a valve and releasing some of the pressure. She could gift that to herself.

"When I dated Caleb Wallace, I believed we were in… well, strong like. At least, I was. Right up until the moment I was a damn cliché, walking in on him and another woman screwing in his office. Then there was Jack Daniel." She laughed and the serrated edge of it scraped her throat. "I know, you don't even need to say it. The name should've been a waving red flag. But you can't let a person's name determine their character. I mean, my little brother named himself after Sonny Bono. And Jack wasn't an alcoholic. Far from it. Straitlaced as they came. And cheap, too. Never wanted to take me out on a date. Preferred to eat at the inn every night so he didn't have to spend money. Even stole the soaps from the guests' bathrooms for his apartment. They were just two on a long list."

"Leo," Owen murmured, his hand rising to cup the nape of her neck.

"They all had one thing in common, though." She swallowed, skin hot, prickly. Blinking, she glanced away from him, focusing on the gazebo Wolf had built several months earlier. "It didn't matter if they broke it off or if I did. None of them had a problem leaving. Didn't even look back. What is it about me that makes it so easy for people to walk away?"

Maybe it was unfair to ask him. After all, he would soon be included on that list. But she wouldn't rescind the question. She wanted to know. *Needed* to know.

No matter how desperate she might appear.

"Why are you asking me?" He squeezed, not hard enough to hurt, but firm enough to get her attention. To demand she look at him. Which she did. "You pose it like I would have the answer. Like there *is* an answer. When you really should be asking, *What is their issue that made them walk away? What was wrong with them? Why are you laying the blame on your shoulders?*"

He shifted closer. She should've scooted back, inserted space between them, but his gaze, his earthy scent and body heat wrapped her in their decadent embrace and held her captive. She breathed him in, deep. Blamed her tiredness on allowing herself to get punch-drunk on his nearness.

"There will come a time when I do leave this town and you, but I won't kid myself. Nothing about it will be easy or simple." His long fingers cradled one side of her neck and his thumb brushed the other. Up and down. Up and down, in a hypnotic rhythm. "I don't know what the fuck was wrong with those other men, but make no mistake, sweetheart, it *was* them. My father is a deacon in our church back home. I ever tell you that?"

His sudden switch of subject had her shaking her head, as much in reply as to clear her thoughts to keep up.

"Well, he is. And one of his favorite sayings is *You can tell if someone has spent time with the Bible because they're changed.* I can't say how much of that is true since I'm not a dedicated churchgoer—something else to disappoint him—" his mouth curved into a self-deprecating twist "—but you… You're like the Bible. Spending time with you is to be changed. For the better."

"I think you're skirting really close to blasphemy," she rasped, blinking back the sting of tears.

He left her breathless.

"You touch people, Leo, and we're not left the same. We're *more*." He tilted his head, studying her face, and by the time his eyes found hers again, there didn't remain an inch of her that hadn't been visually caressed by him. She sank her teeth into her bottom lip to confine the needy sound that would surely escape. "Maybe those other men weren't mature enough to acknowledge what and who they had. Maybe they were too selfish or ignorant to be grateful. Or maybe they were scared of changing. Like I said, I can't answer for them, because I'm not them. I know who you are. I see you."

It seemed she did have breath left in her chest. Because it burst from her on a loud, heavy rush. No one…*no one*… had ever spoken to her like that. Like she was precious. Like they would…miss her.

She closed her eyes.

"No, sweetheart." A thumb gently but firmly tugged her bottom lip from under her teeth. The touch resonated in a wet, aching twinge between her thighs. She hadn't even been aware that she'd bitten the tender flesh again. This time she couldn't contain the whimper from sliding free, and it hung there, suspended between them like the sword of Damocles. "Look at me."

Part of her rebelled against obeying him because she feared what her eyes would betray. But the other part—the stronger, hungrier and more desperate part—didn't give a damn. It gave in to that vein of steel running beneath his smoke-and-sex voice.

She opened her eyes.

"Don't hide your eyes from me," he softly ordered. Or was that order a plea? She couldn't tell. But she could indulge in wishful thinking. "I've discovered over these last few weeks, I like—no, that's too tame a word. I crave looking into your eyes. And not just because they remind me of those rare times when my father took me camping and we'd rise at dawn and sit under that gray-blue sky together at the edge of the lake." He released the back of her neck and brushed a thumb over the thin skin beneath her eyes. "I haven't thought about that in a long time," he murmured as if to himself. With a shake of his head, he lifted his other hand and cradled her jaw. "Yes, your eyes are beautiful, but there's truth here. As hard as you try to mask your feelings, your eyes don't always comply. I *need* to know your truth."

Terror raced through her. No one had access to all of her. And she couldn't give it.

"Why?" she whispered.

He dropped his hands and straightened, huffing out a breath that ended on a jagged chuckle. Leaning back against the bench, he dragged a hand through his hair.

"Maybe I want you to share with me what you don't with everyone else." He let loose another of those dry laughs. "Or it could be I just don't want to end up on that list of people who have hurt you. The people you regret."

"I don't regret you. I couldn't." The truth barreled out of her, and she didn't follow it up with stammered excuses or justifications.

"No?" he asked, a terrifyingly sexy rumble turning his

voice to gravel. Vibrating between her legs, right up against her sex.

"No," she breathed.

Once more he lifted his hand to her. Touched her. And she turned her head into his palm, brushing her lips over his skin. Humming at the faint taste of him.

Regret him? Oh, God, never. She couldn't regret this, either. Just imagining not having the privilege of tasting his mouth, stroking his hard body, of being covered, taken and filled by it… Missing out on that would be a tragedy.

Yet…

She couldn't lie. She would regret not keeping her distance after the first time he closed the door in her face. Because when Owen left Rose Bend, he would carry pieces of her with him. Pieces she feared would be irretrievable.

This knowledge didn't stop her from flicking her tongue against his palm then tipping her head back at his low groan. Didn't prevent her from opening wide for him when his mouth covered hers, his tongue immediately demanding entrance.

And she gave it. Without reservation. With total pleasure.

Thoughts of where they were melted away. She didn't care. Nothing mattered but the slick glide of his tongue over hers, the erotic dance where he led, and she followed. For now.

With a long, luxurious lick and suck, she flipped their roles, wrenched the lead and ordered him to tangle with her, get dirty with her…

A not-so-subtle clearing of a throat penetrated her haze of lust. She stiffened and would've jerked away if not for the hand still cradling her jaw. Owen held her still, captured by both his piercing gaze and his grip. Annoyance flashed in those eagle eyes. Annoyance at her willingness to leap away from him as if caught like a guilty teen, no doubt.

But dammit. Kissing in public. Getting lost in him.

She'd lost her head.

She must have a rule against this, but with her lips still damp and prickling from that passionate siege of a kiss, recalling it proved to be beyond her current capabilities.

"If I wasn't seeing it with my own eyes, I wouldn't believe it. Or at least I'd start to think all those nightcaps were catching up with me," Eva Wright drawled.

Out of habit—and genuine respect—Leo rose to her feet, greeting the handsome older woman with her tight cap of gray curls and lean frame. Embarrassment still sang through Leo, but her joy in seeing Eva outweighed it. She *adored* the older woman. Even if Eva's suffer-no-fools demeanor and generous spirit hadn't endeared her to Leo, her staunch defense of Cole as a member of the town council against Jenna's father and former mayor, Jasper Landon, would have. In a word, Eva Wright was *fierce*.

"Hi, Ms. Eva." Leo wrapped the woman in a tight hug, brushing a kiss over her cheek. "I've missed you. I haven't seen you in a while."

The older woman nodded. "I know. I've been by the inn and had coffee with your mom. You have a lot going on. Turning Rose Bend into *the* premier wedding venue—and from the way Gina Riley is raving about you, I'm of the belief it will happen in no time—taking Moe's place on the spring festival committee and, of course, this pageant business. She even told me about Mr. Strafford here finding a coach for you."

Eva switched her dark, measured gaze on Owen, who had risen as well.

"Ms. Eva, let me formally introduce you to Owen Strafford. Owen—" she turned to him, settling a hand on Eva's slender but wiry shoulder "—this is Ms. Eva Wright, town councilwoman, day-care owner and matriarch of Rose Bend, although she refuses to claim the title."

"Very funny," Eva muttered before accepting the hand Owen extended. "This one's mouthy, if you haven't spent enough time around her to guess."

"Oh, I've noticed." Owen's smile flashed and damn, really? He should be ashamed of himself trying to charm a woman old enough to be his great-aunt. "It's nice to meet you, Ms. Wright."

"Eva." She waved off his formality. "And it's wonderful to finally meet you as well. Nice to verify for myself that you're not a myth." She arched a brow. "I see you're through hiding out in that house, then?"

Owen blinked at Eva's customary bluntness, and Leo tried—and failed—to swallow a snort of laughter.

"Yes, it seems I am," Owen said, coughing into his fist.

"You know, I read about your accident," Eva continued, and as sharp-eyed as she was, Leo had no doubt the older woman caught the subtle stiffening of his tall frame. But Eva studied him with an intensity that could have the children in her care spilling their secrets in five-point-six seconds. Hell, most adults, too, for that matter. "I can only guess you came to Rose Bend to heal and regroup, and it was a smart choice. Like any town, we have some asses, but for the most part that phrase on the welcome sign speaks the truth. We don't know strangers. That is, if you give us half a chance. You should give us half a chance, Mr. Strafford. I think we might surprise you."

"I'm late, but I'm discovering that, Ms. Eva. And please, call me Owen."

"Good." Then she stepped closer to him, eyes narrowed. "But if anyone tries to make you feel embarrassed or ashamed for *surviving*—" she flicked her fingers toward his scars "—then they forfeit the right to the kindness they didn't offer you. Or better yet, call me. I will delight in reminding them where to locate the manners they misplaced."

Love for this woman and laughter bubbled up inside Leo's chest, and she didn't miss the surprise that flashed in Owen's eyes or the warmth that suffused his features. A smile started with a quirk of the scarred corner of his mouth, but it slowly spread until it lit up his face.

Her breath snagged in her chest, and she blinked at that rare expression like a sun worshipper denied her deity for a long while.

Oh, God.

She had some serious damage control to do or else this man was going to leave her an unrecognizable mess.

And she would have no one to blame but herself.

"Yes, ma'am," Owen said.

She dipped her head, waving between him and Leo. "Fine. Now, I'll go and let you two get back to your date."

"Oh, no. We're not on a date," Leo rushed to object, cursing the fiery blush that streamed up her neck to stain her cheekbones. "We're just friends."

"Oh, Jesus." Eva rolled her eyes. "It's been a little over ten years since my Joe passed but I remember quite clearly that we shared friendly kisses like the one I just witnessed. But okay. Friends, it is." Continuing to mutter to herself, she strolled off toward Main Street.

"She's…something else."

"That she is," Leo grumbled, mortification still blazing her from the inside out. Squinting after the other woman's retreating figure, Leo asked, "I was teasing earlier about you being in town during daylight hours, but seriously, what are you doing here?"

Owen didn't answer her, but turned around and strode toward the curb where he'd parked his car. Leo fell into step beside him.

"Because you were here."

Leo stuttered and momentarily slammed to a halt, staring at his wide back. Then she shook her head and picked up her pace, following after him. Owen helped her into his vehicle, even though she could've hopped up into it herself. And considering the way her waist and arm tingled from his gentle handling, she should've insisted on it.

The interior of the SUV carried his scent, and before he entered the vehicle, she inhaled deep, capturing the sexy leather, sandalwood and musk that defined him. But nothing replaced the real thing, and as Owen swung into the driver's seat, his body heat ignited that trio of fragrances, turning them sultrier, earthier...hotter.

Looking toward the passenger-side window, she breathed through her parted lips. As if that would minimize the effect he had on her. One could hope.

Because you were here.

The four words barreled into her head, and once they infiltrated, she couldn't evict them.

What had Owen meant?

Had Celeste mentioned something to him? And he'd what—driven through town looking for her? Not that Rose Bend was particularly huge, but still...

Had Owen, who avoided people and public places like a zombie apocalypse, really ventured out just to find her and make sure she was okay?

Her belly dipped, and a wave of heat that had nothing to do with lust rolled through her. Surely, someone other than her family had placed her welfare, her emotional well-being above theirs before. Certainly, someone not bearing the Dennison last name had sacrificed their own comfort and security to set her as a priority. *Surely*, it had happened in her life. But right now, sitting beside him in his SUV, his scent embracing her, she couldn't recall one person.

Just him.

"Celeste wanted me to invite you to dinner. She said after, you two could go over some things from rehearsal today, if you'd like."

The automatic "Thank you, but no" leaped to her tongue, but "Let me check with Moe to see if I'm needed back at the inn" emerged instead.

Holy shit.

When had she ever *not* wanted to be at Kinsale Inn? It was her safe place, her haven. She slid a glance at Owen, at his relaxed yet confident grip on the steering wheel. At the elegant length of his fingers. Fingers she knew from vivid experience could deliver such exquisite pleasure that even now her thighs quivered. Just like she knew those powerful thighs could hold hers open, control her so easily...

Jesus. She should've said that "No, thank you." But as she dialed the inn, she couldn't bring herself to say it. Chalk it up to the emotional strain from the pageant rehearsal and from his unexpected appearance on the town square, but she wanted to spend more time with him.

For today, at least.

For today, she could grab these next few hours without overanalyzing why or beating herself up. Especially since that would lead to her examining and dissecting the consequences of her actions.

As foolish as this decision might be—hell, *was*—she granted herself permission to just *be*.

A few minutes later she ended her call and glanced at Owen's profile. "I've been assured that the inn will not crumble and fall into ruin if I'm not on the premises for one evening."

The corner of his mouth quirked. "I take it that's a yes for dinner?"

"It's a yes."

"Good." He nodded, shifted his gaze from the road to her. "I'm glad it's a yes."

It required every bit of the worn and frayed self-control she retained to not lift her unsteady fingers and press them to the still-sensitive flesh of her mouth. Because she couldn't trust her hands to obey the orders of her brain, she curled one around the door handle and slid the other under her thigh.

"Me, too," she murmured.

He nodded again, then returned his attention to the road, and she released a low sigh.

Minutes later they approached the Victorian that she'd started to think of as his home. When he eventually left, changing that mentality would be difficult. Who was she kidding? She'd probably avoid this end of town for a long while, unable to stop associating with him—

"Fuck," he growled.

She startled, jerking straight in her seat.

"What's wrong?"

His full lips flattened, and through the light scruff darkening his jaw, a small muscle jumped. His grip on the steering wheel tightened to the point that the skin over his knuckles blanched.

Worry tore through her, and she dragged her scrutiny from him to scan his street, lawn, the front of his house, trying to catch anything that could've triggered this sudden switch in demeanor.

Nothing. The same quiet residential street and houses. Owen's neat front lawn and tidy if personality-barren porch. Sherrod and Celeste's car occupied their usual space in the driveway, as did an unfamiliar black truck… Had that irritated him? Visitors?

"Owen? What's wrong?" she asked again.

He pulled up to the curb outside the house. Jerked the car into Park.

"My parents are here."

CHAPTER FIFTEEN

OWEN GRABBED THE knob of his front door and twisted it, the hated but familiar chunk of ice setting up residence in his gut. Resentment. Anger. Anxiety.

Love.

They all congealed together, and he couldn't begin to separate them if he wanted to. God knew he wanted to. Just take a blowtorch to it.

With Leo's curious gaze burning a hole into the side of his face, he ground his teeth and pushed open the door. Immediately, the murmur of voices from the living room reached him, so he headed in that direction. When he stepped into the high, arched entrance, he paused, that ice spreading like cracks on a windshield.

Celeste lounged on one end of the love seat, and Sherrod settled on the arm. Across from them, his mother perched on the couch, space between her ramrod spine and the back of the sofa, her hands clasped in her lap. His father stood in front of the fireplace, an elbow propped on the empty mantel, posture as stiff as his wife's, expression as warm as the dormant fire behind him.

This was typical—this coldness, formality, underlying tension. What Owen had known for most of his life.

At least until he'd turned seven and his father realized Owen's potential for football.

Then, over the years, his father had slowly stepped back, and Owen had gained a constantly critical coach.

Nothing had changed except geography.

His father just criticized him long-distance now instead of over the dinner table and at the football field.

"Mom. Dad," Owen greeted, voice carefully even. Flat.

Behind him, a delicate hand settled on his lower back. And the scent of lilacs and fresh rain teased him...soothed him. For the space of a heartbeat, he relaxed into that hand, allowed that scent to comfort him, fortify him, for the battle ahead.

Because he didn't dupe himself into believing his parents had traveled the hundreds of miles from Indiana to Massachusetts for a nice family vacation. One, Troy Strafford didn't do family vacations. No time for them when it was either football season or Owen could be training for football season. And two, Owen hadn't given them the location of where he'd gone after he'd left New York. So their unannounced appearance here had a specific purpose.

Owen swallowed a low growl.

You can't throw your parents out of your house. It's rude.

That reminder wavering in his head, he moved farther into the room. His mother rose from the couch, the hazel eyes she'd bequeathed him lighting up. A smile tipped the corners of Charlene Strafford's pink painted lips as she stretched out her hands toward him. Dutifully, he enfolded them in his and, leaning forward, kissed her cheek. Roses and powder. The makeup. The perfume. Even the carefully styled, dark brown, chin-length bob. All the same.

Comfort at the sense of familiarity wrapped around him even as sadness at the stagnation squeezed his diaphragm.

"It's good to see you, son." His mother's gaze flickered

over his scars then quickly resettled on his eyes, firmly staying there.

The gust of pain blew through him. He should have expected this, braced himself for it. After all, she hadn't been able to fully look at him since the bandages came off in the hospital. For over a year, she'd pretended his scars didn't exist. As if by not acknowledging them, she could pretend her perfect, handsome son hadn't been replaced by this marred, ruined one.

He released her hands and stepped back, not returning the sentiment. Refusing to lie. God, that made him a shitty son.

"Owen." His father moved forward, arm outstretched toward him.

One step. No more. Forcing Owen to cross the remaining space to meet him. A tiny power play, but one nonetheless. Acid flooded into his mouth, and the caustic flavor scalded his tongue. Some men shared a comfortable, affectionate relationship with their fathers. Not one strained with tension, resentment and a never-ending competition.

Troy Strafford had traveled half a country to mete out the same old bullshit. As if he needed a masculinity fix and putting Owen in his place was his drug of choice.

Grinding his teeth—Jesus, he wouldn't have any left by the time this day ended—Owen approached his father and shook his hand.

"Dad."

After a tight grip that, thankfully, Troy didn't turn into a pissing contest, Owen dropped his hand and shifted back until he stood in the middle of the room.

"This is a surprise." He slid his hands in the front pockets of his jeans. "Last time we talked, you didn't mention anything about visiting."

"Honestly, Owen, when we do speak, you're on and off the phone so quickly, we barely have time to say hi and bye," his mom admonished with a small laugh.

"And since we didn't know if we would be welcomed, we asked your agent for the address and took the chance you'd be here." His father glanced at Sherrod and Celeste. "It seems you don't mind having company, though," he added.

The *just not ours* hung in the air, silent but deafening.

Fucking Byron. They would have words the next time they spoke.

His mother cleared her throat, her polite smile trembling a little. "Honey, why don't you introduce us to your guest?"

No.

It hovered on his tongue, hot and defiant. Not to be rebellious, but to protect Leo from their attention. Their curiosity, which, from personal experience, could be harmful. But it was too late for that. If he'd been thinking, he would've sent her home before she'd climbed his porch behind him.

Why didn't you?

Yeah, he wasn't touching that question.

So instead, he edged to the side, drawing Leo forward with a gentle hand to the small of her back. As soon as his palm settled on the indent a couple of inches above the delectable curve of her ass, the restless, angry itch nagging at him calmed. It didn't disappear, but it eased to a manageable level. Just from one touch.

"Mom, Dad, this is Leontyne Dennison. She and her family own and run the local inn." Glancing down at Leo, he said, "Leo, these are my parents, Troy and Charlene Strafford."

"It's very nice to meet you both, Mr. and Mrs. Strafford," Leo greeted them.

"You, too…Leontyne, is it?" his mother asked, tipping her head to the side. "As in the opera singer?"

"Yes, the same."

"How unique," Charlene murmured. "I'm sure Owen caught that right away and appreciated it. He didn't think I knew, but he loved opera." Her smile widened, warmth changing it from aloof politeness to genuine warmth. "I always loved that you dared to be different, even in your choice of music, Owen."

His father snorted, the corner of his mouth turning up in a sneer. "I remember you coming home with that crap from your coach about opera music teaching you to concentrate on your body and be more graceful like you were a damn ballerina instead of a football player. Ridiculous then, ridiculous now."

Beside him, Leo stiffened. The movement was small, almost imperceptible. But he sensed it. He rubbed his thumb back and forth along her spine. And by degrees, the rigidity eased from her posture.

"Hmm. I think there are some football greats who would take exception to the ballerina comment since they claim dance did help make them better players." Leo shrugged, her grin and the deliberate nonchalance in her voice barbed. "But hey, I'm totally new to this whole football thing, so what do I know?"

"Aw, look at you. Been studying up, haven't you, Leo?" Sherrod teased, and Owen caught the glimmer of admiration in his eyes.

She held her pointer finger and thumb up an inch apart, squinting. "A skosh."

Celeste snickered, and Owen barely contained his own bark of laughter.

"You're not a fan of football?" Troy frowned, skepticism

heavy in his tone. He switched his gaze to Owen, not even trying to conceal the message there. *Oh, come on. You believe this?* "That's…odd."

And this summed up why Owen shouldn't have allowed Leo to follow him into the house. Why he should've protected her by sending her home. The first time she did something to displease his father—and hell, that could be breathing in a manner he found disrespectful—he would find a way to demean her, cut her down to size. Like now. How dare she contradict him? How dare she commit the ultimate sin of defending Owen?

Now she would be fair game.

Fuck that.

"Not really," Celeste said, chiming in before Owen could order Troy to mind his goddamn business. "When Sherrod and I met, I had zero interest in football. Modeling, pageants and launching my own makeup line for women of color consumed my time and attention. Of course, when he introduced himself to me, he said his name like he expected me to swoon."

"Fact, babe. You should've swooned. By then, I'd already hit the Sexiest Man List."

Celeste rolled her eyes. "Didn't follow that, either. And I hate to break it to you guys, but not everyone's lives revolve around sports. Not when there are so many more important things in the world. Like, I don't know, off the top of my head, Black Lives Matter."

"The Me Too Movement," Leo added.

"AAPI Hate."

"Voter suppression."

"Harry spilling *all* the tea on the royal family," Celeste said, throwing her arms wide.

"Who's going to replace Steve Harvey on *Family Feud*?"

Owen jerked his head toward his mom, astonishment popping his lips apart. His mother blushed as not just he stared at her, but everyone else in the room did as well.

"Well, it *is* important," Charlene insisted.

First, Leo snickered. Then Celeste's chuckle joined in, and then everyone's laughter filled the room.

Everyone's but Troy's. He scowled at all of them, but especially his wife, as if she'd personally betrayed him by jerking the stick out of her ass.

Jesus Christ.

This was going to be a long evening.

"THAT WAS SUCH a delicious meal, Celeste." His mother patted her mouth with her napkin. "Thank you. Where did you learn to cook like that?"

"My mom and grandmother created magic in the kitchen," Celeste said, her smile as soft as her eyes. "And they made it a point to have me in there, learning next to them."

"Sounds like a good upbringing," his father said with a firm nod. Owen briefly closed his eyes and had the urge to pinch his nose—or pinch Troy's mouth shut. "Seems like your mother and grandmother knew how important it is that a woman should know how to cook for her husband and family."

Celeste arched a delicate dark eyebrow.

Oh, shit.

Out of Owen's peripheral vision, Sherrod slowly shook his head.

"Actually, no, that is not why they thought it important that I learn how to cook. It was about tradition, bonding and sharing. For them, food was about more than fuel for the body. It was an expression of love and pride. More importantly, though, they wanted to pass down independence to me. If I could prepare my own meals, I saved money. They believed in my dreams, and while everyone else blew their budgets on fancy dinners, I could budget and spend that money on more essential things. Also, I didn't have to depend on anyone else to provide for me, because I could do it myself. And if a man came along and could enjoy a delicious meal I cooked, well, that was to his benefit, not mine." She smiled but it did not reach her eyes. "But it's sweet that you think so."

If *sweet* had suddenly become a synonym for *misogynistic*, okay, then.

Silence permeated the table, but Troy Strafford would never let anyone have the last word. It wasn't in his DNA.

"It was a compliment," he grumbled.

"Thank you," she said sweetly. So sweetly, Owen's teeth ached with the start of a cavity.

He glanced at Sherrod, who stared at Troy with a look caught somewhere between "I pity the fool" and "You got one more time to talk to my woman like that." Dammit. Owen smothered a sigh. Not even four hours and his father already courted a beatdown.

Sad to say, but it wasn't even a record.

Celeste pushed back her chair and rose. "If you'll excuse me, I'll go get coffee—"

"You did an amazing job tonight, babe." Sherrod shot to his feet, brushing a kiss across his wife's cheek before gently, yet firmly, lowering her back to her seat. "I'll get the coffee and clear the dishes. Relax."

"I'll help," Owen offered, standing, too.

His father's derisive snort scratched down his spine, but he still gathered the dishes with Sherrod and cleared the table. Minutes later they returned to the dining room with cups, saucers and a carafe of steaming, fragrant coffee. A lively conversation punctuated with laughter about some reality TV show greeted them, and once more shock and delight drifted through him, spying his mother's animated face and hearing her usually modulated voice lively with humor and enthusiasm. He hadn't seen his mother this... light in longer than he could remember.

After serving the coffee, he reclaimed his seat, and of its own volition, his gaze wandered to Leo. In the dining room's soft lighting her golden skin appeared even richer, more luxurious. If he leaned over right now and pressed his lips to her cheekbone, would he taste sun-warmed honey? Better yet, if he lowered his head and teased that shallow bowl in the middle of her collarbone, would he sample the unique, irreplaceable essence of her?

His heart thudded against his chest, so loud he slightly winced, amazed no one else could detect its bass. An itch set up under his skin, one he could reach, couldn't scratch. One that would only be soothed by bare skin sliding over skin. Her trembling sighs breathing into his mouth, his ear. Her dangerous curves pressed to his harder frame. Her liquid heat bathing him, welcoming him...drowning him.

Hell.

What was it about dinner tables and him getting hard?

Bad goddamn habit he needed to break.

"Owen, what is this about you coming out of retirement, and why did I have to hear about it from your agent instead of you?"

His father's question dropped into the middle of the room like a verbal bomb, and the shrapnel rained down on Owen, piercing his skin, his heart, his peace.

What. The. Actual. *Fuck?*

He couldn't move, couldn't speak. Couldn't do anything

but stare at his father. As a hint of satisfaction glittered in his father's green eyes, Owen's reaction had obviously been Troy's intention. To catch Owen off guard so Troy could be in control. In his father's world, there was no such thing as an even playing field. That was for pussies.

"My agent gave you confidential information about my career," Owen stated, not bothering to keep the edge out of his voice.

"You got to be kidding me," Sherrod softly growled.

"I'm your father," Troy snapped as if that was enough explanation.

Oh, Owen and Byron were definitely going to have words. And if this shit was true, maybe a parting of ways.

"And as I've told you before, one is personal, and the other is business. They have nothing to do with each other."

"Yes, you've made that abundantly clear." His father's mouth twisted into an ugly caricature of a smile. "You've also made it clear that you don't need my advice even though I've been there for you throughout your entire career. Hell, if it wasn't for me, you wouldn't have one. But fine, what I think isn't important. Got it."

Fuck.

A headache bloomed behind Owen's right eye, but he didn't rub it. That boy who hid his books, who only listened to certain music on earphones so he wouldn't face ridicule, couldn't allow him to ease the growing ache. Again, old habits didn't just die hard. They were poltergeists who refused to go into the goddamn light.

"I thought you hadn't made a decision," Leo said, her even tone a cool balm. Under the table, her hand slid over his thigh, the gentle weight an anchor. "So the conversation might be a little premature."

"You haven't made a decision?" Troy's chin jerked back,

his sneer deepening. Ignoring Leo, he glared at Owen. "What are you talking about? What is there to make a decision about? You have an opportunity to return to the game. There is no other choice."

His voice brooked no argument, handing down the order and expecting it to be obeyed as if Owen was three instead of thirty.

Anger stirred in his gut like a firestorm. He couldn't look at Leo. Or Sherrod or Celeste. Not when this glimpse into his childhood gaped wide like a window thrown open to allow the whole neighborhood to see. His father's toxic masculinity. His mother's eternal struggle between victim and volunteer. Owen's tug-of-war for acceptance and independence.

"Since I haven't made up my mind yet, there is a choice," Owen stated, veins of steel running through his tone. "I'm done talking about this right—"

"You were cleared to play after rehab. I never agreed with the retirement in the first place. But you did it against my wishes. Against everyone's advice. But here is a chance to correct that foolish mistake. You need to return while everyone still remembers who you are. While you're still relevant." He jabbed a finger into the table. "You have what? Three more years as an elite quarterback? You can't afford to waste any more time."

"Is this why you drove all the way here? To dig in my ass about football?" he growled.

"Owen." His mother lowered her coffee cup to the table. "That kind of language isn't necessary. Respect your father and the table."

Damn. It.

"Someone has to." His father's fingers curled into a fist next to his saucer. "I'm sure your friends mean well, but they obviously coddle you. Too afraid to hurt your feelings to tell you the truth."

"No offense, sir, but that's not accurate," Sherrod interjected, leaning back in his chair, crossing his arms over his chest. While his posture might've been relaxed, his best friend didn't fool Owen. Neither did the flint in his dark gaze or the tense set of his shoulders. "We do tell Owen the truth. I've actually encouraged Owen to come out of retirement and return to football. The team isn't the same without him. But I also grant him the space to make up his own mind because ultimately, it comes down to what he wants. I respect him enough to accept his decision."

Warmth and love for his friend surged within Owen. But nothing could choke out the grime that never failed to coat him whenever he spent time in his parents' presence.

Troy waved away Sherrod's words. "That's lip service, and you know it. What else is he going to do if he doesn't play?" His father switched his narrow-eyed attention back to Owen. "What else, son? You *are* football. It's all you've known. What else are you going to do?"

What else are you good for?

Troy didn't voice the question, but it hung there, bright and blinding, like a chandelier, suspended by his derision.

"I guess it's a good thing I didn't enter the draft early, stayed in college and earned my degree, then," Owen drawled.

"That degree." Troy scoffed, as he'd done since the day Owen had informed Troy he would be remaining in college instead of following in several of his teammates' footsteps and entering the draft. "That degree is a worthless piece of paper. You've had that thing for eight years and haven't done a damn thing with it. You are a football player not a businessman." His lips curled around *businessman* as if it tasted like shit on his tongue.

"He's thirty," Leo said, and Owen could easily imagine her using the same overly polite, determined tone with difficult guests at the inn. "People make life changes in careers much older than that. And he's intelligent, driven and a hard worker. Just from what I've googled about Owen since knowing him, all the journalists say the same about him as a player and leader. So conceivably, he could return to school and earn another degree. Open a nonprofit or run a business. He has a world of options open to him. Not just football, if he decides it's not what he wants."

"I don't mean to be rude, but this is a family matter and none of your business."

Leo shook her head, the corner of her mouth tilted. "It's funny how *I don't mean to be rude* really means *Wait for it. I'm about to be rude.* But—" she folded her arms on the table and leaned forward, her gray-blue eyes gleaming "—when you ignored Owen's request to let it go and continued talking about it anyway at this table, I think that made it everyone's business."

Owen didn't dare look at her. Not with his dick hard. God knew what would be reflected in his face. Lust? Admiration?

Gratitude?

Yes, it would be best if he avoided glancing at her. Because of all those emotions, gratitude would be the worst.

No one had ever stepped in to defend him from his father. His coaches, his agent, other players—as unnecessarily hard they thought Troy had been on Owen, it'd still been between father and son, and they hadn't intervened.

But Leo did.

Without hesitation.

She'd done what his own mother had never done.

Beneath the table, he fisted his hands. To prevent them from hauling her onto his lap. From burrowing them through her hair and dragging her close so he could take that beautiful temptation of a mouth.

From clapping together and going under his chin as he begged her to never stop…stop…

Shit. His brain couldn't even form the rest of that sentence. It struck too close to a forbidden desire that wasn't meant to be his. Couldn't be his.

"Let's just…everyone…" His mother spoke into the tense silence, spreading her palms over the table and patting the air. Turning pleading eyes and a tremulous smile to him, she said, "Son, I'm excited for you. This town looked really cute and sweet as we drove through, but this isn't what you're used to now, is it? From the times we visited you in New York, the city seems more your speed. I'm sure you can't wait to return to your life there. You can't hide out here forever."

"I'm not hiding."

Okay, maybe he had been until recently. But in the past few weeks, that had changed. Due to Leo, Sherrod and Celeste, he'd stopped playing the recluse. He'd started to integrate himself into the town through the football team. Through Leo, he'd come to know Sonny and the rest of her family. He'd even ventured onto the town square today without a care about who saw his face.

So no. He wasn't the social creature he'd once been—the center of every party, club or restaurant opening, walking a few red carpets—but he also wasn't the hermit he'd become this past year.

"You know what I mean, honey. I—" his mother murmured, pity coating her voice and softening her gaze. Her hand rose to her throat, fingers fluttering, before she lowered it beneath the table. "I can't even pretend to imagine how difficult it's been with the…" Once more her fingers rose but this time they floated near her face. Right where scars etched his own skin. Flames licked at him, embarrassment searing him. She couldn't even say the word. Couldn't even say *scars*. "But with as much time that's passed surely plastic surgery is an option—"

"He doesn't need surgery. Are you kidding me?" Leo snapped. "He's perfect. As his girlfriend, I make sure he knows that every day. That also goes for whether or not he's a football player. He's. Perfect."

She narrowed her eyes on each of his parents, daring them to say anything different.

Hell, with that glowing light of battle in her eyes, *he* didn't have the balls to say anything different.

Not that he could actually voice a word. Not with the shock racing through his blood like a shot of liquor, leaving him reeling.

Girlfriend?

He's perfect.

A shudder worked through him, and he fought not to let the entire table witness how that fierce avowal shook him. Truth rang in her voice, riding shotgun next to anger. Like earlier, he avoided looking at her, still afraid of what he'd betray. And Jesus…

Girlfriend?

"Girlfriend?" his mother repeated, plucking the word right out of his head. She turned to him, hope shining in her hazel eyes so brightly he damn near strangled on the caustic laughter that scraped his throat. What? Did she fear another woman would never want him? "Is that true?" she asked.

Beside him, Leo tensed.

It didn't require a mentalist to know she waited for him to out her as a liar. And hell, as kind as the effort had been, he should end it before her claim took on a life of its own. God only knew how long his parents planned on sticking around. Probably as long as his father believed he needed to convince Owen to come to his senses. In other words, they could be here for the long haul, and he should save her from the act she didn't sign up for...

"Yes."

Maybe he imagined it, but he heard Leo's relieved exhale.

"Really?" Skepticism dripped from his father's tone. "Why are we just hearing about this? You didn't mention this...relationship when you first introduced her to us."

"She's with me in my house, meeting my parents. Isn't that enough of a hint?" Owen arched his eyebrow.

"How did you two meet? Owen, I can't believe you've kept Leo from us," his mother gushed.

Leo's lips parted, but Owen beat her to it. "We met a little over a year ago. In Boston right after our Super Bowl win."

Her soft gasp stung him, tattooing him with her shock, her disbelief. And it wouldn't be long before her hurt joined them.

He finally turned and looked at her.

He shouldn't have. Now he couldn't glance away. Those gorgeous eyes, like shattered pieces of overcast sky, stared into his. That same shock. Confusion.

And there. Right there.

Hurt.

I'm sorry I'm a coward.

The apology pounded against his skull, an anvil against steel.

"Are you sure about that?" his father drawled. "Leontyne doesn't look too certain about it."

"It's true," she whispered, addressing his father though not removing her gaze from Owen. "I was in Boston for a convention, and we were staying at the same hotel. We met in the bar..."

"And ended up closing it down talking for the rest of the night," he concluded on a murmur.

The hurt and bewilderment didn't fade from her eyes, but heat simmered there, brightening them like flashes of lightning during a summer storm.

"Where have you been for the last year, then?" his father demanded, threads of doubt still lacing his voice.

Leo looked away from Owen, and he momentarily closed his eyes, releasing a long breath. His chest ached, raw.

"I broke it off with her, pushed her away," Owen once again answered for her. "But we reconnected again when I came to Rose Bend."

Silence filled the room. He dared to glance at Sherrod and Celeste, and his friend stared back at him, not a little awe in his eyes. A small, enigmatic smile curved Celeste's mouth, and Owen couldn't begin to decipher it.

And didn't have the inclination to—not when so *much* damn near vibrated off Leo.

Jesus, he needed this circus of a dinner to end so he could talk to her in private. So he could demand to know what the hell she'd been thinking to claim she was his girlfriend.

So he could beg her for one more taste of her mouth, one more touch from her hands, before she walked away from him for being a lying piece of shit.

Goddamn.

"That was the past, and this is now," Leo said to his father. "And like I said, I didn't follow football, so I had no idea about the accident. Because if I had known, you best believe, even he at his asshole worst couldn't have kept me away." She glanced at his mother. "Excuse my language."

His mother smiled, her eyes bright with a suspicious sheen. God, not tears.

"Don't worry about that, Leo," Charlene whispered.

Because if I had known, you best believe, even he at his asshole worst couldn't have kept me away.

For the first time he thought back on the loneliest, angriest and most painful time of his life and wished he hadn't shut everyone out, hadn't insisted on suffering through it alone. No, that wasn't correct. He wished *Leo* had been there so he wouldn't have been there alone.

Wished that he could somehow reverse time, could have gotten her name, could have woken up early enough to catch her before she snuck out of his hotel room. Refused to let her disappear out of his life.

Shit. If wishes were fifths, he'd be fucked up instead of torturing himself fantasizing about what-ifs.

The rest of the evening wrapped up quickly, but each minute dragged as if time itself conspired against him finally getting to Leo.

When Celeste offered to show his parents up to one of the guest rooms, Owen could've kissed her and risked Sherrod's wrath. Leo said good-night, and he guided her out of the house and to his car. Since Celeste had picked her up from the inn for pageant practice, Leo had no choice but to accept a ride home from him. And from the hard set of her jaw as she rounded the hood of his Range Rover, she knew it and wasn't happy about it.

He followed her, opening the passenger-side door. But when she moved forward, he didn't do the smart thing and step back. Instead, he shifted closer until only a breath of space separated them. If he bowed his head, he could bury his face in her thick, silken strands, inhale her scent. If he lifted his hands, he could cup her beautiful breasts, feel her nipples harden under his teasing fingertips, triumph in Leo arching into his grip. Because she would. He harbored zero doubts that she would gasp and grind that beautiful, tight ass against his cock, begging without words for more.

"Leo…"

"Not now, Owen." She shook her head and slid into the SUV.

Inhaling a deep breath that contained her lilac-and-rain fragrance, he dipped his head and closed the door. Within seconds he climbed inside the vehicle and pulled away from his house.

Several minutes passed. The shadowed, quiet residential streets of Rose Bend passed by before she demanded, "Where are you going? This isn't the way to the inn."

"I don't really want to have this conversation on the front lawn of your family's establishment. Do you?"

"I don't want to have this conversation at all."

"Liar," he said softly. "You want to have this out. And I'm going to give you a chance to do it. To lay it all out and let me have it. But I don't want an audience. This is between you and me, Leo."

He fell silent, and so did she. When he pulled up into the vacant lot next to the empty Glen, she barely waited until he shifted the car into Park before whipping the door open and jumping out of the vehicle. He braced himself for her fury, opening the driver's-side door slower and stepping free. Once he closed the door, she whirled on him.

"You son of a bitch."

He slid his hands into the front pockets of his pants. Didn't say a word.

Thrusting her hands into her hair, she dislodged her

ponytail, thick strands falling over her shoulder. Her anger beat at him, and his heart ached to soothe it, to ease the hurt that throbbed underneath. But his palms… His palms dampened with the need to curl her hair around his palms and haul her into him until he could feast on that rage directly from the source.

"You *knew*. All along you knew and yet you didn't say a word." She laughed and the harsh sound rasped in the night air. "You looked me in my eye and pretended not to know me."

"Yes, I did."

"You lied to me. Reduced me to a nameless, faceless fuck who wasn't worth your memory. At least that's what I left your house believing. And you let me."

He didn't answer. Couldn't. Horror choked his vocal cords. If he'd known that was how she'd perceived his silence—no, dammit, his deception—then he would've come clean. Nothing about Leo could be cheapened to a random fuck. She was… She was… Undefinable.

She was…Leo.

"I would've never let you walk out that door if I'd—"

"Save it, Owen." She slashed a hand through the air, jerking her head and sending more hair sliding over her shoulder. "Weeks. It has been weeks since we became friends. You've had plenty of time to tell me the truth, and every day that you've seen me and didn't, you made the decision all over again to lie to me. Even during your request, *your request*, for honesty. What bullshit."

Tunneling her fingers through her hair again, she pivoted sharply on her heel and paced away from him. She whirled back once more, facing him, dropping her arms to her sides.

"Did you get a kick out of making me look like a fool? Or did you…?"

Her voice trailed off and her pain propelled him off the car and toward her. "Did I what, Leo?" he grated.

"Nothing."

"Nothing, hell." He abruptly halted several steps away from her, but his upper body didn't receive the memo, and he leaned forward, his chest rising and falling, breath pitching like a shipwreck victim on a storm-tossed sea. "Say it. Did I what?"

When her full lips curled in, as if trapping the truth inside, he stalked closer, and he flexed his fingers, reminding himself to keep them at his sides. That he couldn't grab her, drag her to him and force her to confess it. On his tongue.

"Say it, Leo," he growled. Or pleaded. Maybe both.

"Did you want me to go away so badly, regretted that night so much, you were willing to lie so I would disappear? Only I didn't. I didn't go away. I didn't disappear. I kept coming back." Another one of those terrible chuckles. "You must've thought I was a serious level-ten clinger. Pathetic."

"Stop it."

One moment he stood watching her shiver with the emotion that coursed through her. In the next, he gripped the disheveled mess of her ponytail, destroying the rest of it. The band tumbled to the ground, and he groaned as the thick, cool fall of her hair streamed over his hand and wrist. He surrendered to the need that had called to him earlier, and he buried his face in the fragrant strands, inhaling deep.

"Stop it," he repeated. Lust and desire ground his voice to the consistency of sand. He lifted his free hand to cup the sweet curve of her hip. Tried to tame his strength so he didn't grab when every instinct howled at him to clutch her close, mark her so any motherfucker who dared to touch—

Goddamn.

He shuddered.

He was reverting to a fucking caveman.

"Feel me shaking, Leo? Just lower your head, sweetheart, and press your ear to my chest. Hear my heart pounding?" He bent his body around her, wielding a control that had to be divinely inspired. "If you're feeling brave, take that perfect little hand and feel me like you did in Boston. Feel me, sweetheart. Feel me, hear me and touch me, and you tell me if I regret you. Don't want you. Think you're pathetic. There's only one pathetic person here, and it's not you."

With his fingers tangled in her hair, he used that leverage to tug her head back so she couldn't hide from him. So for once, he couldn't hide from her.

"You're right. I did want you to go away. I did want you to disappear." When she jerked against him, a soft cry escaping her, he tightened his grip on her hair, her hip, holding her steady. Holding her closer. "But not for what you believed. I couldn't look at you and not remember how you wanted me a year ago. The me *then*. Not the man I am now. Scarred. Brok—"

"You're not," she snapped, irritation mixing with the anger. Irritation for him, not at him. And damn, if that didn't send warmth pulsing through him with each heartbeat. Even mad at him, she defended him. Even from himself.

"I'm not telling you this for sympathy, Leo," he said softly. "I don't *deserve* your sympathy. Yeah, I panicked, but I still made the choice to sacrifice your feelings for my pride, my insecurities. Fuck yes, I remembered you. As soon as I opened the door. I've never forgotten anything about you in fourteen months. Not your scent. Or the dusting of freckles here." He abandoned her hip and lifted his hand to her face, his fingertips hovering right over her check. "And here." The bridge of her nose. "And here." Her other check.

The night air carried the whisper of insects' songs and her short, jagged puffs of breath that crashed on her parted lips. He loved that sound. And when he returned to New York, whether to come out of retirement or find a new path for his life after football, that sound would stay with him forever. His keepsake from Rose Bend. One of many.

"I haven't forgotten how sensitive you are here," he murmured, dipping his head until his lips almost but not quite brushed the fragrant place where neck and shoulder met. "Or the sharp catch of breath when I kiss you there. Or here," he breathed, dropping his hand again in another of those non-touches over her rapidly rising and falling breasts, the hard tips clearly delineated under the white cotton of her shirt. Briefly closing his eyes, he lowered his hand to the small of her back, fisting the hem of her top. "But what's haunted me most? What follows me into sleep and makes a joke of my self-control when I'm awake? It's that low, hungry sound you make when I push into you. Like you can't get enough. Like you won't let me go until I give you everything you desire, you demand."

A shudder rippled through him, and he didn't care that she felt it. He was past concealing his need from her. Hell, he didn't know if he possessed the power to do it even if he wanted to.

"But the instant I looked at you on my doorstep, I also remembered the look of pity—that fucking pity—on everyone else's faces when they saw me after the surgery. And I couldn't handle that from you. Of all people, not from *you*. To see the same eyes that had filled with pleasure now darken with disgust? I couldn't…" He shook his head, his voice broke off, throat working.

"I would ask you what bitch did that and what's her address, but I think it's best that I don't know," she said, mouth flattening and a light he could only call unholy entering her eyes.

God, how could she stir laughter in him at this moment?

"That's not the point, sweetheart—"

"It is," she insisted hotly. "It damn well is. Maybe if the people in your life had spent more time letting you know just how special, gifted, brilliant and just damn good you are—all of you, not only your arm or your face—then I wouldn't be here, in the middle of the night, in a dark parking lot telling you, *you are fucking enough*, Owen Strafford."

Then I wouldn't know you. Then I wouldn't be in Rose Bend.

And I wouldn't trade that for this scar. For that accident. For foot—

Fuck.

He scrambled back from the dusty, crumbling ledge of that thought. His heart raced a hundred-yard dash for the back of his throat. Where the hell had that come from? She was a woman. A remarkable, gorgeous woman, yes. But not one he would change his entire life for. Not one he would place on the same level as the sport that had been his sanity, his purpose…his freedom.

But not one woman—not one person—in his life had ever told him he was enough. Just him. Not because of his arm. Or his money. Or his fame. Or his face.

But just him.

No one but Leo Dennison.

More emotion crowded into him. Too much. Too huge. It filled every bit of him, finding every crack, every crevice, until a visceral fear clenched him. He might not be able to contain this.

A strangled sound shook loose from him and when he would have hidden from her again, she tunneled her fingers in his hair, drawing it back from his face. Giving him no choice but to look at her. He might have been bigger, taller, heavier, but she held all the power here.

"I'm going to kiss you, and I want you to let me," she whispered. "And not because I claimed to be your fake girlfriend to shut up your parents. Not because we once shared the hottest sex of my life. Not because you're an ex- or soon-to-be-again football player. I want you to let me kiss you simply because when you look at me right now you see how much I'm dying to have your mouth on me."

With a groan, he lowered his head, but stopped just short of taking her mouth. She'd declared she was going to kiss him, and he wanted it.

"Show me how much, Leo. I promise you it's not as much as I dream about fucking your mouth."

Her eyes widened, shock flaring in the bright depths before she tugged, pulling him closer.

She didn't make him wait.

Didn't go slow.

Didn't tease.

Leo delivered.

She owned him with her kiss. Did she know? Could she tell that with each glide of her tongue over his, with each lick to the roof of his mouth, each wet tangle and suck, he surrendered more of himself to her? His fingers straightened and flexed in her hair, against her back. Restlessly. Hungrily. He opened wider for her, bending his head lower, cocking his head farther, granting her easier, deeper access.

Whatever she wanted from him, of him, she could have.

In *this*, she could have everything.

"God, I can't get enough of kissing you," she rasped. "I could've done it for hours that night."

"Then you shouldn't have left," he growled, nipping her damp, swollen bottom lip in punishment. "We're going to talk about that. But not right now."

Not when too many decisions bombarded his mind. Like whether or not to draw her nipple into his mouth through her shirt or strip her half-naked so he could finally taste her flesh again. Like whether to lay her back on the hood of the Range Rover, tug her pants off and bury his face between her slim thighs or finger-fuck her first.

Yeah, so many decisions.

Gripping her waist, he jerked his head up, breaking their kiss. He turned and hiked her up in the air. Her surprised cry echoed in his ear, but her legs clamped around his waist. Satisfaction zipped up his spine.

Another thing he hadn't forgotten from that night. Though they'd just met, there'd been an instinctive...trust between them. She'd entrusted him with her body, her pleasure. An unspoken promise not to harm her or abuse her vulnerability.

Maybe they'd torn down one barrier tonight—one he'd erected—but he didn't kid himself. For every guard eradicated, Leo had another in place. With armed sentinels, barbed wire and an electrified fence. He might look like the beast, roaring, turning away visitors and hiding in his castle. But this beauty really bore the secrets and was the recluse—an emotional one.

Except here. In this parking lot with her thighs embracing him as tightly as her arms and her lips, tongue and teeth marking his neck, she didn't hide from him. As in that hotel room that had smelled of lilacs, rain and sex, she opened herself to him. And yeah, he leaped on it like a predator sinking its teeth into an exposed throat. But he did it gently, tenderly.

But fuck, he took.

Walking the few feet to the front of his vehicle, he set her on the hood and moved between her legs, not stopping until his cock pressed against the seam of her pants. And…he ground his teeth together, his head tipping back, eyes squeezing closed. Maybe it was his very active, very ravenous, imagination, but he swore he could feel the heat of her through the linen. Because he couldn't help it—he didn't want to help it—he cradled her hips, holding her tight to him, and rocked his dick over that cloth-covered flesh.

Her lush, uninhibited moan floated on the air like a song. One on which he longed to hit Replay. Repeatedly. Raising one hand to the back of her neck and supporting her, he pulled her even closer, rolled over her again. Elicited that tune from her again.

Blunt, feminine nails trailed down his back and dug into his sides, clutching him, dragging him closer. Leo arched into the clasp he had on her neck, using it as leverage to twist and grind into his dick. Each stroke drew a rough whimper from her throat, and he pressed his lips there, savoring the vibration, the sound.

Perfect. Jesus, it was perfect.

And they hadn't even removed any clothes yet.

"Kiss me," she breathed. "Kiss me, Owen…please."

He lifted his head, stared down into her bright gaze. Brushed his lips over her cheekbones, temple, the tender skin under her eyes, and finally, her mouth.

"You don't ever have to beg me to give you what's yours, Leo. Just come take it."

Even in the dark of the parking lot, he caught a vulnerable flash in her eyes. It had his arms aching to surround her with his body and keep her there. Protect her. But that was impossible. Because he couldn't defend her from what tortured her on the inside.

"No games. I won't use this against you later. This is between us. Trust me again like you did before, sweetheart. Let go," he invited. Maybe tempted.

He hoped.

He wanted to be her temptation. Her ruin. Just like she was his.

"Now, do it," he whispered, lowering his head to just a couple of inches above her mouth. "Come get what you want."

Slowly curling a hand in the front of his shirt, she hoisted herself up those couple of inches and claimed her kiss. Claimed him.

Again.

Hot. Wet. Hard. Wild. Lips bruised lips. Tongues tangled with tongues. Hands tangled in hair, gripped shoulders, clutched muscle. Her nails scratched at his scalp, his back. *Dammit.* He needed…

"Sweetheart." He trailed his mouth over her jaw, nipping the delicate yet stubborn line. Deliberately gentling his touch, he cupped her head, holding her steady for a more tender scattering of kisses. "We—"

"No." She shook her head, reaching up between them and tugging him down. Hard. Her teeth grazed his scars, and she wasn't gentle. She made him feel her. In his chest. His soul.

His cock.

A full-body shiver shuddered through him, and his grip roughened. With a growl, he jerked back and crushed his mouth to hers, fucking it. Undone. He came undone at the seams. Only a last-minute whisper of lucidity cautioned him to take care as he sprawled her on the hood of the SUV.

Sending up an undoubtedly profane prayer for the blessing of his height, he pressed between her legs, spreading them wide and lifting them over his shoulders. Closing his eyes, he buried his face against her linen-covered sex, inhaling her, feeling her, mouthing her. Fuck, he craved her, and the clothing only served to ratchet up the lust clawing at him, demanding he tear the remaining barrier away so he could taste, feast, gorge.

He slid his hands under her shirt, his palms sliding over smooth, silken skin, and his cock throbbed, molten desire flowing through him, unchecked. His mouth followed, rediscovering what his hands revealed.

Even though her scent called to him and his stomach damn near cramped with the hunger inside him, he slowed, appreciating, relishing. Licking, nipping, sucking, he took his time as he raised her shirt over her stomach. Enjoyed a fierce satisfaction as the flat surface went even more concave as he dipped his tongue in the shallow bowl of her navel. Hummed in savage delight as he brushed his lips over her torso, under the curves of her breasts, in the perspiration-dampened valley between those just-less-than-a-handful and perfect mounds. Tilting his head, he captured a nipple, sucking it through the lace of her bra.

"Owen," Leo whimpered, tunneling her fingers through his hair, grasping him to her. She shivered, arching high into him, and he wrapped an arm around and under her. "Please."

Another detail that had haunted him in every erotic, dirty dream. The exquisite sensitivity of her breasts. Her breathless pants and strained pleas were the sweetest caresses on his ears, his skin, his cock as he curled his tongue around that diamond-hard peak and drew on it. With his free hand, he tugged down the bra cup of her other breast and teased and tweaked her flesh, preparing her. And when he switched his mouth to that tip, her nails scratched across his scalp, her vibrating growl a visceral thing.

"If this isn't what you want, tell me to stop," he said, reluctantly releasing her breasts and retracing his path down her torso.

Deliberately, he turned his face to the side and rubbed his scars over her soft skin. Was he still testing her? Maybe. Because a part of him continued to find it shocking that she wanted no part of his money, his name or his connections.

She only wanted him. Just the way he was.

A gentle hand stroked over his hair, giving him tenderness in the midst of this wild, raw storm.

Squeezing his eyes closed against the sudden sting in his eyes, he refocused on the physical aspect of this moment. On the lust—the only safe landscape. He allowed his fingers to guide him. The valleys, dips and planes of her body were burned in his memory. He swept a kiss over the curve of her hip as he deftly released the closure of her pants and removed them, impatiently taking her panties with them. Pausing long enough to slide her shoes off, he moved back between her legs, sliding his palms up her strong, beautiful thighs, not stopping until his fingertips almost grazed the plump, glistening folds of her sex.

Christ, she was gorgeous.

Unable to restrain himself, he dove into her. He didn't hold back, didn't pretend to. Skill gave way to hunger, to raw passion. His thumbs held her wide open for him and he left no part of her untouched. Left no part of her unloved.

Leo writhed and twisted beneath him, her cries and grunts breaking on the night air, on him, like the rain of her scent. She clutched at his head, grasping him to her sex, hips feverishly working, riding his mouth, demanding he give even as he took. And fuck, if that wasn't sexy as hell.

Crossing an arm low on her belly, he exerted force to hold her in place as he latched on to her clit, suckling, pushing two fingers inside her.

"Dammit, sweetheart." He ground his teeth together so hard an ache bloomed across his jaw.

So tight. So hot. So wet.

Closing his eyes, he screwed his wrist, pressing deeper, seeking that spot high inside her. Rubbing it. Chuckling at the loud scream that tore free of her, the wild bucking of her hips. Shit, if his arm didn't tether her, she might slide off his hood. And he loved it. Loved her total abandon. Her fierceness. Her sexuality.

Lapping at the bundle of nerves cresting her sex, he withdrew his fingers, then plunged back inside her, over and over. Her trembling thighs squeezed his head, that keening wail growing in her throat, cresting on the air. And he didn't stop. Not until her feminine walls gripped his fingers, spasming, quivering.

Her cries still echoed around them as he pressed gentle, soothing kisses to her swollen sex. But nothing could soothe his cock or the fire racing through his blood. His whole body throbbed with lust and another, more complicated, tender emotion he refused to focus on. Refused to analyze. That emotion pulsed like an aching wound.

Straightening, he stroked a hand up her stomach, the middle of her breasts, over her throat and to the back of her neck. Cupping the nape, he drew her up. Long brown hair tangled from his fingers, shirt shoved up, and bra yanked below her breasts, pants gone...she'd never been more beautiful to him. No matter who had come before him, this Leo belonged only to him.

"Leo." He almost winced at the serrated quality to his voice, but he was unsurprised by it. Not when need scraped him raw. Waiting until the pleasure glazing her eyes started to clear and she focused on him, he said, "I want inside you, sweetheart. Now. But I don't have condoms on me. It's been...months for me. But I've been tested. Last time I saw my doctor, I had a physical. That said, sweetheart..." He pressed his lips to her forehead, her mouth. "If you want me to grab your pants and pull them on and place you in my car and drive you home, I will. We can end this right here, and it will be okay."

Fuck, that would almost kill him, but he meant it. With everything in him, he meant it.

She didn't answer him. At least not vocally.

With her gaze on him, she lowered her hands to the front of his jeans, unbuttoned and unzipped them, then tugged the denim low on his hips.

His lungs stuttered when she pushed the button through the corresponding hole. They stopped working altogether when she dipped her hand in his boxer briefs and wrapped her hand around his cock.

"I'm guessing that's a yes," he ground out on a huff of laughter. Jesus, how could he laugh right now, with her basically naked on the hood of his car and her hand on his dick? *Only Leo*, his stubborn subconscious supplied. "But I need to hear the words from you."

"Yes, Owen." She squeezed him hard, tugging down the front of his underwear with her other hand. A guttural groan rumbled in his chest as she pumped him from root to tip and a frisson of pleasure tripped down his spine. She pressed an almost tender kiss to the center of his chest, contradicting the erotic hold on his flesh. "And I've been tested, too, and I'm on the pill, but I—"

She closed her eyes, a spasm of emotion passing over her features. She turned her head away from him, her hand abandoning his cock to clutch his waist.

Worry poured into him, momentarily submerging lust. The pain, and maybe grief, touching her face, that took precedence.

"Sweetheart." Though desire still pulsed hot and heavy in his body, in his hardened sex, he waited. And when she tipped her head back and met his eyes, he brushed the backs of his fingers down the front of her throat. And waited some more.

"You're..." She hesitated, her fingers biting into his skin before relaxing. Deliberately, he thought. "You're the first man I've been with without a condom in...years," she whispered. After a long moment where she didn't remove those haunting eyes from his, she shook her head. "I'm scared."

The confession hulled out his chest. And for an instant he couldn't move. Afraid he would shatter.

"Of?"

Her kiss-swollen lips moved, but no words emerged. Then the tip of her tongue slicked over them, and she tried again.

"Of myself."

The aching honesty in the two words dragged out his own truth. Tunneling his fingers into her tangled hair, he tipped her head back. "That makes two of us, then."

She frowned. "I don't..."

"Makes two of us who are scared of you. No, that's not completely true." He inhaled, held it. Exhaled. "I'm terrified of how you make me feel. How you make me...hope. Hope is fucking dangerous. You are fucking dangerous,

Leontyne Dennison." He skimmed his lips over her fore-head before pressing them directly to the middle. "Let's be fearless together."

He kissed her, holding back nothing of himself. Hands in her hair, flowing over her shoulders, back, hips, ass, legs. Body aligned to the front of her, chest to her breasts, ab-domen to her belly, cock to her sex. She widened her legs, twisting them around his waist and reaching between them to fist his dick, notching him to her core.

Accepting him.

Taking him.

Welcoming him.

A whirlwind tore through his head, ripped through his chest and shuddered down his spine as he sank deep, deep into her liquid heat. So tight. So perfect. So…his.

He buried his head in the crook of her neck. As if he could hide from that thought in his head right after he'd asked her to be brave with him.

Her hands grabbed at his back, tugging, scratching, pull-ing him close. Closer.

Needing to look into her eyes, he levered back, staring down at her even as he slowly withdrew, dragging himself over quivering feminine muscles and hissing at the exqui-site pleasure of it before surging back inside, bottoming out.

Another thing he remembered with crystal clarity.

How completely she took him. How…complete he felt when he was inside her.

The heat of her burned away the last of his control, and arms wrapped tight around her, he let go, unleashed. His hips snapped forward, plunging, driving. Over and over, he claimed her, took her. He couldn't get enough. Couldn't get close enough. Even as he hauled her to the very edge of the hood, his arms almost a vise around her as he thrust into her, shoving them both toward a cataclysmic release that already sizzled at the base of his spine.

Reaching between them, he whisked his thumb over her clit, once, twice, and he didn't need a third time before her sex seized him in a brutal grip that had him groaning and struggling not to go over the edge right there and then. He wouldn't. Not until she received the full measure of her orgasm. Not until she received all the pleasure he could give her, that she was due.

She stiffened against him, her lips parting on a soundless scream that, nonetheless, he swore echoed in his head. Covering her mouth and swallowing that nonsound, he wildly thrust into her, her clenching sex hauling him into that sweet, dark abyss.

With her lilac-and-rain scent in his nose, her slender arms supporting him and her sex squeezing him tight, he felt the safest he'd been in over a year.

Even as he surrendered to her, to the ecstasy, a small insidious voice questioned, *For how long?*

CHAPTER SIXTEEN

"WELL, THERE USED to be a time I couldn't get you out of this place, and now I can't keep you *in*."

Leo glanced up from shutting down the computer on the office desk to see her mother leaning on the doorjamb.

She frowned. "Where are your crutches, woman?"

Moe waved away Leo's question then hobbled farther into the room on her cast. "I'm fine without the crutches for a few hours. Besides, they just get in the way."

"Oh, really?" Leo drawled. "Where's Dad? How does he feel about this medical degree you've suddenly acquired?"

"You leave your father out of this, young woman. That man is completely happy in his blissfully ignorant state." Moe jabbed a finger at her. "Now, stop trying to change the subject," she said, lowering to the visitor's chair. "Unless you're switching it to a certain football player dropping you off late last night and you creeping in the kitchen entrance." Her mother arched an eyebrow, lips cranking into a frankly lascivious grin that was seriously disturbing.

Leo's lips parted, then snapped shut with an audible pop. Dammit. At twenty-nine years old, heat should *not* be pouring into her face, setting it on fire as if she'd been caught sneaking in after curfew. Well, technically she'd been caught sneaking in after being out with a guy, but again, *twenty-nine*!

And for the love of God, she was not going to think of

all the things she'd been doing with Owen the night before. Of how he'd laid her out on that hood, rearranged her as if her body belonged to him for the possessing, the marking, the claiming. And damn, how he'd claimed her. Over and over. With his mouth, his fingers, that beautiful, big cock that she hadn't exaggerated in her dreams...

So much for not dwelling on hot, throat-searing, on-a-hood-of-a-car sex with Owen while five feet away from her mother.

God, she had no control. None. Zip.

Sweeping away the fingers of fear that scraped over her skin at that thought, she inhaled a deep breath that did *not* contain the memory of his earthy scent. Slowly, she hitched a hip to the corner of the desk, sitting on it. "I'm not trying to change the subject." *So* changing the subject. "I'm just concerned you don't injure yourself worse. But," she sighed, curling her fingers around the edge of the desk and tilting her head to the side, "are you okay with me being gone so much? Truthfully? I didn't intend for this—"

"Oh, please." Moe waved her hand. "I've run this inn for nearly half my life without you. I think I can manage for several afternoons and evenings."

Well...ouch.

She must've been shit at hiding her dinged feelings because Moe leaned forward and patted her thigh, a small smile curving her mouth.

"Leo, we're long overdue for a talk. Since you're about to head out the door, I'll postpone it for now, but, sweetie, we're going to have it."

Her mother's smile remained, but a glint of steel that every Dennison child recognized entered her eyes. Leo barely contained a shiver of foreboding. One of Moe's infamous "talks." Good God. It would either leave her irritated and uncomfortably introspective or crying her eyes out. Neither appealed.

"I will say this, though," Moe continued. "The inn is important to you. I get that. But somewhere along the line, it's become your everything, and that's not healthy. You're shortchanging yourself. You've thrown yourself into this place, believing it can't leave you, disappoint you…break your heart." Moe's fingers momentarily tightened on Leo's thigh before sliding off and returning to her own lap. "I got news for you, Leo. It can't listen to you when you need to vent about the unfairness of life. It can't hold you when you burst out crying for no damn reason—or for a very good reason. It can't whisper in your ear that everything is going to be all right even when you can't possibly see how. As wonderful as this inn is, it can't love you. And, it will never fill a place inside you it was never meant to fill."

So…irritated but uncomfortably introspective.

Her fingers clenched tighter around the desk's edge, and she glanced away from Moe. "I love you, Moe, but you don't—"

"Understand? Is that what you were about to say?" Moe shook her head, the smile on her lips small, somehow sad.

And Leo suddenly felt like a grade-A ass.

"No, I didn't mean—"

"You were too young to remember—it was after Sinead was born and before Flo came to us." Her mother interrupted Leo with a subdued voice and a distant gaze focused on a point over Leo's shoulder. "But your father and I went through a real rough patch in our marriage. The why of it doesn't matter, but we handled it different. Your father… Well, he was your father. He turned inward, didn't talk about it. Me? I threw myself into the inn. Like you, I prioritized it above all in my life. Because it didn't cause me pain.

It brought me satisfaction, gave me purpose, focus, and as long as I poured my all into it, I didn't feel like a failure."

Leo stared at her mother, for the first time in her life seeing her not as Moe, her parent, her safe place to fall, her provider, her protector. But viewing her as Billie Thomasina Dennison, a woman who'd suffered all the same things other women had—uncertainty in her marriage, fear, loneliness and doubt about who she was, why God had put her here.

How, in this moment, when her mother had ripped Leo's chest wide open, did she feel the closest to her?

"The inn, though—" Moe switched her focus back to Leo, leaning forward in her chair "—it was only a temporary solution to a problem that didn't disappear, no matter how much I prayed it would. When I realized that, I almost lost my family, my marriage and the only man I've ever loved. This place—" Moe waved a hand, encompassing the office "—it's not a panacea for whatever you're running from, honey. These last few weeks, with the festival, the pageant...Owen Strafford, I've been excited that you've finally started letting loose. More, I've been thankful to see the beginnings of the return of my old Leo. It's been so long. And I've been so scared I'd never see her again."

Her heartbeat pounded in her head, her throat, her chest, loud and primal. She battled the urge to break out in a run, escape Moe's way too perceptive stare, that mother's intuition.

Both were deadly when it came to secrets.

"What're you talking about?"

Another of those small, sad smiles that smacked of both love and disappointment. Not disappointment in Leo. But in her obvious deflection and deception.

"Eight years, Leo. Eight years you've carried this heaviness and I've lost the daughter who once laughed loudly and loved freely. I've tried not to push too much, hoping you'd come to me, but now I'm rethinking my decision."

Eight years, Leo. Eight years.

Her mother's words rang in her head like a warning bell. Love, fear and grief churned in her belly. Of course her mother would notice. She might not know the details—no one did—but Moe, being Moe, would've pinpointed the change in her child.

That was what love did.

It saw.

"I need to go or I'm going to be late to this pageant practice," Leo whispered, rising from the desk. "I should only be gone a couple of hours."

"If you need longer, take longer. This inn will be here, but if we've all learned anything in the last couple of years, it's that nothing—not time, not the next moment, not life—is guaranteed. So if something comes up, just call and let me know. We'll be fine."

"Okay, Moe, but I'll be back."

Moe didn't say anything, just nodded. And Leo was grateful.

She didn't want to hear any more wise words or revelations that rocked her world. She just needed to leave and get to practice so she could return to the familiar, the steady, the known. Her mother was right. She'd been spending a lot of time outside the inn. And while Moe had probably meant her talk to convince Leo not to cling so much to their family business and home, it'd done the opposite. It'd reminded her that last night—Owen, relationships—they were fleeting, unstable and ended in disappointment.

But Kinsale Inn...

Moe was wrong. In eight years it'd never failed her.

Never looked at her with frustration then, ultimately, disapproval in its eyes. It'd never broken her heart.

Maybe she'd never have the grand love story with the fairy-tale ending that Cole and Wolf had found. But she wouldn't have pain and loss, either.

To her, that was a good trade-off.

CHAPTER SEVENTEEN

Déjà vu.

Leo stood at the back of the stage again, arms folded across her chest, watching the other contestants practice the evening wear round. Since Scarlett had decided they would enter alphabetically, Leo had already walked, and hadn't done a bad job. Without Celeste there to critique her performance, she rated herself a B. Maybe she had a chance of getting through this thing without tripping, falling flat on her face or completely humiliating herself.

Oh, wait.

They hadn't gotten to the talent portion of this program yet.

She pinched the bridge of her nose, squeezing her eyes shut.

Unfortunately, she couldn't shut out the bombardment of what-ifs that could—hell, given her track record, probably *would*—happen. Her stomach knotted. She and Celeste had finally decided on a talent. And though Leo had agreed to Celeste's suggestion, it still scared the shit out of her. And even now she swallowed convulsively at just the thought of standing on this stage in front of the whole town in another few weeks and…

God, she couldn't even complete the sentence in her head. And if she couldn't do that, how in the world was she going to perform it?

Miracle. She needed an honest-to-God, water-into-wine miracle.

"I didn't think you had it in you, but brava, Leo Dennison." Jenna quietly slow-clapped as she stepped close to Leo.

Yeah, she didn't have the patience or capacity to care for Jenna's shenanigans.

"I have no clue what you're talking about, Jenna."

"Oh, come on," she purred, tilting her head. "I totally underestimated you. You should be proud of how fast you work. Snatching up the millionaire pro athlete in town? Scarred or not scarred, he's this town's top bachelor. I mean, I don't know what he sees—" she slowly scanned Leo from head to toe, disdain heavy in her curled lip "—but maybe he goes for the rumpled innkeeper look. Everyone has their kink."

Swinging on the town bitch wouldn't be good for business.

Damn that. You could put it front and center in the brochure.

God. Things were bad when even your subconscious didn't agree on pacifism.

Leo inhaled and focused on the meat of Jenna's pettiness. Apparently, her and Owen's fake relationship had already started to make the rounds. She shouldn't be shocked. This was Rose Bend, after all. But damn. That'd been quick.

"Uh, thanks?" She smiled wide, flashing all her teeth. Or baring them. "I'm not sure what the proper response to 'You're getting pity dick' is supposed to be, but I'll go with *thanks*."

"Oh, pity dick? Don't you worry, Leo. I'm sure Hallmark has a card for that, too." Flicking her thick hair over her shoulder, Jenna flashed her a pseudo-sympathetic smile.

"But the real reason I came over here was because I was concerned. You're back here looking a little green around the gills. You aren't perchance reliving The Gelding of Mercutio, are you?" Jenna tsked. "After that disaster, I can't blame you for hiding over here looking like you're about to hurl on those fashionably questionable shoes."

Leo met Jenna's mocking gaze. It matched the smirk on her pink-painted mouth. Screw her. Her Wonder Woman–themed patent leather Mary Janes were the shit.

Leo stretched up on her toes, craned her neck to the right and to the left. Giving Jenna an exaggerated wince, she shrugged. "Dang it, Jenna. I'm sorry. I've looked but I can't seem to find where I left that last fu—"

"All right, everyone," Scarlett called from the front of the stage with a single clap of her hands. "That run-through was amazing. Let's practice the Q&A round."

Jenna and Leo didn't move, continuing to stand there, glaring at each other. Part of Leo buzzed with anticipation, silently hoping the redhead would utter just one more catty comment... Since her conversation with Moe, Leo had left the inn scraped raw and spoiling for an outlet.

"Leo, Jenna."

Leo sucked in a breath and tipped her head toward Scarlett. "Coming, Scarlett."

Turning her back on Jenna, Leo joined the rest of the women, but Jenna's glower practically burned. Relief flashed across the coordinator's face—most likely thankful a catfight wouldn't be erupting on her stage. Ah, but the day was young.

"So we're not going over the actual questions that will be asked in the pageant, but I have mock ones. The purpose is to practice how the round will run and to help you be more comfortable with the Q&A. Here are a few things to keep in mind. You have two minutes to answer. Keep eye contact with the judges. Try to maintain your smile, even if you flub the question or lose your train of thought. A smile goes a long way. Listen carefully to the question and don't be afraid to take a few moments to think over your answer before delivering it. And speak clearly. Okay? Ready to go?"

A chorus of *yes*es and *let's do it*s answered Scarlett, and the coordinator beamed. Moments later she instructed them on where they would stand, how they would step forward after their names were called, the placement of the mic and where they should stop behind it. There were a lot of details, but Leo appreciated every one of them. The exacting directions calmed some of Leo's nervousness, offering her something concrete to focus on other than speaking in front of a huge crowd of people and being stared at and judged—her personal nightmare.

She tried not to fidget as Scarlett called woman after woman forward. Not knowing the questions sent her heart pounding. She couldn't prepare an answer, couldn't research, if necessary, couldn't practice what she intended to say.

She possessed no control over the situation.

"Aileen Grayson."

The pretty brunette stepped forward, gliding elegantly across the stage to the mic set near the edge. Leo kept her gaze trained on the younger woman's face, and didn't allow herself to glance below…to Aileen's still-flat belly.

"Mrs. Grayson," Scarlett said, rifling through several small white cards. Settling on one, she smiled up at her friend. "Where do you see yourself in the next five years?"

Aileen paused, obviously taking Scarlett's advice and considering her answer before speaking.

"I am a high school guidance counselor, and I love my job. There's such satisfaction in assisting kids in deciding on the paths that will set the course for their future. And also, there's joy in being their support system as they start to become who they are meant to be. And if I'm lucky, being a part of that process." Aileen paused, clasping her hands in front of her. "The school system is also where I met my beautiful wife, who is a middle school teacher. We share the same passion for education and children, so up until last year my five-year future plans centered around my wife and my career. But that vision changed when we decided to have a family."

A fine tremble shook Leo's hands, and she clutched them together, squeezing tight. She swallowed, but her throat, dry as a desert after a sandstorm, worked against her. There'd been a time when the vision of Leo's future had included a family, too. When she'd believed she could have it all.

She'd been an idealistic fool. And life had cured her of that dream really quick. Brutally quick.

"In five years I still see myself married to the most wonderful woman in the world and working as a guidance counselor, but I will also have an equally important role— as a mother. Very few people know this, but we suffered a miscarriage earlier this year. It was one of the most devastating experiences I've ever gone through. Yet, it also confirmed for me that more than anything, I wanted motherhood in my future…"

A buzzing, like a thousand swarming bees, took up residence in Leo's head. Prickles of ice and heat raced up her spine and migrated over her skin. She alternated between fighting against shivers and needing to slap out imaginary flames licking at her arms, hands and chest.

She stumbled back a step, her legs suddenly the consistency of water. Invisible fingers tore at her throat, and an inarticulate sound crawled inside her, scrambling for release. And only when two of the women peered back at her over their shoulders with worried frowns did Leo realize that sound had made a break for it.

Rhonda Gleason, a hairstylist at A Cut Above, the local salon, turned and extended a hand toward her. "Leo? Hey, you okay?"

Barely hearing the question above the ever-increasing drone, Leo nodded. She lied.

Panic closed in on her like shrink-wrap, binding tighter and tighter, suffocating her...

Scratching at the base of her throat, she battled back the black creeping into the edges of her peripheral vision.

She needed to get out of here before she crumbled. Before she fainted.

Before she broke.

"I—I'm—" She backpedaled, desperation and slick fear stealing her coherence.

"She's fine. I got her." Jenna cuffed her arm in a firm, no-nonsense grip and ushered Leo toward the side of the stage and the stairs that led to the ground.

Oh, shit.

Not her. Anyone but *her.*

In Leo's weakened state, both emotional and physical, she couldn't push the other woman away. It required all her seriously limited focus to put one foot in front of the other and not collapse in a heap right there on the stage.

As soon as she escaped the curious gazes burning into her back—as soon as she reached some semblance of safety—she'd send Jenna away. And have her panic attack in private. The last person she could afford to be weak in front of was *this* woman.

In moments shadows enveloped her, and surprisingly gentle hands cupped her shoulders and guided her down to a chair. Her breath wheezed in and out of her lungs, and those same hands shifted to the middle of her back and pushed so her head hung between her knees.

After several minutes the dizziness started to abate, and her breathing slowed until it no longer rattled in her chest or crashed in her head. She slowly straightened, her muscles pulling so tight they damn near vibrated. Closing her eyes, she dragged in a ragged lungful of air and desperately tried to relax her muscles, one at a time.

And let loose a rough laugh when her body refused to cooperate. Why would it? Why, when fear, anger and a bone-deep, howling grief saturated every tendon, vein and organ? She *hurt*. The panic didn't threaten to strangle her. The hurt did.

A loud scrape coaxed her eyes open, and Leo lifted her lashes to see Jenna pulling a chair back from a folding table and carrying it over to her. The redhead set it in front of Leo and sank down, crossing her legs and folding her hands on top of a knee, appearing for all the world as if she was attending an afternoon tea instead of sitting inside the makeshift tent set up for the festival volunteers. Jenna didn't speak, just continued to gaze at Leo, those blue eyes measuring her. No, analyzing her, peering too deep. Seeing too much.

God, Leo was too raw for this. Having Celeste, Scarlett or any of the other women witness her breakdown would've been humiliating enough, but Jenna? Leo couldn't imagine a worse scenario than Jasper Landon's daughter, of all people, having a front-row seat.

"Thanks, Jenna," Leo murmured, shoving to her feet. "I'm good—"

"When did you lose your baby?"

Leo froze, staring at Jenna. Shock pummeled her, wave after wave crashing into her until she collapsed back onto the seat beneath her. Moisture fled from her mouth, and her lips moved but no sound emerged. Not the first time. Not the second. But on the third, she managed it.

"What?" she rasped.

"Your baby. When did you have a miscarriage?"

Just that word scraped over her soul, leaving bloody gouges behind. Especially with Jenna voicing it so cavalierly, so easily, as if it didn't carry a world of desolation.

Shut up, she silently snarled.

Instead, she said, "I—I don't know what you're talking about." After so many years, denial had become second nature. It wasn't hard at all with this woman. Not when it was self-preservation.

Jenna arched a dark auburn eyebrow. "I may be a bitch, but I have eyes and a brain. When Aileen announced her pregnancy, you looked like you were about to get sick. But today, when she mentioned her miscarriage, that's when you almost fell on your ass. I can add, Leo. And all those details add up to you and trauma over losing a baby."

Terror swept her up in a whirlwind, whipping her higher and higher, even though she didn't move from the chair.

Oh, God. Oh, *God*.

No. *No*.

This was *her* secret, *her* pain. Her guilt.

She'd been hoarding it for so long that admitting it, exposing it, terrified her. It was hers, and hers alone. No one understood her loneliness, her anguish, her heartbreak.

Jenna couldn't have this. No one could ha—

"I got pregnant when I was fifteen."

Leo stiffened at the verbal bomb Jenna just detonated. She

stared at the other woman, who continued to sit as if attending a social event, posture perfect, legs crossed. The casual tone of her voice didn't alter, and she could've been talking about the weather if Leo hadn't looked into her eyes. Eyes that usually contained traces of disdain or smug derision were now darkened by shadows that couldn't hide the pain.

Pain drenched that gaze, and Leo couldn't glance away from it.

"Jenna," she whispered.

"Holden Daniels. Do you remember him?"

"Yes, I remember."

Leo did. Jenna hadn't always been a mean girl. Once upon a time, she, Sydney and Jenna had been good friends. And their freshman year of high school, Jenna had had the hugest crush on a junior, Holden Daniels, a drummer in the marching band. The three of them had plotted ways to catch his attention for Jenna, but nothing had ever come of it. And after their freshman year, Jenna had gone on vacation that summer, and when she'd returned for their sophomore year, so had the "new and unimproved" version of her.

"I never did tell you and Sydney, but we were secretly seeing each other."

"What? You never said a word."

Jenna shrugged. "He didn't want anyone to know since I was a freshman and fifteen and he was seventeen. And given who I had for a father." Her lips twisted at the corner. "Made sense at the time. Anyway, I missed a period toward the end of the school year. Since my first, I'd never missed one. Then I knew."

The shock still crackled through Leo, but it ebbed, sympathy rushing in for the young, frightened girl she must've been.

"Why didn't you say anything?" Leo murmured. "Sydney and I would've been there for you."

Part of her expected a smart-ass answer—that was what the Jenna she'd known for so long would've done. But this Jenna, with the vulnerable eyes, shook her head. And gave her truth.

"Because I was scared. I didn't even tell Holden. I think I believed if I didn't say the words aloud, then I could make it go away. Make it *un*true. So I locked myself in my room for a couple of weeks and pretended…and prayed." She gave a low, harsh chuckle. "But after a nightmare where I woke up screaming, my mother came into my room, and I broke down and confessed to her."

For the first time Jenna's expression reflected the storm in her eyes. Grief spasmed across her face, and she turned away from Leo, staring at the side of the tent. Tendons pulled taut along her neck, and her shoulders could've been carved out of marble. Leo couldn't have imagined wanting to embrace Jenna Landon, but here she was, the need to tug the woman into her arms pulsing within her.

"She immediately told my father, and I expected them to reassure me, tell me everything was going to be okay. To make me *feel* like everything was going to be okay. Because until that moment, they'd always been like that with me. Praising me. Supporting me. Bragging about me. Loving me. But that's not what happened." Another of those rough laughs, and when Jenna turned back to look at Leo, a bitter smile accompanied it. "They got rid of me. I could understand their anger. What parent wouldn't be upset if their fifteen-year-old turned up pregnant? But they were ashamed, mortified over what people would say if they discovered their daughter was knocked up. Horrified over how it would reflect on them. So they sent me away."

"Jenna, Jesus." Giving in to the need, uncaring if the other woman rejected the overture, Leo covered Jenna's clasped hands with one of hers. Jenna's hands were so cold. As if the retelling of that period in her life sapped the warmth from her body. "I'm so damn sorry."

And they'd believed she'd just gone on vacation for the summer. Instead, the girl they'd called a friend had been going through hell. How had Leo and Sydney not known?

"They intended for me to stay with my aunt in Oregon. I was there three weeks before I lost the baby. The doctor told me there wasn't anything I could've done. But I still blamed myself. Blamed my parents. Blamed Holden. Even after my parents allowed me to return home, I stayed bitter, angry. And afraid. Afraid to make another mistake since they revealed to me in the clearest and cruelest of ways that I was only good to them if I was perfect—and they were willing to rid themselves of me if I wasn't."

"We—Sydney and I—would've been there for you if you let us. We would've never judged you, abandoned you."

But Jenna shook her head again. Another spasm flashed across her features, one of such sadness, Leo squeezed Jenna's hands harder, tighter.

"I couldn't. Like I said, when I came back, I was angry. And that included with you and Sydney. I resented the both of you. Sydney with her rebellious spirit and freedom to act out, and no matter what she did, her parents didn't disown her. And you, for always being so perfect. With the perfect family and parents who adored you. Moe and Ian would've never discarded you like you were contaminated. You and Sydney were reminders of my pain, my failure."

"And so you punished us for it."

"Yes, I did," she said, no trace of apology in her voice, just acceptance. "But not just you two. I punished everyone. Myself included."

No one messes with the bitch just like they don't mess with the good girl. They leave both of us alone.

Jenna's words whispered in Leo's head, and she straightened, falling against the chair back. She and Jenna weren't so different. Not in their experiences and not in their motives. Oh, their delivery, definitely, but they both sought to hold people at a distance, to not show their secrets, their pain.

Their truth.

That same truth had been such a weight on her soul for so long, it'd become a companion, and part of her was afraid to let it go. Who would she be without it?

She had to find out.

"When I was twenty-one." Leo inhaled, held it. Then deliberately exhaled the breath, briefly closing her eyes before meeting Jenna's steady gaze. "I was twenty-one when I miscarried my baby."

God.

She'd said it.

She'd never uttered those words. Not when the doctor asked her if she understood what had happened. Not when Moe had asked her why she'd returned home from school so early. Not when the man she'd loved told her he was breaking up with her because he didn't do long-distance relationships.

"I was in love. So in love," she whispered, her heart a wild thing throwing itself against the cage of her ribs. "He was a senior and it was the beginning of my junior year when we started dating. We shared a lot of the same interests and goals, both pursuing business degrees. He was handsome, affectionate, kind, funny..."

"Was he good in bed, though?"

For the first time since she'd fallen apart on that stage, humor bubbled within her. "At twenty-one, I thought so."

"Ah." Jenna nodded. "But you've had pity dick since then."

Chuckling, Leo shook her head then tipped it back to stare at the top of the tent. As the memories rolled in like summer storm clouds, the humor faded.

"He was the love of my life—or so I believed at the time—and I couldn't see my future without him in it. So when I found out I was pregnant in April, yes, I was scared because a baby hadn't been in my immediate plans, but I wasn't upset. I'd been…happy. The baby was ours. And I loved him or her from the moment I saw the plus sign on that stick."

She paused, lowered her head and looked at Jenna again. Unlike Leo, Jenna didn't reach for her, didn't offer comforting words. But in a way, Leo needed that. If the other woman hugged her, or even covered her hand, she might not be able to finish this story. Right now she felt like an open wound, and any touch might make it worse.

Jenna sitting here, listening, was enough.

"After I went to the doctor and confirmed the pregnancy, I told my boyfriend. And he…wasn't happy. Like me, a baby wasn't in his plans, but unlike me, he had no intentions of changing them. That's when he informed me that he'd been accepted into a graduate program at another school, and he wasn't interested in a long-distance relationship. He broke up with me. Abandoned me. Devastated me. And a week later, standing in my shower, the bleeding started. By the time I made it to the hospital, I'd lost the baby."

The desolation and grief swelled within her, yawning so wide she was in danger of never pulling herself free. Though eight years old, the pain's edges remained sharp, its pricks and stabs constant reminders that people easily walked away without looking back. That Leo was expendable.

"Spontaneous abortion, the doctor called it. She said there was nothing I could've done, that it wasn't my fault. But I've lived with this guilt, this shame. Because the week after my boyfriend broke up with me, I didn't eat or sleep. I barely made it to classes. I didn't take care of myself, much less the baby. Maybe if I hadn't been so selfish, he or she would've—"

"Don't do that." Jenna leaned forward, her voice a hard snap. "Don't you dare do that to yourself. Not one more day. Not one more minute. Even the doctors can only tell us why *after* the fact. But they can't give us warning of when it's going to happen or if it's going to happen. As sad and devastating as miscarriages are, they do occur. And it's *not our fault*. And okay, let's go with your theory that the stress of the breakup caused it. Then why are you the only one carrying the blame? What about the asshole coward who broke up with you because he couldn't handle the responsibility of a child he helped create? Why doesn't he get to shoulder any of that blame? No." She paused, clenching her fingers into a fist. "Too often, we assume the shame, the guilt, because it's our bodies. But what if our bodies were protecting us from enduring something more tragic down the line? What if? What if? We'll never know. But one thing we do know. There was nothing you could do. Let that go."

Leo stared at Jenna, lips parted. She blinked.

"Who are you, and what have you done with Jenna Landon?"

A smirk curved the redhead's mouth. "Don't get too excited. As soon as we walk out of this tent, we're business as usual. This conversation didn't happen."

"So we're Mission Impossible now?" Leo snorted. "Well, before this conversation self-combusts in ten seconds, let me... Thank you. For everything."

Jenna waved a hand. "Forget about it. And I do mean—"

"Thank you, Jenna," she repeated, softer, firmer.

The other woman stilled. For a moment, just for a moment, Leo caught a hint of warmth in Jenna's blue eyes.

"You're welcome." Clearing her throat, Jenna rose, brushing imaginary lint from her skirt. "Now, I'll go back out there and tell them you were ill and had to go home. Consider it my last good deed. The very last."

She strode toward the flap and lifted it but then stopped. Glancing at Leo over her shoulder, she arched an eyebrow. "Maybe not so pity after all."

With that comment, she disappeared. Leo slowly stood, her pulse an echo in her head, a throb at the base of her throat. She knew who would walk through that opening before he appeared.

Owen's hazel eyes hit her, and the intensity rocked her. She grappled for the back of the chair, steadying herself.

She ached for him. And not for sex. Well, not *just* for sex, because that heat simmering low in her belly at just the sight of him couldn't be denied. But more than sex, she ached to inhale his scent, feel his solid body pressed against her.

It scared her how much she wanted to lean on him.

Owen closed in on her. His gold-and-green gaze roamed over her face, halting on every feature before returning to her eyes.

"How much did you overhear?" she whispered.

"Everything."

Then he yanked her into his arms, holding her so tight she could barely move.

And it was okay.

It was everything she wanted.

CHAPTER EIGHTEEN

"WHERE ARE YOUR PARENTS?" Leo stepped into the foyer of Owen's home, greeted by silence. She glanced toward the living room entrance, but no one occupied the couches and chairs, and Celeste's and Sherrod's voices didn't drift through the Victorian.

"I told them I had boyfriend duty and was helping you with festival activities. Celeste volunteered to take them on a tour of the town. I owe her. When she and Sherrod return home in New Jersey, there's going to be a car waiting for her in their driveway."

Even tired and emotionally wrung out, she laughed. "Sherrod's going to love that."

Owen flashed her a grin as he took her hand and led her up the stairs. "Even more reason to do it."

After they crested the landing, he cupped the nape of her neck and guided her down the far end of the hall. He opened the last door, and she followed him inside.

A huge, mounted television she was quite sure hadn't come with the house hung over the now-dormant fireplace. Two armchairs and an oval rug created a small sitting area. Beautiful dark gray drapes adorned tall bay windows, and filmy, off-white curtains allowed the afternoon sun to beam through. A heavy four-poster bed with silver, gray and black bedding and pillows dominated the room. More throw rugs scattered around the gleaming hardwood floor.

The effect was clean, masculine and elegant. Yet, the stacks of books on the bedside table and under it surprised her. She reined in the urge to snoop through the titles and discover exactly what Owen loved to read at the end of a long day.

Hell, she had to resist the urge to discover everything about him.

He's leaving. Don't forget that he's leaving.

Right.

She couldn't afford to get lost in the details of Owen Strafford because when he left Rose Bend—left her—those same details would torment her.

She needed to place more distance between them. As transcendent as sex with him had been, she had to find a way to pull back before she resembled that same shattered girl who'd been abandoned eight years ago.

She needed—

His fingers curled around her shoulders, gently tugging her back against him, and she willingly went. Strong arms wrapped around her, crossing under her breasts. Tipping her head back, she turned her face into his neck, resting her arms on top of his. His leather, sandalwood and musk scent teased her, enticed her to sip, to savor. To indulge in it, in him, and forget the emotional storm of earlier.

God, she was tempted. *He* was temptation...

"Tell me what you need from me." His warm breath brushed the top of her ear, and she shivered.

Be here. Be with me. Stay.

She squeezed her eyes closed as if she could block those traitorous words out of her head. Instead, she asked, "What were you doing at The Glen today?"

"Still so hard for you to ask for help," he softly admonished. If he only knew how much she was relying on him right now. "I wanted to see you. I went by the inn, and Moe told me you had pageant practice. I'm sorry, Leo. I didn't mean to violate your privacy. As soon as I heard you talking, what you were speaking about, I should've announced my presence or walked away. But...I froze. I've faced down countless defensive lines intent on knocking the shit out of me, yet I've never frozen like I did today."

"It's okay, Owen."

And it was. She probably should be upset that he'd listened to her and Jenna's conversation, but she couldn't summon the outrage. Besides, she...trusted him.

Maybe too much dark and roiling water under the bridge for her to trust him with her heart or her future, but her truth? Yes, she could place that in his hands and believe he would handle it with care and kindness.

"Are your friend and I the only ones who know about your miscarriage? You haven't told anyone else?"

Leo huffed out a low, dry chuckle. "Jenna, my friend? Our relationship is a bit more...complicated than that. But no, I've never talked about it with anyone before today. Not even with my family. I couldn't stand to see their disappointment in me. And a part of me was embarrassed. I didn't want them to know how stupid, how gullible, I'd been. Moe and Dad always called me the responsible child, the one they didn't have to worry about. Then I went to college, fell for the wrong man and got pregnant. I couldn't stand to see that hurt and disappointment in their eyes. After a while, keeping this to myself became a habit. And it became *mine*, if that makes sense."

"Yes." He dipped his head, and the scruff shadowing his jaw abraded her skin. "It does."

She murmured, "Why don't I feel lighter? In all the books and movies, whenever someone tells a secret or unburdens themselves, they feel like a weight has been lifted off their chests. It's not true. It's still as heavy. Still…there."

"Sweetheart." He pressed his lips to her temple. "You carried this for eight years. It's not going away in eight seconds or eight minutes. Those books and movies—that's fiction. Give yourself time to process, to heal." He loosened his hold to grip her elbows and turn her around to face him. Cradling her face, he tipped her head back, and his dark hair swept forward, he pressed his mouth to hers. "I always knew you were strong, with a beautiful, indomitable spirit, but today I found out just how much. Please, let me be the first to tell you this, Leo." He pulled her back into his arms, molding her body to his. Enfolded in his embrace, his head resting on top of hers, he surrounded her. Shielded her. "I'm so sorry for your loss, sweetheart."

Retelling how her first love abandoned her hadn't brought tears. Reliving the devastating loss of her baby had brought tears. But Owen's heartfelt sympathy breached the wall she'd erected around her emotions. In one second, her eyes stung, and she blinked against the tiny pricks. And in the next, tears streamed down her face, and an almost animalistic wail clawed its way out of her mouth.

Like the earth during a volcanic eruption, she cracked open, and all the pent-up anguish, grief, rage and helplessness poured out, destroying the last of her barriers.

Once unleashed, the torrent of emotion couldn't be contained. And when Owen swept her up and carried her to his bed, she wrapped her arms around his shoulders, burying her face in his neck. In this moment he was her haven, her shelter from this storm. And she clung to him.

Owen laid her down on the bed. With a quiet "Be right back," he disappeared. A soft click, the sound of running water, and he returned with a damp bath cloth. He gently wiped her face clean, taking such tender care of her that it brought fresh moisture to her eyes. Moments later he removed her clothes, leaving her only in her bra and panties, pulled one of his T-shirts over her head. Toeing off his shoes, he climbed on the bed and curled his body around hers.

"Let me take it, Leo," he said, threading his fingers through her hair. "Even if for a little while. Let me take it for you, sweetheart."

She closed her eyes.

And let him.

LEO LIFTED HER LASHES, BLINKING. Holding herself still, she took stock of her surroundings. Of the shadows that stretched across the room that wasn't her own. Of the cotton-like thickness in her head and her arid-dry mouth. The curious weight of her limbs that stretched across a very hard chest and powerful thighs.

A bare chest.

The heat emanating from the taut skin beneath her chin burned away the last foggy remnants of sleep. And with it, memories of where she was and what happened to bring her here rolled in.

Pageant practice. Breakdown. Confession to Jenna. Owen finding her and bringing her to his house. Crying in his arms.

Owen taking care of her.

She deliberately, quietly, released a sigh. In spite of feeling like she'd gone ten rounds with Laila Ali, that crying jag had been cathartic. Her first since leaving the hospital after losing her baby. She paused; how could that be? Surely, she'd... No, she hadn't given herself permission to weep. Again, punishing herself.

What she'd been doing for the past eight years.

Shoving the thought aside to examine later, when she wasn't so…raw, she shifted, and careful not to jolt Owen, eased off him. Propping herself up on an elbow, she studied the slumbering giant beside her. In sleep, he should've appeared younger, more relaxed. But he didn't. The vitality and power that radiated from him when awake didn't dissipate. It seemed to shimmer over him like a glamour. How could this sensual, stunning man ever believe something as superficial as a scar could erode his beauty, his vitality?

She lifted a hand, her finger hovering over the razor-sharp arc of his cheekbone, the patrician bridge of his nose, the carnal curves of his mouth.

Stay.

The forbidden word flickered in her head. Forbidden because she could never ask that of him. Forbidden because fear choked the plea, refusing to allow her to utter it, even if she had the courage. The past had unequivocally shown her she was dispensable and easy to walk away from. And Owen, with his larger-than-life presence and his career, would just be the latest to prove her right.

"What's that right there?"

She jerked her gaze from her blind study of his chin and met his hazel eyes. Hell. How long had he been awake?

"What's what right there?"

"That." He lifted a hand from behind his head and smoothed a thumb just under her eye. "Whatever just passed through your eyes. You were thinking something, and it hurt you."

"Owen."

"No, don't deny it." He continued to caress her, gentling her like a skittish mare. As mortifying as she found the comparison, it wasn't far off. "Tell me what's hurting you. Let me in more than here." He flattened his palm on her belly, and slid it down, granting her time to move, to push his hand away, but she didn't. And when he cupped her sex, applying a firm, delicious pressure, she hissed, the pleasure screaming up her spine and dancing along her scalp. "Let me in here." He moved his hand, placing it between her breasts...over her heart. "And here." He shifted again, cradling the side of her head. "Please. Let. Me. In."

"And what will I have left?" she whispered, fear leaving her voice the consistency of gravel.

"Me." He lifted his other hand and rubbed his thumb over her bottom lip. "If you'll let me have you, you'll have all of me."

A yearning so strong surged within her, her body almost jerked with it. She wanted what he offered, craved it. But reality stepped in swift, bodychecking her, slamming her against an invisible "wake the fuck up" force.

He's leaving.

He's not meant for you, for a life in Rose Bend.

The warnings rebounded off her skull, and she didn't try to shush them. Instead, she cranked the volume up, immersed herself in them as she carefully pushed his hands aside and straddled his abdomen. Spreading her fingers wide over his chest, she slid them up his pectoral muscles, over his shoulders, down his arms. Then she retraced her path, all the while avoiding his penetrating gaze.

"Leo."

Bracing her weight on her hands on either side of his head, she leaned over him and took his mouth. She moaned, loving the immediate tangle of his tongue, lips and teeth. He opened for her, licking the roof and sides of her mouth, before thrusting deep, branding her even as she claimed him. It was the only way she could, so she held nothing back. Not from him, not from herself.

Grasping her hips in his big hands, he inched her backward until her sex rode his cock. Her breath expelled from her lungs along with a long, needy whimper. He rocked her on his length, rolling her up so her clit bumped his plump head, then easing her back down. Flames pirouetted low in her belly, at the base of her spine. Oh, God, it was so good.

"Is this your idea, Leo? Using this pretty little body to distract me?" He bucked his hips, grinding hard against her. He reared up, crushing his mouth to hers in a hot, consuming kiss then fell back to the pillows. But his gold-and-green eyes held her captive. "I'll take what you give me, sweetheart. But don't think for a second that I'm not coming for more."

The silk-and-steel promise reverberated deep within her, and her core spasmed at the erotic threat. She sank her teeth into her bottom lip, attempting to hold back the cry climbing up her throat. But Owen pressed his thumb against her kiss-swollen flesh and tugged it free.

"Don't hold that in. Let me have it." He slid his thumb into her mouth, and she swirled her tongue around it, sucking, licking. "Please don't hold anything back from me here, in this bed."

Pulling free, he lowered his hand to her T-shirt-covered breast and circled one nipple, then the other. Pinching, rolling the tip, he elicited cry after cry from her. She twisted on top of him, each tug a direct line to her sex. The restless circling only stirred the need, the pleasure that threatened to drive her insane.

He stroked an arm up her back, cupped her shoulder and dragged her up and down to his mouth and sucked. Hard.

"Owen," she breathed. "Oh, God."

She crushed his hair between her fingers, the coolness of the strands another sensory detail that added to this feast. And she gorged. She was a wild, sexual thing that gripped his head close, pleaded that he "Please, don't stop," while she writhed on top of him.

Cool air drifted over her lower back and panties-clad ass seconds before a heated hand slid beneath her underwear and long, oh-so-gifted fingers drove into her from behind.

"Owen." She tried to temper the scream, aware of being in his home, cognizant that they might not be alone.

But *Jesus.* She squeezed her eyes shut, lips parted on that non-scream. He released her long enough to whip his shirt over her head and strip her bra off, and then he recaptured her breast. All the while, he finger-fucked her mindless.

"Wait. Wait." She palmed his face and levered back and up. Cool air kissed her wet breasts, and she groaned, her nipples tingling at the additional caress.

Scrambling back between his spread thighs, she stripped off her panties, tossing them over the side of the bed. But she didn't climb on top of him. Instead, she rose to her knees, curling her fingers beneath the waistband of his black, thin sweatpants. Without her coaxing, he lifted his hips and let her tug the pants down, freeing his dick.

Damn. Lust throbbed, hot and heavy in her veins, pooling between her thighs, readying her for this long, thick, perfect cock inside her.

"You're beautiful," she whispered, running a fingertip from the flared head down the wide length to the base surrounded by wiry hair.

Tracing the damp slit at the crest, she collected the small bead of moisture and curled her tongue around her finger, sucking it off. Salty, earthy musk. Him.

"Goddamn, sweetheart." His hips bucked, hands fisting the dark gray sheets.

His reaction—clenched teeth, straining body, quivering muscles—emboldened her, and she bent over him, parting her lips wide and sucking him deep.

"Fuck."

The quiet roar filled her ears, and she hummed in satisfaction.

"Yes, dammit. Yes," he hissed, tangling his fingers in her hair, holding her steady as he thrust into her mouth, taking it as he'd taken her sex the previous night.

She wrapped her hand around the bottom half of him, pumping his length, her lips bumping into her fingers, before he moved her hand.

"Trust me," he ground out.

Then he proceeded to claim her mouth, her throat, with a careful ferocity that shook and aroused her. And all the while, he praised her for trusting him, for giving him this, for her "fuckable mouth." And damn if that didn't have her silently preening even as another rush of moisture coated her thighs.

"That's it, sweetheart." Rolling up in a half crunch, he grasped her under her arms and hauled her back on top of him, crashing his mouth to hers, tongue mimicking his cock. "I'm right on the edge, but I want to come home, sweetheart." He rocked his hips, sliding his dick through her folds, letting her know what he considered *home*.

"Let me come home."

He didn't need to ask her twice.

Lifting on her knees, she gripped the base of his erection, held it at her entrance…and slowly slid down.

Their twin groans filled the room, and at this moment, as he filled her and filled her, she couldn't spare a thought for keeping quiet. Not when she couldn't breathe for the exquisite pressure that teetered on pleasure and pain, a beautiful blending of both.

No one had ever taken her so completely. Branded her so permanently. How would she survive this...this intimate bonding with another person? Tears pricked her eyes, and she lowered her lashes, hiding from him.

Too bad she couldn't hide from herself as easily.

She pulsed her hips, working and working until not one inch of him remained outside her. Shivers beset her, and she sank her nails into his dense chest muscle. He rubbed his hands up and down her back, murmuring low, soothing sounds, praising her.

"Easy, sweetheart. Shh. Whenever you're ready."

Ready? She was ready over a year ago when she saw him in that bar. And she hadn't stopped being *ready* since.

She rose off him, feminine muscles dragging over his thick stalk. Panting, she hovered over him, only the head still lodged in her sex, before sinking back down.

"Wait." He clutched her hips, holding her down so she couldn't move. "Open your eyes. You're letting me have this. Then let me have it. Look at me, Leo."

The softness in his order didn't hide the steel in it. And she obeyed, gazing into his gleaming eyes.

"That's what I want. What we both need." He tunneled his fingers through her hair, his thumb sweeping over her cheekbone. "What you're afraid to give us."

Before she could say anything—or not say anything— he pulled her down and claimed her mouth.

That kiss threw TNT into an already burning fire. Her control became nonexistent, her inhibitions a myth. She rode him, fucked him. And he met every buck and circle of her hips with a thrust and dirty grind that had her whimpering and shaking like a rain-battered leaf in a storm.

He was everywhere on her. His mouth on her breasts. His hands in her hair, on her ass, urging her on. His teeth scraping her neck. It was a rampage of sex, of pleasure, and she chased it like a wild creature set free for the first time.

And when he slid a hand between them, strumming the tight bundle of nerves at the top of her sex, she surrendered to that riot of sensations, of rapture, throwing herself into it with no reservations, no cares.

So this was true freedom.

Even knowing it would come with a high price, she let go.

CHAPTER NINETEEN

"Isn't this a cute little coffee shop," Owen's mother said as they approached the store with Mimi's Café scrawled across the black-and-gold awning in elegant script.

Owen didn't reply, too busy controlling his breathing. The air scraped his lungs with each inhale, and the scars on his cheek burned like a red-hot brand. He lifted his arm, but at the last instant caught himself and lowered it. Instead of dragging his hair forward to cover the marks, he reached for the handle on the door and pulled it open.

I can do this. No more hiding.

"Leo and Celeste rave so much about this place, I thought we should try it before you and Dad leave tomorrow."

The scent of freshly brewed coffee, baked goods and sugar hit him as soon as he stepped inside the packed café. Damn. He'd missed these scents. Before the accident, he used to don a baseball cap and sunglasses and walk to his favorite coffee shop for a grande brew of the day and a blueberry scone. The employees there recognized him, but they treated him like all the other regulars. Nostalgia for that part of his old life threatened to rock him on his heels. In his bitterness and anger this past year, he'd forgotten about those good, sweet moments of his life.

"Well, thank you for bringing me here. This is such a treat, having you to myself, even for coffee." His mother smiled, patting his arm. "Not that I'm complaining. I adore

Leo. And I've enjoyed getting to know her over the past week."

"Thanks, Mom."

He fought to keep his hands in the front pockets of his jeans and not fidget. His pulse thundered in his ears and the skin on his neck and face seemed besieged by fire ants. By sheer stubbornness and will, he kept his chin kicked up and shoulders back.

If he closed his eyes, he could feel the phantom caress of Leo's lips and the graze of her teeth on his scars, loving them, worshipping them. Telling him, without words, that she found him beautiful. That he had nothing to be ashamed of.

We don't know strangers. That is, if you give us half a chance. You should give us half a chance, Mr. Strafford. I think we might surprise you.

Eva Wright's words rang in his head, and he lifted his lashes. Glanced around. Surprise winged through him. Yes, the café was packed, but most of the customers paid attention to either their drinks and baked goods or the company with them. And those whose eyes he did catch just smiled instead of stared.

No horror.

No pity.

No flashing cameras or indiscreet cell phones.

The vise cinching his rib cage loosened, and he breathed deep.

"Owen?" His mom set a hand on his arm. "It's our turn to order. Are you okay?" She peered up at him.

He nodded. "I'm fine. Just lost in thought for a moment."

Shifting forward, they approached the counter, and a lovely young woman with shoulder-length brown curls and freckles sprinkled across her light brown skin greeted them.

"Welcome to Mimi's Café, folks. I'm the owner, Autumn Bryant." She smiled. "You, of course, need no introduction. It's nice to meet you, Owen Strafford. And you're a new face in town," she said, turning to Charlene. "It's a pleasure to meet you, ma'am." Autumn stretched her hand across the counter toward his mother.

"You, too." Charlene glanced at him, pleasure brightening her hazel eyes. "I'm Owen's mother, Charlene Strafford. You have a wonderful café."

"Thank you so much. What can I get you two?"

After placing their order—a caramel latte for his mother, a regular coffee for him and scones for both of them—and collecting it, Owen led Charlene back out into the mid-morning sunshine to the town square. They found an empty bench close to the gazebo, sat and drank and ate in companionable silence.

Owen studied his mom and tried to pinpoint a time when he'd seen her like this…relaxed. Regardless of his father's reasons for descending on him with the wrath of God and football, his mother had seemed to enjoy her time in Rose Bend and benefit from it. She'd smiled and laughed more, teased more. And she'd taken to Leo and Celeste like old friends. Especially Leo. She hadn't even batted an eye when his "girlfriend" had joined them for breakfast the morning after he'd brought her home with him from pageant practice.

And Leo had taken his mother under her wing, introduced her to the rest of the Dennison clan. Moe and Charlene had hit it off like two girls at sleepaway camp. Charlene had driven over to Kinsale Inn for morning coffee with Moe and Leo and even helped cook Sunday dinner. Miraculously, she hadn't allowed his father's more somber and sour mood to affect her.

If for no other reason than to witness his mother's brief

independence and happiness, Owen was glad his parents had shown up unannounced on his doorstep.

"I've missed you, Owen."

He paused, the cardboard cup halfway to his mouth.

She chuckled, shaking her head. "The fact that you look so shocked speaks volumes. Is it so surprising that I would miss you?"

"No," he said cautiously, lowering his coffee cup to the bench seat. "It is surprising that you'd tell me. We're not exactly the most demonstrative of families."

"No, I guess we're not." She clasped her cup between her palms but didn't lift it to her mouth.

Several long moments passed with only the sound of happy chatter on Main Street, lazy traffic and the chirp of birds filling them. He'd lifted his coffee again, believing their conversation had ended, when she spoke again.

"I've always worried about you, you know."

He threw her a sharp glance, disbelief careening through him. "What?"

"I have." She sighed, dipping her head and staring down at her lap. "Your father can be…intense. Actually, it was one of the things that attracted me to him. All that passionate focus concentrated on me? It was breathtaking, and it made me feel so important, so vital, to him." She shook her head, lifting it and looking at him again. A wistful half smile quirked a corner of her mouth. "I feel like I'm making excuses for him. Like I've constantly done. Especially when it comes to you."

"Mom, I don't know what you're talking about."

"Don't you?" That smile didn't fade. If anything, the melancholy behind it deepened. "You have the most sensitive heart, Owen. You always have. Did you know it surprised me when you fell in love with football? I thought you were going to be some kind of artist or writer." Both of his eyebrows winged toward his forehead, and she laughed. The heaviness didn't dissipate, but the delight was genuine. "From the time you were very little, you thumbed through books. Even before you could read them. And you adored music. You would sing and dance with me in the kitchen while I cooked. Those are some of my most precious memories. And though you seemed to put those down after you discovered football, I only mourned them a little. Because you loved football. It was your passion, and I just wanted you to be happy. And I prayed you didn't lose your compassion and sensitivity."

Owen couldn't move, captivated by the picture she painted of them reading and dancing together. He didn't remember any of it, but damn, he wanted to. Wanted to recall a time when he and his mother had laughed together instead of behaving like awkward acquaintances biding their time before they could go to their separate corners.

When had that happened?

How sad was it that he didn't recollect a time when it *wasn't* like that?

"But I should've done more. What's the saying? 'Pray to God, but row to shore'? Your father loves you. I've never doubted that. But his way of showing it—he could only give you what he had. His father was a hard man, and *I love you* was shown with food on the table and clothes on your back, not the words. Troy's way of exhibiting his love was pushing you, helping you be the best, making sure you achieved your goals and dreams. But somewhere along the line, your dreams became entangled with his identity and ego. For so long he was your coach, your adviser, your trainer. And when you left for college and started pulling away, didn't need his advice as much, he suddenly didn't know who he was, because he'd been so tangled up in you."

"But you just said it, Mom," he said, frustration simmering inside him. Dragging his fingers through his hair, he pulled tight until pinpricks of pain scattered across his scalp. Dropping his arm, he huffed out a hard laugh. "He was my coach, adviser and trainer. But I needed a father. And I needed a mother, not a cheerleader or a spectator."

Silence pounded between them at his outburst. His heart beat in time with that deafening pulse, and he stared at his mother, horrified at the words he'd allowed to escape.

Apologize, asshole.

And he parted his lips to do just that, but something held him back. Because the time for truth between them had arrived. They'd lived in a cocoon of silence for so long that they'd perfected it, fine-tuned it into an art form. If they were to have a real relationship, they had to be honest with one another.

"You're right."

He blinked. Yeah, he hadn't been expecting that. More silence, maybe. Even more excuses for his father. But not this quick capitulation.

"When we brought you into this world, we had certain obligations toward you, and they weren't to ensure you made it to championship games or to go pro. They were to parent you, teach you how to be a good man, a man who cares for and serves his community. A man who respects others but is also concerned with how he represents himself in this world. You are this man, but sometimes I can't help but think you've become him despite us rather than because of us. We did our best by you, Owen. Our very best, but I won't make excuses. We fell down on the job in other areas, too."

She reached for him, her fingers hovering over the scar that ran the length of his face. Moisture glittered in her eyes, highlighting the love there. A week, hell, a day ago, Owen would've pulled away from her, rejected her. But today he circled her wrist and pressed her palm to his marred cheek.

A tremulous breath escaped her.

"You are so much more than how far you can throw a ball or how fast you can run down a field. You're the curious little boy who'd lug books around and later hid them, thinking no one saw. You're the boy who danced to Phil Collins in the kitchen and later pretended he didn't like opera when he secretly loved it. We should've honored *all* of you, Owen. All the beautiful parts of you. And you *are* beautiful." She brushed her thumb over his scar. "Forgive me for the times I failed to tell you that. For the times I didn't celebrate the whole man and only focused on one part of him."

Love welled up in him, filling his chest. When he'd invited his mother for coffee this morning, he hadn't expected this. Hadn't expected to bridge a divide that he'd believed almost too impossible to cross.

Standing, he pulled his mother to her feet and into a tight embrace. Closing his eyes, he became that boy she described. The one who'd loved spending time with his mom. And at the same time, he was the man who couldn't wait to discover the people they'd become.

"I love you, Mom. And yeah, I forgive you."

She held on to him, and how long they stood there, he didn't know. Didn't care. They were making up for years of missed hugs with this one.

Finally, she drew back, and he lowered his arms. They

sat back down on the bench, picking up their now-cooler coffee, his mother dabbing at her eyes with her napkin.

"I forgot. There's another mark of a good man," she said, clearing her throat.

He arched his brow. "Yeah?"

She nodded.

"A good man loves his mother."

She smiled, and Owen broke out in a wide grin.

A second later their laughter rang out across the town square.

OWEN PARKED HIS SUV behind his parents' car in his driveway, immediately noticing the additional vehicle at the curb.

So did his mother.

"Leo's here," she said, the delight obvious in her voice. "She must be here for an early practice with Celeste. Moe mentioned they have a couple driving in from Boston to tour Kinsale Inn for their wedding this afternoon. How exciting for them!"

Owen smirked, shaking his head as he stepped out of the Range Rover and rounded the hood to help his mother out. She knew Leo's schedule better than he did.

"I like her for you."

He shut the passenger door behind her. "I'm sorry?"

"Leo," she said, tilting her head and looking toward the house. "I like her for you. That first night she championed you. Most new girlfriends would be more concerned with ingratiating themselves with their boyfriend's parents, but she jumped to your defense, not caring if she alienated your father or me." His mother nodded, a warm smile curving her mouth. "Oh, yes. I like her for you."

He did, too.

God, did he.

That night she'd spent with him, he'd come so close to begging Leo to give him all of her—not just her body, but her beautiful, bruised heart. But he'd seen the fear, the doubt in her eyes. Heard the hesitation in her voice. Felt the tension in her body as she straddled him.

She wasn't ready.

Leo might have shared with him one of the most traumatic periods of her life, but she'd erected a roadblock that she wasn't ready to tear down yet. A roadblock that not only kept him out but also barricaded her behind it. And Owen had to decide if he was okay with that. If he could settle for parts of her.

The answer was simple.

No.

Not when he'd had glimpses of the glorious whole of her.

The loving, self-sacrificing daughter and sister. The fierce warrior who championed those she cared about. The loyal friend. The confident, brilliant businesswoman. The vulnerable yet brave soul who didn't know the meaning of surrender. The passionate, uninhibited lover.

How could he be content with fragments of this woman when he'd touched, tasted, seen all of her? As if Icarus would be satisfied with just seeing the sun instead of flying close to its beauty. Even if it meant tumbling to his doom.

Because Owen had become Icarus, and Leo was his sun.

But even knowing that falling in love with her might mean his heart's imminent breaking, he still couldn't change it. Wouldn't change it.

He loved Leontyne Dennison.

And he'd never been more terrified.

"Owen, I'd like a word with you."

He glanced toward the front porch where his father

stood, hands in the front pockets of his slacks, a frown on his brow. The usual.

"Sure, Dad." Turning to his mother, Owen brushed a kiss over her cheek. "I'll see you inside."

"Okay, Owen." She grasped his hand, squeezing it.

Then, as she passed his father, she murmured something too low for Owen to catch, but his father's lips flattened before he gave her an abrupt nod.

Sighing, Owen followed his mother, but paused on the porch instead of going inside the house. He propped a shoulder against the railing, crossing his arms over his chest. The relaxed, peaceful calm that had filled him at the square with his mother evaporated, leaving a fine tension. The norm for all his interactions with his father. But it'd become more contentious in the past year and a half since his father was injured on his job and forced into retirement. Owen had been helping out his parents with their bills; it'd been his honor, his duty as a son. But every deposit into his parents' account seemed to be a personal affront to his father's pride.

He was damned if he did... Well, he was just damned.

"We're leaving tomorrow," his father began when Owen remained silent. "And you and I haven't had a chance to sit down and discuss your plans regarding returning to football."

Honestly, Owen was surprised his father had held out so long before cornering him. His mother probably had more to do with that than any consideration Troy might have for Owen's request for him to let it go.

"Nothing's changed since you arrived, Dad. I'm still considering my options and I haven't made any firm decisions."

"Owen." His father stalked a couple of steps across the porch before pivoting and facing Owen again. He rubbed a hand over the nape of his neck before heavily dropping his arm down to his side. "I'm trying to understand, son. I really am, but I don't know what you're doing. Other than throwing away this last chance at your career. The draft has already passed. You're not a dumb man, and even if you didn't know what it meant, I'm sure that agent of yours has explained it to you. Teams have chosen players—younger, uninjured players who they don't have to pay as much as you. Quarterbacks, Owen. Did you know the Knights chose that kid from Alabama for your position? All because you've sat around with your thumb up your ass without making a decision that should be a no-brainer."

Well, this discussion had deteriorated quickly.

Owen pushed off the railing and looked at his father. Really looked at him, for the first time in years.

He noted the faint shadows and bags underneath his eyes. The deep grooves bracketing his mouth. More lines etched his forehead and fine, white ones fanned out from the corners of his eyes. Not laugh lines. Because he had the sense his father didn't do a lot of laughing. Didn't enjoy life so much.

What had happened to make him this frustrated, bitter man? One who should be enjoying this stage of his life with his wife, but was instead a man who seemed so... angry with the world.

Owen shook his head. Those were questions he couldn't answer, and even more, as much as he loved his father, a weight he couldn't bear. Being responsible for someone's happiness... That was an unfair burden to ask of anyone. Even for a parent.

Especially for a parent.

"I have spoken with Byron." Damn right he had. And though his agent had apologized for talking about Owen's business affairs with Troy—he'd believed Troy had already known—Owen had let him know in no uncertain terms, that shit could not happen again. If he couldn't trust his agent, what was the point in having one? "And I'm well aware of my options if I decide to come out of retirement. Yes, the draft has passed, and the Knights took a new quarterback. But that doesn't mean my window of opportunity has closed. Since my contract with them was ending at the time of the accident and I was about to be a free agent, they aren't my only choice. There are other teams besides the Knights, Dad. But this is all what-ifs we're talking right now. I don't know what my future looks like. If it will include football or not. Like I said, I have options."

"Options." His father scoffed, slicing a hand through the air. "You said that nonsense at the table the first night we arrived. And that's what it is. Nonsense. Son, you went to college to play ball. You might've stayed all four years instead of entering the draft your sophomore year just to spite me, but that degree was a side benefit. Let's not pretend college wasn't just a stepping stone to the NFL. You are. A. Football. Player. It's all you've been. All you've wanted. Now, stop being a damn coward and go after it."

His father's words pummeled him, verbal fists. Owen remained on his feet, standing steady, but inside... Inside he reeled. Why, he didn't know. This wasn't the first time he'd heard this tirade or a variation of it. Yet...it fucking hurt.

It fucking hurt to hear that his father thought he was a coward.

"Every decision in my life hasn't been about you or to spite you, Dad," he said, voice quiet though pain and anger pulsed inside him like another heartbeat. "I stopped talking as much football with you in college because your advice was contradicting the coaches' and I didn't need that in my ear. It was for the good of the team, my relationship with my coaches and for myself. I decided not to enter the draft early because there are too many stories of football players who are injured or go bankrupt and have nothing to fall back on. I didn't want to be another statistic. I chose my agent on my own because I knew what I wanted, who would be the best for my career, and it was ultimately my decision. Just like this one will be about me and my life and what I need for myself."

"Is this about that girl in there?" Troy jerked a thumb over his shoulder. "Are you actually considering throwing away this chance over her? What are you going to do? Set up a home in this town? Maybe be an assistant coach on the high school football team? Wither away?" His lip curled in a sneer. "Do you seriously believe that story of her not knowing who you were when you met? And are you buying right now that she would be satisfied with a washed-up football player? C'mon, son. Get your head out! You can't throw away your future over some woman you've known five min—"

"Don't say another word, Dad." He took a step toward his father, and then another one. Fury, hard and bright, lodged in his sternum, burning a hole through him. "You want to come at me, call me a coward or whatever name you got in your pocket, do it. But you leave Leo out of this. She has nothing to do with my decision, and she would never make me choose. I might have known her for *five minutes*, but she supports me whether I decide to return to the game or become a businessman or a coach or a fucking street sweeper. As long as I'm happy. In *five minutes*, she sees more in me than you have in thirty years. You're right, Dad. I'm a football player. But that's not *all* I am."

What could've been pain or regret flickered across his father's face. But it was there and gone, replaced by his customary frown.

"Owen, I didn't mean—"

"Yes, you did," Owen murmured. "I'm nothing without my arm. Remember that? I do. It's funny how you might've given me a ton of compliments through the years—I can't say for sure because I really can't recall them. But that? I remember it clearly. And I've spent the years since trying to prove you wrong. But I'm tired, Dad. I don't have a damn thing left to prove. I'm already good enough. It's not my fault if you can't see it."

This time, when the emotion etched itself in his father's expression, Owen had no trouble deciphering it. Hurt. Sadness. Decades of it.

"Son, I—" His father stared at him, a whole conversation in his eyes. He shook his head. "I'm sorry," he whispered.

"Me, too."

Owen strode forward, his intention to pass by his father and go into the house, leaving the ugliness, the brokenness, behind once and for all. But he didn't.

He stopped next to his father, shoulder touching shoulder.

"I love you, Dad."

Owen didn't wait for his father's response. Didn't need one. That was more for himself than for his dad. And as he pulled open the storm door and entered the house, he paused in the foyer. Waited for the easing of that burden. But like Leo had mentioned that night a week ago, the miraculous lifting of the weight didn't occur. This wound with his father burrowed too deep, and the scar—much older than the ones on his face and body—hadn't fully healed. Only time could do that.

But this was a start.

He inhaled, and after a long moment, released it.

Where was Sherrod? Maybe he'd go for a run with him. God knows he could burn off some—

Loud cackles and hoots of laughter—good God, was that a fiddle?—grabbed his attention. What the hell?

He strode down the hall toward the rowdy and joyous sounds. After his conversation with his father, he needed joyous. He wanted to be a part of whatever was going on in his study.

His steps slowed as he neared the doorway, catching sight of the room. As she did every time Leo came over to practice, Celeste had transformed his perfectly respectable man cave into a makeshift dance studio. All the furniture hugged the walls, and from somewhere—he didn't ask— she had unearthed several tall mirrors and lined them up like toy soldiers. Usually, Celeste used his stereo system, but today she'd pulled out her violin and currently played an Irish-sounding tune.

Hence, the fiddle.

But neither the rearranged furniture nor the improvised wall of mirrors snagged his attention. Not even the beautiful woman killing it on the violin could accomplish that feat. No, that honor belonged to the gorgeous brunette in the center of the room, leaping, kicking and spinning in an Irish step dance with a breathtaking smile lighting her face. Hands on hips, upper body straight and feet flying. Breathtaking, hell. He needed breath for that.

For just a second he noted his mother and Sherrod clapping and laughing, rooting her on. But he could only spare those few seconds. His captivated stare jerked back to Leo.

Stunning as the sun Leo.

Bright as a flame Leo.

Courageous as a lion Leo.

So fucking brave.

Taking on a new business venture at the inn. Facing her

fears with this pageant. Telling Jenna and then him the truth about her baby.

And here he stood, watching from the sidelines. Again. Afraid to make a decision about a future he craved. Tasted. Dreamed about. All because he feared the what-ifs.

What if his old team didn't want him anymore?

What if he could no longer play at the same level?

What if he really was washed-up?

What if… What if… What if…

What if his coming to Rose Bend had led him to this moment right here? Standing here, in love with an amazing woman whose purpose was to inspire him to pursue his dreams, to be the best man he could be?

Yeah, what if…

Only God knew the answers, and Owen had no chance of ever finding out if he couldn't take the risk. Couldn't take the leap.

Couldn't be brave.

That lightening of his soul that he'd been waiting on back in the foyer decided to show up. And for the first time in over a year, he didn't just inhale a deep, cleansing breath. He inhaled hope.

He'd made his decision.

He was going back to football.

Whether that was with the Knights or with another team, he didn't know.

Didn't matter. He was returning to the game he loved.

But as his hungry gaze roamed over Leo as she threw back her head, laughter ringing above the violin's tune, he couldn't prevent the shaft of fear piercing his chest.

Would returning to the game he loved cost him the woman he loved?

CHAPTER TWENTY

"Leo, get over here." Sherrod waved her over from his position in front of the grill. He lifted the black hood. "You're the judge. Now, I know you and my wife have this girlmance going on, but I'm asking you to be fair."

Leo groaned, going for a melodramatic swoon, draping herself over the arm of the lounge chair behind Owen's house. All she wanted was to relax and enjoy the pitcher of strawberry margaritas on the small table beside her while waiting on her food to be done. After all, Owen had declared this dinner to be in her honor. The couple who'd traveled up from Boston a week ago had decided to book Kinsale Inn for their wedding in the fall. Excitement and fierce satisfaction soared inside her just thinking about it. So yes, she wanted to celebrate and relax.

Not referee The Next Great Barbecue-Off between Sherrod and Celeste.

"Shouldn't I recuse myself? I mean, Celeste did teach me how to spin without tripping over the hem of a gown."

Sherrod scowled at her, jabbing some kind of paintbrush utensil at her.

"And I saved your ass by being a judge in the chili contest. Who are you more beholden to?"

Leo leaned farther over the arm of the lounge chair to glance around Sherrod and catch Celeste's gaze. "Did he really just trot out *beholden*?"

"Sure did. I'm chalking it up to desperation."

"Just get over here and judge my meat." When Celeste and Leo broke out in snickers, he glared back and forth between them. "And you say I have the mind of a twelve-year-old boy."

Groaning, Leo shoved to her feet and stretched, scanning the wide backyard with its *still*-creepy playset, lush trees and the tire swing that would forever hold a special place in her heart. A golden warmth flooded her, and she couldn't stop the smile that curved her lips. She'd never considered herself a sentimental person, but this place... It was special.

Shaking her head, she switched her attention back to Sherrod.

"Pass." She held up a hand, moving toward the back door. "My mother didn't raise fools. And if she did, it's my brothers. I'm not getting involved in that. I'm going to get glasses for the margaritas."

She twirled a finger toward the grill, before pulling the door open and stepping into the small morning room that led to the kitchen. Still smiling at the good-natured squabbling, she opened the cabinet to grab glasses for the margaritas. After setting two on the counter, she reached for two more when Owen's deep voice echoed from the direction of the hallway.

He'd disappeared inside a couple of minutes earlier on a phone call. She shrugged a shoulder. Though she had six brothers and sisters and eavesdropping had become a tool of survival in her childhood, she'd abandoned the habit in adulthood. He'd finish up the call and return soon. Rising on tiptoe, she grasped the glass...

"...do they want to meet? Did they give us a date?" A pause. "A month from now? Okay, that's doable."

Slowly, she lowered back to the floor. They? A month from now?

Forgetting her rule about eavesdropping, she shifted away from the cabinets and edged closer to the kitchen entrance.

"Byron, stop it. I'm not worried about the quarterback they just drafted." Another pause. "Yeah, I've been working out, but we both know there's a difference between lifting weights and running and being football ready."

Her stomach plunged, her heart nose-diving right after it. She stumbled, her hip striking the edge of the oak island, but she barely felt the impact or the ache. Her pulse drummed in her head, but it couldn't drown out Owen's voice.

God, she wished it could.

"We'll talk to the Knights first. By that time it'll be June and we'll know if there are any teams interested enough to invite me for workouts." Pause. "Sounds good. Hit me back with firm dates. Later."

She blankly stared at the entrance to the kitchen as if gazing into the mouth of a black hole.

He was leaving.

She should've known. Should've picked up on the tiny changes in him. In his schedule. In the past week since his parents had left town, if he hadn't been with her, he'd been at the high school football field or in his gym.

Now she realized why.

Owen was leaving Rose Bend.

Leaving her.

She'd known his stay in Rose Bend was only temporary. Known he had zero intentions of staying here. Known that if she hadn't heeded her rules, she would inevitably end up here, hurt, on the verge of screaming...

But apparently recognizing facts didn't prevent her heart from feeling as if it were shattering into so many pieces it should be littering the floor mat.

When did he plan on telling her? If she hadn't overheard this conversation, when would he have informed her of his decision? Didn't she deserve that? Or had she just been a fling all along? Small-town ass to pass the time while he convalesced in—

Stop it.

She knew better. Knew *him* better. He wasn't her old boyfriends, and she refused to shuttle their faults onto him.

Yet, it changed nothing. He was still...

Owen appeared in the kitchen doorway. His hazel eyes connected with hers.

"You're leaving."

She tossed the flat, hoarse statement between them, and it sat there, a fragile explosive capable of blowing her heart to ash. This was what she'd tried to avoid. Why she'd tried to keep her distance. This bright, red-hot pain in her chest that blared "I told you so" with each rapid beat.

His gaze softened as he moved toward her, his hand outstretched. More than anything, she longed to place her palm in his, watch it enfold hers just as his body had wrapped around hers after they made love—

Sex. Fucking.

Not made love.

Because of all the mistakes and missteps she'd made since meeting Owen Strafford again, she could not have been so foolish as to have fallen in love with him.

She curled her fingers around the edge of the island, clutching it as if it were her one lifeline.

Owen drew to a halt, his gaze dropping to her grip on the wood before lifting to her face.

"Leo," he murmured.

"You're leaving," she repeated.

Because if she said it often enough, drilled it into her head, her heart would get on board and stop this fucking bleeding thing. He'd never planned on staying; he'd never lied about that. So it was up to her to cauterize the wound.

"I'm leaving," he said softly. "I didn't want you to find out like that." He waved a hand behind him toward the hall. "I intended to tell you myself once all the details were hammered out."

"How long have you known?"

He studied her, tilting his head to the side. She hated herself for wanting to cross the floor and thread her fingers through his hair, sweep the strands away from his face.

Hated herself for still wanting him.

"I decided a week ago to come out of retirement. But I didn't tell my agent until a couple of days ago. I haven't told anyone but him. And now you."

Disbelief winged through her, and she glanced over her shoulder toward the windows and the side patio beyond them where Celeste and Sherrod still argued.

"No, not even Sherrod knows. I planned on you being the first person I told."

She closed her eyes. But she couldn't block out his voice, or the news he delivered. Couldn't block out the fear that ate at her like acid. What she'd been most afraid of was coming to pass. When he left, he would only leave pieces of her behind.

All because she'd failed to follow her own damn rules. Again.

"Leo, look at me. Please."

She lifted her lashes and met the sadness in his eyes.

And fuck if that didn't just drive the knife deeper. Twisting it harder.

"I want to touch you," he said.

"No." She shook her head for added emphasis.

And she caught the flash of pain in his gaze, but she couldn't take it back. She was fighting for survival here. Fighting for those pieces.

She drew in a breath. Exhaled it.

"When are you leaving for—" She huffed out an arid dry laugh. "Where are you going?"

"I'm leaving for New York in a week," he said. "I'll spend a month there training and conditioning to get ready for workouts come June. And if I'm lucky, training camps."

A month in New York before he flew off to...wherever. But wherever wouldn't be Rose Bend. A ripple of grief passed through her, and she clutched the island harder. Willed her legs not to let her down.

"I'm happy for you, Owen," she murmured. "I really am. It's what you wanted, and you deserve this chance."

"You mean that, don't you, Leo?"

"Of course I do." And she did. No matter how much she would miss him, she could never begrudge him this opportunity to reclaim his career. "I may not know shit about football, but apparently a lot of people seem to think you're great at it. So there's nothing more I want for you than to go be great. You are meant for it."

"And us?" He folded his arms across his chest, that too-piercing gaze fixed on her when all she wanted to do was hide from it. "What are we meant for?"

Her chin jerked back, his question a verbal tap. "What are you talking about?"

"Just what I said."

"Owen." She thrust her hands in her hair, dragging the

strands away from her face. "You just told me you're leaving Rose Bend. You'll be gone for a month in New York *at least* before you're off to God knows where." She dropped her arms to her sides, shaking her head. "Besides, we never established an *us*, a *we*. If anything, we're friends who were fu—"

"Don't do that, Leo," he snapped. He didn't move, but somehow he seemed to loom larger, taller. It could've been the anger radiating off him in waves. "Find another excuse to blow us up, but don't you dare relegate us to fuck buddies. We're more than that. Much more than that, and you know it. Otherwise, you wouldn't be trying so goddamn desperately to minimize it." He shifted forward, uncrossing his arms and flattening a palm on the counter next to him. "Now, tell me the real reason you're panicking. Because you are, sweetheart. I can damn near hear your heart fighting in your chest."

She stared at him, her fingers fisted at her sides. What did he want her to say? Yes, calling them friends with benefits had been a low blow, but not too far off the mark. They hadn't made commitments to one another. How could they? He'd made no bones about not remaining in Rose Bend and she… Well, no man had ever had staying power with her, so why should Owen be any different?

And it was *okay*. Dammit, it was.

But why did he want his pound of flesh? Why was she willing to give it to him?

"We never made commitments to each other," she said.

"What are we, in high school?" he scoffed. "I thought me holding you in my bed while you cried, and then you riding my dick into exhaustion would've been a clue about our commitment."

Her cheeks flamed. And her sex swelled, ached.

She glanced away from him.

"That was just sex."

"Look at me, Leo," he ordered once more. And like before, she acquiesced. Met the glittering hardness in his hazel eyes. "Now, look at me while you say that lie again."

She couldn't. Her lips moved, but the words dried up on her tongue. Hell, they'd tasted like dirty ash when she'd uttered them.

"Owen," she softly pleaded, out of excuses, out of verbal darts wrapped in deceptions. "What are you doing? Let it go."

"Not until you throw everything you got at me. Keep going, Leo. You're not done yet."

God, she was tired. She just wanted to go home and lick her wounds. Why wouldn't he let her do that?

"Owen, I don't know what you want me to say," she said, unable to keep the weariness from her voice. "You're going back to New York—"

"It's less than three hours away."

"For now," she ground out. "You don't know where you'll end up. It could be across the country."

"So?"

"So?" She shook her head, throwing up her hands. "So, long-distance relationships don't work."

"Is that another one of your rules, Leo? *Fuck*." He barked a sharp laugh, fisting his hair and turning away from her. A muscle ticked along his jaw, and she stared at it, inordinately fascinated. "We work, sweetheart. If you'd give us half a chance outside that box you're determined to fit your life into—fit everyone into—you'd see that."

"Owen," she whispered.

"Do you need me to say I love you? Because I do. But looking at you, seeing that panic—no, worse, that resignation in your eyes—there's no point in me telling you. You've made up your mind that we're over before we ever had a chance to really begin."

"That's not true." She held out her hand in the age-old sign of stop. "You can't... You don't..."

"I can't love you? I can't love a woman who not only loves her family but would sacrifice for them? A woman whose heart is so huge she's earned the respect of her whole community? A woman who is selfless, passionate and so goddamn brave she inspired me to get off my ass, push past fear and pursue my dream?" Leo's lips parted, a gasp escaping, and Owen nodded. "Yeah, you're my inspiration, sweetheart. So the question isn't how can I love you. It's how can I *not* love you."

He moved forward, not stopping until barely an inch separated them. Technically, he complied with her request not to touch her. But his scent, his voice, his gaze—they caressed her, stroked her, held her close.

"You asked me once, what about you makes it so easy for people to walk away. Like then, I still don't have that answer. I want to walk *with* you, not away from you. Hell, if you'd let me walk behind you, I'd do it. I'd have your back and you wouldn't have to constantly be on guard all the time. You have to be so exhausted, sweetheart," he whispered. "I just want to be your soft place to land. Let me in, Leo."

He'd asked her that before. To let him in. But she was not that brave woman he called her. She'd allowed so many people in, and they'd hurt her. Some more than others. Owen. God, Owen. He was a category-five hurricane where the others were summer showers. He would destroy her if she stripped herself bare and he found her lacking and left.

No, she had to put herself first for once.

If she wasn't her priority, she would never be anyone else's.

"I'm sorry, Owen. I can't be who you need."

She shoved away from the island and strode out of the kitchen. Why did the front door loom so far away? It was like a hall in Wonderland. The faster she walked, the farther away it slipped. A sob crawled up her throat. So close. She had to make it out that door, then she could release it.

"Leo."

She froze, her hand on the knob, trembling with the effort it required not to pull open the door and bolt through. Still, she waited even though she didn't turn around to face him.

"I need to know one thing before you leave. Why did you leave me that morning? Can you give me that truth?"

She dipped her chin, not needing him to explain which morning he referred to.

His jagged chuckle filled the foyer. "You know what? Never mind. I don't need your answer when I already know it. You ran because you were scared. You came up against something you couldn't control—what happened between us in that bar, in that hotel room bed—and you didn't know how to handle it. How to manage it. So you ran away. Just like you're doing now. And let's make this clear so there's no misunderstanding. *You* are walking away from *me*. Not the other way around."

His footsteps fell on the hallway behind her, and she pulled open the front door.

The sob didn't wait until she reached the porch to escape her.

CHAPTER TWENTY-ONE

LEO STRIPPED THE sheets from the bed in the Kerry Room and tossed them in the corner with the rest of the covers and pillowcases she'd take down to wash. Turning, she nabbed the fresh sheets she'd brought with her when she'd arrived at the room a half hour earlier to clean it for a new guest who would be checking in tomorrow.

Technically, cleaning the rooms wasn't her job. But in the past two weeks, everything around the inn had become her responsibility. Only Wolf threatening her with spiders in her bed had prevented her from hanging white fairy lights from the eaves out front. Yeah, she didn't put it past him; her older brother might look like a friendly giant with a man bun, but he had a mean streak if pushed.

So that left her changing out linens. Thank God. The constant activity kept her busy and her body so tired, she dropped into sleep at night. Not a dreamless sleep, though. Which meant she lay in bed staring at the ceiling for hours before rising in the morning, eyes dry and grainy, and starting the cycle all over again.

If she occupied her time, those were fewer hours she spent thinking about Owen. Wondering what he was doing. If he was okay. How the training was coming along. If he missed her. If he still...

Don't go down that road.

Busy. Stay busy.

She snapped out the fitted sheet and shifted to each corner, tucking it under the mattress. That done, she returned to the chair for the flat sheet…

"There you are." Sydney appeared in the room's doorway and propped a shoulder on the frame. "Why am I not surprised that you're face deep in sheets again? And not in a fun way."

Leo scrunched her face up. Okay. Eew.

"I'm really not sure how I'm supposed to respond to that." Leo flicked the flat sheet open on the mattress. "But since you're here, make yourself useful and grab the other side."

"No, ma'am. I will not enable you. Besides, I'm here on a mission, not to help you put someone out of a job." Sydney strode into the room and snatched the sheet from Leo's grasp. After tossing it on the bed, she gripped Leo by the arm and marched her toward the door. "Believe me, this is for your own good."

"What the hell—"

"If you weren't so damn stubborn, this wouldn't be necessary, but you are, and now we have to force a girls' night on you. You're welcome." Sydney shut the door behind her. "Or not. But I have strict orders to bring you to the family parlor and to use physical force if necessary." She glanced down at her hand wrapped around Leo's biceps. "I've found it necessary."

Obviously.

"Sydney, listen, I appreciate the thought but—"

"Yeah, you know what takes care of *buts*? Tequila. Lots and lots of tequila." Sydney drew to an abrupt halt and whipped around to face Leo, grabbing her other arm. "We're doing this, Leo. It's happening. You're my best friend, and you're worrying me. Not to mention annoying the hell outta me with all this moping. Let me, all of us, take care of you. At least for tonight. Then tomorrow you can go back to being The Ringwraith of Kinsale Inn."

Leo studied her friend, noted the honest concern in her eyes and sighed.

"Cool points for the *Lord of the Rings* reference."

"Thank you. I've been working on it."

Snorting, Leo followed her friend to the family's side of the inn. And two hours later, surrounded by Sydney, Nessa, Moe and Celeste, she downed her third tequila shot and gorged on homemade loaded nachos. She had to admit it—this was a nice break from working herself to the bone before falling into bed and praying for sleep.

Of course, she had to force herself not to ask Celeste if she had heard from Owen, but every time she managed, it seemed a small victory. Very small. Because she craved information about him. Celeste and Sherrod remained in Owen's home while they stayed in Rose Bend until the spring festival, and without Leo even having to ask, Celeste had offered to move their pageant practice so she wasn't bombarded with memories of Owen every day. So now they met at Wolf's former cottage, which fit their needs since they were focusing more on the Q&A and talent rounds.

God, she was going to miss Celeste—both of them—when they left. They might've started off as Owen's friends, but they'd quickly become hers, and she loved them.

"Nope. Nope, nope, nope." Nessa leaned forward and poured more tequila into Leo's shot glass. "I'm seeing something weepy in your eyes and you know how emotion makes me itch. Drink up, woman."

Laughing at her sister-in-law's antics, Leo obeyed and knocked back the alcohol. Four shots in and she could still think clearly. Bummer. She popped a nacho into her mouth.

"Moe?" Nessa held up the bottle, shaking it back and forth. "More?"

"No, thanks." Her mother held up a hand. "I have to go downstairs in a while and prep food for tomorrow. And drunk sex is not sexy."

"Oh, my *God*!"

"Eeew."

"Jesus be a brain bleach!"

"Get it, Moe!"

Leo glared at Celeste, who toasted her mother before shooting back her tumbler of alcohol.

"Don't encourage her," Leo growled.

Celeste grinned. "What? I want to always be hot and heavy with Sherrod like your parents obviously are."

"You're so evil," Leo hissed.

Celeste cackled. "Jumping subjects." She picked up a nacho and waved it without dropping a bit of sour cream, jalapeños or ground beef. Girl had skills. "Mind you, I'm new to this town, but I've been here long enough to pick up on that Jenna Landon being a, uh, piece of work."

"That's one of the more polite terms for her," Sydney muttered, pouring more tequila.

"But is it me or did she actually snipe less and roll her eyes only two times today at your practice?" Celeste asked Leo and popped the nacho into her mouth.

Nessa widened her eyes. "That must be a personal record. Is Aquarius in retrograde or something?"

Sydney shook her head. "It's not Christmas so her heart hasn't grown three sizes. Oh, wait." She snapped her fingers. "She'd need a heart in order for that to happen."

"She's not that bad," Leo murmured.

The room plunged into a silence so thick Leo could've

choked on it. Four pairs of eyes trained on her, ranging from outright incredulity to curiosity.

"Um, 'scuse me," Sydney said. "Who isn't that bad? Certainly you're not referring to Jenna 'Mean Girl Extraordinaire' Landon? Not after everything she put me through. *Us* through. Do I really need to go back to high school and dig up those files?"

"No, no need for that." Leo sighed. "And in no way am I saying what she did to us back then or to you when you came home was cool. She was a bitch. And she'll be the first to claim it—"

"Whoa, whoa, whoa." Sydney set the bottle down, anger flashing across her face. "She'll be the first to claim it? And how do you know her so well now that you can be assured of that?"

"Syd," Leo said, covering her friend's hand, squeezing. "By no means are we friends, but yes, we have talked—"

"Leo, what the hell is going on?" Sydney demanded.

"Sydney," Moe said softly, settling a hand on her daughter-in-law's back, but her gaze focused on Leo. "Leo, go ahead."

She bowed her head, briefly closing her eyes. The truth pressed on her chest, building and building so it threatened to burst from her. She was so damn *tired*. Tired of hiding. Tired of being something she wasn't.

Perfect.

These women were some of the most important in her life. And she couldn't be honest with them. That was what she needed—what they all needed here.

Honesty.

"Saying Jenna and I are friends is a huge stretch, but a few weeks ago, she was unexpectedly there for me when I had a panic attack at pageant rehearsal. She talked me through it and protected my privacy from the other women."

"A panic attack?" Moe asked, tone sharp. Her eyes narrowed. "Since when?"

Here I go. I can do this. I want to be free.

"I've experienced them on and off for eight years now." She held her mother's gaze, her heart drumming in her chest. She swallowed, wetting her suddenly dry mouth. "Since I had a miscarriage my junior year in college."

No one spoke. No one moved. It seemed like no one *breathed*. That reaction gave her the courage to go on, to allow the story to purge out of her. And she didn't stop. She told them about her ex, the pregnancy, being scared, his abandonment and being alone when she miscarried. About holding that secret for almost a decade.

By the time she finished, Moe knelt beside Leo, and her mother's arms were wrapped around her. Sydney held one of Leo's hands and Nessa captured the other. Celeste rested a palm on Leo's knee. All these beautiful, powerful women touched her, offering her unconditional love and support. And healing.

"I'm so sorry, Leo," Moe said, pressing a kiss to the side of her head.

"You don't have anything to be sorry for. I made the choice not to tell you. That's on me, not you."

"But I knew," Moe insisted, her arms tightening. "I *knew* something was wrong. When you came home earlier than usual that year, I suspected. And all this time since, I've wondered what I missed. You're my oldest daughter. You're more like me than any of my other children, and I *knew*. Yes, when I asked you always told me you were fine and brushed it off, but I should've bulldozed my way in because you were hurting. And I don't know if I'll forgive myself for that."

"Moe," Leo breathed.

"No." Her mother drew back, cupping Leo's face between her palms. "You've always prided yourself on being responsible, on being strong. And I agreed with you, because you are. You're so resilient, so brave, Leo. But I neglected to tell you that strength isn't about never feeling vulnerable or never having moments of weakness. It's not about never being *not fine*. True strength is about having the integrity to admit when you're not. As women, we're afraid to say those three words—I'm not okay. As if it makes us less than, inept, for some idiotic reason. But, honey, that's what we're all here for. When you're tired, when you're at your most vulnerable, we're here to carry the load until you're strong again. I'm not just your mother, and they're not just your friends. We're sisters, and that's what we do for each other."

Leo laid her head on her mother's chest and held her, her limbs weights she couldn't move. Didn't want to move. But as heavy as her body felt, she was...light.

Free from the burden of an impossible pursuit. Because perfection could never be obtained. For years she'd never been truly at peace, at rest.

Until this moment.

But what had the quest for perfection cost her?

Owen flickered across her mind's eye.

She'd bound herself by impossible rules, and in the end locked Owen out. Her not believing he could love her had nothing to do with him, and everything to do with her.

Moe had been right; Leo turned to the inn because it didn't make her feel vulnerable. If she was brutally honest with herself, she'd used the inn as an excuse in her past relationships to avoid being truly intimate with her partners—not with her body, but with her whole heart. She hadn't given anyone all of her since her ex in college.

It was about control. And as long as she remained in control of her emotions, of the parameters of her relationships, then she wouldn't be hurt. She wouldn't be rejected.

Her biggest fear was opening herself to another person, giving all of herself to that person and being abandoned again.

So she'd launched a preemptive strike with Owen. She'd left him before he could leave her.

She'd claimed that she wouldn't make Owen pay for her baggage with her exes, but hadn't she done just that? She'd withheld her love, her trust, because she'd been hurt in the past. Because in the darkest, deepest part of her heart, she feared him deciding she wasn't enough. When in his eyes, she'd always been *more* than enough.

Just as he was for her.

Oh, God, she'd screwed up.

Huge.

Owen had called her brave.

It was past time she lived up to his belief in her.

"Celeste?"

"Yes?"

"How is Owen doing?"

Celeste smiled. "Not good. Not good at all."

LEO STARED AT the sheet of paper filled with her handwriting.

Sure, she could've sent an email. Hell, it would've been easier, faster and, well…more twenty-first century. But this, a letter handwritten and mailed by her, seemed more personal. And that was what she needed to get across to Owen.

She wanted *personal* with him.

Holding the sheet of Kinsale Inn stationery in her hand, she reread the letter.

Owen,

I know you're probably wondering what's up with the paper and pen when a server and email address would've done just as well. But when a woman is attempting a grand gesture, she gets to be a little dramatic, so snail mail it is. I draw the line at dabbing perfume to this, though.

First, let me tell you how proud I am of you. I hope that doesn't come across as condescending because I don't mean it that way. But I am so very proud of you. When we met—again—you were hiding from the world. Which struck me as such a shame that a beautiful, gifted man like you was shut up in that house. Yet, over the weeks, I had the pleasure of witnessing you overcome your fears and return to the game you love so much. You said I was brave? No, Owen. That took courage. *You* inspire *me*.

Second, I'm sorry. I'm sorry for so much. That I hurt you. Rejected you. That I allowed my mistrust in myself to dictate my reaction to you. You were right. I was running scared. Ever since I met you, I've thrown my precious rules out the window. No, that's not true. With you, I have no rules. And that terrified me. My feelings for you—my love for you— terrified me. Because, for me, love didn't equate to safety or security but pain and loss. But just like you buck the rules, I should've known my experience of love couldn't be prescribed to you, either.

You are…everything. Safety. Exhilaration. Security. A free fall. Excitement. Peace. Lust. Love. I can't contain you, and I was a fool for trying. And I've come to realize I don't want to.

Owen, I would love to have you here with me. That was my fear. Seeing you walk away. But I'm not afraid anymore. I love you, so I'm willing to let you go pursue your dream, your career, because it's what's best for you. Even if it means being away from you. You told me that one of the reasons you loved me was because I sacrificed for those I love.

Well, Owen Strafford, I love you.

And I'm willing to sacrifice for you.

Thank you for teaching me the true meaning of love. And for giving me the gift of you.

Remember, home isn't a place, but a person who cherishes you. And you will always have a home here.

With all my love from Rose Bend,
Leo

She reread the letter a second time, and then a third. Before she could change her mind, she folded the paper, slipped it in an envelope and sealed it.

Now, if only she wasn't too late.

CHAPTER TWENTY-TWO

Wow.

Sherrod hadn't lied. Rose Bend took their festivals seriously.

He stepped onto The Glen, halting under the huge purple, yellow and white sign declaring the Honeybee Festival. Taking in the brightly decorated booths, the stage where a blues band played, a partitioned-off section where children played games with bouncy castles and slides, and several yellow tents close to the parking lot...

Yeah, best not to focus on the parking lot at this moment.

More specifically, best not to focus on what went down in that parking lot at this moment.

Dragging his attention back to the rows and rows of booths, he moved forward, searching for one section in particular—the chili contest.

Yet, as he strolled through the aisles, he couldn't help but remember the first time Leo showed up unannounced at his rental home. He huffed out a small, soft laugh. She hadn't lied. There was a hell of a lot of honey to be had in all forms here. Wild honey. Honey soaps and candles and lotions. He had yet to pass the honey cake contest and the illustrious Melba Dinkins, though.

From the amount of people crowded into the field, it appeared her worries about low attendance were unfounded. Damn, the whole town had to be here. And more, besides.

He'd always pictured this as a small, low-key affair. But this… He shook his head. Like Eva Wright had warned him, Rose Bend would surprise him. And it'd constantly done just that.

"Owen?"

He jerked his head up at the sound of his name and met Sydney's shocked gaze.

"Hi, Sydney."

Since Leo's best friend had never been overly friendly toward him, he prepared for a snarky comment or an "I'm watching you" two-finger sign. Or even one finger. He *didn't* expect the petite woman to throw herself at him and hug him tight.

Uh, okay.

"You're back," she whispered. She grinned at him, though tears glittered in her dark eyes. "I knew you would return for her."

Instead of addressing that statement, he arched an eyebrow. "You do know you're voluntarily touching me, right?"

Laughing, she gave him one last squeeze then released him. "Eh, all that's water under the bridge. I like you, Owen."

"Should I be afraid?"

She scrunched up her face. "Maybe?" Then, with another of those joy-filled laughs, she hooked her arm through his and led him forward. "Leo's getting ready for the pageant. It's about to start in another hour, but I'll take you over there—"

"Sydney." Owen halted. "I was headed to see Sherrod."

She frowned. "But…"

"I'm glad you like me now, but at the risk of pissing you off again, this is between me and Leo. We have some things we need to say to each other and work out. Plus, she doesn't need any distractions before the pageant."

Sydney studied him, and after a moment she nodded, smiled. "I got it. Mind my own business. Fine." She turned, looped her arm through his again and resumed walking. "And I still like you."

He snorted. "Well, thank God for that."

She led him to the far side of the field and a medium-size tent. About thirty or so small tables with various pots and warming plates sat under it with contestants for the chili contest standing behind them.

"This must be one of the more popular contests, then?" He surveyed the people stirring pots, adding last-minute spices and tasting their chili.

"Only the honey cakes can compete. But you couldn't pay me to enter that one. They can get vicious over there."

Chuckling, Owen spotted his best friend near the back of the tent. At the same time Sherrod glanced up and saw him. Grinning wide, he murmured something to the older woman next to him then rounded the judging table and strode toward Owen and Sydney.

"Owen!" Jerking Owen forward into a bone-crushing hug, Sherrod pounded him on the back, damn near dislodging a lung. "Damn, man, you didn't say anything about coming back to town last time we talked."

"Last-minute decision," he murmured.

Sherrod's gaze scanned his face, and because they were as close as brothers, he glimpsed answers that Owen wasn't ready to articulate yet.

"I'm glad you made it back." Nodding, Sherrod clapped him on the shoulder. "Come on, we're about to start the judging. I might need a bodyguard."

"Nah, you'll be fine, Sherrod," Sydney said, patting his

arm. "In all the years I've attended the festival, I remember only one fistfight." She frowned, tapping her bottom lip. "But then again, I've been gone for ten years..."

Shrugging, she smiled at them, waved and headed back toward the other booths.

"Have you seen Leo yet?" Sherrod asked, voice low.

Owen shook his head. "Not yet. And she's worked too hard on this pageant for me to throw any distractions at her."

"Yeah. Celeste said Leo's going to win the whole thing. She's that good."

"Never doubted it."

And he didn't. Whatever Leo put her brilliant mind and laser-sharp focus to, she could conquer. That was who she was—the woman he'd fallen in love with. The woman who'd walked away from him, from them, rather than take a chance on that love.

"I saw the press conference announcing you were coming out of retirement," Sherrod said, walking back toward the judges' table. "Every sports station I turned to had it on constant replay. Hell, even the regular news stations aired it. There's a lot of excitement about your return."

Owen snorted. "Byron's happy."

"I bet." Sherrod paused. "Anyone reach out?"

"A few teams. After the meeting with the Knights' head office at the end of the month, I'll know more about where I'm headed."

"I'm happy for you, man. Even if we don't end up on the same team again, I'm so damn glad you're back on that field. You belong there."

Owen smiled. "Yeah, I do."

The first week back in New York had been...difficult. Not only because of the hole in his chest where his heart used to be, but also the press, cameras, interviews. It'd been months since he'd voluntarily sat in front of a reporter or posed for a picture. And there hadn't been a way to avoid the inevitable questions regarding the accident, his recovery and the scars. *Uncomfortable* had been a severe understatement. But he hadn't caved. Hadn't tucked tail and hid in his penthouse. He'd remembered Leo's words, conjured up her face, and he'd survived it.

The jury was still out on whether or not he'd survive loving her.

For the next forty-five minutes Owen shadowed Sherrod as he tasted and rated the various offerings of chili. Good thing the man had a cast-iron stomach, because that was a fuck ton of chili. The winner would be announced at the end of the day, but while the judges tallied their numbers, Owen greeted Ian, Leo's father, who, judging by the bear hug, appeared happy to see him. Owen also signed autographs and talked with everyone who approached him.

He had fun.

And he experienced a pang of regret that he'd wasted months hiding in his rental house instead of becoming a part of this community.

"You ready?" Sherrod clapped his hands, rubbing them in glee. "Celeste just texted me. The pageant starts in ten minutes. Let's go get a good seat."

Owen nodded, his stomach knotting. God, he hadn't been this nervous before the Super Bowl. He slid his hand in his pants pocket, his fingers closing around the folded paper there. Probably because the championship game hadn't been as important as this moment or the woman who would soon be walking across that stage.

Minutes later he perched on a folded chair several rows back from the stage, Sherrod beside him, and the whole

Dennison clan on the other side of him. The twisting in his gut hadn't subsided, and it wouldn't until he laid eyes on Leo. Until he saw her again for the first time in three weeks.

God, he was an addict in full withdrawal.

"Chill." Sherrod elbowed him. "She's going to be fine."

"Yeah, she's got this."

A woman with auburn hair strode onto the stage and stopped behind the mic.

"Hello, Rose Bend! Welcome to the Honeybee Festival and to our annual Lavender Queen Beauty Pageant!" Cheers erupted from the crowd, and she beamed, waiting until the applause died down before speaking again. "Thank you for attending. You are in for an absolutely wonderful show this evening. These contestants have worked so hard, and I'm proud of each of them. Let's give them a round of applause."

Another round of boisterous clapping and yells burst into the air. Wolf and Cole stood to their feet, their dog whistles adding to the noise. Owen grinned as the proud brothers finally took their seats.

"Now, a reminder for newcomers, and even some of you old-timers," she teased. "This pageant isn't just for your entertainment. We're here to raise money for Purple Heart Homes so we can show our love and appreciation to our courageous servicemen and women and their families who have sacrificed so much for us. On your chair you would've found a donation slip. Please make a gift in the name of your favorite contestant or contestants. We're not limiting you. And we guarantee you every single penny goes to our veterans."

Owen had already completed the donation slip in Leo's honor and dropped it into the basket at the end of the aisle. It wasn't the cause alone that was worthy. She so was, too.

The MC quickly introduced the judges, and moments later she moved to the side of the stage and the pageant began.

One by one, women glided onto the stage in beautiful evening gowns as the MC introduced them by name, occupation and a small detail about them. Owen leaned forward in his seat, anticipating one woman, and when she finally walked out, an invisible hand pushed him against the chair back.

Gorgeous.

Her dark hair fell in loose waves over her shoulder and down her back. A strapless, emerald green, mermaid-style dress clung to her breasts, hips and thighs before billowing out around her feet. His blood pumped hot in his veins. His cock pounded behind his zipper.

His heart thudded against his sternum.

Fuck, he'd missed her.

As if she'd been born to the stage, she floated across, slowly spinning in front of the mic before pausing, an easy smile curving her lips.

Their eyes connected.

He sucked in a lungful of air. He couldn't move. Couldn't think. Didn't know if her features would reflect sadness, anger or, worse, absolutely nothing. That moment compressed tighter and tighter until only they existed, and he feasted on her with his gaze even as his chest contracted, apprehension shoving into him, filling his throat.

Then she smiled.

A huge, beautiful smile that lit up her eyes, her face, hell, The Glen.

And it was for him.

"Wow," Sherrod breathed. "That's...wow."

Yeah. Wow.

"Contestant number six is Leontyne Dennison. Leo, as we all call her, helps run her family's business, Kinsale Inn. A fun fact about Leo? She has six brothers and sisters, which means she has the patience of Job and the intercessory skills of a SWAT negotiator."

Laughter spilled from the crowd and Owen caught Wolf's muttered "She's not wrong."

Without her smile dimming, Leo turned and glided off the stage and the next contestant walked out. Leaving him still reeling.

And the fragile seed of hope that had sowed into his heart on receiving her letter bloomed.

The rest of the pageant flew by and then the talent round arrived. His knee bounced, and he crossed his arms over his chest. She and Celeste had kept Leo's act under wraps. As whispers from her family filtered down to him, he realized even they didn't know what she'd planned.

Please, God, let her have this moment, this victory.

Him, Owen Strafford, praying.

By the time Leo stepped onto the stage in a dress that could've come straight out of a black-and-white film noir, with Celeste behind her, violin in hand, he'd gone through the whole rosary. Three times. And he wasn't even Catholic.

After Leo stopped in front of the mic, Celeste lifted her violin and bow, and seconds later the very recognizable theme song to *A Streetcar Named Desire* poured into the silence.

"He was a boy, just a boy..."

Leo started Blanche DuBois's monologue about discovering love and the tragic ending of it. A hush fell over the crowd, and maybe if Owen could tear his eyes away from her, he might glimpse that everyone else was as captivated as he was.

She embodied the frail, insecure Blanche, delivering the slightly disjointed monologue with vulnerable perfection. He believed she was the aging Southern belle. And when she finished, and the audience surged to their feet—led by Owen and the Dennisons—he knew from the tears reflected in her eyes from the stage lights, that Leo had finally conquered that last fear.

She believed, too.

She didn't win.

But from her wide grin as the MC crowned a petite woman with dark curls who'd sung the hell out of "I Come to the Garden Alone," Leo didn't seem to mind her first-runner-up status at all.

He waited at the side of the stage as her family swarmed her after the pageant. Though they hugged and kissed her, Leo's gaze kept returning to him, and each time that connection punched him in the chest.

By the time she approached him, back in her evening gown, he damn near shook with the need to touch her, to tug her into his arms and bury his face in the scented crook of her neck.

"Owen," she whispered.

"Leo," he whispered back. "You were—are—amazing. Fucking amazing."

She smiled, and though it wasn't as wide as the one she'd given him onstage, it struck him just as hard, just as powerful.

"Thank you. I felt amazing. It was…"

"Freeing."

"Yes," she breathed. "Freeing." She shook her head. "I didn't expect to see you here."

"Where else would I be?" He shifted closer because

he needed to. Just inches separated them, and yet he still needed to be…closer. "I received your letter."

"I love you."

Owen blinked.

She shrugged. "I promised myself the next time I saw you, I wouldn't waste any more time in telling you what I should've before you left." She inhaled. "I love you, Owen."

He closed his eyes, allowing those four words to saturate his soul. Of course, he'd read them in her letter. But hearing them? Yeah, it was different. Purer.

"Are you going to kiss me now, Leo?"

"God, yes."

And her mouth was on his.

He tunneled his fingers into her hair, cradling her scalp, taking her tongue and lips as she tipped her head back, offering them up. He groaned; she groaned. He couldn't tell where they ended, only knew they were beginning. Together.

"I love you, Leo. So damn much. That's why I'm back. It's why I never truly left. I'll never leave you, sweetheart. You called it. As long as you're here, I'm home."

"You're my home, too." She placed a soft kiss on his chin, jaw, mouth. "I've already talked it over with Moe and Dad. We're going to hire administrative staff to help out so I can split my time here and with you in New York, or wherever you end up. Because I believe you will end up playing on a team."

"Leo, that's your decision." He stroked the backs of his fingers down her cheek, unable to stop touching her. "But I put in an offer on the Victorian as soon as I got your letter. Rose Bend is going to be my home base, and you factor into my decision about where I land. Because—" he palmed her face, brushing his lips over hers "—you're important and so is your happiness. And your family, Rose Bend and the inn make you happy. We'll make it work, Leo. Together."

"Together." She hesitated. "But…"

He heaved an exaggerated sigh. "What? I'm being really romantic here, dammit."

"I know, I know. And you're really kicking ass with it." She patted his chest, placating him. He snorted. "But I just thought of something. When should we reveal to your parents our initial lie about me being your girlfriend?"

Owen shrugged, lowering his arms to her waist and pressing a long, soft kiss to her lips. "How about our tenth wedding anniversary?"

EPILOGUE

LEO STARED DOWN at the football field from her lower seat on the fifty-yard line. Around her, thunderous noise from the Knights' and Falcons' fans filled E.S. Jennings Stadium until the open-air structure fairly hummed with it. Excitement and a frenetic energy rippled on the air, undulating like a current through the sea of white, green and blue that surrounded her and her family, who sat on either side of her.

This.

This was why she and everyone else had rejected sitting in the glass-enclosed luxury box where some of the football players' families opted to watch the game. They'd wanted to be smack-dab in the middle of the electric energy of the fans. And Leo? She had another reason. She needed to be as close as possible to her fiancé on his first professional game since his return from retirement.

Fierce pride erupted inside her even as nerves tickled her stomach like an irritating feather. Pride for the strong, brave, beautiful man who'd fought to be on this field, the place Owen loved, the place he belonged. Well, only after her. And she knew and believed that because he'd told her. Repeatedly.

She sought him out among the pristine white jerseys accented with green and blue that wouldn't be so clean in just a few minutes. Even though helmets emblazoned with a knight head covering concealed the features of many of the players, she still found Owen. Not just because of the number four on the back of his jersey. But even under the pads and uniform, she would be able to identify that tall, wide-shouldered, slim-hipped, gorgeous body anywhere. As often as she touched it, worshipped it, loved it, she was an expert on the subject.

Maybe he felt her gaze on him, or maybe before he started this momentous game, he needed to seek her out, too. Her heart thudded as his head turned toward the stands, and though she couldn't see his eyes, he found her. Saw her. The press of fingers to his face guard then stretching those same fingers in her direction let her know that.

She grinned through the tears that stung her eyes. Through the still-thudding heart that echoed in the base of her throat. Through the almost overwhelming love that swelled, nearly cutting off her breath.

God, she loved this man.

"Aw, that's so sweet." Sydney fluttered her lashes, but her eyes gleamed with happiness.

Leo snorted. "Whatever." Pause. "Hell, yeah, it is."

Sydney laughed, looping her arm through Leo's. "He's going to have a great game, the team is going to win and then you two can go back home and have hot sex to celebrate."

"Hey!" Wolf and Cole practically wailed from the other side of Sydney.

From Leo's side, Moe and Charlene's laughter did nothing to hide her father's "Good Lord." She didn't need to peek over to see Troy's wince; she could picture it perfectly well.

"I know," Leo agreed, waving a hand at her suddenly prudish brothers. "But not at the brownstone. We're driving back with you guys to Rose Bend. We'll christen his victory in the Victorian."

"Oh, God, *enough* already," Wolf groaned.

Leo and Sydney snickered, co-conspirators. But the thought of returning home tonight filled her with joy as it always did. Not that she spent much time away from her hometown and Kinsale Inn. Owen had made good on his promise; he refused to take her away from the people and place she loved. But she couldn't allow him to do all the sacrificing, all the compromising.

He hadn't returned to New York after the festival that spring. Owen had convinced his trainer to move to Rose Bend and the high school's weight room had received the best, state-of-the-art equipment, worthy of a professional football team's training room. And after he'd re-signed with the Knights at the end of May, he'd remained in Rose Bend, only leaving for training camp in June and again in August. Leo had traveled to New York and stayed the last week with him in June. In August she'd alternated weeks, with both of them returning home when he had off days. With only a three-hour drive, they were never far. And with the added administrative staff at the inn and Moe fully healed and back to her old self, Leo could do some work virtually. And letting go of some of her tightly held control was…freeing.

It left her more time to focus on the wedding venture, which was coming along nicely. Especially since word had gotten out that Sherrod and Celeste had chosen Kinsale Inn as their venue to renew their vows.

She glanced down the row to where her other best friend sat, Celeste and Sherrod's family beside her. As if she, too, sensed Leo's gaze, Celeste turned and smiled. The other woman practically glowed, if possible, appearing more gorgeous. Celeste was proving that myth about pregnant women true.

A whistle rent the air, and Leo jerked her head toward

the field. Owen, Sherrod and another team member strode out onto the field for the coin toss. The referee threw the flip coin in the air and in seconds, the captains trotted back to their sides. The Falcons would have the ball first.

Damn.

"Don't worry." Wolf reached across Sydney and patted Leo's knee. "With Owen and Sherrod playing together again, there's no way the Knights are losing this game. They got this."

"Yeah." Leo nodded, smiling at her brother. Returning her attention to the field, she murmured, "I know."

And they did.

A little over three hours later the game ended, the final score 37–23, a Knights win. Her family leaped from their seats, shouting, hugging her, throwing their arms around each other. Happiness for Owen flowed from her. He'd been...amazing. She didn't even watch football, but she'd watched a true, natural, gifted athlete tonight. Tears stung her eyes. If anyone had doubted him before now, they'd been proven wrong. So wrong. Owen Strafford was phenomenal.

And hers.

An hour and a half passed before he exited the press conference room and walked straight to her, wrapping her in his arms. Leo closed her eyes, ignoring the clicks and flashes of cameras. She inhaled his fresh scent, savored the press of his hard body against her, craved the gentle yet hungry taking of her mouth.

When he lifted his head and set her on the floor, he grinned down at her.

"Nice jersey."

She peered down at her Knights jersey with his number on it.

Shrugging, she said, "Meh. They ran out of Sherrod's."

"Wow." Owen laughed, throwing his head back. More clicks and flashes but for a man who'd hid from the media like it was a religion, he didn't give a damn now. Still chuckling, he cupped her cheek and rubbed a thumb over her skin. "We did it," he whispered, a husky note of awe thickening his voice.

"I never doubted you would. Not for a second," she whispered back, turning into his palm and kissing it.

"I had one thought every time I returned to the sidelines." His hazel eyes lit with an inner light, warming her. The thumb stroking the corner of her mouth stoked an entirely different warmth. "Getting home."

"To Rose Bend?"

"No." He shook his head, his other hand lifting to cradle her face. "To you."

"Well, damn," she muttered, blinking back another prickling of tears. "I love you, Owen Strafford."

"I love you more, Leontyne Dennison."

He covered her mouth with his, taking her under in the sweetest, hottest kiss. She clung to him, loving him more than she thought possible. Feeling at home.

"All right, enough of that. Can we congratulate our soon-to-be brother-in-law?" Cole demanded.

Huffing out a breath, Leo rolled her eyes, but her grin belied her exaggerated annoyance. "Fine. But your timing sucks."

As soon as she stepped back, her family, including Owen's parents, swarmed in to hug and praise him. But a big hand encircled her wrist, drawing her into his side so they were both surrounded by family.

By love.

* * * * *

ACKNOWLEDGMENTS

THANK YOU, GOD, for Your creative spirit and pouring into me with each and every book. You're my co-author, and not only can I not do this without You, I don't want to do this without You.

Thank you to my husband, Gary, who has been my rock and never-failing support. You pushed me and told me I could do this when I doubted myself. This journey wouldn't be the same without you.

To my father, Rev. Wayne L. Alston, Dr. Phil has nothing on you! Thank you for not only being an amazing dad, but also for always answering the phone and giving me insight into the human condition and spirit so I can write these flawed but beautiful characters the way I do. I'm still not giving you any of my royalties, though. LOL!

To my football council—Gary, Konard and Daddy. If not for you three, well, my football players would be scoring home runs and running fast breaks. You set me right and help me sound like I know what I'm talking about! Thank you!

To Rachel Brooks, the best agent ever! Thank you for being my advocate and voice. And in this hardest year of my life, you've been my champion, too. I can't express how grateful I am to and for you. Thank you!

Thank you to Stacy Boyd, my editor and magician! You just wave your editor's wand—or pen—and make every book stronger and lovelier. It never fails that I learn more with each book and become a better writer. Thank you for that guidance and for always putting those little hearts in the comments so I feel all sparkly and unicorn-y. LOL!

And a HUGE thank-you to all of my readers! You are just amazing and I appreciate you for going on all of these adventures with me. Your support, encouragement and joy in my books have meant the world to me. I'm going to keep writing, and I hope you keep reading!

The Love List

The Love List

CHAPTER ONE

KORRIE NOEL SHOVED down the handle on the French door of the restaurant's back porch and hurried out into the cool April night air. She tore her earpiece free, gulping down the air as if it were made of appletinis instead of oxygen.

"God, we need to have a serious talk. I mean, really. You and my father are tight. Like, he's Your guy." She shook her head, grasping the iron railing. The cool of the metal seeped into her palms, but she barely paid it any attention. She held on. Otherwise, she might do something ridiculous. Like climb over it and go on a moonlit power hike into the woods. "So I'm just asking, God—don't I get any kind of brownie points for Your relationship with him? Any kind of leeway? I'm a good person. I tithe. I teach children's Sunday school. My job is helping to bring people together in holy matrimony. I don't even curse unless the situation *really* merits it. So why, God? Why let this happen to me? I think I deserve some kind of answer. Give me a sign or something."

"Sorry, sweetheart. This hideout is taken. Find your own."

"Shit!"

Korrie wheeled around, hand pressed to her chest over her suddenly hammering heart. Fear raced through her veins, her pulse crashing in her head like violent waves. She glanced down, to the side, then to the other side for anything to snatch up as an impromptu weapon. But nothing except for chairs and tables littered the deserted porch. Well, not entirely as deserted as she'd believed. Her gaze lit on the squat candleholder in the middle of the nearest table. It would have to do...

"I guess this is one of those situations that *really* merited a curse."

The drawled words sank in along with the humor just as she reached for the candleholder. She slowly dropped her arm and squinted at the dark corner where a wide grin flashed like an eerie Cheshire Cat. Except, as this figure gradually emerged from the shadows, its toothy smirk was attached to a face of strong, almost stern angles that was somehow starkly beautiful in its symmetry and boldness. Not a subtle or even a kind face, but stunning, nonetheless. Especially when paired with a sharp slant of a nose and a vivid pair of blue eyes that gleamed in the darkness like an inner torch shone behind them. Surely, they were contacts. That color—caught somewhere between indigo and denim—couldn't be found outside of an accidental dye job.

Who was he? In a town the size of Rose Bend, Massachusetts—population 4,815—it was pretty difficult not to know everyone. And everyone's business. Her stomach twisted at that reminder. Still, difficult but not impossible. And she would've remembered him. He was pretty unforgettable.

As if he'd plucked her thought out of her head, his smirk deepened through thick, silky-looking scruff, and a dimple dented a lean cheek, drawing her attention to his mouth. Full with a hard, almost cruel slant that should've been intimidating. Instead, she had the strangest urge to sink her teeth into that slightly thinner top lip and see it swell.

Holy...

She blinked. Leaned back.

Where had *that* thought come from? She glanced to the side, into the woods, as if they held the answer.

"Excuse me?" she finally stammered. *Awesome. Brilliant.* She slapped a mental palm to her forehead.

He arched a dark eyebrow, shifting farther toward the pool of light cast through the French doors. A solid jaw that spoke of epic stubbornness, a wide, clear brow. A dirty-blond mohawk arced over his head. All he needed were two braids on either side of his scalpel-sharp cheekbones to complete the image of a fierce Viking intent on a sacking.

Her belly quivered, an echo of it spasming lower, deeper. What would it feel like to have this man lay siege to her?

He would consume her, completely wreck her and leave nothing but burning rubble behind.

The knowledge whispered in her head with certainty.

"No excuse needed, sweetheart. I saw who was in there." He jerked his chin in the direction of the doors and the restaurant she'd just escaped. "Go ahead and have your breakdown. Your secret's safe with me."

"I'm not having a breakdown." Not a big one anyway. But it was rude of him to mention it, either way. "And please don't call me 'sweetheart.' It's inappropriate since we met five seconds ago." Lord, when had she started sounding like Nana Rena?

"Okay, no breakdown. You were having intercessory prayer." He snorted and tipped a bottle of beer she hadn't noticed he held to his mouth for a long drink. Lowering it, he wiped the back of his hand across his lips. She should've found that disgusting. Any minute, she *would*. "And I apologize for being so forward...Barbie."

"Barbie?" She tilted her head, narrowed her eyes on him. "That isn't my name."

"Oh, I know what your name is, Korrie Noel. Pastor Keith Noel's daughter. Wedding planner. Town darling." His cobalt gaze dipped, roaming down her wholly suitable pale green, inch-above-the-knee sheath and nude heels and back up again.

So why did she feel as if she stood there in a merry widow under his inspection?

"Barbie. Perfect." As the insult wrapped in pretty compliments sank into her skin, he cocked his head, and a corner of his mouth quirked. She tensed, not trusting that hint of smile on that cruel mouth. "Although, maybe not so perfect. Because we both know why you're out here hiding, invoking a God that's too busy to care about your runaway groom showing up at the wedding you're coordinating."

Hot flames of humiliation licked her skin. Not only did he baldly voice what others in this town and her own family tiptoed around as if she were a land mine with a hair-trigger detonator, but he also stated what she feared. God could care less about her problems. Because if He did, wouldn't she be happily married by now? Maybe even expecting her first child? Seriously. Whoever heard of a wedding planner who was abandoned by her own fiancé at the altar? It was a miracle she even had any clients left.

She suspected her business had barely dipped only because of pity. And that stung as much as if everyone had scattered.

The townspeople of Rose Bend were nothing if not loyal.

And it spoke volumes about the state of her heart that she resented them a little for it.

"You're an asshole," she whispered, anger, hurt and embarrassment churning inside her.

"Never claimed to be anything different, Barbie," he whispered back. "And believe me, I merit that curse, too."

"Did that make you feel good?" She drew her shoulders back, notching up her chin. "Anything else you'd like to throw my way before I go?"

Something glimmered in his eyes. With another person she might identify the emotion as compassion, but not on this stranger. Nothing about him was soft.

"Yes." He leaned an incredibly wide shoulder against the iron beam, his beer bottle dangling from his long fingers. "Get your shit together, Korrie Noel. No one, especially not a son of a bitch who pulls a dick move like not showing up at his own wedding and not having the balls to tell his bride-to-be that he's changed his mind, should have you running away. The fact that you're still in this town when he disappeared for six months, leaving you to deal with the fallout, shows you're much stronger than this." He waved a hand, indicating the patio.

"Who are you to lecture me? I don't even know you, and for all the gossip you have gathered, you don't know me, either." She nearly trembled with fury and shame… and pleasure. God, she hated that smoky tendrils of delight swirled low in her belly at his scorn of her ex-fiancé and his claim that she was indeed "stronger than this." Not that she sought or needed his validation. Especially considering she'd met him five minutes ago. "And you're being a bit of a hypocrite, aren't you? I'm not out here in the dark talking to myself. You're hiding, too. Why isn't it good enough for me when it seems perfectly fine for you?"

That grin flashed in his scruff again. "Oh, that's easy, Barbie. I freely admit that I'm avoiding that shit—" again he jerked his chin toward the doors "—like tea at the queen's. I hate weddings."

"Then why are you here?"

"Because I hate people knowing even more."

They stared at each other, his admission ringing between them, enigmatic and revealing. It struck a chord deep inside her. Wasn't that why she insisted on still coordinating weddings? So no one would suspect her ex-fiancé's defection had broken something elemental inside her?

She glanced away from him. From that too-perceptive stare. She didn't want to have anything in common with him.

"I should get back in there," she murmured. "It was nice to meet you…"

"Israel Ford." He chuckled, and it carried an edge so dry, it crackled. "And no need to lie to me. Matter of fact, I'm the one person you don't need to bother wearing that pretense of perfection with at all." He leaned slightly forward, his voice lowering, deepening. The timbre caressed her bared skin, stoked a simmering fire in her belly. "Consider me your confessional. I won't tell a soul."

Israel Ford. Her breath turned to smoke in her lungs, set aflame by the unwanted lust flickering to life in her veins. The shock of it stole whatever air she had left. Since her ex, she'd had no interest in romance and definitely not in sex. Getting through each day and focusing on the tasks at hand had consumed her. Risking trusting another human outside of her father not to hurt, betray or fail her… That lay beyond her, and she didn't know if or when she would be capable of taking that chance with her heart again.

It seemed her body—or more specifically, her vagina—had other ideas.

Spinning around, she strode toward the French doors, not bothering to reply to him. *Get away.* Her mind recognized the danger her rebellious and reawakened sex had not. She grabbed the handle, his gaze heavy on her back. She entered the hallway, grateful it remained empty and no one had witnessed her flight from the reception. Thank God for small favors at least—

"Korrie."

Oh, wow, really, God. Really?

Drawing to a sudden halt, she went ice-cold as she stared at the man who appeared in front of her like a specter who haunted her dreams.

No, her nightmares.

The recurring nightmare where she waits in the daycare turned dressing room of First Providence Ministries, her father's church, in her wedding gown and veil, smiling, barely able to sit still. That is, until her father enters with sorrow in his dark brown eyes and tells her that Derek Boyd, her husband-to-be, hasn't arrived and isn't coming. Then, sitting still isn't an issue. Moving at all is.

Breathing is.

Then she'd wake up, heart pounding, humiliation a cold, wet slick over her skin, bitterness dirty in her throat, as she tried to convince herself it was a dream and not her real life.

But it *was* her real life, and her bogeyman—still handsome—stood not three feet in front of her.

"Derek."

He stared at her, as if he expected her to say more. Anger flashed inside her, a struck match flickering to life. Well, he would have a long wait. *He'd* obviously followed *her. He'd* cornered *her.* She didn't have a damn thing to say to him.

And yes, the situation *so* merited that curse.

"I noticed you in the reception earlier. And I… Well, I didn't want to cause a scene or be the source of any more pain for you…" He paused, but she still didn't say a word and a small frown creased his brow. He shifted forward, a hand outstretched. "But I wanted to speak to you. Needed to speak to you."

"And it's all about what you want, yeah?" A new but now familiar voice joined the conversation. "Forget that she's working right now and they're not paying her to have a reunion with you. She also doesn't need your bullshit or drama."

Both Korrie and Derek stiffened, but for different reasons.

Derek, probably because an unwanted interloper had intruded on his planned ambush. That had always been Derek. A planner. Which was why his abandoning her had been such a twisting knife in her heart. He'd have known for at least days in advance that he had no intentions of showing up to the church. And he hadn't had the decency to give her a heads-up.

Her, because... Well, because Israel's scent, like freshly washed sheets and sun-warmed skin, enveloped her in its own ephemeral embrace.

"Excuse me," Derek said, glaring at Israel, who stood just behind Korrie. "But this is between Korrie and me. It has nothing to do with you."

"Thank you for that update." Israel snorted. "And yet, I think I'll stay."

"Derek," Korrie gritted out, irritation toward both of them sticking to her chest wall like burrs. "Now is not the time. I'm on a job. If—and that's a big *if*—I decide to talk to you, it will be on my timetable. Not yours. Now, you're obviously a guest of either the bride or groom, and I can't do anything about you being in attendance here. But I can do something about you being near me. Which I prefer you not be. Goodbye, Derek."

"Keke—" he murmured, using his nickname for her. As if that would, what? Soften her? Tug on old memories? A cheap trick that wouldn't work.

"Good. Bye. Derek."

Frustration crossed his face, but he dipped his chin, pivoted and walked off down the hall, back toward the main room of the restaurant. As soon as he slipped back through the doors, she turned and faced Israel, the irritation brewing inside her flaming into anger.

Her first glimpse of him in the light tightened her belly like a screw. Pulling. Coiling. Aching. It echoed in her chest, constricting her airways so her breath squeaked past. It pulsed in her nipples, tautening the tips into beads. It spasmed in her sex, tugging hard, leaving her hot and so wet.

He was younger than she'd first assumed. Maybe five or seven years junior to her thirty-four. But…

Good God.

The man was beautiful.

Not in a traditional or conventional way, not like Derek. But with an almost brutal, raw magnetism that fairly emanated from him in waves. In the dark, she hadn't fully appreciated the wide breadth of his powerful shoulders and chest that were barely constrained in a white dress shirt. The sleeves, rolled up to just below his elbows, exposed sinewy forearms covered in colorful tattoos that reached to his wrists. More ink peeked from the open collar of his shirt and crept up the side of his neck. How far did that gorgeous artwork extend? The question popped in her mind as she scanned a flat abdomen, lean waist and thick thighs encased in slim black pants. What did it say about her that even as she debated strangling him with the belt on her dress—her only option since she couldn't possibly get her smaller hands around that strong neck—she wanted to seek out every tattoo on him with her fingers, mouth…tongue.

What. Was. Happening?

Not only was he tattooed, rude and much too wildly beautiful for her comfort, but he was too young. She already had "jilted bride" on her résumé, she didn't need to add "cougar."

Sucking in a much-needed breath, she stepped back. And to be on the safe side, took another step.

Yes, she was angry at his high-handedness. At assuming she was weak. *Focus on that.*

"In spite of what you think you saw out there—" she jabbed a finger toward the porch "—I'm no damsel in distress, and I don't need a knight in shining armor riding to my rescue."

His full lips tightened at the corners, and lightning flashed in his denim eyes.

"Good. Because I'm no knight to the rescue and have no desire to be one for anyone."

"Then it seems we're in full agreement on something for the first time." Embarrassment fed her anger. Embarrassment over him witnessing her initially freezing at the sight of Derek. Embarrassment that for a brief moment, relief had trickled through her like cool water over hot skin, when Israel had appeared and spoken up for her. She didn't need his pity. Hated it. "I can take care of and speak for myself. I don't need saving."

"Duly noted, Ms. Korrie Noel." He saluted her, the gesture as mocking as the tilt of his mouth, then stalked away in the opposite direction Derek had disappeared.

Damn him for looking as good going as he did coming. And *yes*. That curse was merited, too.

CHAPTER TWO

ISRAEL POPPED THE caps off two bottles of Sam Adams and set them down in front of the two women perched at the end of the bar. They both thanked him, and the brunette flashed him a flirtatious smile, giving him a heated look he had no problem recognizing from under her lowered lashes. At any other time, he probably would've picked up that gauntlet.

Instead, he rapped his knuckles on the scarred wood top and moved on to take the order of the next customer waiting on their drink. Road's End, the dive bar where he worked, was packed on this Thursday night. As usual, since Maddox Holt, the owner and Israel's best friend, hired a live band on Thursday, Friday and Saturday nights. Not that business wasn't respectable the other days of the week. As the only dive bar in Rose Bend, most of the stools and tables were usually filled, but there was something about the weekend—or coming weekend—and men and women rocking it out onstage that brought people in droves even from the next towns over. Which meant more tips for him.

Usually, that had him looking forward to the last days of the week. After all, they kept him so busy he didn't have time to think on anything but serving drinks, chatting up customers and collecting tips. Definitely no time to dwell on how much longer he intended to hide out here in a small town in the southern Berkshires pretending to be a late-twentysomething bartender with no other ambition in life but to master the perfect pour. Yep, as long as he could keep occupied, he could make believe he'd never had a life outside of Rose Bend, a completely different career he'd once loved, a wife he'd divorced...

Yeah. He was stellar at pretending.

Or at least he had been until last week and a certain wedding.

It figured it'd be the kind of occasion he avoided like the plague that would be the catalyst for this restless itch that refused to go away.

If Doug, one of the bartenders here, hadn't invited him to his wedding, and Maddox and Cherrie, Maddox's wife, hadn't guilted Israel into going, he'd have never met a certain wedding planner out on a deserted patio. Wouldn't have engaged in verbal sparring that equated to the hottest foreplay of his life. Wouldn't have been so distracted by a certain planner that a blatant invitation from another woman didn't entice him at all.

Distracted, hell.

Fascinated. Enraptured. Fucking whipped.

He shook his head. Talk about an exercise in futility. If he laid out a map and penciled in his name on one side of the country and her name on the other, it still wouldn't begin to describe the divide between them.

Pastor's daughter. He hadn't stepped foot in a church in years.

Rose Bend native and town good girl. He was a transplant who worked in the local dive bar.

Wedding planner. He'd rather walk over live coals and then frolic in a pool of alcohol before having anything to do with weddings or, God forbid, *love*.

She hated the sight of him. He wanted to fuck her until neither one of them could move.

See? Different.

"Iz?" Maddox nudged his shoulder as he built a Guinness. "You've been requested at the other end of the bar."

The gleam in his eyes should've been enough of a warning before Israel set the shot of whiskey down in front of a customer and turned in the direction of the entrance.

Yeah. Nothing could've been proper enough warning.

Korrie.

He stared. Wasn't even any point in denying it. He openly stared at the woman who'd refused to get the hell out of his head this past week.

In his other life, he'd been a wordsmith. Words had been the tools of his trade and arranging them to paint literary pictures had been his absolute pleasure. But after the hellscape of his divorce, they'd abandoned him. Like a lobotomy, that part of him, that almost magical, creative stirring he'd always counted on had been sliced off. He hadn't written a word in two years. Yet now, as on that dark patio, that stirring returned. Just a mere whisper. But when it'd been absent for so long, that whisper had nearly knocked him on his ass like a lion's roar. And the common denominator?

Her.

He'd heard musicians talk of muses before. And yeah, whatever worked for other people, but he'd never bought into that.

Until a week ago.

Until her.

No, he still hadn't written a word. And the thought of opening up his laptop again, sitting in front of it and pulling up a blank document had a cold sweat breaking out over his skin. But it couldn't smother the embers of hope from burning.

What if...

He squashed those cinders, extinguished them before they could take spark. How many times had he wished— even went so far as to pray—that the words would return? But they hadn't. He wasn't setting himself up for that again. And no face, no matter how beautiful, could return that gift to him.

He forced his feet forward, because part of him yelled he should wheel his ass around and head in the opposite direction. The woman *disturbed* him.

But he headed toward her anyway. Because he'd always been a stubborn shit.

"Korrie Noel." He added a drawl to her name guaranteed to send irritation flashing in her dark brown eyes. Just. Like. *That*. "What brings you to my world? Slumming it? Or are you out here to evangelize to us sinners?"

Another bolt of annoyance flickered in her gaze, but she simply arched her dark brows and leaned forward on her crossed arms. "That depends. Are you willing to turn from your wicked ways?"

He propped his arms on the bar top and met her halfway. This close, her delicate scent of lavender and something sweet like almonds teased him. Tempted him. He curled his fingers, pressing the tips hard into his muscle. "Why would I ever do that, when my wicked ways are so much fun, Barbie?" he murmured. "Don't knock 'em 'til you try 'em."

She didn't immediately reply, but stared at him, her eyes meeting his without flinching. Goddamn, those eyes. Pure, melted caramel with shards of a darker chocolate. He could peer into her gaze and, like a chameleon, always find something different. Something intriguing.

Clearing her throat, she straightened, breaking the taut silence that had descended between them. Tension hummed through him, alive, loud and *demanding*. He mimicked her action, slowly straightening, edging away from her lest he do something ill-advised. Like wrap his hand around the back of her neck, haul her forward and take that cock tease of a mouth.

"Speaking of trying them..." she said.

Israel frowned. "Trying what?"

"Your wicked ways." She cleared her throat again, glanced to the side. Down at her hands, which twisted a napkin. Then back up at him. "I want to."

"I'm lost." Like Hansel and Gretel meeting a cannibal witch in the woods lost. "You want what?"

She inhaled a breath and splayed her fingers wide on the bar top. "I want you to teach me to...to..."

"To?"

"To not give a fuck."

He blinked.

Shock rippled through him, its waves like sonic booms that rocked him. Surely, he hadn't... She couldn't have said... No, she wouldn't have...

And at some point, he was going to complete a sentence.

Spinning on the heel of his work boot, he strode over to Maddox and clapped his shoulder. When his friend turned around, he didn't waste any time. "Hey, can you get Daphne to cover me while I take a fifteen-minute break?"

Maddox scanned the crowded bar and the tables and dance floor beyond. But when he returned his narrowed gaze to Israel, he gave him a sharp nod. "I got you covered. Make it fast, though, yeah? We're only going to get more swamped."

"I promise. And thanks, man."

"Sure thing." The corner of Maddox's mouth quirked. "Are my eyes deceiving me, or is that Pastor Noel's daughter?"

"Don't trust your lying eyes, Maddy."

Clapping him on the shoulder again, Israel strode to the bar hatch, lifted it and passed through. In moments, he stood next to Korrie, cupping her elbow.

He lowered his head next to her ear and tried to ignore the tickle of her dark brown curls on his cheek and nose. "Come with me outside?"

After a brief hesitation, she nodded and slid from the stool. He guided her through the throng of people, putting his body between her and them until he reached the entrance and pushed through the door. As soon as he stepped outside, he dropped his hand as if her skin burned through her long-sleeved white shirt. He was half-convinced his palm carried a brand, but he refused to look.

Moving far enough away from the door so they wouldn't hinder anyone from entering, but close enough to remain in the light so she wouldn't feel uncomfortable, he leaned his back against the brick building, crossing his arms and studying her.

And damn, did he like studying her.

They might not have officially met before that night on the patio, but he'd immediately recognized her.

Or his dick had.

Hell, all it took was one look at that smooth, gorgeous skin only a couple of shades darker than her eyes, those striking cheekbones sharp enough to etch glass, a patrician nose with flared nostrils and a wide, sensual mouth that God surely couldn't have had anything to do with. Nothing holy or innocent about those plush lips. Thank the Lord.

His gaze dipped lower to the simple white cotton shirt and dark jeans that her petite, curvaceous body transformed into elegant couture straight off a New York Fashion Week runway, sexy as one of Victoria's Secret's newest fashions.

Full, firm breasts that pushed against the top. Hips that enticed hands to grip, hold on to...bruise. An ass that made him want to drop to his knees in prayer. And thighs. Jesus. Thighs so thick and toned, he ached to sink his teeth in before wrapping them around him.

In a word, she was...flawless.

Inhaling a long breath through his nose, he mentally withdrew from the temptation of her even if he couldn't physically distance himself.

"I have fifteen minutes for you to convince me I didn't hear what I think I just heard."

She heaved a sigh and thrust her hand through her tight curls, and he flexed his own hand. Jealous. Yeah, he wanted to sift those strands through his own fingers and discover their texture for himself.

"Let me start over because that came out wrong back there."

He snorted. "You think?"

"I haven't been able to stop thinking about our meeting last week."

Join our illicit club of two.

Bending his knee, his pressed his foot against the building and waited.

"More specifically, I can't stop thinking about how you described me. How you...perceive me." She frowned, and Israel stiffened, his stomach cranking tight at the uncertainty that wavered across her face. "Perfect. Pastor's kid. Town darling. Uptight."

"I didn't say that."

Her mouth twisted into a parody of a smile. "You didn't have to. It was more than implied." When he parted his lips to object, because dammit, he was going to object, she held up a hand. "No, you're right. I am uptight. I am all those things you called me—or I've tried to be. Or tried to make people believe I am. It's…exhausting. I don't know why I'm telling you this." She huffed out a dry chuckle, her gaze shifting to the ground between them. Several moments passed, and then she lifted her gaze to him, spearing him with those toffee-colored eyes. "I'm thirty-four years old and I've never made a decision based solely on my needs, my wants. I've always weighed how my choices will reflect on my father, his church, my image, on my marriageability and later, Derek. And when Derek…"

She wrapped her arms around her waist and a fire seethed inside him. He itched to hunt down her coward ex and kick in his balls to show him where they were located.

"When Derek left, it became important to show everyone I wasn't affected. That I wasn't broken. So I was—I'm still—making decisions for others and not for me. And I'm done with that. At least for tonight."

Another laugh, but this one more real. And goddammit, why did his arms ache to hold her? He wasn't the *holding type*.

"What do you need from me, Korrie?" Korrie. Not Barbie. Because this wasn't a teasing moment. She'd stripped herself in front of him, a relative stranger, and he'd honor that courage. "Make it plain."

"Teach me how to…" Her face scrunched up as if she now scrounged for the words that had seemed to tumble out of her moments ago. "Teach me how to be me before I allowed myself to be tied up by so many restrictions. Show me how to let loose and have…fun. Please."

He swallowed back a bark of laughter at that seemingly involuntary addition of "please." Always mannerable, even when asking him to school her in being wild.

"Korrie…"

"Before you make up your mind, I don't expect you to give me your time for free. I'll pay you."

His head jerked back, almost cracking the wall behind him. Arms and leg dropping, he pushed away from the wall and stalked forward, eliminating the small space that separated them. He stopped just short of looming over her. The anger glinting inside his chest like a hard diamond was not sharp enough that he'd abuse his height and strength to intimidate her.

"I may be a lowly bartender in your eyes, but I can't be bought. I don't need or *want* your money."

Her eyes widened a fraction before what appeared to be shame shadowed them. "I'm sorry, Israel. I didn't mean to offend you. I just didn't want you to think I was taking advantage of you."

"If I agree to this—and that's a huge *if*—it will be because I *choose* to. Your first lesson in letting loose? Let go of the concept of people only wanting to be around you for what they can get out of you. I'm not here for that."

His words throbbed between them like a heartbeat.

"Are you going to be here for me, then?"

Her voice didn't tremble, didn't waver, but her eyes... Shit, they were going to be the death of him. They had a language all their own, and they pleaded with him.

"Why me? Hell, you don't even like me," he said, grasping at straws. Because he hovered on the edge of a *yes* that wouldn't be wise for either of them.

No way in hell he didn't end this without being balls deep inside her.

And with her regretting she'd ever laid eyes on him.

Call him insane—and no, it wouldn't be the first time he'd called himself that in the last two years—but he didn't want to be one more regret on her list. Right under her ass-hole of an ex.

"And you don't like me, either."

"I wouldn't go that far," he muttered.

He didn't know her, not really. But he didn't need to be able to pick out her favorite flavor of ice cream in order to have her screaming his name in his ears.

She loosed a low, rough laugh. "As odd as it sounds, it's nice that you don't really care for me," she murmured. "It means you don't have a problem being honest with me. I need that in my life. It's...refreshing."

He didn't bother disabusing her of her idea regarding his feelings toward her. It was probably safer for both of them that she believed it.

"And to answer your question of why you..." She held up her hands, her delicate pale palms facing upward. "Because no one else would do it. They would worry more about handling me with kid gloves than helping me. And I want this too much to let their well-meaning interfere. No." She shook her head. "I need you."

Those three words stroked right down his abs and wrapped around his cock. But they also reached inside his chest and squeezed his heart. A heart he'd sworn no longer did things like hurt or even beat. He'd believed it'd atrophied a long time ago.

"I told you before, I'm no knight in shining armor."

"And I told *you* that I'm not a damsel in distress. I don't need you to save me. I need you to show me how to save myself."

He scrubbed a hand over his hair then down the shaved sides of his head.

Aw shit.

"Fine."

A smile lit up her face, glowing like the sun breaking over the horizon. Damn. He just managed to stop himself from stumbling back away from her. That smile was lethal.

And he was in danger.

Oh, yeah, this was *not* going to end well.

But too late now. He'd rather run naked through the field at the end of town in the middle of January and suffer severe shrinkage than steal that beautiful light from her face.

"When do we start?" She rolled to the balls of her feet and back to her heels, rocking back and forth.

He grabbed his cell from his back pocket and glanced at the screen. "I have to get back to work. Here." He opened the phone and brought up a new message. "Text me so I have your number. I'll get in touch with you tomorrow."

"Okay." Her fingers flew over the keypad then she handed the cell back. "Thank you, Israel," she said. "I really appreciate this."

"Yeah." He turned to go but then jerked to a stop. Glancing over his shoulder, he murmured, "You're welcome."

Then he walked back into the bar, losing himself in the noise of the music and the crowd before he did something stupid.

Like tell her he was proud of her.

CHAPTER THREE

"I'M GOING TO be honest. This was not what I pictured when I asked you to help me let loose."

Perched on a chair at a high table, she scanned the place that looked more like a dance club than the dive bar she'd ventured into only a week earlier. After having never stepped foot in a bar in her life, she'd visited two in two weeks.

When she went rogue, she went *rogue*.

"Do tell what you were imagining, Barbie." Israel plunked a glass containing golden-brown alcohol with a lighter foam on top along with a bottle of beer on the table between them. "Did there happen to be a sex dungeon and a red room involved? C'mon, it's a safe space here. You can admit it." He waggled his dark eyebrows.

She wrinkled her nose at him and picked up the glass, assuming the Sam Adams wasn't intended for her. Sipping the drink, she hummed, pleasantly surprised when the creamy, butterscotch flavor flowed over her tongue. "Wow. That's delicious." She took another sip then set it down on the table. "What's this called?"

"A buttery nipple."

A sputtering cough burst from her, spraying alcohol over the tabletop. He calmly reached over and patted her on the back, as if women choking and wheezing through a spasming fit were an everyday occurrence for him. She swatted his hand away. He disappeared and moments later, returned with a glass of water. Snatching it up, her first impulse was to gulp it down. But her tight throat wouldn't allow it. She sipped the water, and after a couple of moments, lowered the glass and sucked in a deep breath. And threw him a death glare.

"You did that on purpose," she rasped.

He widened his eyes trying for innocent and missing it by a country mile. The only thing missing was him clutching his pearls.

"I have no idea what you mean. As a bartender, I thought you might enjoy this particular drink. Butterscotch and Irish cream liqueur, what's not to love? And I was right. Tell me I was wrong." He nudged the glass with his finger.

"I swear to God, I'm being sexually harassed," she grumbled, patting down the table with a napkin.

A big, long-fingered hand covered hers, and she glanced up, meeting his denim gaze. "If I made you uncomfortable, Korrie, I apologize, and I'll do better. I didn't intend any offense."

She stared at him, frozen. Other than her father, had another man been so concerned with her comfort, her feelings? Maybe Derek had, in the beginning of their relationship. The very beginning but not after. God. What did that say about her?

That you're so desperate to not be old and alone that you'll put up with not being valued and appreciated as you deserve.

Well…okay, then.

That truth stung. Didn't make it any less accurate.

"You do make me uncomfortable sometimes, but not because you offend me. You're fine."

His hand pressed down on hers for a brief moment. Then he slowly leaned back in his chair, his fingers trailing a fire-licked path along the back of her hand. Why flames didn't spring up in their wake, she had no idea. She drew her arm under the table, unobtrusively rubbing her thumb over the suddenly sensitive skin.

Or maybe not so unobtrusively, she amended, when his gaze dropped as if he could peer through the wood.

"How else, Korrie?"

"What?" For the life of her she couldn't grasp their conversation past the heat evaporating all the blood in her veins.

"How else do I cause you…discomfort?"

She paused, then almost winced. Yes, she'd said that. And couldn't take it back now that he'd called her out on it.

"You are…different from other men I've known."

"Different," he repeated, tipping the bottle to his mouth and studying her over the rim. "Now I'm the one who doesn't know if I should be offended." His tone remained easy, but she caught the slight tightening of his fingers around the beer, the telltale firming of his mouth.

Or at least telltale to her.

Probably because she'd become an expert in the study of his hard but incredibly soft-looking mouth.

Drink up, girl. There's courage at the bottom of this glass.

Obeying her subconscious's order, she picked up her buttery nipple—*Lord, that name!*—and downed more liquor.

"As I'm learning, different isn't bad. Derek was my norm." She inhaled. "The way you look at me. Talk to me. Behave toward me…" A shimmering wave of heat undulated low in her belly. And she steeled herself against the shiver that worked its way through her. "It's blunt and like a lot of drinks you probably serve—straight up with no chaser. Yes, it's uncomfortable. But it's also the most honest conversation I've ever had. So yes, you are different. And it's good. At least, good for me."

Something quicksilver and dark flashed through his eyes. What was that? What had she said? She ran her words through her head but couldn't pinpoint what would elicit that particular reaction. An emotion that she couldn't decipher but reminded her of pain, of anger, or a volatile mixture of the two.

But in the next instant, it disappeared, hidden behind his hooded gaze and a lazy smile.

"Let's see if you're saying that by the end of the night, Barbie." He tipped his head toward the front of the bar. "Tonight's 'I don't give a fuck' assignment."

Just then, the music cut, and a woman's voice boomed over a mic. Korrie spun on her chair and located the source on the raised platform.

"Welcome to karaoke night at the Bull's Head! Who's ready to get their Beyoncé on?" The older woman with her tight Bull's Head T-shirt—complete with horns shooting out of either side of the logo—and tighter jeans and boots, held up her hands. Hoots and hollers broke out all around Korrie, and the woman grinned. "Well, let's get it started. Tammy, you're up!"

A girl with beautiful sister locs bounced up the stairs onto the stage and accepted the mic. She waved to the crowd, and Korrie honestly expected her to break out in jazz hands. Then the music kicked in, she opened her mouth and belted out the first lyrics of "Wanted Dead or Alive" by Bon Jovi.

Korrie's jaw dropped. She might look barely old enough to be in the bar but the pipes on her…

Her head snapped around to Israel.

"I'm not doing that."

He shook his head. "Of course not."

She exhaled, relieved. Maybe he just expected them to watch tonight. To ease into this whole letting loose thing—

"I picked a different song for us."

Shit. *Shitshitshitshit.*

And yes. This situation *so* merited a curse. Several of them.

"No."

"Now, don't knock—"

"No way."

"Korrie."

"I can't."

In spite of the performance and cheering around them, silence hummed at their table, louder than the din in the bar. Or so it seemed to her. And her very telling *I can't* vibrated between them.

After several moments where her impassioned, humiliating plea sat there, he simply asked, "Why not?"

"Why?" She splayed her hands wide on the table. "Because I'm not a college student. I'm too old to get up there."

The opening notes to Patsy Cline's "Crazy" filtered through the speakers and a pretty but creaky-with-age voice did, too.

"Next."

Korrie briefly closed her eyes. *Why me, God? Why?*

She pinched the bridge of her nose, panic crawling up her throat like a spider with the light suddenly thrown on.

"That's not me. I don't do—" she flicked a hand in the direction of the stage "—that."

"You don't know what you do. What you're capable of. Isn't that the whole reason you sought me out? So next excuse. But—" he propped his folded arms on the table and leaned forward, his indigo eyes not allowing her to look away "—to save time, why not try the truth this time?"

"I'm scared." The admission came out quiet, small. Ashamed.

"Scared of what? Name it, Korrie."

"Embarrassing myself. People booing. People saying nothing at all." She started slowly, but the more she talked, the more her words toppled over themselves faster and faster. "Me forgetting the words even though they're right there on the screen. Feeling the stares. Freezing. Failing," she whispered. "Again."

"Korrie, look at me."

She jerked her head up, not realizing until that moment that her gaze had drifted away from him, staring sightlessly over his shoulder.

"Do you trust me?"

Did she? She barely knew him. And she'd quietly asked around before seeking him out at Road's End. A twenty-eight-year-old bartender who'd shown up in Rose Bend two years earlier. Jesse Ford, co-owner of Auto World, the local auto parts store and garage, with his father-in-law, was Israel's brother. Maddox Holt, owner of the dive bar, his friend. That's it. No other info. And the people of Rose Bend were experts at digging into others' business.

Yet…she *had* sought him out. Because yes, she did trust him.

At least in this.

That honesty she'd mentioned minutes ago assured her he might carry secrets, but he didn't intend to abuse her or the faith she'd placed in him.

"Yes."

His wide shoulders didn't slump, but his big body did

visibly relax. As if her answer had filled him with tension. As if it'd been important to him.

"Then get this." He pressed his palm to hers, his long fingers grazing her wrist. She bit the inside of her cheek to trap the gasp that tried to escape at the skin-to-skin contact. He'd briefly touched her before. But this… This somehow seemed more intimate, like a kiss, a mating. A promise. "I won't let you go up there alone. I won't disappear on you. I won't fail you."

His voice, low, almost fervent, rumbled through her, leaving her pulled taut and loose-limbed, on fire and wet. And his words… His words were so much scarier.

Because they left her feeling secure.

The last time she'd depended on, trusted a man, he'd abandoned her in the most humiliating and devastating way possible.

And yet, she nodded. Then slipped her hand out from under his. And ignored the tingling that refused to abate.

Turning back to the stage, she forced herself to relax and focus on the karaoke entertainers rolling onto the stage one after the other. And soon, she didn't have to force anything. The sometimes good, sometimes downright awful singing, as well as the deafening applause and good-natured laughter and cheering swept Korrie up in their contagious fun. She laughed and clapped along with everyone else, and only when Israel stood next to her did she remember that, right, she wasn't just a spectator.

Oh, God.

Her stomach bottomed out and panic swirled in like an eddying tide. She sucked in air through her lips. Deep breaths. Passing out in a bar full of people wasn't a good look.

"You got this." Israel wrapped her hand in his, squeezed. And as he led her toward the stage, he didn't release it.

"I do. I got this," she repeated, heart lodged in her throat, furiously beating there.

She could barely swallow, much less speak—or sing. But she was getting up on that stage. Even if Israel ended up doing most of the singing, she was dragging her behind up there and going through with this. If she wanted to break out of the too-tight, ill-fitting mold—out of the chains she'd had a huge part in cuffing to herself—then she had to start here.

With karaoke.

"Do I want to know what song you chose?" she muttered as they climbed the steps.

He glanced at her over his shoulder, the blue, green and white spotlights swirling over his mohawk, face and shoulders. And when he grinned, he reminded her more than ever of that Viking.

"Oh, just a little song about premeditated murder."

Without giving her time to dwell on that, he pulled her up behind him and led her out to the mic stands and the karaoke monitor. He pressed a mic into her numb hand, and only reflex kept her from dropping it.

"What's up, folks," he drawled, and whether people whistled and yelled in response to the big, gorgeous man or the greeting itself was a toss-up. "I brought my friend up here and she's a karaoke virgin so give her some love, yeah?"

The applause broke out again, but louder this time, complete with stomping that made it sound like they had only seconds before the floor caved in under them.

The panic spiked as Korrie stared at Israel, eyes wide, but underneath the sharp edges of that terror trickled humor and maybe, just maybe, excitement?

Good Lord, she was doing this.

Summoning a shaky smile, she finally shifted her gaze from Israel to the dark crowd beyond the stage. Even though she could only see the first few tables, she gave everyone a small wave, and received more cheers. The panic loosened its grip, and her heart started returning to its normal place in her chest. She inhaled a breath, held it.

Ready? he mouthed.

She nodded. As she'd ever be.

Then the title of the song he'd chosen appeared on the screen, and she choked out a bark of laughter. Her grin spread so wide, her cheeks hurt, and Israel returned it with a wink that shouldn't have been sexy, but, well, this was Israel.

The opening notes of the song about two best friends who off one of their husbands with poisoned black-eyed peas because he's an abusive asshole blasted through the speakers.

For a moment, her throat seized, and nothing came out.

But Israel didn't have that problem.

Taking her hand in his, he started singing in an exaggerated twang that, again, shoved back the panic. The sheer ridiculousness of it had amusement bubbling up inside and before she realized it, she joined him—without the Texas drawl.

By the time they hit the second chorus, she'd forgotten all her fear, all her insecurities, all her doubts and belted out the lyrics with an abandon that she'd never, ever known.

She was…free.

When the last guitar riff echoed in the room, she turned to Israel and threw her arms around him. Burying her face into the crook of his neck. And laughed.

Laughed long, loud and hard.

Simply because she could.

CHAPTER FOUR

"You're a bit of a drama queen."

Israel's mouth quirked as Korrie's eyes widened then narrowed on him.

Delight fluttered inside his rib cage like trapped butterfly wings, and it stunned him. Delight? When was the last time that effervescent thrill had filled him? Definitely not in the last two years.

Definitely not since his marriage ended.

Not since he'd last written a word.

Seeing Korrie come alive up there on that stage. Seeing her laugh and dance before that crowd and how they ate that shit up.

Feeling that tight, curvy body pressed to his, those firm breasts crushed to his abdomen, thick thighs tangled with his…inhaling that lavender-and-almond scent… It'd required everything in him not to hike her up in his arms, wrap those legs around his waist and take that dick tease of a mouth…

Speaking of her mouth…

He tore his gaze from those lips and dropped his focus to the darkness of the parking lot and the trees beyond the porch where they stood.

What was it about them and porches?

"What're you talking about?" she asked.

He tipped his beer for a long sip before answering, trying to swallow down the lust swarming inside him, hungry, loud and almost angry. It didn't work, but at least it dampened his throat so he could speak.

"Acting all nervous and scared. But then you get up there and blow like you're Jennifer Hudson. The preacher's kid's been holding out."

"I might have been in the church choir when I was younger."

He snorted. "You were definitely holding out." He cocked his head, stared at the small smile flirting with those full lips. "Did you have fun?"

She leaned a shoulder against the post. "I did. I really did," she murmured, and he didn't miss the note of awe in her voice.

"I hate to break this to you, Barbie. But you're kind of a badass."

A laugh escaped her, and she shook her head. "Thank you. I think."

"It's a compliment." He paused, wondering if he should ask the question that had been plaguing him since their conversation in the bar earlier. Part of him loathed bringing up anything that might steal that gleam from her eyes, but… But the other half needed to know what was in her head. That had become a compulsion for him lately. "Back there you said you were scared of failing again. What did you mean?"

The light in her gaze dimmed, the faint smile fading from her lips. "Do you really need to ask?"

"You can't possibly tell me you believe him being a fucking runaway groom was your fault." He slowly straightened, disbelief sharpening his voice.

She released a sound that struck him as impatient yet vulnerable. "Logically, I know Derek abandoning me wasn't my fault. But emotionally? In the middle of the night when I can't shut my brain off? Then, I don't always know that."

Just ask me, and I'll give you something else to distract you in those hours in the middle of the night. My mouth, my body, my cock. Just. Fucking. Ask.

The plea shoved at his throat, demanding to be released. But he locked it down, crossing his arms over his chest as if that could confine it.

"It's more than that," she continued, squinting into the darkness and not meeting his eyes. "I'm thirty-four. All of my friends are married, have their own homes, are raising their children by now. That was supposed to be me. It's what I always imagined for myself. And I thought I could finally have it with Derek. Instead, I'm still single, still alone. And every day I wake up, questioning more and more... Who am I? How sad is it that at nearly thirty-five, I'm still doing that?"

"There's never anything wrong with asking that. How else are you going to find out the answers? How else are you going to know if the answers that were one thing yesterday are different today? Because out of everything you've just claimed to imagine for yourself—the husband, home and kids—you never said if you *wanted* them."

Her head jerked toward him, lips parted, but nothing emerged.

Sucking in a breath, he turned, gripped the railing and gave it his weight. Self-preservation screamed at him to play this off with some platitude, to assure her that it was all good and to walk back into the bar, go on with the night. But he couldn't move.

Her vulnerability, her honesty deserved—no, demanded—his. He could choose to be a coward in this moment, but it would not only shame him, but also her gift of opening up to him, a relative stranger she'd trusted with a truth he sensed she didn't give to many.

Why me? What about me makes me trustworthy?

The question nagged at him, but he put it aside to dissect later. Much later when his heart wasn't trying to cut bait and run.

"I get feeling like a failure, Korrie. Feeling like even though you colored within the lines, followed the rules, said all the right things, made all the right moves that, in the end, none of it meant shit. You still have nothing to show for it. Not friends. Not a house in the most affluent neighborhood. Not a wife. Not a career."

Her soft gasp whispered in the night, but he didn't glance at her. Couldn't. Underneath his long-sleeved cotton shirt, his skin itched. An insane craving to shed it all and just disappear surged within him. Anything to avoid the inevitable shame and pain that crawled through him when he thought about the last few years.

"Israel." A soft, delicate hand settled on his arm, and it soothed the restlessness like a balm. "You don't have to do this."

"Yes, I do." He stared out across the parking lot and into the trees as if the ghosts of his past would wander out. "I once had what you described, except for the kids. But I wanted them, too. One day. But I found out I was alone in that dream. At some point, the woman I married, the woman I'd loved, and planned on spending the rest of my life with, had changed her mind. About all of it. The marriage, the family, our future…me. Except she didn't clue me in until I arrived to the home I bought for us with my first big royalty check and the locks were changed and my supposed best friend was telling me through the door that my wife had filed for divorce—so she could be with him."

"The hell you say."

The bitter dregs from that day swirled in his chest like dirty coffee grounds. Memories damn near trampled him, so he didn't even call her out on the cursing.

"Yeah. How cliché is that? My best friend and my wife, fucking behind my back. And me, the clueless dupe, who didn't even notice. But it wasn't enough for them to steal my trust, they tried to come after my livelihood, too. Everything I worked my ass off for, sacrificed for. They tried to strip me of what made me *me*. I would say thank God I had a hell of an attorney, but by the time the divorce papers were signed, I was so empty, so done with it all, she might as well as have taken me for everything because I had nothing left to give. My heart, my soul, my creativity, my faith in people... I was done."

He scrubbed a hand over his hair, down the shaved side of his head, the shorter strands abrading his palm. Risking a look at her, he glanced over his shoulder. And immediately closed his eyes.

Sympathy darkened those brown eyes, and he both hated it and wanted to bask in that warmth.

"Is that when you came to Rose Bend?"

He nodded. "I had nowhere else to go," he admitted quietly, hearing how sad that confession sounded. "I won the house in the divorce, but I didn't want that shrine to a dead future, false dreams. So I sold it and came here. My parents had retired to Florida, and my brother had lived here for years. I'd visited once or twice and met Maddox on one of those visits. He offered me a job in his bar and so..." He shrugged.

"You mentioned a royalty check and how your ex had

stolen your creativity…" She tilted her head. "There is absolutely nothing wrong with being a bartender, but that's not who you are, is it, Israel?"

"It is now." His jaw worked and he half turned, leaning his hip against the railing, crossing his arms. "I was I. M. Kelly."

She stared at him. No, gaped. Then slowly shook her head, frowning. "I. M. Kelly. The number one *New York Times* bestselling author? *That* I. M. Kelly?"

"Same."

"Shut. The. Front. Door."

For the first time since he started his pathetic trip into his past, genuine humor swelled inside him and a grin tugged at his lips. Jesus, how was that possible? Nothing even remotely surrounding his divorce or his former career had ever stirred amusement within him.

Korrie.

The answer flickered across his mind, there and gone before he could grasp it.

A fissure of alarm raced through him. She shouldn't have that kind of influence over his emotions. Not this woman with the soulful chocolate eyes and danger written all over her. Danger to his status quo. To his vow of distance from people, from life.

"You are *not* I. M. Kelly. There's no way that's possible."

He arched an eyebrow. "Yeah? Why is that?"

"Because one, she's a romance writer. You, Israel Ford, don't have one romantic bone in your body."

I did once. They were all broken.

"Hate to break it to you, Barbie, but not all romance authors are romantics. That's a stereotype. Kind of like the one about Black people not blushing. And since I've seen those cheeks of yours fired up all pretty once or twice in my company, we both know that's a lie."

"See?" She jabbed a finger at him, scowling. "That right there. That's what I'm talking about! The taunting Barbie. Riding the edge of political correctness. The blunt, 'I don't give an eff' demeanor. That's so far from the beautiful, sensitive, haunting prose of I. M. Kelly, they're not even in the same hemisphere. Nope." She shook her head again, then threw him a disgruntled glower. "Besides, I refuse to believe I've been in the presence of one of my favorite authors all this time and didn't know it."

"One of your favorites, huh? Who beat me out?" When she glared at him, he chuckled. "So sorry to disappoint, but…" He gave her another shrug, but then his smirk died on his lips. "You're right. I'm not I. M. Kelly. Not anymore. The truth is…"

He hesitated, the words lodging in his throat out of fear and shame. How would she view him if he admitted this fault, this weakness? He uncrossed his arms, dangling them at his sides. Letting go. He was letting go with this particular woman when he hadn't spoken of this with anyone else—not his brother, not Maddox. He didn't pause to analyze why. Afraid to.

"The truth is I haven't written a word since the divorce. Two years. *Two. Years.* It's like a part of me has been amputated. That part I took for granted. That part that has always been there for me. Every writer has those times when the words play hard to get. But this? It's as if they disappeared, abandoned me. My ex-wife, the divorce, they broke more than my heart. They broke *me*."

Silence filled the vacuum left by his hoarse confession. Only the muted music and din of conversation and laughter from the bar filtered into the night.

Shit. He shouldn't have said anything. Shouldn't have laid his soul bare.

He needed to get out of here—

"You're wrong, you know."

His head jerked toward her, his pulse so loud in his ears, it almost drowned her out. But he caught it.

"I'm wrong about what?"

"You said that you *were* an author. You *were* I. M. Kelly. You're wrong—you couldn't stop being a writer any more than you could stop willingly breathing. A lack of written words doesn't change that. It's who you are. And your ex can't steal that from you. It's not hers to take."

Frustration spiked hard within him, and he slashed a hand between them. "You don't know—"

"Don't know what I'm talking about? Know how you feel? Understand?" A faint smile teased her mouth, and he shoved his hands into his pockets, preventing himself from rubbing his thumb across that full bottom lip. Stopping himself from feeling that slight smile against his skin. "How is it that despite the mohawk, muscles, tattoos and smart mouth we're pretty much the same person? We've both been betrayed by someone we loved. Both have had our worlds shattered and reshaped by them so we're feeling our way, searching for who we are in the aftermath. Both are hiding behind façades so other people can't see the real us because we're afraid to be hurt again. Afraid people won't accept or love the real us."

The moisture fled his mouth, and for the first time in years he felt...seen. And it wasn't comfortable. At all.

"I don't know what it is to have an amazing talent like yours. To be able to create such gorgeous love stories with mere words. But I do know what it is to have what you love most suddenly be the most painful thing in your life. I'm a wedding planner, for God's sake. I love my job—everything about it. Yet, I was a bride left at the altar. Love became a dirty four-letter word, and I couldn't stand to see people have what I lost. What Derek ruined for me."

She thrust her fingers through her hair, pushing the thick curls away from her face. Pain flashed across those stunning, sensual features. His palms tingled with the need to cradle those elegant, sharp cheekbones, trace the sensitive skin beneath her eyes. Wish he could've been there to dry the tears that would've wet it in the darkest of those days.

"For a while, I thought I'd have to find a different career. But I'd given him my heart, my pride, my dreams. I couldn't give him one more thing. So I'm faithing it until I make it. Some days, I'm dying a little inside as I watch two people find their happily-ever-after. And then there are days when I'm okay. Days when I know he bruised me, but he didn't break me. And your ex didn't break you."

"Then why do I feel like I'm in pieces? And as if those pieces will never again form the person I once was?"

Another of those almost-there smiles graced her lips, and she tilted her head, her gaze steady on him.

"Call it the PK in me, but I don't believe God gave you such a gift of beauty and power, only so it can die on the vine. Every injury needs time to heal. And that's what you're doing—healing. You'll write again."

"How can you be so sure of that? I thought you and God were on the outs? Remember the 'Why have Thou forsaken me?' conversation you were having with Him when we met?"

Instead of frowning at his dangerously close to heretical comment and the teasing about their original meeting, she smiled, shaking her head.

"We've come to an understanding. I was so focused on

escaping my past, He was already leading me to what I needed. It just took me a minute to see it."

Israel arched an eyebrow. "Yeah? What's that?"

"You."

Shock blasted him, and if not for the post at his back, he would've rocked on his feet. That one word punched him in the chest, and he inhaled a shallow breath that scraped his throat.

He didn't believe in that divine intervention shit she seemed to accept, but damn if hearing her claim he was part of her path didn't resonate in his soul. Damn if it didn't touch that part of him that he'd just told her was atrophied.

As the icy shock ebbed, molten heat flowed in, so hot it should've cauterized his veins. Instead it swept through him like an open valve, and any moment, he feared—anticipated— erupting with this dark, greedy desire.

He was already leading me to what I needed.

His mind argued she probably meant that in some spiritual, figurative way; his body didn't give a fuck.

"Why do you need me?" he asked, voice churned-up gravel.

She hesitated a beat, and if he hadn't been watching her as if his very existence depended on her next breath, he might've missed that slight pause. But he didn't. And the hunger in him dug deeper, burned hotter.

"For that." She turned and waved a hand toward the closed porch double doors. "If you hadn't agreed to help me, I would've never had the guts to get up there and sing tonight. I wouldn't have experienced that kind of fun and... freedom. So no—" she shook her head so hard, her curls grazed her shoulders "—I don't believe someone who has given so generously of himself won't receive it in return.

That's not the way this works. So you'll write again. I believe in you."

"So now you accept that I'm I. M. Kelly?" he teased.

I believe in you.

Not even during their happiest moments had his ex-wife ever stated those words to him.

They trembled through him, and he shook.

She rolled her eyes. "You just want your pound of flesh, don't you? Fine. You're her—or him. God, this changed my whole world," she mumbled.

"Not the first time I've heard that from a woman."

She scowled at him, but ruined it with a snicker.

"Ready to head back in?" She turned toward the doors, but stopped, glancing over her shoulder. "How old are you, Israel?"

"Twenty-eight. Why?"

A wince shadowed across her features. "Why are you here with me? Why aren't you hanging out with women your age or younger?"

"Because they don't have social security checks I can fleece."

A beat of silence pulsed, then her crack of laughter burst on the night air.

He grinned.

And for the moment, he decided not to dwell on how the joyful sound squeezed a heart he'd believed no longer capable of feeling.

CHAPTER FIVE

"I STILL CAN'T believe you arranged all this."

Korrie stared in awe at the huge screen set up several yards in front of them. Somehow, Israel had commandeered the screen, and she didn't know what shocked her more—the projector propped on top of his black Ram 1500 pickup truck playing *Robin Hood: Prince of Thieves*...or the simple but beautiful split-level log cabin surrounded by trees and acreage. It seemed the bestselling author masquerading as a bartender preferred his privacy. And he'd bought himself an oasis out here on the outskirts of Rose Bend.

"It's not a wild and crazy outing, but you did mention how much you love eighties movies. I thought this might be a cool surprise."

Israel passed her a slice of pepperoni and sausage pizza from the grease-stained cardboard box bearing the name of Rossi Pizza Palace, the best pizzeria in Rose Bend. She accepted it on autopilot, schooling her features into a smile, while inside...inside her belly quivered. She'd uttered that throwaway comment in passing, yet he'd remembered; he'd paid attention.

The man not only stoked her body's hunger. He seduced her mind.

There was no part of her that didn't ache for him.

And in the last three weeks that she'd become partners-in-crime and even friends with him, she'd become adept at hiding her ever-increasing need.

In other words, she'd become a consummate liar.

"Do you like it?" Israel asked, sliding a paper plate under her pizza.

"Of course." She bit into the slice of pepperoni, sausage and cheese heaven, groaning at the explosion of flavor and spices on her tongue. "Rossi's is always delicious."

She opened her eyes to catch his hooded gaze on her mouth. Noted the firm set of his wide, full mouth. The stretch of skin over his sharp cheekbones. And all of that intensity was focused on her.

The breath stalled in her lungs, but every nerve ending jolted to strict attention, vibrating like a tuning fork. And he was the perfect pitch she sought.

This…*greed* for him had only deepened, intensified since their first outing at the karaoke bar. Yes, they'd bonded on the stage, but he'd slid under her defenses, etched himself on her very psyche out on that porch with his low, careful admission. An admission that had pulsed with pain, frustration, bitterness and an aching vulnerability that had crept inside her and refused to leave.

He scared her.

No, that wasn't correct. That was her passing the blame.

She terrified herself. Because she'd allowed herself to want another man who was emotionally unavailable.

Want. She latched on to that word like a mountain climber clinging to a rope dangling off the side of a cliff. As long as she could remember that this was strictly about the physical, she could control this reaction. Control herself.

Control your heart.

"But as for everything else?" She found a smile, upped the wattage on it to cast the thoughts in her head in the shadows. "Karaoke. A motorcycle ride through the mountains. Zip-lining. And now Kevin Costner and Morgan Freeman and pizza in the back of a pickup. I'd say it's definitely a contender." She took another bite of her pizza. "Matter of fact, a winner."

"Good," he murmured, switching his attention back to the screen, where Robin of Locksley returned to England to find his father dead and his land in ruins.

She turned to the movie as well, trying to lose herself in it, since the film was one of her favorites. But for the first time, she couldn't. Not with Israel sitting next to her, his big body's warmth combatting the coolness of the April night.

What would he do if she moved the pizza out of the way, closed the space separating them and curled up against him? Would he stiffen and gently push her away? Would he ask her what the hell she was doing? Or would he lay her down on the blanket he'd used to cover the pickup bed, and slide between her thighs, cover her…take her.

Her chest rose and fell on labored breaths, and she inhaled a deep one, holding it. But heat swirled low in her belly, and lower still, wetting her sex. Readying her for a possession that might never happen.

"Korrie."

She startled, her head jerking to the side.

"What's wrong?" he asked, his denim eyes nearly black under the night sky.

"What? Nothing." *You. You are what's wrong.* "Why do you ask?"

"Because you're not watching the movie." He shifted, leaning his wide back against the pickup bed and raising his leg. Resting his wrist on his knee, he stared at her, and she struggled not to avoid it. "What's going on? Do you want me to stop the movie?"

"No." She shook her head. "I love that you did this. Please don't stop it."

He cocked his head, and God, that gaze. It seemed to penetrate right through skin and bone to the heart of her. No, deeper. The hungry, needy soul of her. Could he see? Did he know?

Lord help her, she'd been dumped at the altar, was commitment shy, didn't trust and was now officially a cougar. So far, she and Israel had done the impossible in a town the size of Rose Bend—kept their...relationship a secret. But if it got out that she, Pastor Keith Noel's daughter, had rebounded with a younger man—the bartender from the local dive bar—she'd never hear the end of it.

But sitting in the back of his truck, staring into his indigo eyes, those thick thighs encased in dark denim and spread as if inviting her to come claim her space between them, she couldn't give a damn.

Curse *so* merited.

She briefly closed her eyes. Did she have the courage to claim him for herself, though? Wasn't that what these last three weeks had been all about? Letting loose? Being brave? Finding the *her* that had lived within all along and allowing her to reign?

Heart slamming against her sternum like a drum, she slowly slid her plate aside and turned to more fully face him.

"Truth?"

"Between me and you? Always."

"Out of all the tasks that I've tackled—singing in front of people, zip-lining down a mountain—nothing scares me as much as this." She waved a hand back and forth between them.

He didn't move, but she sensed the shift in him, from casual to alert. Relaxed to vigilant.

"This?" he murmured.

"Yes." She pressed a fist to her belly. "This thing I wasn't expecting, and if I'm brutally honest, part of me doesn't really want. Because it's messy, ill-advised and doomed. But I can't explain it away. I can't deny it. I can't ignore it. And I don't want to anymore."

He still didn't move, and yet he seemed to go even more rigid. Tension entered every inch of his body until he fairly vibrated with it. Though shadows enveloped them, his eyes gleamed with...

Need.

A furnace of lust blasted out of her, lighting her up. The same need that surged inside her, glittered in his eyes and scorched away her doubts.

"You still haven't defined what *this* is," he said. "But tell me over here." He crooked a finger at her. "Come here, Korrie."

She should've balked at that imperious command. Instead, she rose to her knees and shuffled over to him, not stopping until she knelt between his thighs. He spread his legs wider, providing more room for her.

And her heart constricted so hard, pain bloomed behind her rib cage. A warning. Because that place he'd made for her felt too perfect. Too custom fit.

She couldn't afford to allow that thinking to take root.

"Closer," he said, his voice a coarse caress. She obeyed, moving nearer until her knees butted up against the back of his thighs and his scent—clean, fresh soap and *him*—embraced her. And when his big hands clasped her hips, steadying her, she shuddered, pleasure rocking her on her moorings. "Good. Now tell me. Define 'this,' Barbie."

"Need. Hunger. Desire. You."

"Then conquer it just like everything else we've done together. Conquer me."

He threw the dare down, a carnal gauntlet between them.

She picked it up.

Gripping the edge of the truck on either side of his head, she leaned forward and took his mouth.

She groaned, immediately drunk on him. Insatiable for more. Tilting her head, she parted her lips, then parting his with her tongue. His grip on her hips tightened, holding her steady—or maybe holding himself steady. She didn't know. But he met her, stroke for stroke, lick for lick. Suck for suck.

Oh, God.

She might have started this kiss, initiated the conquering, but with one growl that vibrated over her nipples and echoed lower in her clenching sex, he took over. He lifted an arm, and his big hand sank into her hair, fingers tangling in the strands. She gasped into his mouth, prickles dancing over her scalp. Her lashes fluttered at the pinpricks of pleasure pain, and she curled into him, her elbows bending so her breasts pressed into his, nipples beaded so tight, they ached. And rubbing them against the hard wall of his chest only heightened the sweet pain, not alleviated it.

Not that she wanted it to be eased. No, she wanted him to make her hurt more.

"You're so sweet, Barbie." He nipped her bottom lip, soothing the tiny sting with a lick. "I could get a sugar rush from you. Fucking crash from you."

He crushed his mouth to hers again, and the kiss burned, turning wilder, rawer. Though she hovered over him, he was in full control, consuming her. And she loved it. Was a willing supplicant to this pleasure that already branded her. Changed her. Like she knew it would.

Like she'd been afraid of.

His mouth abandoned hers and brushed over the line of her jaw, his tongue and teeth tracing the same path. She shivered, the desire sizzling through her, dissolving all thoughts except his lips and hands.

She should only be focusing on this moment. This man.

With a tug to her hair, he tipped her head back, dragging a whimper from her as he tongued her neck. Her fingers curled tighter around the rim, and she sank into him, urging him to kiss and suck harder.

He lowered his hands to the bottom of her sweater, and pausing a beat, he lifted his head, meeting her eyes. When she didn't object, he jerked the top over her head. The cool night air whispered against her bare skin, but she barely felt it. Not when his heated gaze roamed over her, touching on her shoulders, her navy blue lace-covered breasts, her slightly rounded stomach. A small voice whispered that she should possess some modesty given the whole PK thing, but she didn't. Nothing about that stare impelled her to cover up.

"I knew you were beautiful." He set his knuckles at the base of her throat then drew them down the center of her chest. "But even my most vivid, dirtiest fantasies—and believe me, Barbie, they got pretty dirty—could compare to the reality of you."

She clasped his hands in hers and lifted them to her breasts. Pressed them to her.

"Show me how dirty."

His gaze never leaving hers, he squeezed her flesh, molded her to his hands, and she sank her teeth into her bottom lip to contain her cry.

"None of that," he admonished, whisking the pads of

his thumbs over her nipples. "Let me hear you. Don't hold back on me."

And when he pinched the tips, she gave him exactly what he requested. A sharp cry escaped her, and she shifted her hands from the truck to his shoulders. Frustrated, she plucked at his sweater. She wanted to touch him, feel his taut muscles under her fingers, her nails. Leaning back, she gripped the hem of his shirt, but he gently brushed her hands aside and hauled it up and off himself.

Sucking in a breath, she stilled, soaking in his beauty. The breadth of his shoulders and chest. The strength of his arms. The ridged ladder of his abs. And then there were all the tattoos. They covered almost every inch of him. Gorgeous artwork—ornate calligraphy, colorful landscapes and portraits, bold black and gray geometric patterns—over a body that was a work of art on its own.

She couldn't help herself. Surrendering to an impulse she couldn't contain, she leaned forward and traced the *g* in "imagination" from the *Charlie and the Chocolate Factory* quote inked across his sternum with her tongue. Israel cupped her head with one hand, whispering encouragement and praise as she stroked a caress over his skin, faithfully following the lettering. With his other hand, he tugged down the cup of her bra and caressed her breast, circling the taut nipple, rubbing it, tweaking it.

A shiver rippled through her, and she bit into his dense muscle, then sucked, needing to mark him like his tattoos.

"Fuck." He gripped her hair, none-too-gently tugged her head back and slammed his mouth down on hers. "I'm trying to have control when it comes to you," he muttered against her lips. "But it's damn near impossible. I want you too bad. I fucking hurt to be inside you."

She got it. God, she got it.

Maneuvering her backward, he lowered her to the well-padded bed of the truck. In moments, he had removed her remaining clothing…and had his mouth between her legs.

Pleasure ricocheted through her, hard, bright and unforgiving. Digging her heels into the truck bed, she pressed her head into the blankets, back arched tight, hands clutching his head. To push away? To hold him to her? The answer slipped her grasp. Along with her sanity as he licked a path up her folds to her clit and sucked.

Her cry rode the air, and she was thankful he didn't have any close neighbors because she couldn't trap the sounds he ripped from her. Not when he devoured her like a man served his last meal. Hungry, that's how he went at her, licking and sucking every part of her, dragging his teeth over the engorged nub of flesh at the top of her sex. She jerked, shook, rocked against his mouth, begging with her body and a garbled tumble of words to "don't stop." Please, whatever he did, just never stop.

He palmed her thighs, spreading her wider, and with one hand holding her open, he thrust two fingers inside her.

She splintered.

And as the pieces of her reassembled themselves, she was dimly aware of Israel moving above her, stripping and then rolling a condom down his cock. Though ripples of pleasure still echoed through her, and she twitched with the aftershocks, a renewed, hot punch of lust surged within her.

With clothes, he was a large man. Without them, he loomed even larger, a giant made flesh. And his dick… Unbelievable how it, too, could be beautiful, but it was. Long and thick with a flared tip that had her swiping her tongue over her lips. She wanted to take him inside her— her mouth, her hands, her body.

She wanted to worship him.

And yes, that was blasphemous, but she couldn't bring herself to care.

Especially with him prowling over her, crouching between her spread thighs. He'd just gifted her with a mind-numbing orgasm, yet her body hummed for more. An emptiness yawned deep inside her, and instinctively, she knew only he could fill it.

A spasm of fear quivered underneath the lust.

A mistake. She was making a mistake that would change her forever.

"Korrie." He pinched her chin, tilted her head back so she had no choice but to meet his dark blue eyes. "You still with me?"

Even now if she told him no, that she couldn't go through with this, he would stop. She harbored zero doubts about that. But she wanted him inside her, and the rest… Well, the rest would handle itself.

Stretching a hand toward him, she cupped his cheek. "I'm with you. Now." She levered up, taking his mouth in a swift, hot kiss. Tasting herself on his lips, his tongue. "Inside me."

He didn't give her time to change her mind. Burying his face in the crook of her neck, he thrust home.

Her head tipped back, and her lips parted on a silent scream. All her limbs tightened around him even as she opened for him. She'd known he would fill her, but she hadn't anticipated how he would mark not just her body but her soul. Branded. He stretched her, almost to the point of too much, but nothing had ever felt this wonderful, this important, this…perfect.

In this moment, she was his Eve, and he was her Adam. Created for each other.

And she sensed they would curse each other as that couple had done, too.

"On you, Barbie," he rasped, lifting his head and pressing a firm but tender kiss to her lips. "I'm yours to take. So take me."

Take him. He couldn't know the effect those words had on her. How they tempted her to grab for so much more than what he offered. So much more than she knew better to wish for.

So she seized what she could.

Sliding her hands over his shoulders, down his sides and over his taut ass, she cupped him and hiked her knees higher. She hissed out a breath as he notched deeper inside her.

"Yes," she whimpered, arching her back, pressing her breasts into his chest. "Give me all of you."

With a rumble that vibrated over her nipples and high inside her, he withdrew, dragging his cock over fluttering feminine muscles that seemed to protest his leaving. But with a snap of his hips, he drove back inside, powering the breath from her lungs. Her cry and his groan mated along with their bodies, and she shuddered under the pleasure that rippled through her.

"So goddamn wet for me. So tight. How're you so fucking perfect?" he said in her ear, planting stinging kisses along her jaw, raining them on her mouth. He tangled a hand in her hair, yanking her head back for more even as she gripped his ass harder, digging her nails into his taut flesh. He grunted, hammering into her with short, bruising, delicious thrusts that had stars bursting behind her closed lids. "Open those pretty eyes, Barbie. Look at me. See what you're doing to me. You're fault. All for you," he praised, or maybe accused, on a growl.

She obeyed him, staring into his eyes, his fierce face stamped with lust, and it ratcheted the desire in her when she didn't believe that possible. All vestiges of control shattered, and she let go. He reached behind him, grasped her wrists, and tugged her arms above her head, tangling their fingers together. Pressing their joined hands down on either side of her head, he took her mouth and rode her, consuming her with the passion that blazed a path down her spine to the soles of her feet and back up again.

Over and over, he buried himself inside her sex, molding it so only his cock would ever satisfy her, make her complete. Tears stung her eyes, even as an orgasm swelled bigger, harder and higher, threatening her. She wouldn't survive this. Physically, sure. But not emotionally.

And she fought the release. Even as he reached between their straining bodies and swept his thumb over her clit, rubbing, circling, she shied away from the crumbling edge that would inevitably give way and hurl her into that dark abyss.

But there was no escape. Not from pleasure. Not from his touch. Not from herself.

And as she screamed his name and detonated, she didn't want to escape.

Not as long as he was there, falling into oblivion with her.

ISRAEL JERKED AWAKE, jackknifing to a sitting position. His breath heaved in and out of his lungs as if he'd been running a marathon at full speed. But a survey around revealed his property and the blank projector screen. Korrie lay beside him, her curls concealing half of her face, her body lax in sleep.

One glance down at Korrie, and *why* he woke up so suddenly flooded him.

Images.

Some flashes. Some in movie reels. Some in montages. But so many images.

His heart hammered against his rib cage, and his heavy breath thundered in his head like waves crashing against a rocky shore. This was how ideas for books always came to him. In dreams. And he'd always kept a notebook on the dresser next to his bed so he could jot them down.

But there was no notebook. Hadn't been for two years, because there hadn't been any dreams, any ideas. There hadn't been the urge to write.

There was now.

God, there was now.

Urgency screamed through him like a car careening on rims. He scrambled for his pants, standing and jerking them on, tugging the zipper up but forgoing the button. Chest rising and falling on his harsh breaths, he bent and picked up Korrie in his arms, blankets and all, and eased out of the bed of the truck.

Barefoot, he stalked across the yard and climbed his front porch, only pausing long enough to open his front door before hustling inside and settling her in his bedroom. She didn't stir as he laid her on his mattress, and his gaze roamed over her once more, soaking her in, savoring her.

His muse.

He'd called her that once but then scoffed at the idea.

Now he knew for sure he'd been right.

The stirring that had fluttered in his chest, in his gut when he'd seen her weeks ago hadn't been a fluke. She had unlocked something in him. All this time she'd thanked him for giving her freedom when she'd given him his.

Because for two years he'd been in the jail of his mind, the most essential part of him locked up tight behind a prison of bitterness, hurt and anger. Who could've guessed—least of all him—that all he'd needed was to travel to a small town in the southern Berkshires and stumble onto the pastor's daughter to find the key?

Bending down, he brushed a kiss over her forehead then wheeled around and exited the room, softly pulling the door closed behind him. He hurried down the hall to the second bedroom he'd converted to an office when he'd bought the cabin with the proceeds from his old home. At the time, he'd been hopeful the change of scenery would stir his creativity. But as the weeks and then months had passed, that hope had died, and he'd stopped coming in here. Now, though...

Excitement whipped inside him as he entered. Rounding the desk, he gingerly sat down in his chair. Part of him—the part that had died a thousand deaths over the last two years—expected the images swirling in his head to disappear as the laptop went through its paces. But even after it booted up and he pulled up a blank document, they remained. As did the anticipation, the little trickles of fear that always accompanied starting a new project and, of course, the joy.

That joy he'd missed and now welcomed like a prodigal friend.

Lifting his hands, he settled them on the keyboard.

And began to write.

CHAPTER SIX

KORRIE CLOSED HER car door, scanning the church parking lot. She didn't spot the vehicle of the couple she was supposed to meet to go over the wedding rehearsal this Friday. Then again, she was early. She hit the alarm on her key fob. The crime rate in Rose Bend was relatively low, especially compared to other towns and cities, but she'd gone to college in New York City. And only an idiot left her car unlocked. The habit hadn't abandoned her. So she locked up tight—even if it was in the parking lot behind her father's church.

The pastor's daughter had a suspicious mind.

She shook her head, a faint smile curving her mouth. Surprise skated through her that she found even that bit of humor. Amusement of any kind had been a major feat since early Saturday morning when she'd crept out of Israel's house.

Pausing midstep, she pinched the bridge of her nose and beat back a wave of guilt and embarrassment. Two days later, she still couldn't explain why she hadn't said anything to him—not even a goodbye—before she'd left his home.

She'd awakened alone, in his bedroom, buried under his sheets, his scent wrapped around her as snugly as his blankets. And it'd felt...natural. Normal. Like she belonged.

Dangerous.

That had propelled her out of his bed like she'd been on

fire. Fear had pumped through her, metallic on her tongue. She couldn't do this. Couldn't allow herself to be fooled again by her heart. Couldn't allow herself to trust that same heart again. God, what was she doing? It'd only been six months since Derek dumped her.

But it'd been longer than that since she'd started having doubts.

Then, when that sly, insidious voice had slid inside Korrie's head, she yanked a blanket from his bed, wrapped it around her and ran from his bedroom. She'd momentarily paused when the sound of typing had reached into the hallway from the cracked doorway of another room. But it hadn't held her up. She'd raced from the house, gathered her clothes from the back of the truck and driven away, glancing in her rearview mirror the entire time.

But now, as that slick voice once again whispered to her, she didn't try to escape. This time, she sat and examined her relationship with Derek through a more objective lens rather than one clouded by pain and resentment.

"Korrie."

She stiffened. What the...? Had she conjured him?

Slowly, she turned and faced her ex-fiancé.

"Hello, Derek. What're you doing here?" She didn't add that when they'd been dating, he'd had no use for her father's church—well, for church, in general. He'd joined her for Sunday service at the beginning of their relationship, but after a while, he'd come less and less often, then stopped altogether. "Are you here to see Dad?"

Derek slipped his hands in the pockets of his black slacks, shaking his head. "No, I was hoping to talk to you." He dipped his head in the direction of the parking lot exit. "You passed by me at the corner of Main and Elmer. I honked, but you didn't hear me, so I followed you here.

We haven't had an opportunity to speak since the wedding, so I thought…"

"So you thought you'd ambush me in the church parking lot?" She scoffed. "I'm sorry—" *not even a little bit* "—but I have a meeting with a couple in a few minutes. So if you'll excuse me…"

"That's all I need," he said, an urgency in his voice. "Please. Just a couple of minutes and if you don't want me to bother you again, I promise to leave you alone."

She hesitated, studying his still-handsome features. It didn't seem fair that someone who'd behaved so cowardly and had hurt her so deeply shouldn't wear that somehow. Maybe a bad outbreak of acne on the chin or an unfortunate bald spot. A spurt of humor caught her by surprise, and she blinked at the welling of warmth. As a matter of fact, his presence hadn't dragged out the usual bitterness or painful humiliation. Instead, a blank nothingness filled her. When had that happened?

Apparently taking her stunned silence as acceptance, Derek shifted closer. He blew out a hard, long breath and rubbed his palms together.

"Let me start off by apologizing. I'm so sorry for hurting you, Korrie. That wasn't my intention—"

"Stop right there." She shot up a hand, palm out. "If this conversation is going to continue, then you're going to have to cut out the platitudes and be honest. Because I'm not accepting that 'I didn't intend to hurt you' b.s. What did you think would happen when you didn't show up on our wedding day? How did you think I would feel when you abandoned me for six months afterward to face the sad, pitying looks and gossip of this town alone as if it were my fault you didn't show? Was there an alternative emotion to feel other than hurt and betrayed?"

"Oh, sweetheart, it wasn't your fault, though," he said, holding his hands out, as if to grasp hers. "It wasn't you."

She snorted, stepping back just in case he had the bright idea of touching her. "Of course it wasn't. I'd never done anything but love and respect you. And I certainly would have never humiliated you like that. If I'd changed my mind about marrying you, I would've had the decency to come to you before our wedding day and tell you. Not let you and our guests show up and leave it to your parents to deliver the news."

The bitterness and anger might not consume her any longer when she looked at him, but that didn't mean she was letting him off the hook. It didn't mean she had a problem letting him know what an asshole he'd been to treat her like trash he'd casually tossed out the window.

And oh, yes. That curse was *most definitely* merited.

He winced slightly, turning away from her.

"You're right, Korrie. About all of it. I was a coward and I treated you abominably. You didn't deserve it. I own my actions, and I don't have an excuse other than I woke up a couple of days before our wedding scared. Scared I couldn't live up to the man you needed me to be. Scared I wasn't ready to be married. Just scared. And I couldn't do it. My biggest regret is hurting you, because I never stopped loving you, Korrie."

"Love me?" A sadness stole through her, and the heaviness of it sat on her chest. "I'm not going to tell you how you feel or don't feel. But I will say this—your kind of love isn't good enough for me. It isn't dependable or kind or secure or unshakable. I deserve a love that endures, that strengthens, that lifts, and most of all, is faithful, committed."

This was why tiny seeds of doubt had taken root, and she'd ignored the signs. Even after several premarital counseling sessions that Derek had been late to and barely participated in, she'd made excuses for his behavior. Even after her father had gently tried to warn her to slow down and rethink her decision to marry him, she'd gone forward with the relationship and the wedding.

All because she'd been in her thirties and in a hurry to obtain a standard society had set for her.

So while Derek abandoning her hadn't been her fault, her not heeding the big, flashing caution signs had been.

"You're just saying that because you're upset with me," Derek said, his brown eyes soft with understanding but also hurt. He, once more, stepped forward and reached his hands out toward her. But she didn't take them. On a sigh, he dropped his arms to his sides. "Korrie, I came back for you. For us. We have a history, a relationship behind us. Please don't throw it away because I made a horrible mistake."

"I forgive you, Derek."

His face brightened, a smile pulling at his generous mouth and relief darkening his eyes.

"Sweetheart—"

"Forgive, Derek, but I don't forget. And I forgive you for myself, not for you. I refuse to walk around chained to the past. I've learned some things about myself since you left. Especially in the last few weeks. I don't need a relationship or a man to be fulfilled or to be whole. I'm complete all by myself. And for the first time in my life, I'm discovering who that person is, and I'm starting to really love and appreciate her. And I don't need anyone's approval or partnership for that, either. So I'm sorry you returned to Rose Bend for an 'us' that doesn't exist anymore, but that's your decision. Just as it was yours to leave in the first place without consulting me. I'm not throwing away a relationship. I'm choosing to save myself."

No, she didn't need a man to be happy, but she wanted one in her life. A very specific one. And it'd taken confronting the past and the burden of shame and doubt that she'd been lugging around these last six months to realize it. She'd blamed herself for Derek's defection. Had believed there'd been something defective in her that had made him run. Had thought it was her fault because she'd placed her trust in the wrong person. She'd doubted herself, so how could she possibly trust others?

But Israel had done nothing but prove himself trustworthy.

And dependable. And kind. And unshakable.

Everything she'd told Derek he hadn't been.

Which was why in the few weeks she'd known the author moonlighting as a bartender, she'd fallen in love with him. Did that terrify her? Oh, yes. Because Israel might want her body, but he'd never once said anything about desiring her heart. And as someone whose past when it came to love resembled a war zone, chances were he would reject any mention of the word.

And yet...

Yet, he was worth the risk. Her pulse roared in her head. Fear, most definitely. But also a sense of exhilaration that was as freeing as getting up on that stage and singing karaoke or zooming on a motorcycle through mountain roads.

She loved Israel Ford.

Maybe from the moment he'd held her hand and sang in that godawful twang.

Maybe when he'd stripped his soul bare and shared his own pain and secret with her.

Maybe when he'd first called her Barbie.

Maybe all of them.

Preordained, her father would call it.

Fated, the romance writer would call it.

She'd call it a beautiful amelioration of both.

"Does this have anything to do with that bartender?" Derek demanded, a sneer curling the corner of his mouth. "There have been rumors going around about you two. Really, Korrie. He's younger than you. It's embarrassing. What would your father say?"

"People have been gossiping about us?" She grinned, then turned as a car pulled into the parking lot. Recognizing the couple inside, she waved then returned her attention to Derek. Lighter than she'd been in, God, longer than she could remember, she grinned wider at her ex-fiancé. "Good. As for my father? I believe he'd say, 'Go thy big, or go thy home.'"

Waving, she headed toward the church, humming the song she'd sung with Israel during karaoke.

And barely managed not to dance.

Because that's what happy people did.

CHAPTER SEVEN

"HERE YOU GO." Israel served up the two beers to the regulars at the end of the bar. "Putting those on your tab?"

The older guy with the grizzled gray beard and surprisingly great smile nodded and picked up his Sam Adams. "Yep. Thanks, Iz."

"You got it, Rex."

Rapping the bar top with his knuckles, he walked off, stopping next to Maddox, who poured two glasses of Moscato.

"Not that I don't love live music, but it's Wednesday night. Why is the band here tonight?"

Maddox glanced up at him, arching a dark red eyebrow. "Maybe I called them in to celebrate losing a great bartender to the publishing world."

Israel snorted, although pleasure bloomed in his chest. "Yeah, I'm sure that's it." He cocked his head. "You do know if you ever need me to pinch-hit, I'll be here. And besides, this book will take me a minute to write, I don't mind picking up hours—"

Maddox cut him off with a short bark of laughter. "We both know that's bullshit. You might not have put anything out for some time, but you're far from broke and don't need the money this job brings in. No." He shook his head, recorking the wine bottle. "You focus on writing that book, and when you finish, you can come in here for a celebratory shift."

"Sounds like a plan." He paused, cleared his throat. "And thanks, Maddy. For everything."

"You got it, man. And just so you know, I never had any doubts you'd find your way back to doing what you love." He picked up the wineglasses and squinted at Israel. "Now, your bartending skills…"

Israel laughed, the sound hoarse with emotion but genuine. At one point in his life, he'd believed the number of friends, cars and houses determined a man's success. Only when he'd lost all of that had he discovered quality really did trump quantity every time. He had a cabin in the woods, a lone pickup truck and could count his close friends on one hand with a couple of fingers left over.

And he was good.

Better than good.

Well, almost.

As it'd done damn near hundreds of times in the past few days, his mind drifted to Korrie. And how, when he'd emerged from his office, tired but energized and excited to share with her about the twenty-two pages he'd just pounded out, she'd been gone. At first, he'd been confused, thinking she'd just gone to the bathroom or maybe out to the truck to get her clothes. But it hadn't taken long to accept that she'd left. And an even shorter time to realize why.

Korrie was running scared.

Literally.

Initially, he'd been pissed. But after another furious writing session where he poured all of his emotion into his new work-in-progress, a bout with his punching bag and about four cups of coffee, the anger had dissipated. And awe had seeped in.

Korrie was running scared.

And there could be only one reason behind that.

He mattered more than a fuck buddy. She had feelings for him, and she'd been unprepared for that. Once his anger had cooled, it wasn't a shock to him. Korrie wasn't the type of woman to do casual sex, to give herself to a man without emotional attachment. And he'd known that when he'd invited her to kiss him, to take him. Yes, a part of him had damn well known that and accepted it. Had wanted it.

It'd been four days since his revelation and since he'd heard from her. He planned on giving her just a couple more before he tracked her down to her house or even her father's church and laid out the truth.

She wasn't alone in this.

He'd fallen for her. Hard.

He still bore the scars from his past proudly because through them he'd learned what love wasn't and how to recognize it.

He loved Korrie, and if she needed time to heal from her own past, he would give that to her. But she owned his heart, and he intended to let her know.

"All right, ladies and gentlemen, we have a treat for you tonight. A special guest of honor who's going to sit in with us for a song. Put your hands together for our very own Korrie Noel."

Israel jerked to a halt, his hands locking around the glasses he'd been pulling down to fill with the local IPA. Everything in him went silent, and he caught the raucous cheering in the bar as if from down a long tunnel. Shock might have dulled all his other senses, but his eyes—they were as sharp as an eagle's, and as Korrie stepped onto the stage and up to the microphone, he noted everything about her. The thick dark cloud of curls. The lovely face that had haunted his dreaming and waking hours. The petite body with its wicked curves clothed in a frilly yet sexy blouse, tight jeans and black ankle boots that did unlawful things to her already gorgeous legs.

Jesus, he'd missed her.

He carefully set the glasses down on the bar top, knowing he should be serving drinks, but he couldn't move. All he could do was stare at the stunning woman who flashed the band's lead singer and guitarist a shy smile. He remembered that smile. Had seen it on another stage only weeks ago, and the urge to charge through the crowd packed on the dance floor to gather her in his arms punched him in the chest.

But again, he couldn't move.

"Hey, everyone," Korrie said, her husky, sexy voice echoing through the bar.

Goddamn, that voice. The timbre of it reminded him of how it sounded raspy with pleasure after screaming his name. Shit. He couldn't think about that here. Serving drinks with an erection tenting his jeans wasn't a good look.

"Thanks to Maddox and the guys of Breaking Even for letting me horn in on their set tonight. I know it's not their usual night to perform, but because they're great guys they agreed to play so I could do something that frankly scares the hell out of me." She chuckled, holding up her hands. "Being the center of attention, stepping outside of my box, taking risks. But when someone is worth falling on your face over, you have to take that risk. So—" she spread her arms wide "—to that someone. You are worth the fall."

She turned and nodded to the band behind her, and they started playing the opening notes to a song he didn't recognize. Probably because he couldn't immediately hear them past the rush of blood in his ears and the jackhammering of his heart.

But as soon as she started singing, he recalled the love song by The Chicks. The lyrics spoke of not being okay and having lost her way without the person she loved.

When he'd slid out from behind the bar, he didn't remember. Nor did he recall moving through the throng of people to the front of the stage. By the time she hit the last note and the music died away, he'd climbed the steps and had her face in his hands. And his mouth on hers.

She opened for him, thrusting her hands into his hair and holding on to him, kissing him back with as much passion as he gave her. The crowded bar melted away, leaving only her taste, her scent, only *her*.

Korrie.

"You did that for me," he rasped against her lips. "I think you might like me just a little."

She laughed, and the breathless sound was pure joy to his ears, to his heart. "Like you a little bit? Yes. But I love you so much more."

He closed his eyes and pressed his forehead to hers, the last knot in his chest loosening and unraveling. "I was giving you two more days, Barbie."

"Two more days for what?"

"Before I hunted you down, told you that I loved you and you needed to find your way to admitting the same thing. So thank you for hunting me down instead."

A grin slowly spread across her face, ramping up her beauty from stunning to blinding.

"Anytime."

"Shut up and kiss her," a loud, deep voice boomed from in back of the bar. A voice that sounded suspiciously close to Maddox's.

The crowd picked up the chant, and tilting her head back, Israel smiled down at her.

"I'm going to shut up and kiss you."

"I'm going to shut up so you can."

He brushed his thumbs over her cheeks. "Thank you for coming out on that porch and finding me. For leading me out of the darkness and giving me light again."

"No, Israel, thank you for being on that porch when I needed a friend and a champion until I could champion myself." She nuzzled his palm. "I love you."

"I love you, too, Barbie."

Then he shut up and kissed her.

* * * * *

More unmissable romance from...

NAIMA SIMONE

The last thing Sydney needs is trouble...
Except trouble just walked in the door!

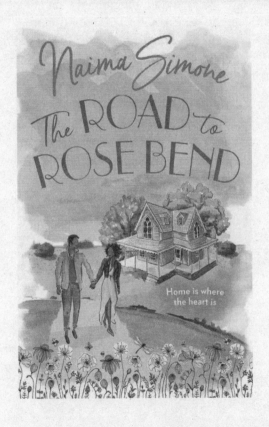

OUT NOW

MILLS & BOON

More unmissable romance from...

NAIMA SIMONE

Can the festive magic heal her broken heart?
There's more than one surprise in store...

OUT NOW

MILLS & BOON

Fall in love with the Rose Bend series from

Naima Simone

MILLS & BOON

Discover more from
NAIMA SIMONE

From our Desire series

Secrets and scandal...

OUT NOW

MILLS & BOON